THE SURVIVOR

Novels by Vince Flynn

VINCE FLYNN

THE SURVIVOR

A NEW **MITCH RAPP** NOVEL

BY KYLE MILLS

SIMON &
SCHUSTER

London · New York · Sydney · Toronto · New Delhi

A CBS COMPANY

First published in USA by Atria Books, an imprint of Simon & Schuster, Inc., 2015
First published in Great Britain by Simon & Schuster UK Ltd, 2015
A CBS COMPANY

1 3 5 7 9 10 8 6 4 2

Simon & Schuster UK Ltd
1st Floor
222 Gray's Inn Road
London WC1X 8HB

www.simonandschuster.co.uk

Simon & Schuster Australia, Sydney
Simon & Schuster India, New Delhi

A CIP catalogue record for this book
is available from the British Library.

Hardback ISBN: 978-1-47114-199-7
Trade paperback ISBN: 978-1-47114-200-0
eBook ISBN: 978-1-47114-202-4

This book is a work of fiction. Names, characters, places and incidents
are either a product of the author's imagination or are used fictitiously.

Printed and bound in Australia by Griffin Press

MIX
Paper from
responsible sources
FSC
www.fsc.org   FSC® C009448

To Vince Flynn
A man who touched so many lives

ACKNOWLEDGMENTS

THANKS to my agent, Simon Lipskar, for thinking of me when the subject of continuing the Mitch Rapp series came up. To Sloan Harris and Emily Bestler for their confidence, encouragement, and insight. To my mother, a Rapp fan for many years and always an honest reader. To Rod Gregg for keeping me straight on all things relating to firearms.

And finally, to Vince's friends, family, and fans who took the time to reach out to me. It was your enthusiasm and trust that kept me going when the task of writing *The Survivor* seemed insurmountable.

THE SURVIVOR

PRELUDE

SCOTT Coleman turned away from the color monitor and glanced right. The panel van seemed almost like a toy by American standards, barely large enough to fit him and his surveillance gear in the back. Even tighter was the front seat, where Joe Maslick's 220-pound frame was wedged behind the wheel. Raindrops were collecting on the windshield, blurring ancient row houses and a street narrow enough that passing required having two wheels on the sidewalk.

After days on the move in a city where good driving etiquette meant clipping fewer than three people a week, they'd resigned themselves to the impossibility of staying with a pedestrian target. Since then, they'd been bouncing from illegal parking space to illegal parking space trying to maximize their surveillance camera's signal strength. No small feat in a city constructed almost entirely of stone.

"How you doing up there, Joe?"

"Fine."

It was a lie, of course. But it was the expected lie.

In fact, the former Delta soldier had recently been shot in a Kabul ambush that had left a hell of a lot of Afghan cops dead, put Mitch Rapp way too close to an explosion of his own making, and forced an agonizing alliance with Louis Gould, the assassin who had killed Rapp's family.

Maslick should have been at home rehabbing his shoulder but he'd insisted on being included on this op. Bringing him along had been a tough call. The doctors were concerned about permanent nerve damage, but sometimes it was better to get back in the saddle as soon as possible. Before doubt could creep in.

"Glad to hear you're having such a good time. Right now our feed looks solid, moving north on a pretty open street. We should be able to stay here for a little while, but be ready to move."

"Right."

Maslick's one-word answers had nothing to do with what must have been the considerable pain in his arm. He'd always resisted stringing more than two or three together unless it was absolutely necessary.

Coleman turned his attention back to the screen secured to the side of the van. The image rocked wildly as the purse the camera was hidden in swung from its owner's hand. Sky. A feral cat lounging on a dumpster. Thick ankles overflowing a pair of sensible shoes.

The legs and Hush Puppies belonged to Bebe Kincaid, a plump, gray-haired woman who was the most unlikely employee of his company, SEAL Demolition and Salvage. She'd spent her adult life as an FBI surveillance expert based on two considerable natural gifts. Her bland features, formless figure, and slightly bowed shuffle made her as anonymous as a fire hydrant. But more important, she had a photographic memory.

It was a label that was often thrown around to describe people who didn't forget much, but Bebe was the rare real thing. In fact, it was her flawless memory that had gotten her eased into early retirement by the FBI's psychologists. The older she got, the more she struggled to differentiate between things that had happened yesterday and things that had happened years—even decades—ago. To her, the memories were all equally vivid. She was perhaps not Bureau material anymore, but Mitch Rapp had been on the phone to her before she'd finished cleaning out her desk.

Coleman had to admit that he'd been a little irritated when a woman who reminded him of his mother showed up at his company's nondescript door to thank him not only for the job but for the generous mental health benefits. As usual, though, Rapp had been right. Bebe was worth her considerable weight in gold.

Coleman glanced at a second screen that displayed a satellite image of Istanbul with a single blue dot representing Bebe's position. It suddenly took a hard left and started down a set of stairs toward the waterfront. "Okay, Joe. She's turned east and we're going to lose her. Can we close in?"

"Old lady gets around," Maslick said, grudging respect audible beneath his irritation at having to wade back into city traffic.

Coleman smiled as they pulled away from the curb. His men were all former special forces, primarily SEALs, Delta, and Recon marines. With the right set of support hose, though, it was possible that Bebe could run them all into the ground.

He wedged a foot against his state-of-the-art electronics to keep them from shifting as the van struggled up a rain-slickened hill. On the main monitor, Bebe's camera swept briefly across the man they were following. He wasn't much to look at. Five foot eight, a slight Asian tilt to his features, and a mediocre suit pulled closed against the rain. In reality, though, Vasily Zhutov was the CIA's highest-placed mole in the Russian Foreign Intelligence Service. Code-named Sitting Bull, he was among the Agency's most clandestine and hard-won assets.

The problem was that no one was sure if his identity was still a secret. Worse, it wasn't just *his* cover that had potentially been blown. It was the cover of virtually every CIA asset recruited in the last quarter century. Teams like Coleman's had been deployed across the globe—spread way too thin to do any more than make educated guesses as to who might be targeted.

And it was all because of one man: the late Joseph "Rick" Rickman.

Rickman had been stationed in Jalalabad for the last eight years and had pretty much run the CIA's side of the war in Afghanistan. Word was that he had an IQ just north of two hundred and based on

Coleman's interactions with the man, he had no reason to dispute that figure.

The better part of a billion dollars had flowed through Rickman's hands over the years, funding weapons purchases, bribes to local politicians, and God knew what else. Rick had a relationship with virtually every player in the country and had an uncanny ability to track the complex forces tearing the region apart. If asked about the economic effect of the heroin trade on the insurgency, he could lecture like a Harvard PhD. Conversely, asked about some minor family dispute between two mountain villages no one had ever heard of, he'd speak with equal authority. The only person at the Agency who could even hope to keep up with what was going on in that man's head was Irene Kennedy, and she had too many other things on her plate to try.

Unfortunately, the house of cards Rickman had built all came crashing down the previous month when he completely lost his mind. Whether it was the pressure of the job, family problems, or just the chaos and hopelessness of Afghanistan, no one knew. What they did know, though, was that Rickman had hatched a plot with Akhtar Durrani, the deputy general of Pakistan's ISI, to betray the CIA and the people Rickman had fought with for his entire career.

Rickman had killed his bodyguards and faked his own kidnapping, going so far as to release a gut-wrenching video of himself being tortured by two men posing as Muslim extremists. It had been like setting off a bomb in the U.S. intelligence community. With his incredible intellect and decades of CIA ops under his belt, there was no way for anyone to know what information he was privy to and how much of it he'd give up when the hot pokers came out. Panic ensued, with countless undercover assets requesting extraction, demanding asylum at U.S. embassies, and generally drawing a lot of unwanted attention to America's spy network.

During his faked interrogation, Rickman had blurted out a number of names, but one in particular had generated a wave of dread in Langley: Sitting Bull. Russia hadn't been Rick's theater of operation and the identity of the man was one of the CIA's most closely held secrets. Was it a red herring? Nothing more than a couple of meaningless words he'd overheard and socked away in that magnificent brain of his? Or had he actually gotten hold of enough information to compromise the Russian?

Zhutov turned left into an alley and Bebe hung back. Istanbul's streets were generally packed with people this time of afternoon but they were moving into a neighborhood made up of dilapidated, unoccupied houses. Based on the shaky camera feed, there were only a couple of people on the street.

"Joe," Coleman said. "Are you watching the map? He's cutting north. Can we get ahead of him?"

"Maybe. Lots of traffic," Maslick muttered, rerouting onto the sidewalk to get around a delivery truck.

"Bebe, we're coming around," Coleman said into a microphone clipped to his collar. "Give that alley a miss and take the next one. They end up on the same square."

"Roger that."

The money was good, but Coleman was starting to wonder how much longer he could stand being stuck on a surveillance detail that was looking more and more like a waste of time. Both Rickman and Durrani were dead, which should have been the end of it. On the other hand, it didn't pay to underestimate Rickman's ability to plan fifteen steps ahead. Everyone at the Agency believed that there was more classified information floating around than was on the torture video Rickman had posted to the Internet. Kennedy had gone one step further, though. She was concerned that Rickman might have figured out a way to keep his vendetta against the Agency moving forward from beyond the grave. It seemed a little paranoid to Coleman, but then he was just a soldier. Better to leave the strategizing to Kennedy and Rapp. They were good at it.

"Scott," Bebe said over the radio. "Are you getting this?"

The swinging image that Coleman had become so accustomed to stabilized as she aimed the purse-mounted camera toward a man wearing a leather jacket and jeans. He was lighting a cigarette and looked pretty much like the other million or so Turks his age living in the city.

"I've seen him before," Bebe said. "Two days ago. By the trolley up on the shopping street. He came out of a store and followed the subject for six and a half blocks before turning off."

Coleman cursed under his breath as the man started casually down the alley the Russian had disappeared into. Normally this was when he'd ask if she was certain, but there was no point. As far as anyone could tell, Bebe had never made a mistake with regard to a face.

"What do you think, Bebe? Any chance it could be a coincidence?"

"Million to one."

"Okay. Continue to the next alley and let's see if this guy trades off to someone else you recognize."

"On it," she said.

Coleman reached for a secure satellite phone, feeling a vague sense of foreboding. Rapp was not going to be happy.

CHAPTER 1

THE safe house was beginning to take on the feeling of a prison for Kennedy. She'd sat through too many of these post-operation debriefings to begin to count, but over her thirty-plus-year career at the CIA it was safe to say the numbers were in the triple digits. The pungent smell of cigarettes, too much coffee, not enough sleep, and too few workouts combined to throw off an all-too-familiar funk. For her part she got to leave. Had to, really. As director of the CIA, she couldn't simply vanish for a week straight.

She spent her days locked almost entirely behind the soundproof door of her seventh-floor office at Langley trying to sort out the mess that had come to be known as the Rickman Affair. And even that had raised some eyebrows. The damage was bad, as it always was with this type of thing, but the question was how bad.

Kennedy didn't fault Rapp for killing her Near East black ops chief. Getting him out of Pakistan would have proved problematic, especially after that duplicitous bastard Lieutenant General Durrani was killed. Had Rapp managed to keep Rickman alive they would have been left with a man whose twisted intellect was capable of sowing so many seeds of disinformation and dissent that the CIA would have been eating itself from the inside out by the time he was done. No, they were all better off with Rickman out of the picture. As Hurley was fond of saying, "Dead men tell no lies."

They also offered no information, which was what Kennedy had been trying to assess during her days locked behind her door. Rapp had recovered a laptop as well as some hard drives from General Durrani's house. They were Rickman's, and her best people were poring over the encrypted CIA files, trying to determine what assets, operatives, and . agents may have been compromised. One operation, due to its current sensitivity, had her particularly worried, and there were already some signs that things might be going off the tracks, which in this particular case was a very appropriate metaphor.

"What are we going to do with him?"

Kennedy slowly closed the red file on the kitchen table, removed her brown glasses, and rubbed her tired eyes.

Mike Nash set a fresh cup of tea in front of her and took a seat.

"Thank you." After a moment she added, "I'm not sure what we're going to do with him. I've left it up to those two for now."

Nash looked out the sliding glass door where night was falling on Mitch Rapp and Stan Hurley. Kennedy had forced them to go outside to smoke. Nash couldn't tell for sure, but they probably were also drinking bourbon. "I don't mean Gould. I mean I care about what we do with him, but for the moment, I'm more worried about what we're going to do with Mitch."

Kennedy was growing tired of this. She'd talked to their resident shrink about the tension between Nash and Rapp and for the most part they were on the same page. Rapp was Nash's senior by a few years, and through some pretty impressive maneuvering Rapp had been able to end Nash's covert career. The how and why were a bit complicated, but in the end it was plainly a noble gesture. Nash had a wife and four kids, and Rapp didn't want to see all that thrown away on a dangerous life that someone else could handle. Nash for his part felt betrayed by Rapp. Their closeness was a natural casualty as Rapp began to share fewer and fewer operational details with his friend, who now spent his time at Langley and on Capitol Hill.

"I know you're worried," Kennedy said, "but you have to stop trying to control him. Trust me, I've spent twenty years trying and the best I can do is nudge him in a general direction."

Nash frowned. "He's going to end up just like Stan. A bitter, lonely old man who's dying of lung cancer. Look at Stan . . . even now he can't put those damn things down."

"Don't judge, Mike," Kennedy said with a weary tone. "He's been through a lot. How he chooses to go out is no one's business but his own."

"But Mitch . . . it's as plain as day. That's the road he's on."

Kennedy thought about it for a long moment, taking a sip of tea. "We're not all made for white picket fences and nine-to-five jobs. He most certainly isn't."

"No, but each time he goes out the odds are stacked against him."

"I used to think so." Kennedy smiled. "And then I came to a very simple conclusion . . ."

"What's that?"

"He's a survivor."

CHAPTER 2

THE CIA's Gulfstream G550 started a lazy banking maneuver and Mitch Rapp peered out the window. The Bosporus was directly below, streaked with boat wakes and divided by a bridge linking Asia to Europe. It was a familiar view—the densely packed buildings, the traffic-choked streets, and the ancient mosques representing a religion that had been subverted by evil men.

A light fog condensed around the plane, obscuring his line of sight. He leaned back in his seat, closing his eyes and letting himself drift back to the first time he'd been there. To his first kill so many years ago.

The man's name had been Sharif. By outward appearance, he'd been a successful and widely respected real estate investor. In fact, his extensive property portfolio was nothing more than a way to launder the hundreds of millions of dollars he made selling arms to anyone willing to meet his price. Strangely, the particulars of the assassination remained more vivid in Rapp's mind than all the others that had followed. He could still smell the tiny apartment that had been rented for him through a maze of CIA shell corporations. He could recall how the Beretta 92F he'd favored at the time felt heavier and colder in his hand than it had during training.

The memory of the operational details brought a barely perceptible and slightly embarrassed smile to his face. He'd completely discarded Stan Hurley's plan, partially out of youthful arrogance and partly to stick his middle finger in the man's face. His pursuit of the target into a park that he had only superficial knowledge of seemed hopelessly amateurish to him now. And his use of multiple rounds when a single properly placed one would have sufficed was something Hurley still rode him about when he'd had too much to drink. Well deserved, unfortunately.

At the young age of twenty-four, Rapp had been one of the most highly trained and talented assassins on the planet. Two decades later, though, he could see how inexperienced and overconfident he'd been. No wonder he'd had the old cuss pulling his hair out.

Normally, planes put Rapp to sleep. He preferred the roar of a C-130, but what the Gulfstream lacked in white noise it made up for with its plush leather seating. On this occasion, though, he'd been awake for the entire trip from the United States. . . . Too much on his mind.

At the forefront was Stan Hurley—a man he'd once despised and who had undoubtedly wanted to quietly do away with the Orion Team's newest recruit after the Sharif job. Rapp had never asked, but he could imagine the knock-down, drag-out Hurley and Kennedy had over that. The old man screaming that Rapp was already out of control and Kennedy calmly extolling their young recruit's potential. It would have been interesting if she'd lost that particular argument. Who would have come out on top? Him or Hurley?

It was a question that would never be answered. His old friend would be gone soon. Rapp could smell death a mile away and Hurley stunk of it. Just like everyone did eventually. Just like he would one day.

Rapp opened his eyes, but didn't bother looking out the window again. Dwelling on Hurley's cancer was a waste of time. It was beyond his control and he had bigger fires to put out.

Scott Coleman's update two hours ago suggested that the Russian surveillance on Sitting Bull was getting more intense. As problems went, that was only the tip of the iceberg. What worried him was *why* the man was suddenly being tailed. Certainly not solely because of the brief mention of a code name on the Rickman video. Russia's internal security agency, the FSB, would have no way to connect it to Vasily Zhutov. No, the only answer was that Rickman had leaked additional classified information before Rapp had put a bullet in his head. But how much more?

The hum of the landing gear lowering filled the cabin. Rapp cleared his mind of the thousand disaster scenarios fighting for his attention and focused on the problem at hand. The FSB had undoubtedly been following Zhutov to see if he would lead them to anyone interesting, but now Coleman's team was seeing activity that suggested the Russians were setting up for a rendition.

The question was what to do about it. Zhutov didn't know anything particularly useful about the CIA's network, and his cover appeared to have already been blown. That made sitting back and letting the FSB snatch him the option that most of the desk jockeys at Langley would go for. Just another casualty in the game they'd been playing with the Russians for nearly three-quarters of a century.

In Rapp's mind—and to a slightly lesser degree in Kennedy's—that was an unacceptable sacrifice. Sitting Bull had put himself in harm's way to help the CIA contain Russia's unpredictable and often self-destructive impulses. Rapp had worked with many moles over the years—traitors who betrayed their homelands for money, or sex, or revenge. They could be useful but were never to be trusted or regarded with anything but contempt.

Zhutov was different. He was a patriot who loved his country and believed in its potential to be a positive force in the world. He'd made it clear from the beginning that he would never give up military secrets and he refused any kind of compensation. Rapp admired him, and there was no way he was going to leave the man twisting in the wind.

How many more Sitting Bulls were out there? All the assets Rickman had given up in his phony torture video were accounted for in one way or another—either vanished, dead, squirreled away in a U.S. embassy, or covered by a team like Coleman's. What else had Rick known? Who else had he given up before Rapp had killed him?

The rain started as they touched down on the private airport's only runway. Rapp walked forward as they taxied, grabbing a duffel from the closet and waiting for the plane to roll to a stop next to a parking lot scattered with cars. The cockpit door remained closed, as was his preference, so he opened the hatch himself and jumped down.

A quick scan of the area turned up no movement. The cars all appeared to be empty and, as promised, no one from the airport was there to greet him. He turned up the collar of his leather jacket to obscure his face not only from anyone looking down from the tower, but also from his own pilots.

The weathered Ford was right where Coleman said it would be, isolated on the east corner of the lot. Rapp tossed his bag in the back and slid behind the wheel. The keys were in the ignition, and a well-used passport identifying him as Mitch Kruse was in the glove box with all the proper entry stamps.

He started the engine and pulled out onto the road, staying well within the speed limit as he dialed his phone. It was picked up on the first ring.

"How's the car?" Scott Coleman said.

"Fine. What's the situation? Are our competitors looking to make a move?" The phone was encrypted but neither of them trusted the technology. In light of the NSA's obsession with vacuuming up every cell signal on the planet, it was best to keep the conversation in line with his cover as a sales executive.

"An hour ago I would have said the situation wasn't pressing. Now, though, things are starting to look more urgent. I'm glad you're here to help close the deal."

Rapp managed to cover the fifteen miles to the center of town relatively quickly. Coleman had sent his coordinates to Rapp's phone, and the turn-by-turn instructions were being fed to an earpiece camouflaged by the intersection of his beard and shaggy hair. Parking tended to be opportunistic in Istanbul, so he pulled in behind some disused scaffolding and stepped out into the cool drizzle.

The sidewalk was typically crowded with pedestrians, but no one gave him a second glance as he lit a cigarette and started up a side street. The leather jacket and dark jeans were right down the center of Istanbul fashion. Combined with his black hair and dark complexion, he became just another local hurrying to get out of the rain.

The clouds were too thick to get a precise bead on the sun, but Rapp guessed it had sunk below the horizon about five minutes ago. Headlights were coming on around him, glaring off wet stone and prompting him to pick up his pace. This is when it would happen—the short period of disorientation when the primitive part of the human mind adjusted from day to night.

The foot traffic thinned as he entered an area lined with closed stores devoted to electronics and construction materials. Sitting Bull would certainly be aware of the Rickman video, but he didn't know his own code name and would have no reason to believe that a man working in Jalalabad would have any knowledge of his existence. Because of that, he was still comfortable routing through this relatively quiet part of Istanbul to get home from his job. Sharif had been cursed with a similarly careless habit of walking his dog in the same park at the same time every morning. And look what happened to him.

The mechanical voice was still giving him directions through his earpiece. Another three minutes and he spotted the hazy but unmistakable outline of Joe Maslick crammed behind the wheel of a white panel van.

Rapp slowed and casually dialed Coleman, looking around as though he were lost.

"Have you arrived?" Coleman said by way of a greeting. "The meeting is about to start."

"Thirty seconds out."

"Why don't you come in through the back?"

Rapp disconnected the call and skirted around the rear of the van, opening the door and slipping into the cramped space. Maslick didn't look back, instead continuing to watch the street through the rain-soaked windshield. Coleman pulled his earphones partially off and pointed toward a shaky image on one of the monitors.

"Bebe's still following Zhutov. Based on what we've seen over the last few days, he'll cross another two streets and then go diagonal into a small square. There's a van parked at the north end with two men in the front seats. No way to know if anyone's in the back. They've been there for a half an hour, which is about the variation in Zhutov's schedule depending on if he stops for coffee. Luckily, he did today."

Rapp nodded. "Tie me into Bebe."

Coleman flipped a switch on the console in front of him and held out the microphone that had been clipped to his collar. The heavily encrypted radio signal didn't travel very far, so Rapp felt comfortable being more direct than he would be on the phone.

"Bebe. Slow down when you start to approach the square. I don't want you anywhere near this when it goes down."

"Thanks, Mitch." The relief in her voice was obvious even over the static. "I'll keep eyes on the subject as long as possible and let you know if anything changes."

Rapp handed the microphone back to Coleman and went forward, slipping into the passenger seat. "All right, Joe. Let's roll."

CHAPTER 3

DR. Irene Kennedy scrolled through an email on the tablet in
her lap, skimming over the details of the Istanbul situation. Sitting Bull's life or death, once one of the CIA's top priorities, was now
largely irrelevant. What mattered was that his situation was more evidence that her worst-case scenario was playing out. More and more it
seemed to be the way the world worked. What could go wrong, inevitably did. Horribly, catastrophically wrong.

She shut down the tablet and set it on the seat next to her, staring
straight ahead at her own hazy reflection. The limousine's bulletproof
glass was heavily tinted, cutting her off from the driver and turning
the sunny streets of Islamabad to a dim blur. She knew that there were
two cars in front and no fewer than three behind, all filled with well-
armed and well-trained men. The streets had been partially cleared
for her motorcade and a Bell AH-1 Cobra attack helicopter was flying
close enough overhead that the thump of the rotors vibrated the vehicle around her.

The modern state of Pakistan had been established in 1947, carved
from the Muslim regions of British India. In the decades since, it had
become the sixth most populous nation in the world, with more than

180 million citizens. But while India had worked to modernize and democratize, its neighbor had toiled for much of its history under the rule of dictators and religious extremists.

Now the massive country was on the verge of being a failed state. Powerful fundamentalist currents were undermining the government, countless terrorist organizations had moved in, and control of the north had been almost completely lost.

With the economy in shambles, terrorists growing increasingly violent, and paranoia about India reaching a fevered pitch, it was hard to blame the Pakistani people for seeking order and stability from any organizations willing to peddle such hollow promises.

Unfortunately, those organizations were the army and the Pakistani intelligence apparatus. Both had grown in influence to the point that it was nearly impossible for the civilian government—and indeed the United States—to keep them in check. The chaos in Pakistan was becoming an impossible situation. A looming disaster that Kennedy no longer believed could be averted.

Normally, the circumstances would cause her to push Washington toward a policy of containment. For a number of reasons, that was impossible in the case of Pakistan. Movement of American men and matériel through the territory was critical to the war on terror. The country had one of the largest and most poorly controlled armies in the world. But both those issues paled when compared to the fact that the Pakistani government possessed more than a hundred nuclear warheads.

In many ways, it was a textbook example of the unintended consequences of America's foreign policy. The United States had funneled billions of dollars into the country to fight the Soviets during their invasion of Afghanistan, but in its anticommunist fervor, it hadn't paid attention when much of that money was diverted to Pakistan's WMD program.

It was a self-destructive behavior that persisted to this day. America continued to pump money into the country that had created—and still quietly supported—the Taliban. A country that had sold nuclear technology to Libya, Iran, and North Korea. A country that had hidden Osama bin Laden and now hosted the most dangerous terrorist organizations in the world.

The simple truth was that the increasingly dysfunctional men and women in Washington weren't interested in making the difficult choices necessary to win the war against extremism. Pakistan would continue to demand U.S. dollars under the auspices of keeping its nuclear arsenal secure, and the American politicians would continue to blindly hand it over, hoping that it would be enough to keep the lid on the pot long enough to get them through the next election cycle.

But *was* it enough? The danger posed by Pakistan's nuclear program now came from every angle: an accident that India could mistake for an attack, one of the many local terrorist organizations acquiring a warhead, or even a coup that put the entire arsenal in the hands of a fundamentalist government.

And at the center of it all was the organization headquartered behind the nondescript gate her motorcade was approaching. Pakistan's Inter-Services Intelligence, or ISI.

Her driver didn't slow as they headed for a group of men with dogs and low, mirrored carts meant to check for explosives. Instead of being alarmed by the vehicles barreling toward them, they moved back and offered a sharp salute as Kennedy passed. Undoubtedly, this would be portrayed as a courtesy—an acknowledgment that an American of her stature was above normal procedures. In actuality, it was an admission that slowing could make her vehicle vulnerable to a rocket attack.

Once inside the walls, Kennedy rolled down her window and looked out over the manicured lawns, fountains, and carefully maintained adobe buildings. It always struck her that the facility looked more like a university campus than the headquarters of one of the most dangerous and secretive intelligence agencies the world had ever known. Maybe someday one of her successors would come here to find it inhabited by young people with backpacks full of textbooks. She hoped so. But right now that idyllic world seemed a thousand years away.

Her lead cars broke off and the limousine pulled up in front of a large, modern building with a lone man standing in front of it. He hurried to open her door, nodding respectfully as she stepped out.

"Dr. Kennedy. Welcome. I'm General Taj's assistant, Kabir Gadai." He held out a hand and she took it. His grip had a practiced feel to it, as did the warmth of his smile. According to his CIA file, Gadai was an extremely well-educated moderate Muslim who had just celebrated his thirty-fourth birthday. A top college cricket player, he'd spent five years in the military after graduation, two with the special forces. To top it off, his wife was stunning and his children earned perfect marks. An overachiever in every sense of the word.

With the exception of his still-solid physique, Gadai's military background was no longer evident. His suit looked like Brooks Brothers, his stylishly cut hair was just a bit over the ear, and his admittedly handsome face was devoid of the mustache favored by many of his colleagues.

"If you could please follow me," he said, leading her into a massive circular lobby with a single security guard who seemed unwilling to even look in their direction. Gadai's voice echoed slightly as he spoke about the building's architecture, the founding of the ISI by a British army officer in the late 1940s, and the organization's importance to what he optimistically described as Pakistan's continued success.

Of course, he was careful to keep the history lesson non-controversial, a light entertainment for his guest as the elevator rose toward the top floor. He didn't mention that the massive expansion of the organization had been funded with dollars that were supposed to have gone to supply the mujahideen's resistance to the Soviets. Or the S Wing, a loose confederation of largely retired ISI operatives in charge of liaising with terrorist groups. And he certainly didn't touch on the fact that the power of the ISI had grown to such proportions that a former Pakistani president had once referred to it as a state within a state.

The elevator doors opened and Gadai led her through a richly appointed hallway that had been cleared for her arrival. Ahmed Taj's suite was at the far end and Gadai led her through the outer office.

"It's been a pleasure meeting you," he said, before opening the ISI director's door for her. "I hope to see you again soon."

Kennedy smiled politely before stepping across the threshold. Ahmed Taj immediately rose from his desk and strode toward her with a hand outstretched.

"It's wonderful as always to see you, Irene. I thank you for making the journey. I trust it wasn't too tiring."

"It was nice to get away from the office, Ahmed. I imagine you're one of the few people who can understand."

"Indeed," he said sympathetically and then motioned toward a group of couches set up in front of one of three stone fireplaces. The office was an opulent affair entirely at odds with the modern architecture of the building. At least four times the size of her own, its walls were covered in rich wood paneling. Numerous bookcases were arranged with photos and other memorabilia, but few actual volumes.

"Tea?"

"Yes, thank you."

Kennedy examined Taj as he poured. The man was a stark contrast to the imposing surroundings, which she knew to be the work of his predecessor. At the Pakistani president's urging, Parliament had chosen the ISI's new director not for his ruthlessness or cunning but for his spectacular mediocrity.

Taj's gift for military supply logistics, as well as his ability to navigate the egos and agendas of his superiors, had allowed him to rise to the rank of air force general. When compared to even his own young assistant, though, Taj came up wanting. His suit was of average quality, he stood barely five six, and his stomach seemed to expand a little more every time she saw him. He had never been an athlete, and his grades had been good, but far from spectacular. Most notable, though, was the fact that whereas Gadai met her eye and spoke in a clear, confident tone, Taj had a tendency to mumble and look at the floor.

At first, she had been surprised when he'd been named and thought that it was perhaps meant as a tacit apology for the Osama bin Laden fiasco. What she'd come to learn, though, was that Taj possessed the one quality that the country's president needed. He was controllable.

Whether this was a good thing or not was, like everything related to Pakistan, a complicated matter. The ISI was heavily factioned. It wasn't unusual for one branch to be hunting a particular terrorist group while another funded it. That incohesiveness weakened the organization and benefited the civilian government, but it also contributed to the dangerous chaos Pakistan was descending into.

Mitch Rapp summed up the ISI situation as a simple question of whether organized crime or disorganized crime was preferable. In his words, would she rather deal with the mafia or a bunch of shiv-wielding junkies?

"I'm glad you agreed to come," Taj said as he finished pouring and took a seat across from her. "I think a face-to-face meeting is better to put this matter behind us."

"So do I."

She picked up her cup and took a sip, making it clear that she wasn't inclined to offer more.

"In our last meeting you made a number of accusations."

"'Accusations' seems like a strong word, Ahmed. I would say 'concerns.'"

His dull eyes fell to the coffee table. "Concerns, then. I'm afraid they were largely justified."

"Indeed?" she said, keeping her expression passive.

"Yes. I've been authorized to tell you everything we've been able to determine about your man Joseph Rickman."

She didn't respond, letting the silence draw out between them until he felt compelled to start speaking again.

"He did not die in the video released on the Internet."

She let the surprise read on her face, despite knowing that Rickman had met his end like so many before him: at the hands of Mitch Rapp. "I'm sorry, I don't understand."

"He was, in fact, transported to Pakistan. Specifically, to Akhtar Rani's private compound."

"The deputy director of your external wing? To what end?"

"His death video was a ruse to ensure that both you and I would stop looking for him. He was transported to General Durrani's home and held there to give Akhtar time to extract everything Rickman knew about the CIA's operations."

"And you're telling me you had no knowledge of this?" Kennedy said, making it a point to allow a bit of skepticism to creep into her voice.

"None," Taj said emphatically. "It seems likely that Durrani wanted to use this information to inflate his own power and unseat me as director."

Of course that is how he would see it. In truth, Durrani had been a thug. Not a stupid man per se, but hardly clever enough to be behind this scheme. No, Rickman had been in charge the entire time. He would have allowed Durrani the illusion of control while he used the man and his organization to carry out his plan of gutting the CIA's worldwide operations.

"Can I assume you'll be turning Rickman over to me immediately?"

Taj's dark skin took on a pallor. "I'm sorry to inform you that he's dead."

"As is Durrani," Kennedy said. "The press release I read said a heart attack."

"In fact, both appear to have been shot by Durrani's man Vazir Kassar, who gained access to his compound with an unknown accomplice. Of course, we'll turn Rickman's body over to your embassy as soon as we can make arrangements."

Kennedy brushed her dark hair behind her ear and leaned back into the sofa. Taj's story explained his forthrightness. The operation against Durrani was highly professional and he had been unable to identify Kassar's accomplice. He would have no choice but to consider the possibility that the CIA had been involved and that she already knew about Durrani's plot. Better to confess and place the blame on a dead man than be caught in a lie that could implicate the entire ISI.

"Can I also assume that the men who were killed in Switzerland were ISI assets?"

"Yes," Taj said, looking increasingly miserable. "Durrani's men. They were interested in the banker Leo Obrecht, who, as you know, seems to have been deeply involved in what was happening. The one who escaped was Kassar. We are trying to find him but so far have had no luck."

It was an unlucky streak that would continue. She had Kassar. He'd declined her job offer, opting instead for a new identity, a U.S. passport, and enough money to start a new life.

"What information did Rickman provide Durrani before their deaths? Was there anything beyond what we saw in the video?"

"I'm afraid I have no idea. All the computers were missing from Durrani's house. I assume taken by Kassar and his man. An exhaustive search of his home turned up nothing of interest. Currently we're working on his Internet usage, bank accounts, and known associates. Rest assured that we're doing everything possible to dissect Durrani's plan and determine whether he passed sensitive information to any of his people. I'm not aware of any additional revelations since their deaths and my assumption is that Rickman's knowledge was limited to your network in Afghanistan. My hope is that this incident is behind us."

Kennedy sat quietly on the sofa. Unfortunately his hopes and her own would be dashed. Rickman's genius and years in the clandestine services had left him with knowledge far beyond his theater of operation. And the situation with Sitting Bull suggested that at least some of that knowledge had made its way into the wrong hands.

"I appreciate your forthrightness, Ahmed."

"We understand the seriousness of this situation and acknowledge the friendship you've showed our country. We are entirely to blame for this incident and can only hope you understand that both I and President Chutani are doing everything we can to mitigate the damage."

She decided to ignore what was undoubtedly meant as an apology, instead changing the subject.

"And Qayem?"

Lieutenant General Abdul Rauf Qayem had ordered an attack on Mitch Rapp that had led to the death of one of Rapp's men as well as twenty-one Afghan police officers.

"We're trying to locate him, but it will be difficult. My understanding is that he believes your Mr. Rapp is hunting him and because of that, he has fled to the mountains."

Taj's information paralleled her own. Rapp had Commander Abdul Siraj Zahir of the Afghan police looking for the man, but Zahir reported that the general had disappeared into the hinterland and abandoned all electronic communication. Of course, Zahir was a sadistic psychopath who had changed sides in the Afghan conflict more times than anyone could count, so who could say for certain?

"My problem, Ahmed, is that the Afghan police are blaming Mitch for attacking their men without provocation. Can I assume you'll use your network to set the record straight? The rumors and animosity are making it difficult for my people to do their jobs."

"Of course. We'll begin spreading that message immediately."

She doubted that was true but, at a minimum, his failure to grant her request would be something she could use against the ISI in their future dealings.

"I'd like to make something very clear—" Kennedy started but then fell silent when the door to Taj's office opened. When she caught a glimpse of the man in the threshold, she immediately rose to her feet.

Taj did the same, but didn't seem to share her surprise.

"I don't think we've had the pleasure," President Saad Chutani said, shaking Kennedy's hand and then indicating toward the sofa. "Please accept my apologies for intruding."

She lowered herself back into the cushions. "No apologies necessary, Mr. President. I'm honored."

Chutani was a head taller than his intelligence chief and seemed to dominate the man in every way.

"I don't have much time, but I wanted to personally reaffirm my confidence in Ahmed."

"Thank you, Mr. President."

Chutani slapped him on the back, seemingly unaware that he'd spoken. "Could you excuse us for a moment? I'd like to speak privately with Director Kennedy."

"Of course, sir."

They both watched Taj retreat across his own office and close the door. When he was gone, Chutani took a seat across from Kennedy and appraised her. The intensity of his stare was both impressive and unsurprising. He'd been one of the country's top generals for years before entering politics. Somewhat unusual for Pakistan, he had become president through an election and not a coup. Since then, he'd managed to marginalize the country's prime minister and Parliament, gathering more and more authority for his office. In many ways, he had become little more than a dictator, but as pro-American a dictator as could be reasonably hoped for in this part of the world.

Kennedy just sat quietly. Some of the most powerful people in the world had tried to stare her down, and she found it was best not to react. Politicians were creatures controlled by passion and it was most effective to quietly absorb that energy without actually giving ground.

"I'd like to extend my personal apologies to you and to ask you to relate that to President Alexander."

"Of course, sir."

He smiled. "I'd heard that you're difficult to ruffle, and it seems those reports are accurate."

"Sir?"

"I'd like an honest assessment, Director Kennedy. How badly has this hurt our relationship?"

"I know that our secretary of state is going to be visiting Islamabad soon. I think she would be a more appropriate person to ask that question."

"But you're here now, so I'm asking you."

It was a position Kennedy felt uncomfortable in. She wasn't a politician and had no desire to be one. Having said that, refusing to answer a direct question from the president of Pakistan seemed impolitic.

"First bin Laden, now one of your people kidnaps our top operative in Afghanistan and tortures him for information," she started, careful to state only the public story. "It's been a difficult time for U.S.-Pakistan relations. An era that I think we'd all like to bring to a close."

"It has indeed been difficult. But you forgot to mention your CIA agents brazenly killing our citizens. And that your embassy is shielding Pakistani citizens accused of spying by your Joe Rickman. Also, there are the constant drone attacks. None of this is easy for me. I answer to the people of Pakistan."

"President Alexander has been clear that our drone program could be significantly scaled back if you think it's necessary."

The politician's smile lost a bit of its gleam. They both knew that he was using America's drones to destroy fundamentalists targeting his regime and not those threatening the United States. It was another nuance that she'd found Congress impervious to understanding. Insofar as scoring political points went, one dead terrorist was as good as another to them.

"You're not a naïve woman, Director Kennedy. You understand what I'm dealing with in trying to reinvent Pakistan as a modern country. Taj is very reasonable and more intelligent than you perhaps give him credit for. But many of our enemies aren't reasonable. Indeed, many of the men working at this very organization aren't reasonable. Unfortunately, men like Durrani and your Mitch Rapp are valuable in their ability to understand our terrorist enemies and, if necessary, to match their brutality."

"With all due respect, Mr. President, Mitch has never betrayed me or his country."

"Then he's a unique man. The skills he and Durrani possess usually come with ambition. Taj didn't watch Durrani close enough. It's a classic mistake, really—to judge others' rationality based on one's own. I assure you he won't make it again."

"I trust then that Durrani's replacement will be easier to work with?"

Chutani frowned. "Concessions had to be made. The new man is not as volatile as Durrani, but he's still very strong. He has to be able to control certain elements within the ISI. Elements that it will take time to eradicate."

"I'm certain he was an excellent choice, and I look forward to meeting him," Kennedy said, making sure she sounded sincere.

"Cooperation and stability, Director. That is what will be good for both our countries. Pakistan needs economic growth and education. Those are the only things that will break the influence of the radicals. People with good lives are hesitant to jeopardize them. People who have nothing, on the other hand, are often no better than wild animals."

She nodded and took a sip of now-lukewarm tea. "I'll be happy to deliver your message to President Alexander, sir. I know how much he values your friendship and the friendship of your people."

CHAPTER 4

VASILY Zhutov skirted close to the building next to him, ignoring the dim display window full of electronics. The rain was coming down harder, but instead of pulling the umbrella from his briefcase, he just walked faster.

His masters in Moscow had thought he was insane when he'd volunteered to fill an open position in Istanbul. It was technically a demotion, but he needed a break if he was going to stave off the middle-aged heart attack suffered by so many of his colleagues.

Everything in Turkey didn't revolve around vodka and heavy food, and his new position didn't rate a car and driver. He'd mapped out this four-kilometer path home from his office the first week he'd arrived. It wound through an area that closed down by the time he got off and was thus devoid of pedestrians who could slow his pace. In less than a month, he'd lost two kilos and cut the time it took to cover the hilly course by almost two minutes.

He turned left into a cobblestone alleyway and glanced at the numbers counting down on his digital watch. It wasn't a record speed, but considering the weather and descending darkness, it was respectable.

More important to his health than the weight loss, though, was the fact that he was two thousand kilometers from the Kremlin, where career advancement was a universe unto itself. The job became not so much protecting the interests of Mother Russia as it was protecting one's own interests. His days had devolved into a blur of questionable political alliances and elaborate plots to destroy his rivals while they hatched similar plots against him.

That was what had driven him into the arms of the Americans. Of course, Russia's leaders would loudly condemn him as a traitor if they found out, but deep down they knew it was they who had betrayed their country. They who were turning it into a corrupt basket case barely kept afloat by natural resources gouged from the land.

There was no innovation, no plan for the future, no attempt to meaningfully engage the West. Only the occasional flexing of military muscle to stir the people's nationalism and blind them to the fact that they had no more hope now than they did under the communists.

Zhutov was forced to divert around a van moving across the entrance to a square dominated by an empty playground. He looked through the rain at the rusting equipment and once again considered how it could be used to enhance his daily exercise routine. Would a pull-up be achievable before he was recalled to headquarters? His doctor had urged caution, but at forty-three it seemed in the realm of possibility.

The van began to move and Zhutov adjusted his trajectory to cut across its rear. When he did, the driver slammed on the brakes, fishtailing on the slick cobbles. The back doors were thrown open and he stumbled to the right, barely avoiding being hit by one.

Despite extensive training in his youth, Zhutov froze. He found himself unable to resist as a man leapt out of the vehicle and grabbed him by the front of his suit jacket. The Russian was nearly lifted from the ground as he was driven into the vehicle's cramped cargo space. Somewhere in the distance, he heard the wet squeal of tires, but the sound seemed to disappear when he looked into the dark eyes of the man preparing to close the doors from his position on the street.

"No!" Zhutov shouted before he could be closed off from the outside world. His heart rate, already elevated from adrenaline and his evening workout, shot up again when he managed to put a name to the face. "Stop! I haven't betrayed you! I swear I haven't!"

He tried to fight into a sitting position but someone behind him grabbed his shoulders and held him down. Zhutov looked up at the disarming grin and neatly trimmed blond hair of Scott Coleman. "Relax, Vasily. We're the good guys."

"Go!" Rapp shouted, slamming the doors. He was sprayed with water as Maslick gunned the van's anemic engine and drifted it onto a winding street leading north. The safe house was less than three miles away and Coleman's team would hole up there for a few days to debrief Zhutov and build him a new identity.

A more pressing problem was the similar van barreling down on Rapp from the other side of the square. Behind him, there was a narrow walkway between two buildings. It would be an easy getaway since he wasn't aware of a single Russian operative who could even come close to keeping up with him on foot. It would also leave a lot of questions unanswered.

Too many, Rapp decided. Kennedy would just have to deal with the fallout.

He slipped his Glock 19 from beneath his jacket and sighted over the silencer toward the van now just over twenty yards away. The windshield wipers were running at full speed, giving him a clear view of the two men in the front seat. He aimed at the driver and squeezed off a round. The Winchester Ranger Bonded wasn't his normal go-to ammunition, but it was ideal for this scenario. Subsonic to eliminate the crack caused by the round breaking the sound barrier but with excellent penetration capability.

A spiderwebbed hole opened directly in front of the driver's face, but the bullet didn't find its mark. It wasn't entirely unexpected. The deflection of even a hard-hitting bullet could be significant. In his career he'd experienced everything from shots that went straight through to the target, to one that had veered so violently it had sheared off a side-view mirror.

The van swerved as the driver instinctively raised his hands to protect his face from the tiny shards of glass. Rapp fired a second shot at the damage made by the first. The softened glass reduced deflection and a spray of blood erupted when the driver's forehead was torn away.

The vehicle slowed as the man's foot went limp and Rapp moved left, bringing the side door into view. These tended to be three-man operations and that suggested the last team member was out of view in the cargo section. It was a prediction that was proved right when the door slid open and a bulky man with an unsuppressed Russian 9A-91 assault rifle started to leap out. Rapp blew the back of his skull off and watched as he pitched forward into the street. One of his feet got tangled in a seat belt and he was dragged along, leaving a broad streak of blood and brain matter on the wet cobblestones.

The surviving man in the passenger seat grabbed the wheel and turned the vehicle toward Rapp, desperately trying to get his foot past his dead companion's leg in order to slam the accelerator to the floor. It was a vaguely pathetic sight, and Rapp just stood there as the van rolled to a stop a few feet in front of him.

"Get out!" he yelled as the Russian stared at him wide-eyed and raised his hands.

He did as ordered and Rapp indicated toward the corpse hanging halfway out the door. "Put him inside."

The dead weight looked significant but the Russian managed. The square and the windows of the buildings around them were still empty, but it wouldn't last. One local with a cell phone was all it would take to bring the police down on them.

"You're driving," Rapp said, keeping his weapon lined up on the man as he dragged what was left of the original driver into the cargo area. Rapp climbed into the passenger seat and pulled the door closed, pressing the tip of his silencer into the man's ribs.

"Go. Nice and easy. No need to attract attention."

The Russian seemed reluctant to lean back into the blood-soaked headrest and instead hunched over the wheel as he steered the car past an empty playground.

"What's your name?" Rapp said.

"Vadim Yenotin."

"Do you know who I am?"

The man swallowed and nodded.

"Then you understand your situation."

"Yes."

They turned onto a broader avenue and were immediately surrounded by the glare of headlights.

"You have two options, Vadim. The first is that I take you to a safe house with a soundproof basement. Things get ugly and you tell me everything you know."

"I do not like this plan." His accent was thick but understandable.

"You're smarter than you look. Good. Option two is for you to answer all my questions completely and truthfully. After that, my boss calls your boss and they do a little horse-trading. You know the drill—we give up a little information and maybe pad a few of your superiors' retirement accounts. A week later, you're sitting in your apartment drinking vodka."

"Yes. I like this very much. This is what should be done."

"Why were you sent to pick Zhutov up?"

"The FSB received an email saying that he was being paid by the Americans."

"Who was it from?"

"Joseph Rickman."

"And you just believed it?"

"There was a great deal of information. The names of his handlers, information he'd passed to the CIA, dates, places. It said that he is the Sitting Bull that Rickman spoke of on the video."

"When did you get the email?"

"Five days ago."

Rapp pulled his gun from the man's ribs and jammed it into his crotch. "I thought you weren't going to lie to me, Vadim. Option one is now back on the table."

"No! I was informed five days ago. I saw the email myself. Our people checked the servers to confirm the date and to try to find where it came from. I swear!"

"Pull over on the next side street and park, Vadim. I don't want you to run over anyone when I blow your nuts off."

"I have no reason to lie to you about this! We arrived four days ago and began watching Zhutov to see if he would lead us to any of his contacts. We flew in on a commercial airliner and went through passport control. I can give you the names we used."

"Joe Rickman died two weeks ago, Vadim. So unless he's figured out a way to stuff his brain back into his skull, you have a serious problem."

"Impossible! Please. Check my story. The CIA can do this easily. You will find that I am telling the truth."

Rapp kept the silencer pressed into the man's crotch, but his desire to pull the trigger began to wane. He had a nose for lies and the overwhelming impression he was getting from Yenotin was that he was very fond of his testicles. The Russian wasn't one of the fanatics Rapp had spent his career dealing with. He wasn't looking to get his fingernails pulled in an effort to please Allah. He was a professional who understood the zero-sum game played by world powers.

"You said your people tried to determine where the email came from. What did they learn?"

"Nothing. It traveled all over the world. There was no way to trace its source."

Rapp let out a long breath and indicated for the man to turn right at the next intersection. Things had just gone from complete crap to insurmountable disaster.

CHAPTER 5

THE Land Cruiser's front wheels dropped into a muddy ditch, and Ahmed Taj heard the whine of the engine as his driver gunned the vehicle toward the low bank on the other side.

Taj didn't bother to look outside. He'd grown up surrounded by such places, and little had changed over the years. Unmaintained dirt roads still threaded haphazardly through tent cities and mud brick huts. The clear sky was still obscured by smoke from cooking fires. The only anomaly was the absence of people. Normally, the area would be filled with children not yet bowed by their circumstances and adults trying desperately to find a way to fill their bellies. On this day, his security detail had coordinated with the local Islamic militias to clear his entry and exit routes.

The SUV he was in was painted white and emblazoned with the logo of one of the aid agencies active in the area, allowing for a certain amount of anonymity despite being the only vehicle on the street. He glanced upward through the moon roof and saw nothing. It was an illusion, though. The Americans were ever present, watching with sat-ellites, drones, and co-opted security cameras. Their mastery of technology was their greatest strength. But their utter reliance on it was, ironically, their greatest weakness.

Areas like these had been slowly taken over by various radical groups with the help of Akhtar Durrani and his notorious S Wing.

The task of relocating these groups from the rural areas to the cities had been as critical as it was monumental. Here, mixed into the general population, even the most surgical drone strike would generate substantial collateral damage. The Americans were uncomfortable with civilian casualties and absolutely abhorred photographs of the blackened bodies of women and children.

It was all part of the bizarre web of lies and hidden agendas created by his country's long relationship with the United States. Many of the politicians in Washington believed that the quagmire in Afghanistan had been caused by the U.S. abandoning the region after the Soviets fled. It was a naïve and arrogant view—an example of how the Americans saw the world as revolving entirely around their fleeting experiment with democracy. Afghanistan had simply reverted back to what it had been for a thousand years. An inevitable and easily predicted outcome.

The money originally earmarked for the mujahideen, though, continued to flow. In the last year alone, the United States had supplied almost $5 billion in aid to Pakistan, most of which had been quietly absorbed by the military and ISI. In fact, the army was now the country's largest holder of commercial real estate, owning condominium complexes, shopping malls, and office buildings throughout the world. Pakistan's generals were some of the wealthiest men in the country.

While the situation was hopelessly complicated, its fundamentals were simple: Pakistan's military-industrial complex and intelligence apparatus had become addicted to American dollars. The only real threat to that massive source of funding was the eradication of terrorism in the region. This left the ISI in the twisted but wildly profitable business of publicly fighting the terrorist threat to America while privately supporting it.

It was a situation that had to be handled with the utmost care. Enough fires had to be ignited to keep the Americans chasing after them, but no single fire could burn so brightly that it garnered too much attention. Unfortunately, that line had been recently crossed.

Durrani had pressed Afghan general Abdul Qayem to set up an assassination attempt on Mitch Rapp. It had been a largely foolish enterprise, turning entirely on successfully killing a man who had proved countless times to be immune to such actions. Now Rapp was leaving no stone unturned in his search for Qayem, including pressing into service Abdul Zahir, who was as shrewd as he was loathsome.

Arrogance was a trap that had killed countless powerful men, and it was one that Taj had promised himself he would never fall into. Mitch Rapp was not someone to be trifled with. Only a fool would refuse to acknowledge that he usually got what he wanted. And what he wanted was to hunt down and butcher his enemies.

Local militia began appearing on the street—dirty men with Kalashnikovs and faces obscured by scarves. They watched his vehicle pass but made no move to block its progress. The Land Cruiser threaded through a narrow gap in a mud wall and stopped on the other side. Taj stepped out, looking down to hide his face from potential surveillance drones. The stone hovel was only a few meters away, and he covered the ground quickly, passing through a door that had been cobbled together from materials scrounged from a landfill.

Inside, the heat and stench of excrement condensed into a humid fog. The single room was empty and he crossed to the back of it, descending a set of rickety stairs to a basement carved from the earth. It was, in fact, one of the many entrances to an elaborate maze of fetid tunnels designed to obscure the movements of the insurgents inhabiting the area.

Near the base of the stairs was a lone man, naked except for a black canvas hood secured around his neck. His hands and feet were wired to the chair he was in and his head moved with birdlike jerks as he tried to track the movement his ears had picked up.

Taj stopped in front of the man, letting his gaze sweep from the stomach resting on thighs thick with hair, to a tray arranged with knives, pliers, and a single propane-fueled torch.

"Ahmed!"

Taj turned toward the figure of General Qayem as he emerged from a tunnel beneath the stairs.

"Abdul. It brings me joy to see you."

They embraced, and when Taj pulled away he pointed to the naked man in the chair. "You found him."

"He's a clever little cockroach," Qayem said. "He has many rocks to hide beneath, but his main tool is fear. Fortunately, some of his men are more afraid of me than they are of him."

He pulled the hood off and Taj looked into the terrified eyes of Abdul Zahir. His hair and beard were shoe-polish black, contrasting the gray streaks of his body hair. It was the custom of Afghan men to try to look younger than they were in a country where age was often seen as a sign of weakness.

"Are you pleased?" Qayem asked.

It was hardly the right word. He was angry about Qayem's attack on Rapp, but it was impossible to blame the man. He was an old and loyal friend who had only been following Akhtar Durrani's orders. The great lengths the ISI went to in order to ensure unquestioning loyalty could at times have drawbacks. Qayem would have never even considered questioning the orders of the deputy general of ISI's external wing.

"Please," Zahir said through chapped, swollen lips but then seemed to lose his train of thought. "Please . . ."

"And what would you have me do for you?" Taj said. "You are a pig who believes in nothing. Who serves neither God nor his people. Who allies himself with whoever pays the most."

"It's not true!" he said, the lack of force in his voice suggesting that even he recognized the absurdity of the denial.

"You were never of any importance, Zahir. I would have been content for you to just die of old age, surrounded by the things your treachery allowed you to acquire. But then you allied yourself with Mitch Rapp."

"Malik al-Mawt? No! That's a lie!" Zahir said. Malik al-Mawt roughly translated to *the angel of death*, a moniker that the Afghans had given Rapp years ago.

"I believe you know him as Mr. Harry."

Zahir's eyes widened. "It can't be. I . . . I didn't know."

Taj could tolerate liars, but there was nothing that disgusted him more than a coward. By all reports, Zahir had tried to insert himself into the investigation of Rickman's kidnapping thinking it was being run by the CIA's pathetic station chief, Darren Sickles. Instead of the bowing and scraping he'd become accustomed to, though, he'd found Rapp's pistol pressed to his forehead. Ever since, the man had been tracking Qayem in hopes of saving his own pathetic life.

"I am deeply sorry about Rapp," Qayem said. "It was my failure and my responsibility."

"No, old friend. This was Durrani's failure. And he's paid for his incompetence."

In fact, it was likely that Durrani had died at the end of Rapp's infamous Glock. Taj had extensive audio surveillance set up at Durrani's house, but cameras had been impractical. This left him with only a general description of Kassar's accomplice in the killing of Durrani and Rickman. Digital recordings of the man's voice had confirmed an American accent but they were of insufficient quality for comparative voice printing.

It was this uncertainty that had left him no choice but to tell Irene Kennedy far more than he'd wanted. There was no way to know what Kennedy had learned or what she suspected. He couldn't afford to be caught in a lie. She was a clever bitch and he needed to build trust between them—to blind her until it was too late.

"Please," he heard Zahir say behind him. "You have to believe me. If I had known who he was, I would have never helped him. I would have—"

"Silence!" Taj screamed, spinning and running at the man. He snatched a meat cleaver from the tray and swung it down onto Zahir's wrist where it was secured to the arm of the chair.

The hand remained wired where it was, but Zahir's arm was suddenly free. He screamed like a woman as he drew back the stump, spraying blood across Taj's white polo shirt.

The ISI director retreated out of range and Qayem snatched a piece of wood from the dirt floor, swinging it full force into the side of the wailing man's head. Silence once again descended on the cramped underground chamber. Only Qayem's elevated breathing and the sound of Zahir's life leaking from him intruded.

"Rapp is coming for you, my friend," Taj said. "I have a man inside his organization who I believe will be able to eliminate him, but our ability to communicate is limited. Once again, we find time working against us."

Qayem was smart enough to understand that he would eventually be found and humble enough to know that he would eventually break. No one could resist what the CIA man would unleash.

"You know what has to be done," Taj said.

"Yes."

The dirt floor had been turned to mud by Zahir's blood, increasing the humidity as Taj returned to the tray and picked up the traitor's .40-caliber Smith & Wesson. A gift from the Americans.

He raised the weapon and pressed it against his old friend's forehead.

God is great were the last words to pass Abdul Qayem's lips.

CHAPTER 6

BY design, the gravel road that cut through the forest never stretched more than fifty yards before taking a hard turn. The contractor who'd built it was a bit baffled by the routing and even more baffled when he'd been asked to do a purposely lousy surfacing job. In the end, though, the finished product had been exactly what Stan Hurley wanted: a road that even the world rally champion couldn't drive at much more than twenty-five miles an hour.

Despite its all-wheel-drive system, Mitch Rapp's black Dodge Charger was limited to about half that. The 5.7-liter Hemi had no problems handling the extensive modifications he'd made but dialing in the suspension had been more problematic. The biggest casualty, though, was the sound system. Most of the speakers had ended up in a dumpster to make room for multiple layers of Kevlar.

He came over a steep rise and frowned when the front spoiler scraped. He'd have to tell Hurley to order the next round of recruits to smooth the peak of that one. A perfect activity to shoehorn in between a twenty-mile run and shooting the local rapids on their backs.

It took another ten minutes to reach the interior gate, which opened automatically when he approached. A few seconds later, he was on butter-smooth pavement bisecting a manicured lawn dotted with flower beds.

The property was nearly an exact copy of the one he'd trained at as a youth. The barn was red instead of white, built to look like it was half a century older than its actual age. The wraparound porch on the farmhouse was a little broader and the outdoor furniture a little more modern. That was about all that met the eye. Below the surface, though, updates were more substantial. The house's basement was far larger, more elaborate, and secure. The sensors that crisscrossed the hundred acres were an order of magnitude more advanced. And most of the lawn was mined. Kennedy was against the last one, but Hurley had convinced her that the computer-controlled system was foolproof. Having said that, Rapp noticed she stayed to the road and walkways.

The property was a monument to the dysfunction inside the Beltway. Every seven years or so, Hurley's clandestine training facility would "accidentally" burn to the ground and another one would be built on a new piece of property paid for with black funds.

If all this effort was to keep ahead of America's enemies, it wouldn't bother Rapp. In fact, it was done to keep ahead of the politicians sniffing around for off-the-books CIA activity they could use to make political points. Displaying fake indignation had become Congress's primary job description.

It was a game the CIA was forced to play with full knowledge that there was no way to win. If Rapp did what was necessary to keep members of Congress and their constituents safe, he was in danger of being indicted. If he followed the rules and allowed America to be attacked, he was in danger of being publicly crucified.

Ahead, Stan Hurley was standing on the porch watching through the same aviator glasses he'd been wearing when Rapp had rolled in as a naïve college kid. The old cuss was probably close to eighty now, but no one seemed to know for certain. He had a bourbon in one hand and, despite advanced lung cancer, a cigarette in the other. No point in turning into a health nut now.

"You're late," he said as Rapp stepped out of the vehicle.

There was actually no specific time he was scheduled to arrive, but Rapp let it go. Hurley had a way of getting under his skin like no one else and it had been a long flight from Turkey.

"Good to see you, too, Stan."

Rapp walked around to the back of the car and opened the trunk. Vadim Yenotin threw his hands up defensively and squinted into the sun.

"Out," Rapp said.

The man was understandably stiff as he eased his legs over the rear bumper. The Charger didn't have much of a trunk, and the weapons case Rapp had built into the bottom made it even smaller.

He grabbed the Russian by the collar and marched him toward the house as Hurley looked on with a bored expression. "Put him in a hole and meet me in the bar. Irene touched down an hour ago. Based on my conversation with her, you're probably going to want something to take the edge off before she gets here."

Rapp stayed behind the Russian as they cut through an incongruously modern kitchen and entered a pantry lined with canned food and baking supplies. It doubled as an elevator, and a click of the key chain in Rapp's pocket caused the floor to begin dropping. A moment later, they were in a long cinder-block room lined with doors—all bare steel with a single hatch just big enough to pass a food tray through. Rapp opened the first one and shoved the Russian inside.

"Wait!" he said, stumbling, but catching himself before he fell. "What are you going to do with me? I told you what you wanted to know. You said you'd send me home."

"What are you complaining about?" Rapp said. "This is the presidential suite."

There were six cells in total. They ranged in comfort from this one, which boasted a sofa bed and big-screen TV, to a concrete cube with dripping pipes and a bucket for a toilet.

"Stop!" Yenotin said as Rapp began closing the door. "I demand that you let me talk to my embassy."

"Consider yourself lucky, Vadim. If it weren't for Irene Kennedy, you'd be spending the week in my trunk."

The door clanged shut, and Rapp took a step back but made no move to leave. Instead he turned and stared at the door to the left of the one he'd just closed. The cell beyond contained Louis Gould, the professional assassin who had blown up Rapp's home, killing his family and leaving him in the hospital with multiple broken bones and swelling on the brain.

He was suddenly aware of the weight of the Glock hanging beneath his right shoulder. It could be over in a few seconds. All he had to do was open the door, aim, and pull the trigger. Normally, killing affected him very little, but how would it feel to end Gould's life? To rip him away from his own wife and daughter? Would it finally put Anna's ghost to rest? Or would it just leave him with nothing to cling to?

"Vodka's on the pool table." Hurley's voice behind him. He hadn't even noticed the elevator go up to get the man.

"Yeah," Rapp said, trance broken.

The door opposite the holding cells led to the bar—another thing that got more elaborate with every iteration of the CIA's clandestine training facility. Hurley seemed to have plucked this one directly from his memory. With the exception of the contemporary pool table centered in it, the space felt like a mid-seventies Morocco dive. The far wall was exposed stone framing an antique mahogany bar imported from France. Asian-style lamps, a few antique ceiling fans, and Hurley's collection of framed World War II–era photos completed the illusion. As the old man's life came to a close, he seemed more and more comfortable in the past.

Rapp picked up the vodka and took a healthy slug before grabbing a cue and slamming the six ball into the side pocket. His thoughts turned to their situation, and once again the anger began to burn in the pit of his stomach. What had Rickman been thinking? Why would a man turn on his country? On his comrades in arms?

It was a question Rapp doubted he'd ever be able to answer. At his core, he was a soldier. A man who located and killed the enemies of his country and who would give his life to protect any member of his team. That was it. Simple.

When Irene Kennedy finally walked in, she was looking a bit haggard. Most people would have seen only what she wanted them to—the neatly pressed skirt, the impeccable white blouse, and the brown hair carefully pulled back. There was something around her eyes, though. Something that said this wasn't business as usual.

"Two Russians dead, Mitch. *Two.*"

Rapp fired the one ball into the corner but didn't otherwise respond.

"Are you telling me there was absolutely no other way to handle that situation?"

He turned his head and stared at her. They locked eyes for a few seconds before Hurley intervened.

"Come on, Irene. The driver tried to run him down and then another guy jumped out with a 9A-91. What did you want Mitch to use? Harsh language? Those Russian pricks were a day late and a dollar short and they knew it. They should have just crawled back under the rock they came from. It was a tactical mistake on their part and now they're dead."

She walked to the bar and poured herself a glass of red wine, using it to wash down two pills. Tylenol, Rapp knew. Ever since the Rickman thing had blown up, she'd been getting headaches.

He put down the cue and leaned back against the table. As much as he despised being second-guessed on operational details, he felt a pang of guilt. She'd become like a sister to him and he was worried about her.

"What Stan left out was that the 9A-91 wasn't even suppressed. That guy was about to do a spray-and-pray in the middle of a city full of fourteen million people, Irene. He had to be dealt with."

She drained half the glass and then put it down on the bar. "I know. But I have five messages from the head of the FSB literally screaming into my voice mail."

Hurley shook his head in disgust. "Mikhail's just playing the victim so he can work you over for two men he doesn't give a rat's ass about."

She shook her head slowly. "A few years ago, this would be a career-defining crisis. Now it feels like a mild distraction. How sure are you that Yenotin is telling the truth, Mitch? That the Russians got the email *after* Rick's death?"

"Ninety-nine percent. He wasn't in a lying mood."

"I was afraid of this."

"What?" Hurley asked.

"Akhtar Durrani has a reputation for killing people who are no longer useful to him. And Rick was terrified of Mitch. If I'd been in his position, I'd have had an insurance policy."

"What kind of insurance policy?"

"Someone to release the information in the event I died. It would have created an incentive for Durrani to keep him alive and it would have ensured that no matter what, the damage he wanted to do to us would happen."

"I could see the little pencil dick doing something like that," Hurley said, lighting a new cigarette off the embers of his old one. "But how?"

"More like who," Rapp said. "Who did he give his files to and who released the information on Sitting Bull? Some foreign agent who has it in for us? A mercenary who's just in it for the money?"

Kennedy shook her head. "Too unreliable. If it were me, I'd en-crypt the files and hand them over to a lawyer. I'd tell him I was going to check in with him every week and if I didn't, he should open a set of instructions I'd given him and follow them."

"What would those instructions say?" Hurley asked.

"They would be a schedule for sending individual files. They'd go to someone less reputable—someone who knows how to send emails and post things to the Internet without being traced. The lawyer would never know what was in the documents and the person releasing them would be the type who doesn't care."

There was a knock at the door, and a moment later a young man with an impressive Afro peeked in. "I found something."

Marcus Dumond was a thirty-four-year-old computer genius with a bit of a checkered past. The young cyber-wiz had run into some trouble with the feds while he was earning a master's in computer science at MIT. He was alleged to have hacked into one of New York's largest banks and then transferred funds into several overseas accounts. The part that interested the CIA was that Dumond wasn't caught because he left a trail; he was caught because he got drunk one night and bragged about his activities to the wrong person. At the time, Dumond was living with Steven Rapp, Mitch's younger brother. When the older Rapp heard about Dumond's problems, he called Irene Kennedy and told her the hacker was worth a look.

"Come in," Rapp said. "What have you got?"

Dumond entered a bit hesitantly, setting up a laptop on the pool table. Rapp recognized it as being one he'd taken from Durrani's house. It was still stained with Joe Rickman's blood.

"I've cracked the encryption protecting all the files on here," Dumond said.

"Really?" Kennedy replied, sounding surprised. "I thought Rick would make it harder than that."

Dumond shook his head. "Just the standard stuff that came with the computer. His password was one of his kids' birth dates."

"I sense that you're about to tell me the bad news."

"Yeah . . . There isn't really anything in them. Mostly personal stuff—his passwords to Amazon, checkbook registers, bank records. That kind of thing."

Kennedy picked up her glass again. "That makes more sense to me. Anything we can access that easily is something Rick either didn't care about or he wanted us to see."

Dumond started to look uncomfortable again.

"What?" Rapp said.

"I figured I'd connect it to the Internet. You know, download any outstanding emails, see if anything interesting happened."

"That's kind of a risk, isn't it?" Rapp said. "It could have been set to wipe the data."

Dumond frowned. He liked being questioned about his work even less than Rapp did. "I mirrored the drive first. And like I said, there's nothing interesting on it anyway."

"So what happened?" Hurley said.

"It automatically downloaded a video."

"What kind of video?" Kennedy asked. "Did you watch it?"

Dumond shook his head. "I figured it was stuff I didn't really want to know."

Rapp slapped him on the shoulder. "Good job, Marcus. Now why don't you go back to work and see what else you can dig up."

When he was gone, Hurley and Kennedy came over to the pool table and Rapp clicked on the video file in the middle of the laptop screen. A window opened, showing Joe Rickman sitting in his Jalalabad home office. He was wearing tooled leather boots, which were propped lazily on his desk. The location and the fact that his soft body and face were uninjured suggested that the recording had been made before his faked kidnapping.

"Hello, Mitch. If you're watching this, me and Akhtar Durrani are dead. And if that's the case, I figure you did it."

Kennedy reached out and paused the playback. "Interesting. How many of these videos do you think he made?"

"What do you mean?" Hurley asked.

"What if Durrani was still alive? What if we'd captured and not killed him? How many scenarios did he have covered?"

"About a thousand if I know that little weasel," Hurley said.

She pressed the play button and Rickman came to life again.

"I have to admit that I thought Gould had a good chance to take you out. I mean, if not him, who? He's one of the top private contractors in the world and he already blew the crap out of your wife and kid."

Rickman's face broke into a wide grin as Rapp's darkened. He wished the son of a bitch really could come back to life. Because then he could kill him again.

"Look over at him, Irene," Rickman continued. "Does he look pissed? Well, how do you think I feel? I'm dead. Anyway, where was I?

Oh yeah. Mitch. Lord knows you're not the sharpest tool in the shed, but you do have one undeniable talent: not getting killed. When it comes to you surviving and your enemies ending up with a bullet in their skulls, you're an honest-to-God genius. Or maybe I should say idiot savant."

He laughed a little too wildly. As though he knew he no longer had to contain it. That he no longer had anyone to fool.

"Afghanistan will drive you nuts. You know that. We've talked about it. A thousand years of culture, man. You could kill everyone here except one cute little seven-year-old girl and you know what she'd do? Stab you with a pair of scissors the minute you turned your back. You might as well try to create a democracy in a rattlesnake den. And now the politicians are giving money and jobs to the people who a few years ago were trying to kill us."

What he was saying was true. Congress had decided that if they just threw enough money around, everyone in Afghanistan would learn to get along. In reality, the politicians just wanted out in the most face-saving way possible. Kick the problem down the road until they were retired and hitting golf balls in Florida.

"This place ruined my life, my family, my health. I have nothing left. A little pension so I can spend my old age sitting alone in a one-bedroom apartment while these bastards sit in their mansions and eat caviar with their kids."

He pulled his feet off the desk and leaned into the camera. "You destroyed me, Irene. So I'm going to return the favor. The leaks are going to keep coming. When I'm done with you, you'll be in jail and the CIA will be an embarrassing little entry in a history book. The world is chaos, punctuated by brief outbreaks of civilization. Mitch, you know that better than anyone. Where you go wrong is thinking you can change it."

He leaned back in his chair again, flashing another insane smile. "See you again soon."

The screen went black and Kennedy took a hesitant step backward. She'd offered to promote him, to pull him out of Afghanistan. But he'd repeatedly declined. Had the warning signs been there? Had she ignored them out of fear of losing his unique skill set?

Rapp seemed to read her mind. "We're all crazy, Irene. It's a prerequisite for the job. No one saw this coming. Not me, not Stan, and not Mike. Even the people who worked with Rick every day were completely blindsided."

"It wasn't their responsibility to see it coming. It was mine."

"Spilt milk," Hurley said impatiently. "You make things too complicated. All we have to do is find the people who have Rick's files and kill them. Problem solved."

"What did he know?" she said. "Sitting Bull was well outside his sphere of influence. How long had he been collecting intelligence on our network? How long had he been planning on using it to inflict maximum damage? And it's not just what he knew. He could lie, too. He could establish his credibility by handing over some legitimate assets, then start mixing in disinformation by naming people who aren't on our payroll."

"If he was going to release it all at once, he'd have done it by now," Rapp said. "No, he's going to dribble it out. Use it to torture us. That gives us time. Stan's right, we just have to find who has the files and stop them. Then it's over."

"And how do you propose we do that?"

"We follow the only lead we have."

"Obrecht," she acknowledged.

Leo Obrecht was a Swiss national who controlled Sparkasse Schaffhausen, a boutique bank based in Zurich. His name and that of his organization had been coming up since Rickman first disappeared. It was he who had accused Rapp and Rickman of depositing illicit personal funds in his bank.

Most interestingly, though, he was Louis Gould's handler. Vetting offers and accepting payments for an assassin wasn't exactly a common side project for a reputable banker.

"If I recall correctly," Kennedy said, "getting to Obrecht didn't work out well last time."

When Rapp had gone to Europe to get answers from the man, he'd run into a carload of ISI agents with the same mission. Three ended up dead and the other, Kassar, had been captured. Later, he'd proved critical to the operation against Rickman and Durrani.

"Obrecht's personal security is tight as hell," Rapp agreed. "And it's gotten even tighter since the incident with the Pakistanis. He doesn't leave his property at all anymore. But based on the amount of encrypted Internet traffic running between his mansion and the bank, he's keeping busy."

"Busy wiping all evidence of his involvement in this thing from his company's records," Kennedy said.

"A good bet."

"Can you two get to him?"

"Not easily," Hurley said before Rapp could answer. "Our best option would have been to take him while he was on the move."

"But you're saying he doesn't move anymore."

"He has to eventually."

Kennedy nodded thoughtfully. "Rickman's files are going to keep coming. When and how I can't say for certain, but I guarantee that it will be in the most damaging way possible."

"Can we absorb the hit?" Hurley asked.

"I honestly don't know, Stan. I ask myself, why did he do this now? He was still relatively young, he doesn't appear to have been ill, and I had no plans to pull him out. Rick never guessed, he planned. He analyzed. The only reason I can think of is that he believed he had enough to take us down. And when Rick believed something, it was usually because he was right."

"So if waiting isn't an option, we go for Obrecht at his house," Rapp said.

"With what?" Hurley responded. "A few Abrams tanks and an Apache?"

Rapp pushed himself up onto the edge of the pool table. "We're running out of time, Stan."

"Don't say it," Hurley pleaded.

"Look, I could probably figure out a way to get in there and kill the man, but that's not what we're talking about. We're talking about getting him out of his compound alive and transporting him somewhere we can interrogate him. I like it even less than you, Stan, but without Louis Gould's help, I don't see a way to make that happen."

CHAPTER 7

AHMED Taj looked between his two security men as the densely populated slum gave way to open highway. He would eventually be transferred to a nondescript Suzuki Mehran that would take him to a private jet registered in the name of a local extraction company.

It seemed almost impossible that his plan was finally going into action. He'd spent the last decade developing it, poring over every detail, examining every potential pitfall. And in many ways it extended even farther back than that. The groundwork for what was to come had been laid almost from his birth.

He had been raised in a modest neighborhood surrounded by the poverty that continued to plague Pakistan. Despite accumulating significant power and wealth, his father had been an unassuming man who deferred to those around him and rarely looked anyone in the eye.

It was the lesson that he beat into his son. Present nothing of yourself that the world would take note of. Build up others while diminishing yourself. Let the endless supply of egocentric men stand in the spotlight they craved while you remained in the darkness. That was how lasting empires were built.

Taj had quickly lost count of the men who had underestimated his father. The men whose bodies still littered the countryside surrounding his childhood home.

Eventually, he had been sent to America for college. The custom of wealthy Pakistanis at the time had been to send their children to their former oppressor, England, for their education. His father had recognized that the United Kingdom was weakening while America's influence grew. A devout Muslim, he understood that the massive Christian country would become a formidable enemy to the followers of Allah, and he wanted his son to understand its ways.

Taj had studied business and economics at an academically competent but unremarkable school in Virginia. In honor of his father's life lessons, he'd sat at the back of the classroom, writing all the correct answers on his tests before changing them to maintain a B-minus average. He'd made no real friends, though he was polite and reasonably well liked. In the end, he'd been satisfied to study American society from its edges.

What he'd seen disgusted him. Women who used the freedoms they were given to turn themselves into whores. Intellectualism that not only marginalized God, but often denied his existence. And the hopeless, endless arrogance.

He had recognized the seeds of America's decline and now those seeds were beginning to grow. Like the Soviets before them, the United States had been deeply wounded by its pathetic effort to conquer countries favored by Allah. Its insatiable greed for all things material had led to a financial collapse that was already in the early stages of being repeated. And its uncanny cohesiveness—the thing that was the secret to its strength—had devolved into petty squabbling and government paralysis. It was the fundamental flaw of democracy: Power found its way into the hands of liars and mobs instead of the cunning and the strong.

Upon graduation, Taj had returned to Pakistan and enlisted in the air force at his father's insistence. The path to power in Pakistan wasn't through the private sector, he knew. Certainly great wealth could play a part, but the country's soul was its military.

Taj had gone into logistics and made a name for himself as a competent and respectful officer. He'd made the right connections and, more important, done away with his rivals by manipulating them into destroying themselves. Eventually that led to his first star and to Saad Chutani foolishly giving him the helm of the ISI in an effort to gain control of the organization.

Now the unassuming Ahmed Taj was positioned to become one of the handful of men who ruled the world. He would turn his country into an enemy of America that would make what they'd experienced during the Soviet era seem trivial.

In fact, it should have already happened. As often was the case, though, even the most carefully laid plans could be derailed by unexpected events. In this instance, the actions of Akhtar Durrani.

Durrani had been a man of great hubris, violence, and ambition. He generated the fear necessary to rule over the ISI's S Wing and was a convenient tool to insulate Taj from the potential blowback generated by its operations.

Durrani had been instrumental in hiding Osama bin Laden, allowing the Saudi to hold al Qaeda together for years longer than would have been possible otherwise. He coordinated the resistance to American forces in Afghanistan and kept track of the insurgent groups that based themselves in Pakistan. Most important, though, he kept those insurgents under control, preventing them from mounting attacks inside Pakistan without ISI consent.

Durrani's alliance with Rickman had come as a rare surprise. Fortunately, Taj kept close tabs on everyone in a position of power at the ISI. It had been through this surveillance that he'd become aware of Rickman and decided to delay the implementation of his own plans. The value of the information the CIA man possessed was beyond calculation, a prize Taj never imagined when he'd first started scheming.

His first instinct had been to simply do away with Durrani and take Rickman when he arrived in Pakistan. Upon further consideration, though, he realized it would have been a mistake. Rickman was too brilliant, his mind too twisted. Even under extended interrogation it would be impossible to sort truth from lies.

Taj had no choice but to stay in the background and wait for the man to reveal what he knew. The trick would be finding the right moment to step out of the shadows. While his and Rickman's goals were similar, they were not the same.

Rickman wanted to punish the CIA, but Taj wanted to co-opt it. If he could gain access to what Rickman knew—his encyclopedic knowledge of every informant, traitor, and double agent in the region—he would have the ability to take control of the massive intelligence network while Irene Kennedy remained completely unaware. Before allowing the CIA to implode under the weight of its sins, he would siphon off its power. He would make the ISI, already swollen with billions of U.S. dollars, the most feared intelligence agency in history.

Unfortunately, between Durrani's stupidity and Mitch Rapp's brutality, the situation had become more complicated. In the end, though, it might be better this way. In every disaster lay opportunity.

He'd been watching Rickman long enough to know that the man was aware of the possibility of his own assassination and had made provisions to protect the information he'd so carefully compiled. That witch Kennedy was undoubtedly devoting her organization's entire capability to locating it but she was at a significant disadvantage. The CIA was just starting its search while Taj's men were nearing the completion of theirs.

CHAPTER 8

THE intercom on Irene Kennedy's desk buzzed and she picked up immediately.

"Dr. Kennedy, Senator Ferris just arrived."

"Thank you. Tell him I'll be just a moment."

She pulled up the security feed of her outer office and examined the man walking awkwardly toward a wing-backed chair. The notoriously tardy politician was right on time, and the large taxpayer-funded entourage he normally traveled with was conspicuously absent.

Carl Ferris had been consolidating his power in the Senate since she was in college, finally rising to the chairmanship of the Judiciary Committee. Surrounded exclusively with yes men and lobbyists, his ego had expanded to proportions unusual even by congressional standards. It gave him a gift for pontificating convincingly on any subject, ingratiating him with his constituents who tended to prefer simplicity and certainty to the more nuanced arguments of experts. The intelligence and military communities, though, saw him for what he was: an ignorant and ultimately dangerous blowhard.

He sat staring straight ahead, forgoing his normal demands from her staff for everything from coffee to the removal of a spot from his tie. It was a side of the influential senator that she had never seen, but that wasn't entirely unexpected.

Ferris had spent the last two years building a web of disgruntled CIA, FBI, and State Department employees to help him in his quest to bring the Agency under his control. Combined with information fed to him by a contact high up in Pakistan's ISI, he had been attempting to assemble enough damning evidence to hold public hearings designed to raise his own stature at the cost of America's security. Those plans had come to a grinding halt when she and the FBI had wiretapped one of his little cabal's meetings and arrested a number of his co-conspirators.

"How does he look?"

She glanced up at Mitch Rapp, who was sitting at one end of the conference table centered in her office. "Nervous. But reasonably healthy."

His eyes narrowed. The CIA possessed information on heart problems that the increasingly overweight senator was keeping quiet in hopes that he would be his party's next presidential nominee. She was convinced that the first thing Rapp did every morning was check his newsfeeds in hopes of finding a story about Carl Ferris dropping dead.

"I'm going to say again that I'd rather you weren't part of this meeting, Mitch. Based on what we've learned about the Rickman situation, it's time for a deescalation between us and the senator."

"I'm staying."

Kennedy sighed quietly. Ferris was scared, and that was something she could use. Panic, though, was a very different emotional state. It could create an environment where the politician turned desperate and unpredictable.

She reached for the intercom, resigned to the fact that nothing she could say would change Rapp's mind. "Please send him in."

Ferris entered a moment later, but froze when he saw Rapp. "What's he doing here?"

"Please close the door behind you, Senator."

"Are you crazy? He threatened to kill me! He said he was going to sneak into my house and—"

"Senator!" Kennedy said, allowing the volume of her voice to rise slightly. "Close the door."

He hesitated, but finally recognized that he had no choice. Kennedy indicated toward the conference table and Ferris kept a wary eye on Rapp as he took the chair farthest from him.

For her part, Kennedy remained at her desk. It would be seen by the politician as the same power play he himself used daily, but the truth was simpler. She was repulsed by the man and preferred to maintain physical distance whenever possible.

Kennedy didn't immediately speak, letting the politician sweat for almost a minute. He had undoubtedly gone over this meeting in his head a thousand times by now, crafting an exhaustive script of the lies and spin he was so well known for.

"I'd like you to tell us about your relationship with Pakistani intelligence," Kennedy said finally.

"I don't have one!" he protested. "This is ridiculous."

"Then you're telling me the emails we found on your maid's computer were hers? That she was corresponding with Akhtar Durrani, the deputy director of the ISI's external wing?"

"No, of course not. But I've never met the man. I swear. He started a dialogue with me and made a number of accusations about illegal CIA activity."

"And you lapped them up," Rapp said. "Figured they'd sound great on TV."

"Absolutely not! But there were too many allegations to ignore." Ferris finally conjured enough courage to look directly at Rapp. "Money diverted into Swiss bank accounts, people murdered . . ."

Rapp leaned forward over the table. "You sit there on Capitol Hill and tell us to set up a coalition government in Afghanistan. You completely ignore our warnings and force us to bring in every scumbag terrorist, warlord, and drug dealer in the region. If it stays together, you'll take the credit. But if it blows up in everybody's face like we've been telling you, you'll act shocked and hold hearings to deflect the blame."

"The CIA must work within the law!" Ferris almost shouted. "You answer to the government. The elected representatives of the American people."

"My ass," Rapp said. "You're like a four-year-old. When you're scared, you cling to my leg, crying and demanding that I protect you by whatever means necessary. But when I succeed, you start to feel safe again. Then you want to show everyone how brave and independent you are."

"This is a country of laws!" Ferris exclaimed, obviously unable to come up with anything more original or to the point.

"Why didn't you come to me with these suspicions?" Kennedy asked, hoping to regain control of the meeting. Rapp looked like he was about to explode and that wouldn't be constructive. Not yet.

"What?" Ferris said, having trouble tracking for a moment. "Why? Because some of your people were implicated. I was concerned that you might lack objectivity."

"I see. In that case, can I assume you discussed this with the president?"

He looked down at the table. "My inquiry hadn't progressed to the point that it would be worth the president's time."

She nodded. "I see. And what do you know about Akhtar Durrani, Senator?"

"He was a respected member of the Pakistani intelligence community and has served with distinction at the ISI for—"

"So you're not aware, for instance, that he was the man responsible for hiding Osama bin Laden from us?"

Ferris fell silent and just stared at her with a stunned expression. Obviously, the mental script he'd prepared didn't include a response to that particular piece of information. "I . . . I don't believe you."

Rapp slid a file across the table with enough force that Ferris was barely quick enough to stop it from slamming into his stomach. He opened it and paged through, hands shaking visibly. "Why have you kept this secret? Why haven't you told—"

"Because we were going to hold it over his head, you moron," Rapp said.

"But—"

"I have to admit that the tone of your emails isn't particularly skeptical," Kennedy said. "In fact, you seem to be strongly siding with Durrani. I wonder what the American people would think of your close relationship with one of al Qaeda's strongest supporters?"

Ferris closed the folder but remained silent. For the first time in his long career, he seemed to have run out of things to say.

"It's my understanding that you're going to be part of an upcoming congressional fact-finding mission to Pakistan."

"In preparation for the state dinner," Ferris muttered.

He was referring to a reception hosted by the Pakistani president in honor of a new billion-dollar humanitarian aid package to his country. Ferris, along with Secretary of State Sunny Wicka, would be two of the American dignitaries attending.

Normally, the senator would consider this kind of preparatory trip beneath him and it seemed likely that he had been planning to use it as an opportunity to meet personally with Durrani. Now that the man was dead, Kennedy couldn't figure out why Ferris hadn't canceled. She'd considered ordering him not to go, but then decided she could learn more by giving him a bit of rope.

"Who are you scheduled to meet with, Senator?"

"No one in particular," he said a little too emphatically. "I'm just following the itinerary set up by the State Department."

Kennedy considered revealing more of what she knew about his activities, but it seemed unnecessary at this juncture. Her point had been made. Maybe including Mitch Rapp in the meeting had been beneficial after all.

"You've had a long and illustrious career, Senator. But continuing to escalate your vendetta against the CIA is dangerous to both the country's security and to you personally."

He gave a contrite nod.

"Then I can look forward to an improved relationship with your office?"

"Of course. My only concern is the safety and prosperity of America and my constituents."

Rapp laughed out loud but she remained serene. "Then enjoy your trip to Islamabad, Senator."

He was unaccustomed to being dismissed and just sat there with a confused expression until Rapp spoke.

"She means get the fuck out, dipshit."

That set him into motion. He stood, took one last look at the file on the desk, and then hurried to the door. Rapp waited until it was closed to speak again.

"I looked at the official schedule for his trip. Just another excuse for a bunch of congressmen to ride around in limos and go shopping."

"Maybe."

"You think it's more?"

"He's a man used to power, Mitch. Is his ego really going to allow him to subordinate himself? To admit that he's lost this battle?"

"If he's smart it will."

"But he's not—he's a good politician. Like you're fond of pointing out, there's a difference."

"If we're going to make a play for him, we should do it while he's over there. It'll be easier to cover up. We could make it look like a heart attack." He paused and smiled in a way that made even her feel a little uncomfortable. "Or we could go for irony. Make him the victim of a phony terrorist attack."

"I didn't hear any of that."

"No? Well, hear this, Irene. If you want to watch him and try to turn him into your lapdog, fine. Right now Carl Ferris is just a pathetic joke to me. But when I stop laughing, he stops breathing."

CHAPTER 9

ONCE again, Mitch Rapp found himself standing in front of the cell holding Louis-Philippe Gould. And once again, Stan Hurley was watching.

"Want me to hold on to your gun?"

It was a noticeable change in his friend's attitude. A few days ago, he'd have paid money to walk in there and execute the Frenchman. Now they needed him. Hurley perhaps more than anyone.

"Turn off the cameras, Stan."

"Irene was pretty specific about that. She says they stay on."

"Don't make me repeat myself, old man."

Hurley swore under his breath and took a seat in front of a computer terminal at the end of the corridor. He wasn't exactly from the digital era, and it took him a few moments with the mouse to find the right application. Finally, he turned back to Rapp.

"I've still got the image, but it's not recording. You need to leave him alive, Mitch. But if you can't, do it close range and sloppy. That way we can tell Irene he went for your gun."

Rapp reached for the door, trying to shut off his emotions as it swung open. This wasn't about him or his past. It was about his job and the countless people who would die if he failed to do it.

The former French Foreign Legionnaire was sitting sideways on the cell's only cot, his back against the concrete wall. He was just a bit shorter than Rapp with longish dark hair tucked behind his ears. The bruising on his face from their last meeting had mostly faded but a line of stitches was still visible on his right cheek.

"Are you here to kill me?"

Despite being a French national, there was no hint of an accent.

"That's up to you."

"Are Claudia and Anna all right?"

His wife and daughter. The reason Rapp hadn't put a bullet in the man years ago.

"What do you care?"

The calculatedly disarming smile Gould always wore faded. It seemed likely that he didn't want to go too deeply into the subject of family—the thing he'd stolen from the armed killer standing in front of him.

"I care," he said finally.

"When I had a gun to your head, you told me you were getting out. That you were going to be the husband and father I couldn't be."

"I needed the money," he said reflexively.

"Don't lie to me, Louis. We track your bank accounts—even the ones you thought were so well hidden in the UAE. You wanted back in the game and now you sit there and tell me you care. Did you think about what would happen if you screwed up? Did it ever occur to you that the men who hired you would go after your family? Or did you overlook that?"

He remained silent. Glaring. Inside, Rapp was daring him to get off that cot. Hurley was willing to lie but it would be so much easier if Gould really did make a move.

"Irene had to track them down in New Zealand and put them in protective custody in Greece," Rapp continued. "If she hadn't, your wife and daughter would be dead now."

Gould gave a submissive nod. "Thank you."

It was exactly the right body language and tone to stave off a confrontation that Gould knew he couldn't win. To say the man's reaction was calculated, though, would be an oversimplification. It was a natural facet of his survival instinct. He could become whatever he needed to be.

Many people had called Rapp a psychopath over the years, but they had no idea what they were talking about. He did what was necessary to protect innocent people from fanatics. If that threat ever disappeared, he'd put his guns in the attic and find another line of work. Gould killed for very different reasons. Money, certainly. But there was more. Like so many assassins for hire, he had a pathological need to dominate those around him.

Having said that, there was no denying the skills he possessed. The general consensus in the profession had long been that Gould was top four. And Rapp's killing of the second best six months ago moved the Frenchman into a podium position.

"Leo Obrecht," Rapp said simply.

"Did you get him?"

"He wasn't a priority."

"Until now."

Rapp nodded.

"What do you want to know?"

The last time they'd discussed this subject, Gould had been less than forthright. It had been impossible to conduct an effective interrogation because Rapp hadn't known anything. Now, though, the CIA had finished compiling a file on the banker. The job of teasing lies from truth would be significantly easier.

"The security at his mansion is a lot tighter than you described."

"I told you what it was last time I was there."

Probably accurate. Obrecht was smart enough to see his position deteriorating and would have reacted by locking down his property.

"Tell me about him."

"Leo? He's an interesting guy," Gould said, putting a foot casually up on the edge of the cot. "He's the controlling shareholder in a little bank that's been in his family for more than a hundred years. It was pretty profitable and had a fairly select clientele until Leo took over. Now it's very profitable, and its clientele is downright exclusive."

"Criminals."

"Yeah. Drug lords, corrupt politicians, dictators, tax dodgers. You name it. People who get Leo's blood pumping and who are willing to pay a premium for anonymity."

Rapp had suspected as much. Sparkasse Schaffhausen was a black hole. The problem for Obrecht was that it was impossible to hide in darkness that deep. The darkness itself gave you away.

"That still doesn't explain *you*," Rapp said. "How does a shady banker go from dodging international financial regulations to being the handler for a hired assassin?"

Gould shrugged. "Leo's a born crook. If he could make a thousand dollars legally or ten dollars illegally, he'd take the ten. Did your people figure out that he had his own father killed when it looked like he was going to sell the bank and cut him out?"

"And who took that contract?"

The easy smile returned. "I figure you know the answer to that question."

Gould was right. Rapp knew the answer to that question and a lot more. So far all of the assassin's responses checked out.

"Obrecht's stopped leaving his property," Rapp said. "He seems to be running the bank remotely."

"That doesn't surprise me. As much as he's attracted to the excitement of the criminal lifestyle, it's just a game to him. He's a coward who likes to see other people go down but never takes too many risks himself. He probably knows you're after him—the guy's intel is flawless. If you manage to get hold of him, you should ask him where he gets it. I've never been able to figure it out."

"And how would I do that?"

"Get ahold of him? How would I know?"

"Because you killed your last handler for skimming money from you."

The disarming mask flickered.

"Come on, Louis, we've been watching you for years. We know every hit, every place you've ever lived, and every woman you've been with right down to that nanny your dad got for you. Trust me when I tell you that you don't have time for games."

"Look, Obrecht is different. He—"

Rapp pulled his Glock from the holster beneath his arm and aimed it between Gould's eyes. "Then what do I need you for?"

What Gould was saying was a load of crap and they both knew it. The first thing he would have done when he got involved with Obrecht was figure out how to do away with him if it became necessary. Rapp had made similar plans for Hurley, Thomas Stansfield, and even Kennedy when he'd first started out—studying their house plans, security, travel routes, and personal habits. It would have been careless not to. And while Gould was a sociopath and general waste of skin, he wasn't careless.

"I might have some ideas about how to access his compound."

The Glock went back into its holster.

"What's in it for me if I help?"

Rapp would have thought there was nothing that could make him laugh in Gould's presence, but the sheer stupidity of the question proved him wrong.

"I've got a shady spot picked out for you in the woods out back. Nice soft dirt. What's in it for you is a chance to avoid lying in it covered with the bag of lye I bought yesterday."

"I want guarantees."

"You picked the wrong business."

"What about Kennedy?"

Rapp folded his arms across his chest. He saw no reason to lie. "She thinks you could be useful. If you help us get Obrecht, she wants me to put you on retainer and send you home."

Another slip in his mask, this one more obvious. It was an offer that any sane man would take. Stay aboveground, be reunited with his family, and continue in the business he needed to feel alive. The question was, just how sane was Louis Gould?

Rapp pulled the door behind him open.

"Where are you going?"

He didn't answer, instead stepping silently into the hall. Hurley turned and looked at him, an expression of mild disappointment on his deeply lined face.

"What?" Rapp said. "You told me not to kill him."

"Yeah, but I didn't think you'd listen. I freed up the next three hours for cleaning his brains off the wall. Now what am I going to do with my afternoon?"

"Hey!" Gould shouted as the door clanged shut. He ran up to it and peered through the open slot three-quarters of the way up. "Come on, guys, don't leave me like this. I've been in here forever. The boredom's killing me. You got a magazine? A newspaper? I'll take anything."

Hurley grabbed a *Washington Post* and shoved it through the slot before sliding the hatch shut. "Now shut up."

He looked at Rapp. "I could turn the fire sprinklers on in there. We could say it was a malfunction."

"No. Leave him alone. Give him some time to think about his options."

"Suit yourself. In the meantime Irene wants to talk to you."

"She's here?"

Hurley shook his head. "Her office."

"She wants me to go back to Langley? I was just there this morning."

"Insisted on it."

Rapp let out a frustrated breath but then managed a shrug. "I hear Marcus is having trouble with the map we've got him working on. I guess I can use the trip to straighten him out."

• • •

Screw you very much, you old geezer.

Louis Gould gathered up the papers scattered across the floor, keeping his expression passive for the cameras.

By all reports, Stan Hurley had been quite a badass back when people still told time with a sundial. Now, instead of playing bingo at the nursing home, he got to play the tough guy. How big a man would he be without that steel door between them and Mitch Rapp backing him up? He'd be peeing in his diaper.

Gould retreated to his cot with the newspaper and began leafing through it, making sure he displayed nothing but bland interest despite the adrenaline Mitch Rapp's visit had sent coursing though him.

Rapp was the pinnacle. Most people had become resigned to the fact that he was unkillable. Gould was one of the few people on the planet who had tried and lived to tell the tale—and even he had to admit that he'd been lucky. Twice.

Rapp wasn't just unkillable, he was in many ways unstoppable. Gould kept track of whatever details were available about the CIA man's hits, and there were a couple that even he couldn't figure out. One in Damascus in particular. The takedown had been vaguely doable but getting out alive afterward seemed impossible. Everything he knew about this business, which was more than just about anyone, suggested that Rapp should be getting picked over by buzzards somewhere near Syria's border with Lebanon.

Gould spent the next few hours reading every story in the paper Hurley had provided in case he was asked about them later. Not that it was at all likely, but he hadn't lived this long by not being thorough.

Finally, when every other section was piled on the cot next to him, he turned to the pages that had been his target the entire time: the classifieds. Going straight for them would have been suspicious and he maintained his bored expression as he leafed through them.

Based on the increased security Rapp had mentioned, Leo Obrecht knew the CIA was after him. That Swiss jackass had undoubtedly thought that getting involved in framing Rapp for corruption would make for a nice ego trip. Now he'd be hiding behind his guards, sniveling like a little girl and looking for a way out.

Obrecht would have detailed reports on what had happened in Kabul and that meant he knew Gould was being held by the Agency. His degenerate little mind would come to the conclusion that the CIA might try to recruit Gould to help them get their hands on his old handler. And in that, he would see an opportunity.

On the third page, Gould found what he'd been searching for— a familiar logo printed in the corner of an ad for a personal assistant. He glanced up at the camera bolted near the ceiling and sagged a little farther into the cot before starting to read.

The candidate must be ready to fill the position immediately. Work will be done primarily at the owner's home in Switzerland. Personal and work history will be verified through Interpol. We are looking to take the most obvious route to finding a good fit. The successful candidate can expect a salary of 150,000 euros. Please send resumes to Roaspap@gmail.com.

Gould tossed the paper on the floor and closed his eyes, feigning an attempt to go to sleep. In reality, he would be up all night, staring at the dark ceiling as he ran through scenarios and turned details over in his head.

The same ad in various languages would be running in newspapers and magazines all over the world. It was a simple cipher, used by Obrecht numerous times in the past to contact him with jobs.

The candidate must be ready to fill the position immediately.

The contract was to be fulfilled as soon as possible.

Work will be done primarily at the owner's home in Switzerland.

Obrecht knew that Rapp would have to try to take him at his mansion and was prepared to help Gould in any way he could.

We are looking to take the most obvious route to finding a good fit.

This was a way of saying that if Gould had a hand in planning the assault, he should use an obvious strategy that Obrecht's people could anticipate and prepare for.

The successful candidate can expect a salary of 150,000 euros.

Compensation would be the largest payment he'd ever received—fifteen million euros.

Please send resumes to Roaspap@gmail.com.

The email address would be live so that applications wouldn't bounce back, but in fact it was the simplest part of the entire message. Remove every other letter and you got the name of the target. Rapp.

The only line that confused him was the one about Interpol verification. It wasn't a code word that they'd agreed on and it didn't have context that could help him decipher its meaning. Normally, he avoided any kind of uncontrollable risk or uncertainty but in this case it didn't matter. And neither did the fifteen million euros. All that mattered was that he would be the man who killed Mitch Rapp.

He would finally be accepted for what he had always known himself to be. The best of all time.

CHAPTER 10

MITCH Rapp gunned his Dodge through the underground parking garage, finally pulling into an empty spot labeled DAVID SANDERS. He had his own designated space, but never used it. The Charger was weighed down with a lot of armor but not enough to park beneath a sign with his name on it. Better to choose one at random. He assumed that when the people whose spaces he took saw his car, they just found a spot in the outdoor lot, but he'd never bothered to find out. All he knew for certain was that no one had ever been stupid enough to lodge a complaint.

Rapp activated the elaborate car alarm that a friend of Marcus Dumond had installed and walked briskly up the ramp, avoiding eye contact with the people he passed. Once inside Kennedy's private elevator, he relaxed a bit. He hated coming to Langley. About half the people working there—the sensible half—used any available excuse to scurry away when they saw him coming. The rest wanted to slap him on the back and drone on about what an honor it was to work with him. The only thing he despised more than people recognizing him was being touched.

"Is she alone?" Rapp said as he entered the director's suite. All three of Kennedy's assistants were on the phone, but one gave him an energetic nod and motioned toward her door. Rapp banged on it a few times before entering.

Like her assistants, Kennedy was on the phone, but she stood and offered her cheek to Rapp. He gave it a quick kiss and then dropped into one of the chairs in front of her desk. She looked like she'd finally gotten some sleep. The dark circles beneath her eyes had faded, but the deep lines at their edges remained.

She wrapped up her call and slid a manila folder toward him. "I'm sorry to drag you out here, but I thought you'd want to see this."

He pulled out two eight-by-ten photos taken in low light. The first was immediately recognizable—the naked corpse of Abdul Zahir wired to a chair. Judging by the lack of damage to his body and face, he hadn't been interrogated. Someone had simply cut off one of his hands and then smashed him in the side of the head with a blunt instrument.

No great loss to the world. Zahir was a violent, backstabbing piece of human refuse even by terrorist standards. Unfortunately, he had been an occasionally useful violent, backstabbing piece of human refuse.

The second photo was of a man lying on a dirt floor with about a third of his face missing. The combination of the damage and his thick beard made it impossible to ID him.

"Who's this?" Rapp said, holding up the photo.

"That is your friend Abdul Qayem."

Rapp looked down again at the man who was responsible for sending the better part of an Afghan police precinct to kill him. "Are we sure?"

"Our people did a digital comparison with photos we have on file. Ninety-nine percent."

"And who sent us these?"

"They're a peace offering from Ahmed Taj."

Rapp threw the eight-by-tens back onto her desk in disgust. "Amazing how quickly he was able to track Qayem down when it was suddenly in his best interest."

"I don't think we should jump—"

"Where were they?"

"He says his people caught up with them in a small village in Afghanistan."

"And the ISI went in personally instead of calling in a drone?"

"He said they wanted to take Qayem alive so he could be questioned."

"That worked out well," Rapp said sarcastically. "Ten bucks says Qayem knew too much. Maybe it wasn't just Durrani who ordered that hit on me. Maybe it went higher and people at the ISI didn't want me to catch up with him."

"It's something I've considered."

"Well, then I've got another ten bucks that says he was inside Pakistan. Probably Lahore. The S Wing is moving more and more terrorists into the cities to give them cover from our air strikes. About all that's left in the countryside are the groups that they can't get a handle on. We kill the people who are a danger to them and then they publish pictures of the aftermath to whip up anti-American sentiment."

"Ahmed and President Chutani are trying to get control of the ISI."

"And I'm supposed to feel good about that?"

She held up a hand. "Right now the only thing that matters is that, for better or for worse, Qayem is dead. That leaves Leo Obrecht as our only window into the Rickman situation."

"So?"

He knew that Kennedy could have just emailed those images to the Farm. But she hadn't. That meant she had something on her mind other than Qayem. Something that demanded a face-to-face meeting. It wasn't hard to guess what it was.

She reached for a mug at the edge of her desk and took a sip from it. Twinings Earl Grey, he knew from the dossier he'd created on her when he was just starting out. When she was under a lot of stress, she went with the decaf version.

"Where do you stand with Louis Gould, Mitch?"

"I haven't killed him yet, if that's what you mean."

"Do you think he can help you get to Obrecht?"

"I don't know."

"But he's good. Even by your standards, yes?"

Rapp didn't answer.

She held the cup in both hands as though she was trying to warm them. "I'm sorry, Mitch. I don't want to have this conversation any more than you. But if we don't do something, the situation is going to get worse. Good people are going to die."

"He's a sociopath, Irene. He doesn't care about anything or anyone but himself."

"Sometimes sociopaths aren't that difficult to control. You just give them what they want."

"Yeah. But what exactly is that?"

"His life? To be returned to his family?"

Rapp wasn't so sure, but he'd already decided he had no alternative to bringing Gould in on this. What he was in no mood for, though, was sitting around the seventh floor talking about it. He stood and started for the door.

"I'm going down to see Marcus. If you get anything else from Rickman, you know how to reach me."

CHAPTER 11

AHMED Taj sat behind his massive desk, staring at the wall. The headphones covering his ears were plugged into a secure laptop and the voice of the late Akhtar Durrani was audible above the hiss of static.

"*Now, you have many stories to tell me.*"

"*Not yet,*" Joseph Rickman replied.

"*You made a promise. I have arranged everything. You are safe in my country. I have even gone so far as to arrange a new identity for you. You must follow through on your side of the bargain. I want the names of the American spies.*"

"*When Vazir gets back from Zurich, we will see how things are, and then I will decide when and how I will begin sharing that information.*"

"*That was not our deal!*" Durrani shouted, and the low growl of Rickman's Rottweiler became audible.

"*The deal has changed. You did that when you decided to interfere with Louis Gould's assassination of Rapp. Now we will have to wait and see.*"

"*I could have you killed,*" Durrani hissed. "*Or better yet, I will nurse you back to health and have you beaten to a pulp again. How would you like that, you stupid American? You think you are so smart . . . well, you are not so smart. I hold all of the cards here. I am the one who decides if you will live or die."*

Rickman's laughter had a distinctive gurgle to it. Undoubtedly the result of his self-inflicted injuries. *"You think you have me by the balls, General?"*

"I could have you killed right now."

"Yes, you could, and then in a month or so you would die as well."

"What are you talking about?"

"You are so naïve, General. Do you think I'm foolish enough to put my life in your hands and not have an insurance policy?"

"You are bluffing."

"No, that's not my style. I plan, I don't bluff. I have taken certain precautions. I've hired a law firm and given them very specific instructions that if they don't hear from me at prearranged intervals they're to begin emailing files to Director Kennedy and a few other select people."

"What kind of files?" Durrani said, cautiously.

"Very detailed information that, among many other things, implicates you in all this."

"What could you possibly be thinking? That is reckless . . . what if these lawyers take a look at the information?"

"It's encrypted, and don't worry, they are people I trust. You have nothing to worry about as long as you honor our agreement."

"You are the one who needs to honor our agreement. Senator Ferris says he needs the information so he can move against Rapp and Kennedy."

"Let's see how things go in Zurich."

"You are a fool."

"Really," Rickman answered in an amused tone. *"I think it is actually very pragmatic of me."*

"I'm talking about giving such valuable information to people I cannot trust. It's foolish."

"It's actually very smart, although probably not all that smart considering your history."

"What is that supposed to mean?"

"It's pretty obvious that you have a habit of killing the people you work with."

"That is an exaggeration."

"Not really, so the fact that I took a few precautions is just common sense. It's not particularly smart."

Taj reached for his keyboard and shut down the recording, returning it to its encrypted folder. There were hundreds of hours of audio from the listening devices in Durrani's home, and he'd allowed no one—not even his personal assistant, Kabir Gadai—to listen to them. In the intelligence business, the control of knowledge was all.

While there was a great deal of interesting information on the tapes, this brief passage was by far the most critical. When he'd first heard it, he'd thought Rickman's threat was entirely credible and immediately began looking into law firms the man could have used. Now he had confirmation that his investigation had been worthwhile. That very morning Taj had received proof that Rickman was telling Durrani the truth about his "insurance policy."

The ISI's network had picked up chatter about an email Rickman sent to the FSB exposing a high-level agent stationed in Istanbul. This had been confirmed by a rendition attempt thwarted by Mitch Rapp that left two Russians dead. Most critically, the email had been sent *after* Rickman's death.

Taj smiled thinly. It was hard not to appreciate the man's brilliance. From beyond the grave, he would set fire after fire, running Kennedy and her people ragged. It was a plan that had gotten off to a rousing start. Even if that whore prostrated herself in front of the director of the FSB, the already tense relations between America and Russia would further worsen. There was little doubt that plans for reprisals were in the works at the Kremlin.

It was tempting to just let Rickman's strategy play out. To sit on the sidelines and watch the CIA blow itself apart. Tempting, but impossible.

Rickman's plan for revenge against his former employer was

akin to an IED—powerful, but indiscriminate. If Taj could possess the information—particularly if he could do so without Kennedy knowing—it could be transformed from an explosive to a scalpel. With it, he would not only ferret out every traitor in his own government, but co-opt the Americans' entire network. Under the threat of exposure, he could quietly turn the CIA's most sensitive assets and monitor or kill the others. Critical spies they believed to be loyal would in fact be working for the ISI. They would provide him with an endless stream of information about U.S. intelligence efforts while feeding back a carefully formulated mix of truth and lies. He wouldn't just blind the world's most powerful spy agency, he would enslave it.

Kabir Gadai was personally leading the team trying to track the law firm Rickman had spoken of but the task had proved difficult. The CIA man hid his activities with incredible care and also created countless false trails, each of which had to be diligently followed. Now that he was dead, though, Rickman's maze had stopped expanding. The picture began to clear.

There was a knock on the door, and Taj took off his headphones before closing the laptop on his desk.

"Come."

Kabir Gadai strode in and closed the door behind him. Most people were unaware that they were second cousins, and looking at them would offer no hint of the relationship. Gadai was good-looking, well dressed, and outwardly accomplished. He was truly devoted to his three gifted sons and portrayed the necessary fondness for his daughter. His wife was beautiful and charming but, more important, willing to overlook his extramarital affairs in return for a life of privilege. It was an immoral lifestyle that Taj had learned to tolerate in light of Gadai's competence and loyalty.

Of course, like all men, Gadai had weaknesses. While his infidelity was problematic, his egocentric need for those around him to be aware of his accomplishments was far worse. Taj excused it as the exuberance of youth, but until Gadai matured, he would have to be watched with extra care.

"Do you have news about Rickman's attorney?"

They had traced the Sitting Bull information dump to the general area of Rome, but that left hundreds of individual firms to investigate.

Gadai laid a dossier on Taj's desk and the ISI director opened it. He immediately recognized the name of the Italian law firm.

"We already looked into them, no? They were helping Rickman create anonymous financial trusts with money he'd siphoned off from the CIA's Afghanistan operation. To benefit his children, if I recall correctly."

"You do," Gadai said. "After we confirmed that his connection with the firm related to personal affairs, we moved on."

Taj felt his grudging admiration for the CIA man grow further. More of Rickman's complex web. He hadn't hidden his personal activity as carefully as he could have, calculating that anyone who found the firm he used would assume that it wouldn't also be involved in his plot against the Agency.

"Then you have him? You know the identity of the lawyer?" Taj said, trying to keep his voice even despite the excitement he felt.

"I'm afraid it isn't that easy, Ahmed. It's a very large firm, and Rickman didn't use the same lawyer that he used for the trusts."

"What about the managing partner? Can we interrogate him?"

"He's a very public and very well-connected man in Italy. Also, I very much doubt he would know anything. While we understand the importance of the files, this arrangement would be unremarkable to the firm. Essentially just a schedule of electronic documents to be sent if certain criteria are met. It's unlikely the attorney handling the details would even know that his client is dead. And it's almost certain that he would be in the dark as to the contents of the files."

This time, Rickman had displayed his cleverness by taking a page out of Taj's own book. Make everything too commonplace to attract attention. It was infuriating. He was within a hair's breadth of closing his fist around Irene Kennedy's delicate throat.

"So, you're telling me that we have to investigate hundreds of individual lawyers whose careers are predicated on confidentiality in hopes that they left some clue about a client they never met? That's unacceptable, Kabir."

The younger man smiled, his eyes shining with an arrogant light that Taj was very familiar with. Gadai knew something but had withheld it for effect.

"Don't make me wait, Kabir. I've indulged your sense of drama in the past, but my patience is at its end."

"My apologies, Director. Our research suggests that this firm has a dedicated division that handles these kinds of arrangements—scheduling, payments, requests for information, notifications . . ."

"How many people are in this division?"

"It's largely automated. Most of the work is done by computer or—"

"How many!"

Gadai opened the dossier again, shuffling to a photo of a plump woman with dyed blond hair. "Isabella Accorso runs the entire enterprise with a single administrative assistant."

Taj picked up the photo and examined the woman's face. She was probably in her mid-thirties, wearing a blouse that clung to her breasts in an obvious attempt to facilitate the faceless, nameless sexual encounters so enjoyed by Western women.

It was hard to believe that this female had the keys to America's heavily guarded intelligence apparatus. That she unwittingly possessed more information on the CIA's operations than anyone outside Langley's executive offices.

"What do we know about her?"

"She's divorced. Clean. No drugs or illegal activity. No affairs or significant financial problems."

Taj just glared at him. Again, his assistant's expression suggested there was more.

"She does have a daughter, though. A sixteen-year-old who attends public school. Quite an attractive young woman."

"Can I assume she's accessible to us?"

Gadai smiled. "Easily."

CHAPTER 12

"DID you get it put back together?" Rapp said as he walked into the Farm's basement bar.

Hurley was standing next to the pool table with the ubiquitous drink in his hand while Scott Coleman was beneath the elaborate scale model with a screwdriver.

"Just finishing," the old man said, lighting a cigarette. "The little twit outdid himself."

He was right. It was an impressive effort even by Marcus Dumond's standards. The computer genius had used a drone-mounted camera to take more than a thousand high-definition photos of Leo Obrecht's property. After stitching them together in Photoshop, he'd fed them to the railroad-car-sized 3-D printer at Langley.

Rapp had been expecting a two-foot-square monochrome model with enough detail to make some general strategy decisions. What he'd gotten was a full-color model so large it had to be cut into three sections to jam it down the elevator shaft. Resolution was detailed enough to differentiate individual plants in Obrecht's garden.

The portion of the model that represented the house was built in detachable layers so that each floor could be removed in order to examine the layout of the one beneath. The only thing missing was furniture—an omission that Dumond seemed genuinely embarrassed about. He still hadn't been able to crack the banker's encryption and tie into his security cameras.

"Voilà," Coleman said, connecting the last section and crawling out from under it.

Rapp let his eyes drift from the mansion grounds out to the mountainous forest surrounding it. Every tree and rock, every road and stream, was faithfully represented. While he was normally suspicious of technology, this was an advance he could get used to.

Hurley set his drink down on a section of open meadow already covered with rings from his glass. "I remember when we'd have planned this op on the back of a napkin."

"The world moves forward, Stan," Coleman said, stepping back to admire the model.

"You're wrong," the old man replied, cigarette smoke rolling from his mouth as he spoke. "The world stands still. All that changes is the window dressing."

"That's why I've always liked you, Stan. Your sunny disposition."

"What do we know about the place?" Rapp said before Hurley could formulate an expletive-laced response.

"The estate itself is about a hundred acres, and beyond that is a whole lot of rugged, heavily forested public land," Coleman said. "I have Wick over there watching the place, and I can tell you that we'd be better off trying to break into Fort Knox."

"Does the public use the area for recreation?"

The former SEAL shook his head. "No trail system. What you see on the model are just game trails or natural features."

"The good news," Hurley said, "is that Obrecht is no different than all the other royalty wannabes. He doesn't want to mix with the unwashed masses. It's miles before you get to his first neighbor."

Coleman agreed. "There's just the one road. It's twenty-one miles long from where it turns off a two-lane rural highway. Obrecht's at the end. The nearest house is nine miles south, and the owners aren't using it right now. One caretaker. Guy's older than Stan and just as deaf."

"Fuck you," Hurley said.

Rapp returned his attention to the model of the banker's property. It was a common mistake made by men like Obrecht. The best security was to be packed in with a hundred neighbors who knew the rhythms of the area and would notice any change. Those kinds of densely populated subdivisions also tended to have solid police coverage with short response times.

"What's the story with the fence?" Rapp said.

"It's more of a wall," Coleman replied. "A little less than a foot thick, constructed of cinder blocks covered with adobe. We talked to the contractor who built it and he said the whole thing is reinforced with concrete."

"Height?"

"About twelve feet. One main gate about fifteen feet wide and one small delivery door. Both look like they could stop a tank. Add to that floodlights, cameras, hardened positions along the wall, and you've got the makings of quite a party."

"What about the men?"

"We're out of luck. The former special ops people Obrecht originally had in there are all gone. The guys he replaced them with look to be Middle Eastern and Eastern European."

The personnel change was bad news. Their best bet had been to get to the Western contractors protecting Obrecht through their military contacts. Most were former special forces and that was a very small and very interconnected fraternity.

Coleman seemed to read his mind. "So, we can't get them to hand Obrecht their resignation and open the gate for us, but I knew one of the GSG 9 guys he canned. He gave me good intel on stuff in the house that didn't make it to the architectural plans. The highlights are that all the glass is bulletproof and Obrecht has a safe room in the basement."

"How many men does he have now?"

"Twelve that we can individually identify. It's possible that there are more inside who never come out, but I doubt it. Also five civilians. A butler, a cook, and three maids."

"Dogs?"

Coleman shook his head. "We hav—"

The door to the bar opened and Louis Gould stepped through, followed by Mike Nash. The assassin had been cleaned up and was wearing a donated pair of slacks and a blue dress shirt. No shoes, though, in case he was stupid enough to try to run.

Coleman started to stretch out a hand but stopped under the force of Rapp's glare. Gould had saved his life in Afghanistan and while he knew it was just because the assassin couldn't afford to lose a good gun, there was no denying that he owed the man. There was also no denying that he wouldn't live long if Rapp ever had reason to question his loyalty.

"I don't think introductions are necessary," Nash said, trying to cut through the tension. He had a gift for such things, but this time it didn't work. Rapp remained silent, tracking Gould as he approached the model on the pool table.

"Wow," he said, leaning over it. "They always said you guys had the best toys. Now I believe it."

No one dared respond as Rapp continued to stare at the man. Gould was the only person he had ever felt conflicted about in his life. Sometimes he found himself wanting to trade places with him—living out a quiet retirement surrounded by his family. Other times he wanted to make Gould's wife a widow and leave his daughter fatherless.

For now, though, they needed him.

"Welcome aboard," Rapp said, finally.

The other men in the room relaxed and Gould nodded respectfully. "Thanks, Mitch."

"Now start earning your keep," Hurley growled.

"Okay," Gould said, folding his arms across his chest. "The wall is a lot stronger than you think it is. It goes down three feet and Obrecht had the cinder blocks filled with cement. The windows are bulletproof, and he's got a safe room in the basement."

Coleman had already covered those bases, but the fact that Gould wasn't starting out with his normal string of lies was promising.

"What about dogs?" Rapp said. Coleman hadn't had a chance to answer the question.

"I'd bet against it. Obrecht got attacked by one of his father's Dobermans when he was a kid. You can still see the scars on one side of his jaw. He's terrified of them."

Rapp glanced at Coleman, who gave a subtle nod, confirming the information.

"What's he got by way of guards?" Gould asked.

"Twelve men," Coleman said. "All serious operators."

"That's more than he's had in the past. You must have spooked him. Can you get to any of them?"

"He canned all the Americans and Brits," Hurley said.

Gould nodded. "He figured you might be able to turn them. That's the problem with Leo. He's not an idiot."

"How secure is the safe room?" Rapp asked.

"It's set into the bedrock in the basement. Foot-thick steel walls, separate oxygen supply, separate heating and cooling systems. You could burn the house down around it and Obrecht would never break a sweat."

"So at the first sign of a breach, Obrecht's going to lock himself in there and wait us out," Rapp said. "Scott, what about his communications?"

"We'll jam his wireless and cut his hard lines, but the amount of firepower we're going to have to use to get in there isn't going to go unnoticed no matter how far away and deaf his neighbors are. We can clip into the police station's line and head off any phone traffic but that's only going to buy us another fifteen minutes or so."

They all fell silent, staring down at Dumond's model. Finally,

Gould spoke. "Since I've passed all the tests about bulletproof glass and dogs, let me tell you something you *don't* know. The safe room isn't all Obrecht has in that basement."

He grabbed a pool cue and pointed to the base of a wooded knoll southeast of the wall. "There's an entrance to an escape tunnel that comes out here."

Rapp looked at Coleman, who shrugged. "It's not on any plans, and his former guards don't know anything about it."

"Obrecht doesn't trust anyone. The safe room's good for the most likely threat—that some crook he works with decides he knows too much. The tunnel is there in case his own guards or a government comes after him. I got lucky and stumbled across it while I was prob-ing for weaknesses in his security. The access is hidden inside a small natural cave."

Mostly lies, of course. Obrecht used that tunnel to smuggle in con-traband that he wanted to make absolutely certain authorities never discovered. Usually attractive young boys snatched from the streets of third-world countries, but occasionally also criminal associates like Gould.

"I can have my guys take a look," Coleman said.

Rapp gave a short nod, authorizing it. "Can we get into the tunnel from that cave?"

"Shouldn't be a problem."

"Okay, then," Rapp said. "As tempting as it is to just kick up a bunch of dust and wait for Obrecht to pop out, we can't risk it. With Rickman involved, there's always a chance that one of the guards is compromised and will take Obrecht out before we can get to him. Even more likely, he'll go for the safe room. In the end, the only way to be sure we get him out of there alive is to drag him out."

CHAPTER 13

F OR this excursion, the aid agency Land Cruiser had been traded for an equally nondescript delivery truck. The vehicle was positioned in the middle of a regularly scheduled supply convoy, and Ahmed Taj was sitting in the passenger seat. The road was well maintained and the surrounding landscape stretched—empty and windswept—to the horizon. A stark contrast to the crush of Pakistan's overcrowded cities.

The facility coming into view had been designed to be unremarkable, and it remained so despite recent events. The warehouse-style building was fashioned from local materials, making it blend into its surroundings to the degree possible. The razor-wire-topped fence surrounding it was a commercially available variety, indistinguishable from millions of similar chain-link structures throughout the country. Most important, the facility actually did produce the textiles described by the placard on the gate—albeit by trusted men sourced from Pakistan's armed forces.

"I want to examine the damage myself," Taj said as the lead vehicle eased to a stop in front of the gate. "I'll get out here."

His driver's stoic expression turned fearful. "We have no way to know if the terrorists who carried out the assault have all been captured, Director. There could still be armed men in the area."

His reaction was understandable. The Pakistani Taliban, bent on bringing down the government, had attacked the facility less than eight hours before.

Despite that, the ISI director threw the door open and stepped onto the running board, not bothering to acknowledge his man's concerns.

"May I send a team with you, sir?"

"No."

The skies were typically clear and a group of men encircling him could draw the attention of American satellites. According to his intelligence, the CIA was still ignorant of this and nineteen similar properties scattered across Pakistan. In light of the extreme challenges associated with building and maintaining them, he wasn't anxious to jeopardize that ignorance.

The army had managed to regain the appearance of normalcy with workmanlike speed. The massive hole in the fence to the east of the gate had been strung with wire in a way that, while not secure, would obscure the fact that a truck full of explosives had struck it just before dawn. A second weaponized vehicle had failed to detonate and was resting on its side barely ten meters from the building's main entrance. Now covered with camouflage netting, it would be invisible from above.

The bodies of the nine guards and sixteen Taliban fighters who died in the attack had been dragged inside and would be hidden within a shipment of fabrics when the convoy left. Even bloodstains and burn marks had been eradicated—covered with fresh dirt before the sun had fully cleared the horizon.

Taj slipped through a gap in the damaged fence, paying no attention to a soldier hidden in a stack of discarded pipes. The army sniper would have been made aware of his arrival.

Taj passed through a rusted door in the side of the building and found himself in a dilapidated office that stunk of the chemicals used on the factory floor. The man sitting behind the only desk wore the threadbare shirt and tie of a factory manager but was in fact the special forces officer in charge of security. He averted his eyes in well-deserved shame for what had happened and pressed a hidden button near his leg. The lock on the door across the room buzzed and Taj pushed through it.

The shop floor contained little to dispel the illusion of a legitimate factory. Workers manned a variety of industrial machines and massive plastic-wrapped bolts of fabric were stacked around the walls. It would take a well-trained eye to see the irregularities in the concrete floor that hid four of Pakistan's 117 nuclear warheads.

These in particular were attached to Shaheen 1A ballistic missiles developed with the help of the North Koreans. They were currently Pakistan's most technologically advanced, with a range of almost two thousand kilometers and the rudimentary ability to evade missile defense systems.

The building's sloped roof was attached with explosive bolts that, when detonated, would cause the entire assembly to slide away. This would allow the missiles to be raised and launched within minutes of an attack order.

Ironically, much of the money for this structure came from the Americans. They were so fearful that terrorists might gain access to a WMD that they were willing to pump nearly unlimited funds into Pakistan's nuclear program. All the U.S. politicians asked in return was that the army maintain the illusion of improved security.

The phone in his pocket began to vibrate and he glanced around him before picking up. The workers were taking great pains to ignore his presence.

"Go ahead," he said, inserting a Bluetooth headset into his ear.

"You requested an update before I got on the plane to Rome," Kabir Gadai said, his voice barely audible over the noise of the machinery.

He was on his way to convince Isabella Accorso to turn over the computer files her law firm had received from Joseph Rickman.

"Quickly," Taj said, continuing toward a door on the far side of the expansive building.

"Per your instructions, Obrecht is running ads in all the major newspapers worldwide as well as the agreed-upon websites and magazines. He's also left encrypted messages in all the predetermined drop sites. So far no response."

Disappointing, but in no way surprising. It was certain that the CIA had captured Louis Gould, but no information was available on his fate. Based on the assassin's history with Mitch Rapp, it was very possible that he was dead.

Kennedy was a clever female, though. She would be desperate to capture Obrecht and the most promising strategy would be to offer Gould his life in return for assistance. That presented an opportunity for getting rid of Rapp.

"We're prepared to deal with an attack on Obrecht's property, then?" Taj asked.

"Yes. Though he's lodged endless complaints about being used as bait."

Taj was forced to step aside to let a front loader pass. Obrecht was less than nothing. A criminal who fed off the excitement of his debauched lifestyle but only if the risks were laid at the feet of others.

"I assume you've offered him money to put his mind at ease."

"Among other things."

"And the American and British guards have been replaced?"

"Yes, sir. With men who have no history with the CIA or U.S. military, and no love for America in general. All experienced."

"If anything should go wrong, it will be time to deal with Obrecht. Under no circumstances is he to fall into Mitch Rapp's hands."

"It would be a shame to lose him," Gadai said. "He's become very useful. But understood."

Taj slowed as he approached the door at the back of the shop floor. "I expect another report when you land in Europe."

"Of course."

He disconnected the line and put the headset back in his pocket. Gadai was right. Obrecht had indeed been useful. Billions of dollars in Afghan heroin revenues had been laundered with his assistance. More than half of the profits had already been paid out by Taj to secure the loyalty of the many militant groups operating in Pakistan. Fortunately, Louis Gould was significantly cheaper.

In fact, it would have been amusing to offer him nothing for killing Mitch Rapp. Taj suspected the assassin would have agreed enthusiastically. But this was no time to take unnecessary risks. In the event that Gould saw the ad and managed to succeed, the fifteen million he'd been promised would be money well spent. While it seemed absurd to put this many resources toward killing one man, it would be even more imprudent to underestimate Mitch Rapp's ability to interfere with his plans. With the CIA man gone, Kennedy's teeth would be pulled. She and her pathetic country would be blind and defenseless in the face of what was to come.

Taj entered a broad corridor and saw President Chutani speaking with Umar Shirani, the army's chief of staff. They turned toward him and Chutani raised a hand in greeting.

"Ahmed. Thank you for coming. I trust your journey was a good one?"

"It was," Taj said, avoiding the man's gaze. "Thank you for asking, sir."

Shirani looked on with disdain and then enveloped Taj's hand in an unusually deferential grip. The general was one of the most influential men in the country and, like so many others, considered Taj weak. Today, though, he found his position diminished. The security at these nuclear sites was his responsibility and this was the second attack on one in as many months. Taken together with Chutani's growing stature and recent American threats to reduce military aid, the aging four-star's relevance was beginning to slip.

"What has the ISI learned?" the president asked.

"A great deal," Taj said. "The attack was perpetrated by a Taliban group based in Bannu. Their leader blew himself up when my men attempted to capture him, and a number of his people are attempting to make it to the Afghan border. Obviously, we're trying to take them alive in order to carry out interrogations. Discovering whether further facilities have been targeted is our top priority."

This was, of course, completely untrue. Taj's S Wing operatives would put on a worthy show, but the surviving Taliban would die when an IED they were assembling detonated. They'd understood the inevitability of their martyrdom from the moment that Taj had provided them with the location of the nuclear facility.

"Good work, Ahmed. As always, I'm grateful to have you."

"If identifying these groups is so easy," Shirani said, "perhaps the director would be so kind as to give me a warning next time one is planning something like this."

The general's attempt to deflect blame was desperate and pathetic. Clearly he had become too comfortable hiding behind the power of his office.

"You must accept my apologies for not having this information in time for you to fortify your defenses," Taj said deferentially. "Rest assured that we are redoubling our efforts to penetrate these radical groups."

While Shirani and Chutani would assume it was unintentional, the message was clear: It was the army's job to be in a constant state of readiness. The ISI wasn't responsible for rousing them from their stupor in time for them to perform their duties.

"It's possible that there could be secondary attacks," Taj continued. "I would strongly urge you to make certain your men are on alert."

"They are always on alert," Shirani said, a bit too forcefully.

President Chutani frowned noticeably. "All evidence to the contrary, Umar. You should be grateful to Ahmed for his support."

Shirani's voice sounded a bit strained when he spoke again. "Of course, I'm grateful for any assistance the ISI can provide. We all have the same goals."

"Indeed," Chutani agreed. "We're all dedicated to keeping these facilities secure. Unfortunately, much of the money earmarked for that task has been spent on other projects."

"Sir, I must protest," Shirani said. "You seem to be implying some kind of impropriety on the part of the army. Terrorists like these are undoubtedly a danger but clearly not the only one—or even the most significant one. Creating the kind of security that would be unbreachable by a small terrorist group would be a simple matter if we weren't concerned about being discovered by the Indians and Americans. Our primary goal must be protecting ourselves from a first strike by one of those countries."

"I am not naïve in these matters, Umar, but I wonder if our concern over foreign enemies is devolving into paranoia. If we lose a warhead to one of these groups and it's used, the Americans' retaliation would be the end of our country as we know it. No. Pakistan has a chance at greatness but we're squandering it with these games. America learned its lesson in Iraq and Afghanistan, and India doesn't need to attack to defeat us. They're already winning with their progress. They've outstripped us in everything from education to economic growth to diplomacy. That's the future, Umar. It is from those things that security flows. Not weapons."

Shirani opened his mouth to object, but Chutani held up a hand, silencing the soldier. "It's convenient to fan the flames of extremism in the short term but now we're in danger of being engulfed ourselves. Changes must be made. The country has to modernize and come together. Our future can't be financed with charity from countries that fear we're on the verge of collapse. Trust. Respect. Wealth. These are the things that must be cultivated."

"What are you proposing?" Shirani said suspiciously.

"The expansion of the Khushab reactor will be halted," Chutani said with a tone that suggested the decision wasn't up for debate. "As will all production of weapons-grade fissile material. The weapons we have are more than enough to deter an attack."

Shirani was too stunned to respond, so Chutani continued. "Further, the defense of our nuclear arsenal will be shifted from the army to the ISI, effective immediately."

Taj feigned surprise, though it was the outcome he'd been working toward for more than two years. "Mr. President, I don't—"

"It's done, Ahmed. You and General Shirani will start coordinating the transition right away."

"Yes, sir," Taj said, watching Shirani's face out of the corner of his eye. It was an incredible insult but the soldier managed to hide his rage. Undoubtedly he was calculating the extent of his own power versus Chutani's and the feasibility of engineering a coup.

Shirani's gaze finally shifted to Taj and this time he didn't bother to hide his contempt. Instead of looking away, as was his custom, Taj met the man's stare. It was time to allow Umar Shirani a brief, unobstructed glimpse into the heart of his new master.

CHAPTER 14

LOUIS Gould pretended to study the enormous scale model but was actually concentrating on the other men in the room. He had to stay calm and professional. The smallest slip was almost guaranteed to end in his death.

Mike Nash, whom he knew very little about, had been called away. That left three men. Stan Hurley wasn't just old, he was ancient. It was hard to separate legend from fact with regard to his past, but if even half of the information out there was true, Hurley had at one time been very dangerous. Now, though, he was just a bag of bones with a death hack and a perceptible limp. Taking the geriatric bastard seriously would require some effort, but completely dismissing him would be careless.

Coleman was a different matter. He was probably pushing fifty but still looked like he was chiseled out of stone. As a former SEAL, it was a given that he was a top operator. The fact that Rapp chose to work with him suggested he was a standout in a fraternity that only accepted standouts. The difference between qualifying for the Olympics and walking away with gold. If he had any weaknesses, they were psychological. He came off as a bit of a Boy Scout—a man who believed too much in God, country, and the camaraderie of battle.

Finally, there was Mitch Rapp. A man in a category all his own. No discernible physical or mental weaknesses. Uncanny instincts, no hesitation, no remorse. Decades of experience and training. Simply put, one of the most dangerous men who ever lived.

Despite all that combined history, the three killers were hanging on his every word. It would be easy to start thinking of them as idiots. To let his well-earned arrogance kick in and categorize them as typical marks.

He'd tried to kill Rapp twice before and failed even though he'd had the element of surprise both times. It was a fact that Gould was already beginning to rationalize away, and he fought against that tendency. The day he forgot who he was up against was the day he ended up with a bullet in his head.

"I know you've been planning this since the day you signed on with Obrecht," Rapp said. "What have you got?"

What he had was an entire plan from start to finish. Ironically, though, it was entirely inspired by Leo Obrecht—the man Rapp incorrectly believed was the target of this operation.

Work will be done primarily at the owner's home in Switzerland. We are looking to take the most obvious route to finding a good fit.

Obrecht knew the CIA was after him and assumed that they would have no choice but to mount an assault on the mansion. Clearly he hoped that Gould could convince them to carry out the operation using the most obvious strategy. It would be an easy sell, particularly to Coleman. Soldiers tended to look at battlefields in predictable ways, and the navy man would have a strong bias toward the KISS principle: Keep It Simple, Stupid.

Gould used a pool cue to tap a rocky knoll to the west of the property's iron gate. "This is the highest point in the area and it's right where you want it. Range to the wall is just over six hundred meters, and the wind tends to get disrupted by the ridgeline to the south. Easy sniper range."

Coleman nodded. "My guys have been up there. It's the only place high enough to get a good view over the wall and you can see right through the gate. Cover's good, and there are multiple lines of retreat if it comes to that."

"What about the tunnel?" Hurley said.

"I had Wick crawl down there and take a look. He found the entrance but didn't go inside in case there were sensors. Based on the pictures he took, the door's steel. No way to know how thick, no visible way to open it."

Gould nodded. "There's a hidden keypad with a twelve-digit combination. I tracked down the man who installed it and convinced him to put in a back door when he serviced the unit. The tunnel comes out behind a shelf in Obrecht's basement."

"Convinced him?" Coleman said

In truth, Obrecht had given Gould a personal code that could be temporarily activated should the assassin ever need to access the mansion.

"People tend to get real cooperative when you have a gun in their mouth."

Hurley took a swig of his bourbon. "True that."

Gould pointed at the representation of the tunnel entrance. "I'd suggest that me and Mitch go in through there just before five o'clock."

"Why five?" Rapp said. "That's still daylight."

"Yeah, but it's also happy hour. Obrecht's careful about never creating identifiable routines outside the mansion, but inside he feels safe. As near as I can tell, he opens a bottle of expensive French wine and lights a Cuban in his study at five on the dot every day. We grab him there, slip him back out the tunnel, and he's on your plane in an hour."

Gould let his eyes linger on Rapp, but the man was impossible to read. Was he buying all this?

"In my experience, wine snobs like to choose their bottle based on their mood," Rapp said. "Wouldn't that put him in the basement with us just before five?"

It was yet another reminder of why the CIA assassin was not to be underestimated. Gould would have asked the same question, but he wasn't sure he'd have come up with it that quickly.

"Good thought, but Obrecht had an auxiliary wine cooler installed in his den. He picks his vintage from there, and if he restocks it on a regular schedule, I don't know what that schedule is."

"The twelve guards we've identified mostly stay outside," Rapp said. "Are there dedicated interior guards that we don't know about?"

"Not that I've ever seen," Gould said. "Obrecht likes his privacy and sticks to a few servants who've been trained to stay out of his way. But since you're telling me he's laid on additional security, I can't swear to that."

"I think there's a good chance you're right," Coleman said. "We've been watching the windows and we're not seeing anyone we don't recognize as a member of the core security team."

"So we have twelve men, primarily in outdoor postings," Hurley said. "All well-armed, solid operators in defensible positions. All recently hired, so not one of them is going to be bored or complacent. That's not a great scenario for us."

"I agree," Gould said. "Trust me when I tell you that I'm not happy about being half of a two-man team if something goes wrong and all those guys come running through the door with guns blazing. But I'm not seeing a lot of alternatives."

The men across from him looked at each other for a moment. Finally, Rapp spoke.

"Three."

"What?"

"You're not half of a two-man team. You're a third of a three-man team. A while back, Hurley knocked on the gate and gave one of Obrecht's guards a fake Interpol business card. He told him to let Obrecht know that Interpol was interested in talking to him about you. Obrecht's secretary just called and set up an appointment at the mansion for the day after tomorrow."

Gould allowed a smile to spread across his face. Not for the reason the other men in the room thought, though.

Personal and work history will be verified through Interpol.

That line in the *Post* ad had perplexed him. Now it was crystal clear. Obrecht had figured out who Hurley was and would be ready for him.

"What time?" Gould said, still processing how this new piece of information would affect him.

"Three o'clock," Rapp said.

It was perfect. The entire thing was starting to look like child's play. Obrecht and his men would not only know that the "obvious route" would be Gould coming through the tunnel and putting his backup on the high ground, but they'd know the time of the breach.

"That works even better," Gould said, finally. "He'll meet with Stan in his office, which is easier to access from the basement than his den. And we have a third man that no one's going to expect. Heck, if it comes to it, we could even play like we've taken Stan hostage."

"So you can use me as a human shield?" Hurley said. "My ass."

"You just follow my lead, pops. I won't let anything happen to you."

Hurley lunged, but Rapp saw it coming and held him back.

The Frenchman stood his ground, a broad grin on his face. He was starting to feel almost giddy about the situation. Everything was lining up in his favor. It was beginning to feel like fate. He was going to be the man who killed Mitch Rapp.

"Careful," Gould said, leaning over the plastic representation of Obrecht's estate. "We don't want you breaking a hip before we even get there."

"Keep talking, kid. While you still can."

Gould laughed and walked to the bar.

"Maybe we should talk about what I get when I pull this off?" he said, reaching over and retrieving a beer from the refrigerator on the other side.

Of course, the real answer was fifteen million euros and the undisputed status of being the best in the world. But these morons didn't know that.

"I thought we already covered that subject," Rapp said as the others looked on.

"You not killing me? That doesn't seem like much for me handing you a man like Leo Obrecht."

"Seems like a lot to me," Hurley said.

Gould shifted his gaze to the old man and twisted the top off his beer. At first, he'd thought this nursing home reject would be a nice cherry on top of Rapp's corpse. Doing both of them at once would be something people in the business would talk about for the next hundred years. After thinking about it, though, maybe he'd just cripple the man. Let him spend the rest of his short life sitting in a wheelchair crapping himself and knowing that he wasn't even worth a bullet.

"If I remember right, Kennedy said something about putting me on retainer."

Rapp didn't answer immediately, instead just staring through him with those black eyes. Gould wouldn't allow himself to look away, but he felt his confidence falter.

"But *I* didn't," Rapp said finally. "All I'm offering you is a chance to go back to your wife and daughter. If you ever take another contract, you won't live long enough to collect the money."

"Seems like you could use someone with my skills," Gould said.

The conversation was meaningless but he refused to back down. Who was Rapp kidding? He'd gotten lucky in Afghanistan. If Gould's employer hadn't betrayed him, the great Mitch Rapp would already be dead. And him surviving the explosion at his house years before had been a combination of dumb luck and Gould overcomplicating the hit by trying to make it look like an accident.

"Listen to me, Louis. Take the deal. Watch your daughter grow up. Get old with your wife. Stan's right. That's a lot."

CHAPTER 15

K ABIR Gadai checked the map on his phone as he strolled casually up the sidewalk. The weather was sunny and cool, allowing
for a collared coat and bulky sunglasses. Neither provided sufficient
anonymity to make him feel comfortable.

Sending him personally to Rome was one of Ahmed Taj's rare tactical mistakes. There were any number of well-trained ISI operatives
who could have successfully completed the mission. It was impossible
in the digital era to travel unphotographed, and too risky for someone
with Gadai's high profile to enter an EU country under an alias. So the
Italians had a record of his arrival under the rather thin guise of a security review being carried out at Pakistan's London embassy.

Taj's obsession with the Rickman files seemed to grow with every
passing day. Admittedly, accessing the information they contained
would be the greatest intelligence coup in the last seventy years, but
Taj seemed to be forgetting that his plan had never required them. His
focus was beginning to wander and, for the first time, Gadai could see
his insatiable greed for power affecting his judgment.

It was this that made Gadai's physical presence in Rome even more
dangerous. Their preparations were at a critical juncture, and he was

very much needed in Islamabad. Someone had to monitor the endless details of Taj's plot, and he was the only man other than the director himself who had knowledge of all its facets. Further, arrangements for the U.S. secretary of state's delegation were in motion and were proving to be more time-consuming than he had anticipated.

A former Secret Service executive named Jack Warch was spearheading the American side of the security measures and he seemed almost childlike in his need to question every detail. The state dinner was the key to Taj's plan and Gadai would not let it be endangered by a single dangerously inquisitive consultant. He had taken to dealing with the man personally and being outside the country was jeopardizing his control over the situation.

Across the lightly traveled street, a turn-of-the-century apartment building gave way to a football pitch. The open field was separated from the sidewalk by a chain-link fence designed less for security than to keep errant balls out of the road. Beyond the well-tended grass was a modern concrete structure that stood in stark contrast to the ancient suburb surrounding it. Behind the rows of reflective windows was the middle school attended by Isabella Accorso's sixteen-year-old daughter.

No children were visible, which was to be expected at that time of the morning. They would briefly appear between classes at various points during the day, with a somewhat longer break for lunch. In the afternoon, sporting activities that these Westerners happily allowed their daughters to participate in were held.

Gadai dug his hands into his pockets and resisted shaking his head in disgust. They cared nothing for purity or chastity. The women in this country were allowed to do whatever they wished. The very thought of his own daughter running across that field with bare legs and arms filled him with rage. He would beat her to death without a moment's remorse and the Islamic courts would support his decision wholeheartedly.

Gadai cut across a cobbled courtyard and entered the lobby of the apartment building at the back of it. He ignored the elevator and instead took the stairs, climbing five stories before exiting into an unoccupied corridor. He walked purposefully toward the fourth door on the right, adjusting his collar and letting his eyes sweep the intersection between wall and ceiling to confirm the reported lack of cameras.

He used the key he'd been provided to enter, immediately closing the door behind him and examining the small space. It was typical of the area—plaster walls, a wood floor warped with age, and a small galley kitchen full of cheap appliances. Having been leased only days before, it was devoid of furniture. The only sign of habitation was a few boxes of food on the countertop and a teapot on the stove.

Lateef Dogar appeared in the entrance to the bedroom and nodded respectfully. "Captain Gadai. How was your journey?"

He ignored the question, striding across the living area and brushing past the man. In the bedroom there was a sleeping area consisting of blankets piled on the floor and a wall covered with photos. Each depicted the same young girl. Most were close-ups of her playing football in front of her school, the focus often not on her face but on her young body and obscene shorts.

"Where did you get these?"

"They were left by the surveillance team, Captain. I—"

"Are you so stupid that you need them to recognize your target?"

"No, Captain."

"Then destroy them."

"Yes, sir."

Perhaps Taj hadn't been so unwise to send him after all. The fact that these photos were ever printed was inexcusable, but hanging them on the wall verged on insubordination. It would be something he would have dealt with quite harshly if Taj hadn't already arranged for these men to disappear when they returned to Pakistan.

The shades were almost completely closed and Gadai knelt to peer through the three-centimeter crack at the bottom. It offered an unobstructed view of the school at a reported range of 212 meters. The fence would have the potential to deflect a shot, but that wasn't important. It was the video image he was interested in, and it would be quite acceptable.

Gadai went to a long metal case resting against the wall and turned the combination dials on it. Inside was a rather unusual item that he held out to Dogar. The assassin took it, turning it over in his hands with a confused expression.

"This . . . This isn't a gun."

He was entirely correct. It was a shortened plastic rifle stock with a handgrip at the front, designed for bird-watchers to hold cameras and spotting scopes steady. It had been far easier to bring into the EU than a firearm and was impervious to both accidents and the stupidity that the Pakistani team had displayed thus far.

Dogar examined the video camera mounted on it, taking inventory of the controls and noting the crosshairs on the zoom lens. "Am I to continue surveillance with this?"

Gadai retrieved the laptop that had been sharing the case and turned it on. "Has the broadband connection been installed?"

"Yes, as you requested. We've verified upload speeds of four megabits per second."

"Turn on the camera and aim it out the window."

He did as he was told, and the image of the school appeared on the laptop screen.

"Do you see the woman on the sidewalk? Line up on her head."

Gadai watched as the crosshairs centered on her right temple. It was all but indistinguishable from a rifle scope.

Perfect.

CHAPTER 16

THE screen on the van's dashboard had been built to look like a normal GPS but was in fact something far more sophisticated. Mitch Rapp watched the video feed being beamed to the screen from a drone controlled by Marcus Dumond.

Most of the image consisted of steeply rolling, heavily forested terrain. The empty rural highway they were driving along cut across the left edge, running north to south. Five miles to the east, he could see the winding road that dead-ended into Leo Obrecht's mansion, also devoid of traffic. It was Wednesday morning, and this area was primarily a weekend retreat for Switzerland's wealthy set.

"We're coming up on the drop site," the driver said. "Three minutes."

Rapp didn't know much about Maria Glauser other than she spoke German with the appropriate Swiss accent and knew the area like the back of her hand. Nash had worked with her in the past and said she was one of the most exacting people he'd ever met. It was a quality Rapp demanded in anyone supporting his ops. So far, she hadn't disappointed.

The activity in the rear of the van intensified, but Rapp didn't look back. Instead he began stripping off his sweatpants and jacket, revealing camouflage fatigues beneath. Nothing about this operation was ideal and the fact that they had to set out in broad daylight to coincide with Hurley's appointment was just one of a long list of problems.

There had been a fair amount of debate as to whether to go in posing as hikers but he'd finally decided against it. There were no trails in the area, making the tried-and-true lost-backpacker cover a little far-fetched. And while Rapp's beard and shaggy hair made him a little hard to pin down, Coleman and his men looked exactly like the elite soldiers they were.

"The bridge is just ahead," Glauser said.

"We're a go," Rapp said loud enough for the men in back to hear. "The video feed looks clear. No cars in sight."

They crossed over a slow-moving stream about five yards wide and Glauser eased onto the shoulder.

"I'll have vehicles at the designated extraction points," she said, keeping her eye on the side-view mirror. "But we're not going to bring them in until the last minute. It could attract attention."

"Just make sure they're there," Rapp said, throwing open the passenger door as his team piled out of the back. "We'll be moving fast and there could be people behind us."

"They'll be here. I guarantee it."

Rapp and his team were already running down the steep stream bank toward the water when she pulled away. The grass had grown to almost the height of a man beneath the bridge, and Rapp sank a good six inches into the mud as he pushed through. The backpacks were exactly where Glauser said they'd be, each subtly marked to identify their owners: Rapp, Gould, Coleman, and Joe Maslick.

They started east, taking advantage of the sparser foliage near the water to keep their pace up. The team split at a fork in the stream twenty minutes in, Maslick taking the south branch, which would lead him to a position above the entrance to Obrecht's escape tunnel. With his injured shoulder, he was a potential liability in a running fight. Dug in with a rifle on a tripod, he'd be close to one hundred percent effective.

The rest of them took the north fork, heading for the high point west of Obrecht's mansion. There they'd rendezvous with Charlie Wicker and Bruno McGraw, who had been reconning the area.

Eventually, they were forced to abandon the streambed and start up the knoll. The angle of the terrain and the dense foliage slowed their progress to a seventeen-minute-mile pace. It felt painfully slow but it was roughly what Rapp had planned for.

They kept to the west, putting the bulk of the knoll between them and Obrecht's property. Wick hadn't found any surveillance equipment or sensors, so they didn't have to worry about staying completely silent.

"Closing in on your position," Rapp said into his throat mike as they crested the ridge.

"Come on," Wicker responded.

They slowed, organizing into a single line with twenty-five-foot intervals. Gould had been solid on the climb and fell into second position, with Coleman keeping a close eye on him from behind. Rapp was pretty sure Gould was a few cards short of a full deck, but even he wasn't crazy enough to make a move with that kind of firepower on his six.

The slope started to descend slightly, and Rapp raised a fist before coming to a stop. Something felt wrong but he couldn't put his finger on it. What little wind there was beneath the clear sky didn't have enough force to penetrate the forest. The gurgle of water had been left far behind and they hadn't seen any sign of the deer that were indigenous to the area. Nothing but silence and the scent of pine. What was it?

His question was answered a moment later.

"On your eleven o'clock, Mitch." Wicker's voice over his earpiece. "Don't shoot."

A bush covered in wildflowers rustled about twenty yards away and then blended back into the landscape. Rapp started forward again, covering the first thirty feet to Wicker's position in a crouch. When the roof of Obrecht's mansion came into view through the trees, Rapp dropped and slithered the rest of the way on his stomach.

Even less than an arm's length from Wicker, the sniper was nearly invisible. He had created a tube from woven sticks and covered it in live plants before sliding in. All Rapp could see was part of his rifle's silencer and the vague outline of the Unertl scope the man favored. At five foot six and barely 140 pounds, Charlie Wicker wasn't what most people would picture when they thought of SEAL Team Six. In a fight, though, Rapp considered him one of the deadliest men alive.

"What have we got, Wick?"

"Not much has changed. Twelve guards, each with a sidearm and an assault rifle. No vehicles in or out. A delivery truck comes every few days but they don't let it inside. Supplies are passed through the small gate to the south. That's where the servants come in and out, too, but not very often. Most seem to be living on premises."

"Any pattern?"

"Nope."

The Swiss banker had clearly gone to ground. He was expecting the CIA to make a play, and if he couldn't stop it, he was going to make sure things got bloody.

Rapp pulled out a small spotting scope and scanned the property. Gould was right. The knoll they were on had an excellent line of sight. The main gate was in full view and they were high enough to be able to take in a significant portion of the courtyard. Not that there was much to see. A few fountains, some tasteful landscaping, and a handful of armed men.

"I only see four guards," Rapp said.

"That's the minimum. If we can choose our moment, we can probably get six. That still leaves the other half, though."

Rapp frowned. "The plan is quiet in and quiet out—leave those guys guarding their dicks. But if we do have to start shooting, I can guarantee you we're not going to be choosing the moment."

"Then I'd count on having to deal with at least eight serious bad guys."

"You've been down to the tunnel from here?"

"Yeah."

"It's clear all the way?"

"Too much wildlife for sensors or tripwires. They'd be dealing with false alarms all day."

"Any surprises?"

"You've got to be really careful in the last couple hundred meters. That's where the guys on top of the wall have a view of your position. Because of all the animals, you could brush a bush or two on your way in, but three or four might get you in trouble."

Rapp nodded and started slithering backward, making sure the building was out of view before standing and returning to the clearing at the apex of the knoll. Coleman had pulled a large piece of netting from his pack and was collecting plants that he'd use to build his own camouflaged position. Gould was crouched next to a tree, blending in with the gnarled trunk. Rapp motioned him over.

"Wick says two hours. Scott, I assume that's going to be enough time to set up here?"

The former SEAL nodded. "We'll be locked and loaded well before you get there."

"All right." He looked at Gould. "You ready?"

The Frenchman had smeared his face with green paint, making it difficult to read his expression. "Yeah."

"You've been down there before," Rapp said. "So you lead out."

In truth, Rapp knew exactly where they were going, having studied both the detailed overhead photos and Dumond's model. But there was no way he was going to let Gould get behind him without Coleman watching.

The former French Legionnaire moved well. He kept a solid pace down the steep slope, silent and eyes constantly moving. His attentiveness to their surroundings was especially critical because Rapp was focused on the silenced Glock 17 in Gould's hand. Coleman had suggested loading it with blanks, but Gould wasn't going to miss something that obvious. Besides, if things went wrong, his skills would be very much in demand. The hope was that his instinct for self-preservation would keep that weapon aimed in the right direction.

• • •

Scott Coleman kept collecting plants for another five minutes after losing sight of the two men and then switched to a frequency that Rapp had set up to exclude Louis Gould. "Okay. We're clear."

He started replacing the plants while Wicker slipped out of the shelter he'd built and disappeared into the trees with Bruno McGraw on his tail.

Coleman finished with the plants and used a dead branch to scrape away any boot prints that had defined themselves too clearly in the soft earth. A quick look around the clearing suggested it was more or less back the way they'd found it. Not that it would fool anyone like him, but in the unlikely event the Swiss cops came up here, they wouldn't find anything unusual.

Coleman grabbed a spotting scope and slid into Wicker's shelter, smiling when he realized that his feet just barely touched the back. Wick was a full five inches shorter than him but, knowing the plan, he'd made the shelter a perfect fit for his boss.

With the scope to his eye, Coleman swept the courtyard below. This was undoubtedly the best seat in the house and he wasn't sure surrendering the high ground was a good idea. It was going to cut the effectiveness of his team by at least seventy percent, but there was nothing he could do about it.

A little less than a half an hour passed before Bruno McGraw's voice crackled over his earpiece. "We've reached the secondary site. Starting setup."

Hopefully the radio signal reached Rapp—they'd identified a few dead spots on the way to the tunnel entrance. There was no way to confirm, though. Gould thought he was getting all the radio chatter and a response from Rapp would tip the man off.

"Roger that," Coleman said.

It was another twenty-three minutes before he spotted an old Citroën driving up the road below. Stan Hurley had the window open, and the cigarette smoke flowing from it was visible through the scope. Right on time.

A guard came out of the door-sized steel grate south of the gate and signaled for the car to stop. It was exactly how Coleman would have set it up. Don't let the vehicle get too close in case it contained explosives.

Hurley stepped out and held up a set of fake Interpol credentials. Coleman couldn't hear what was being said, but he could clearly see the irritation on the old man's face while he was being frisked.

Along the wall, the guards were all paying attention, but not getting overly focused on the man in case it was a diversion. Coleman let out a quiet breath. They looked to be even better than he'd expected. Reason number ninety-eight to hope that this didn't turn into a shooting war.

Hurley was led to the gate, where another armed guard let him through. After that, Coleman lost line of sight.

"Hurley's in. I'm starting to break down the shelter now. Should be approaching your position in approximately thirty."

"Roger that," Wick responded.

Coleman switched to the frequency accessible by Gould. "Hurley's inside the wall and we're ready to rock."

CHAPTER 17

THE heavily reinforced gate swung open and Hurley shuffled through with a stoop meant to make him appear even older than he was. It didn't have the intended effect of making Obrecht's security overconfident, though. The man behind him maintained a careful interval and had his hands wrapped firmly around a Heckler & Koch G36 assault rifle. The one in front kept the gate between them as Hurley passed. Ten yards away, another armed man watched through mirrored sunglasses. The remaining guards were focused elsewhere and were positioned in a way that would make the most of their manpower.

The gate closed behind him and he used the loud clang as an excuse to glance back. The wall seemed higher than the reported twelve feet and it was as smooth inside as it was out. There were strategically placed scaffolds along it, some hastily framed out of unpainted lumber and others more professionally executed from steel and concrete.

Cover was nearly nonexistent. The largest tree was about six inches in diameter, leaving nothing more than a few widely spaced fountains and a couple of parked cars. A sprint across that courtyard—particularly at the speed his new hip would allow—wasn't going to end well.

"Sir?" the guard behind him said in accented English. "If you please."

Hurley limped to an X-ray machine that looked like a more sophisticated version of something you'd find at JFK. "Is this really necessary?"

"I'm sorry for the inconvenience," the man said in a tone that suggested he wasn't. "If you could please remove your jacket and shoes, and empty your pockets."

He did as he was told and then turned to walk to the other side of the conveyor, but was immediately stopped.

"Your belt, too, sir."

He smiled accommodatingly but felt a surge of nervousness as he removed it. It had been made to order in Asia back in the seventies. The buckle was secured to the leather by a two-inch-long metal strip that had been sharpened on all sides. It was sewn in with permanent stitches, but the pattern and thread were purposely weak. One hard jerk and it would break free, giving him a weapon that was complete crap but still better than nothing.

"A lot of security," Hurley observed, trying to distract the man looking at the X-ray screen. The belt had been all over the world, passing through even Israel's airports more times than he could count. Still, this rundown was anything but routine.

"Yes, sir," he said, not looking up. The conveyor paused for a moment and Hurley focused on the man's gun. It'd be a hell of a way to go out—grabbing the guy's weapon and spraying down the courtyard. Just wishful thinking, though. If he so much as raised his voice, they'd immediately harden up on Obrecht. The operation would be finished before it even started. No, if they questioned the belt, he'd tell the truth: that he'd bought it outside a Thai whorehouse before most of the men around him were even born. What did he know about how belt buckles were attached to belts?

It turned out to be unnecessary. His things came rolling out of the machine unchallenged while he was being wanded. A moment later he was fully dressed and moving toward the mansion.

The guard was two paces ahead as they started up the broad marble staircase leading to the front door. He had a sidearm that was within reach, but he wouldn't give it up easily. Even with surprise on his side, Hurley questioned how he would fare against the man. Twenty—even ten—years ago, he wouldn't have given it a second thought. A quick twist of the neck accompanied by the quiet crunch of vertebrae, and it would be done.

The chemotherapy and the hip surgery had taken more out of him than he let on, though. If Rapp knew the real extent of it, he'd have left him in West Virginia. But there was no way Hurley was going to fade away in a rocking chair while that piece of shit Louis Gould replaced him.

They stayed on the first floor, walking through a palatial entry hall lined with antique furniture and original portraits of people spanning a good five centuries. Most were probably Obrecht's ancestors and all looked like they were posing with sticks up their asses. Yet another reminder that crime actually did pay.

"Wait in here."

"Thank you," Hurley said, stepping inside a spacious parlor. "Do you know when Mr. Obrecht will be available?"

One of the few advantages of being his age was that hearing aids were expected. His were tied into Coleman's tactical radio setup and had microphones that picked up his voice as well as the ambient sound around him. He depressed a button on the key fob in his pocket to toggle the transmit function and broadcast the man's answer to Rapp. They wouldn't be able to coordinate the op to the second, but if Obrecht was as anal-retentive as he was reputed to be, they'd be able to nail it to within a minute or so.

"I don't know."

"Could you give me some idea? I need to be back fo—"

The door closed, leaving Hurley staring at the ornately carved back of it. Prick.

He walked around for a few minutes, pretending to look at the expensive furnishings and finally settling into a chair near a set of west-facing windows. Two guards were visible, but there was nothing to see that Dumond's drone hadn't picked up.

Hurley suspected the room was full of hidden cameras and microphones, making it a bit challenging to communicate. He stood and depressed the key fob button again.

"Just one time, I'd like it not to be hurry up and wait," he muttered angrily, as if to himself. "I don't know how long Obrecht expects me to sit by the door watching the sun go down. Like I don't have better things to do."

"Confirm," Rapp said over his fake hearing aid. "You're alone on the first floor, windows facing west."

"Yeah. Just great."

"Understood. Stand by. We're three minutes from the tunnel entrance."

Hurley began pacing, feeling the irritation he was supposed to be faking turn real. He was accustomed to being on the action side of these ops and being dead in the water while Rapp crawled through the dirt and Coleman set up sniper positions was driving him insane.

He got a little satisfaction from imagining opening the door and smashing that Eurotrash merc's head in with a priceless statuette. And the image of Rapp and that frog showing up to find Obrecht already tied and gagged was downright uplifting.

The mission he'd been charged with, though, was very different. Nothing more than confirming the banker's location in the house and keeping him occupied with conversation until the two younger men could come to the rescue. But that wasn't the worst of it. In order to create even more confusion, he was to act like a second hostage if they were confronted by Obrecht's security. The theory was that it would give Hurley the element of surprise, but he wasn't sure that Rapp really believed he was still capable of taking out anyone tougher than a Girl Scout.

He sat again, staring at a blank section of wall and thinking back to when the twenty-two-year-old Mitch Rapp had showed up at his training facility. Some college boy lacrosse player who didn't know one end of a gun from another.

Hurley had wiped the floor with the sniveling little puke. And despite decades of friendship and countless ops, he'd like nothing more than to do it one more time before he died.

CHAPTER 18

UMAR Shirani, Pakistan's army chief of staff, unlocked the cabinet and pulled out a bottle of gin. The kitchen lights were off but the illumination filtering in from the hallway created a dim reflection in the window over the sink. At seventy-one, he was still a bull of a man. An expanding waist was evident behind the casual slacks and golf shirt, but so were the thick arms, barrel chest, and broad shoulders. The scar acquired in the 1971 war with India was still visible—a puckered line that started on his right temple and disappeared into his thick mustache.

Saad Chutani had no such scar. Nor did that pathetic fool Ahmed Taj. They were nothing more than useless bureaucrats. Bookkeepers whose talents were limited to flattery, intrigue, and speechmaking. They had never fought for their country. They would never shed a single drop of blood for Pakistan. All they could do was maneuver in the shadows, quietly chipping away at men greater than themselves.

Shirani put the glass to his mouth and felt the rare sensation of alcohol burning his throat. Allah had put a great hurdle in front of his loyal servant. He would understand.

The aging soldier exited the kitchen and started for his study. The house was nearly ten thousand square feet, decorated and redecorated countless times by his young wife. The wildly expensive furniture and art had recently turned modern, and while he despised it, he knew it wouldn't last more than a few years. Soon she would use U.S. dollars meant for fighting terrorism to create a new theme.

The house seemed unusually quiet as he strode through it. His wife had wisely withdrawn to the east wing. She'd learned to read her husband's moods and knew that her presence would only create a convenient target for his rage.

But where were his security men? Had they too retreated in the face of his anger? Sometimes he thought the younger generation consisted of nothing but pampered cowards. How was his country to survive when he was surrounded by nothing but traitors and weaklings? Men like Saad Chutani and Ahmed Taj?

Shirani could not dispute that the president was a skillful politician. His ousting of the formidable former ISI director in favor of Taj was a first step toward bringing the powerful intelligence agency to heel. Underestimating Chutani's abilities would be extremely dangerous, but overestimating them could lead to paralysis. While in some ways impressive, nothing the politician had accomplished would have been possible without the constant involvement of the Americans.

The critical difference between Shirani and Chutani was that the president actually believed in America. He genuinely treated its leaders as friends and partners. He took their money like they all did, but instead of subverting it, he used it on Washington-sanctioned programs. It was all part of his twisted dream of turning Pakistan into a U.S. clone. Into a place where Shirani's daughters would be free to behave like prostitutes and Allah would become a quaint mythology.

Chutani was dangerous but also far too impressed with himself. While he had been successful in infiltrating Pakistan's intelligence apparatus and bribing the poor with public projects, his position was not unassailable. His American-sponsored drone attacks and commando raids had strengthened Pakistan's growing fundamentalist insurgency. And he was not the master of the army. Not yet.

The truth was that Pakistan had been controlled by a civilian government for too long. The country had a lengthy history of coups and the undeniable fact was that Pakistan performed better under military rule. The time had come to act.

Shirani climbed the stairs lost in thought but by the time he reached the top landing, the continued silence began to intrude. The army provided numerous servants and guards—men he'd handpicked for their skill and loyalty. While the size of his home had the ability to obscure them, it was unheard-of for him to travel its full length without at least a glimpse of the people tasked with keeping his household operating.

Shirani felt a dull surge of adrenaline. Had he underestimated Chutani? Had the politician managed to defeat his security? Was he looking to do something more tangible than just humiliating the commander of his army?

Shirani slowed, staying on the carpet runners as he continued toward the back of the house. The overhead fixtures had been removed in the last remodel, leaving the hallway lit only by weak, widely spaced lamps. He told himself he was being paranoid—that Chutani didn't have the courage to do something this overt—but it did little to steady his nerves.

He put his drink down on a low chest and opened one of the drawers. Inside, he found one of the many guns that had been strategically placed around the house. The mechanism was well oiled, and the round entering the chamber made almost no sound at all.

Shirani found himself wanting to call out, to discover that his men were just giving him space. He wasn't confident enough to do so, though. Instead, he crept forward, taking a deep breath before stepping into his study with the Heckler & Koch P7 stretched out in front of him.

"I hardly think that will be necessary," Ahmed Taj said in Urdu.

He was sitting near the unlit fireplace, legs crossed and hands steepled in front of him. Like at the end of their last meeting, he refused to avert his eyes.

"Where are my men?"

"I wanted to speak privately."

"How . . ." Shirani started, but then fell silent. While Taj was still dressed in his familiar rumpled suit and faded tie, he seemed completely transformed. His posture was ramrod straight and his normally dull eyes had turned cunning. Was it possible that everything Shirani knew about the man was a lie?

The realization that he had seen only what Taj wanted him to see came like a blow to the chest. It seemed so clear now—the increasing sophistication of Taliban activity, Durrani's death, the well-coordinated attacks on the army's nuclear facilities. How had he been so blind?

Taj calmly pointed to the weapon in Shirani's hand. "Put the gun down and sit, Umar. We both know that if I wanted you dead, you would have been long ago."

Taj watched the man as he laid his firearm on an ugly Western table and sat. Umar Shirani was in many ways his polar opposite. The general was a creature of privilege, having been born into a wealthy family with strong ties to the military. It was this that had made him complacent and all too easy to undermine. In the end, men like him possessed a fundamental belief in their own superiority. To them, life was a competition they couldn't lose. An endless game of jockeying for position in an entitled hierarchy.

"First, let me apologize for the army being relieved of its duties guarding our nuclear arsenal. It was certainly not my intention."

It was a lie that Shirani would immediately see through. The goal was less to convince the army commander that the ISI had no interest in reigning over Pakistan's missile capability than to set a civil tone. Taj needed an ally, not another competitor.

"Of course," Shirani responded noncommittally. He looked around him, undoubtedly out of a futile hope that he wasn't alone. That his men would enter and help the old soldier retain the upper hand he was too arrogant to realize he'd lost years ago.

"Our country is rotting, Umar. From both inside and out. The regional instability caused by the Americans is spreading. Sectarian violence has grown to a point that it's at the edge of our control. And while we've been successful at subverting U.S. financial aid, we've also been seduced by it."

Shirani just nodded.

"President Chutani has given me the responsibility of protecting our nuclear arsenal but ordered me to ignore the external threats from the Americans and Indians, both of whom will stop at nothing to wipe out our capabilities and leave us defenseless."

"How can Pakistan survive this?" Shirani said, finally gaining enough confidence to join the conversation. "I fear that God is judging our weakness, Ahmed. Losing faith in our commitment to His will."

"As do I. America's corrupting influence cannot be overestimated."

"Allah be praised."

Taj smiled. Shirani's whoring was legendary and he had been drinking alcohol only moments before. He was like so many others throughout human history—a man who used God as an excuse to pursue his own ambitions.

It was this that would eventually make it necessary to get rid of the man. But not yet. In order for chaos to be averted, Taj's coup would have to preserve as much of the existing political structure as possible. The illusion of normalcy was critical in the short term.

"I assume you're here with a proposal?" Shirani said, gaining still more confidence. He would know that whatever Taj had planned, it would be impossible without the consent of the army. Nothing in Pakistan happened without at least the army's pledge not to interfere.

Fortunately, the general was a simple man. Utterly untrustworthy, but interested first and foremost in protecting his own position.

"I will be taking control of Pakistan soon," Taj said simply.

Shirani's surprise at the boldness of the statement was obvious and anticipated. He'd undoubtedly expected to be recruited for some subtle plan to undermine the civilian government's authority. Not an admission that an ISI coup was in the works.

The general laughed uncomfortably, undoubtedly concerned that this was a trap constructed by Saad Chutani. "You're talking treason,

Ahmed. I have disagreements with the president's relationship with America, but it's my job to tell him my opinion and then obey his orders."

"I admire your sense of duty, Umar, but how much longer will you be able to hold on to that job? You're experienced enough to know that Chutani is maneuvering to remove you as head of the army."

"I know no such thing."

It was Taj's turn to laugh. "I assume you remember what happened to my predecessor."

It was impossible to forget. He had been marginalized with fabricated scandals publicized in media outlets beholden to Chutani. The unrest in North Waziristan had been laid at his feet, and he was vilified every time there was a terrorist attack within Pakistan's borders. Finally, he'd been forced out over accepting bribes that were no different than ones taken by every government executive in the country. He was now facing a lifetime of prosecutions that would leave him penniless and his family disgraced.

"We're at a turning point, Umar. The Middle East is disintegrating. The world is ready—in fact desperate—for a Muslim superpower to fill the vacuum created by the Americans. The Saudis are children obsessed with toys, and the Iranians are backstabbing women with no nuclear capability. Pakistan is the only country capable of becoming that superpower. We have a unique opportunity, Umar. We can neutralize America, take control of the region, and close our fist around the oil they rely so heavily on. We can bring their economy to its knees and stop the drone attacks on our soil. The humiliations can be brought to an end. All we need is our own strength and Allah's blessing."

Taj fell silent and leaned back in his chair. It was Shirani's turn to speak.

"What is my position in all this?"

Predictably, his thoughts immediately turned to himself.

"Under my leadership, you will retain your rank as well as the authority to do what needs to be done with our nuclear arsenal."

"And what is that?"

"The expansion and modernization of our missile technology. Like you, I understand the importance of having weapons capable of reaching the United States. . . ." He paused and allowed himself a smile. "I'm sure America's Congress will be willing to finance the effort."

For the first time, there was a flicker of interest in Shirani's eyes. Self-interest, no doubt, but Taj wasn't naïve. No matter what the general promised by way of support, his army would in fact stay as neutral as possible. The general would wait to see who won and then determine whether the power struggle had been bloody enough to make the victor vulnerable.

And that was all Taj needed—for the army to remain docile until he could do away with President Chutani and consolidate his leadership. Then, and only then, would he move to deal with Umar Shirani.

CHAPTER 19

MITCH Rapp made a show of activating his throat mike, though in fact he was constantly transmitting on the frequency Gould had been excluded from. "Joe. Have you acquired us?"

"Not yet."

That was probably a good thing. Maslick was in an elevated position specifically looking for them and hadn't yet picked them up. If that was the case, it was almost certain that Obrecht's men were still completely ignorant of what was going on outside their wall.

The trip from the knoll had taken longer than Wicker's estimate but Rapp had anticipated that. Gould was good—making no mistakes that Rapp could see from his position five feet behind. He wasn't fast, though. The assassin had been operating primarily in urban environments since he'd left the French Foreign Legion. It was no surprise that he couldn't hold the pace expected by an elfin former SEAL who had been creeping around the woods since he was in diapers.

Gould wriggled between two trees and Rapp followed, thoughts of Anna intruding on his mind. Her courage during the White House op. The depth of her green eyes. How different his life would be if she had lived.

He cleared the trees and the bottom of Gould's boot came into view again. What Rapp saw, though, was the whitewashed front of the man's house in New Zealand and the sun reflecting off the ocean below.

It was a stark contrast to the dilapidated apartment Rapp called home. He'd been building a new house on a couple of acres just outside the Beltway when Anna died. Or more precisely, when the man in front of him had murdered her in a botched attempt to get to him. Construction had immediately stopped, along with everything else in his life.

The burned-out bones of his old house were still there. Kennedy and Mike Nash had tried to convince him to have the lot cleared so it could be sold, but so far he hadn't been able to bring himself to do it.

In light of all that, why did he still feel conflicted about Louis Gould? Why had he passed up every opportunity to take the man out?

Tom Lewis, the CIA's shrink, had gently suggested an answer: When Rapp looked into the Frenchman's eyes, he saw a reflection of himself. Of course, he'd dismissed it as psychobabble, but there was no denying that Lewis was right more than he was wrong.

A small rock outcropping appeared ahead and Rapp took cover behind it. The entrance to the tunnel was just a few yards away, but they were the most exposed of the journey.

"Joe," Rapp said into his radio. "I'm at the feature we designated echo three. Look six feet behind it."

He put a boot against a sapling and gave it a gentle nudge.

"I've got you," Maslick came back immediately.

"Any activity nearby?"

"A nice six-point buck about one twenty-five to the west. That's it."

Rapp started out again, using his elbows to drag himself forward at a pace that would allow him to close the gap to Gould. The light breeze was traveling from west to east, making it unlikely that the deer would be spooked by their scent.

It took an excruciatingly long time to cover the distance, but finally both men were lying in front of the cave's entrance. Gould slid through the tight opening and Rapp put his head partially inside to let his eyes adjust to the lower light.

The Frenchman pried a piece of stone from the dirt wall, revealing the promised keypad. He glanced back before punching in the code. "Keep your fingers crossed."

Rapp counted, confirming that the string of numbers was the twelve Gould had reported back at the farm. Not that he thought a pathological liar like him would make such an obvious mistake, but it made sense to keep close tabs on the man.

There was a quiet click and Gould pressed a hand against the rusted steel at the back of the cavern. It swung inward, revealing dim red emergency lighting beyond.

Rapp adjusted Hurley's Kimber .45 holstered in the small of his back and activated his radio again. "We're about to enter. Figure ten minutes to get to the mansion."

"Roger that," Coleman responded.

"Stan?" Rapp said.

The muttered response was barely intelligible. "Waiting, waiting, and more waiting."

It wasn't what Rapp wanted to hear. They needed Hurley to pinpoint Obrecht's location in the building. A room-by-room search was not part of their quick-in, quick-out plan.

"Roger that. Do what you can, Stan. We're moving."

CHAPTER 20

ONCE again, Allah had blessed their enterprise. Despite a forecast for rain, the sun was in full force, with only a few distant clouds to obscure it.

Kabir Gadai strolled casually along the gravel walkway, led by a leashed Labrador retriever puppy. He'd purchased it only a few hours ago and was already looking forward to putting its dead body in a dumpster as soon as this was over. Westerners' affinity for these filthy creatures was inexplicable, but not acknowledging that affinity would be stupid. Nearly everyone who passed looked down at the animal and smiled. More important, Isabella Accorso had two Labradors of her own—the latest in an unbroken series of similar dogs going back to her childhood.

The park was long and narrow, bordered on the left by a busy Roman road and on the right by the ongoing excavation of an ancient square. Gadai examined the columns and crumbing walls that recalled a time when the Italians ruled the known world. Later Catholicism would take hold and the people of this region would embark on the Crusades, a genocidal rampage against the followers of Mohammed. The same people who were now so critical of violence had burned his people at the stake, imprisoned them in unimaginably cruel conditions, and forced them to endure tortures unparalleled in their creativity and savageness.

Now the Americans were sending their Christian soldiers marching across the Middle East in an effort to remake it in the name of a false faith that they themselves seemed largely uninterested in. They would never understand what it was to have God in one's heart—for Him to be part of their very being. For the Americans, the Creator was nothing more than an occasional convenience. A being to be called on in difficult times and to be briefly acknowledged on public holidays.

"ETA one minute," the voice said over his Bluetooth headset. "Her preferred position is fully open."

Gadai acknowledged the message with a barely perceptible nod.

Conveniently, Accorso ate lunch at the same time as her daughter. On clear days like this one, she left her office at noon and came to this park to eat a sandwich brought from home. There were multiple benches to choose from, but she was biased toward the one closest to her building. If it wasn't available, she would select the next in line.

Her daughter, Bianca, was even more predictable. She sat on the same low concrete wall at the front of her school every day. In the time they had been watching her, even the order of the people she ate with hadn't varied. An example of the inviolable social hierarchy that all adolescents adhered to.

He spotted the blond hair and dark coat of his target just as the puppy found something of interest at the base of a garbage can. His first instinct was to jerk the animal away, but instead he paused until it was ready to move on. The bench Accorso had selected was visible to him now, and it was still completely empty. Again, Allah had blessed him.

He started toward her, setting his pace so that they would reach the bench at the same time.

"Oh, I'm sorry," Gadai said, stopping in front of it. "Were you going to sit here?"

Fortunately Accorso spoke fluent English—a prerequisite for her job administering contracts and trusts for her law firm.

Like the others, she barely noticed him, instead beaming at the dog. "What's his name?"

"Her, actually. And I don't know yet. She's just Puppy for now."

"I was going to eat lunch," she said, pointing at the bench. "Feel free to join me. There's plenty of room."

"That's very kind of you."

They both sat and she leaned forward, rubbing the excited dog's head. It nipped at her leg, and instead of pulling back, she laughed. "I have two just like her at home. Older now, though. You forget how cute they are at this age. Like children."

It was all going exactly as planned. While he'd always been quite successful with women, striking up a conversation with one on a park bench was an unpredictable enterprise. If the attention was unwelcome, their interaction could cause her to move on. Or worse, it could attract the notice of people walking past. The animal solved all those issues.

"Here," Gadai said, pulling out his phone. "Let me show you something."

The woman assumed he was going to show her a photo of the puppy and frowned when the screen came to life. "I'm sorry, what is that?"

He leaned into her so he could speak quietly. "It's a video of your daughter Bianca taken through a rifle scope."

She froze, her expression turning from confusion to recognition and then to terror.

"Smile," Gadai said, slipping the phone back in his jacket.

She began to stammer like some half-wit and he leaned into her ear again. "I said *smile*."

She forced the corners of her mouth upward, still trying to get intelligible words out. "I . . . What . . ."

"Be silent and listen to me very carefully. I have no desire to see your daughter harmed. It can only attract attention to me and my people. Whether she lives her life never knowing this happened or dies today is entirely up to you."

"But what do you want? I don't have—"

"Silence!" he said in a sharp whisper. Still, the people passing by paid little attention. To the degree anyone looked in their direction, it was to admire the dog playfully attacking Accorso's shoe.

"Your firm administers a set of files I'm interested in."

"We administer many files. How—"

"This particular client would have made an unusual request. He would have asked you to send files out over the Internet in the event you didn't hear from him on a particular schedule."

She didn't respond, but the subtle shift in her expression told him everything he needed to know.

"You're familiar with this arrangement?"

"Yes."

"Then return to your office. Load the files and any instructions you were given onto a thumb drive."

"Thumb drive," she repeated numbly.

"That's right, Isabella. You're doing well. This will all be over soon." He pointed to a hotel across the street. "Bring the files to me there. Room two hundred. It's an easy number to remember. Repeat it back to me."

"Two hundred."

"Very good. Do it quickly, Isabella. Your daughter's break from class won't last much longer, and my man has orders not to let her out of his sight. If I don't call him off by the time she gets up to go back to class, he will kill her. Do you understand?"

The woman's eyes were fixed and a tear had formed in the corner of one of them, but she managed to nod.

"Then go."

She broke from her trance and stood, walking unsteadily toward her law firm's building.

The dog bounded after her, but Gadai gripped the leash firmly. He, too, would have liked to follow. The uncertainty—and indeed danger—of sending her back to her office unaccompanied was an unacceptable risk in his opinion. But Taj's orders had been clear.

After a few more moments he rose, glancing at his watch. Just enough time to get rid of the filthy beast before picking up his room key.

CHAPTER 21

SCOTT Coleman came over the top of a rocky outcropping and leapt to the steep slope below. His thighs burned and his heart pounded powerfully in his chest as he half-ran, half-skidded down twenty yards of loose dirt.

"Approaching your position," he said, making sure he didn't sound out of breath. Despite a training program designed and monitored by a soulless Norwegian coach, he was feeling the relentless grade and the weight of his pack. The passage of time was hard on men in his profession. Better than the alternative, though.

"Roger that, Scott. We were wondering what had happened to you." One of Wicker's veiled jabs. See how he felt when he was pushing fifty.

The clearing he entered was probably only thirty feet in diameter, bordered with dense trees choked with even denser bushes. McGraw was in a tree on the north side, barely visible in camouflage fatigues and hat. He was holding the modified hunting rifle that he preferred for shorter ranges, scanning through a Schmidt & Bender scope.

"What have you got, Bruno?"

"Garbage."

Coleman moved toward the east side of the clearing, stopping when he caught a glimpse of the gray wall surrounding Obrecht's property. After carefully moving a few leafy branches, he got an unobstructed view of what McGraw was talking about. They were stuck in a trough between hills. From Coleman's position on the ground, nothing more than the wall and the top of the mansion's roof was visible. The gate was a complete write-off—too far south for even McGraw to see.

"Do you have a view into the courtyard?"

"Barely."

"How many guards do you have eyes on?"

"I'm down to two. Intermittent."

Coleman swore under his breath and pulled out a range finder. Just over 450 yards to the wall. To make matters worse—if that was even possible—they were no longer blocked from the wind. The gentle right-to-left breeze they'd had on top of the knoll was now being accelerated to eight knots as it funneled through a canyon to the east.

To say their new position was a tactical disaster would be the understatement of the century. He might as well have brought a cooler and some beach chairs for all the use they would be stuck in this hole.

"Can you hit either of them?" Coleman said.

"Eighty-twenty. It's starting to gust."

"Wick?"

He knew roughly where his top sniper was, but didn't bother to look for him. Wicker had a custom-built tree stand with telescoping arms painted and textured to look like tree branches even from a few feet away. His camo was modified with fabric leaves and real bark that perfectly matched the tree species he was in. Even his rifle would have been custom painted for this particular contract.

"I've got a little more height than Bruno, but I've set up to prioritize my line of sight on our former position. I might be able to take one guard. Depends on timing, though. I'm maybe thirty percent."

Coleman pulled back to the center of the clearing and began emptying his pack. Best-case scenario, his guys would leave nine highly trained men and no less than two hundred yards of wide-open ground before they hit twelve feet of dead, smooth wall. He hated this plan even more now than when Rapp had first proposed it.

There was nothing he could have done to change it, though. He was comfortable arguing with Kennedy and would even mix it up with Hurley from time to time. Rapp was a different animal. Fighting with him was like taking a swing at a hornet's nest. You weren't going to win, and in the process of losing you were going to be in for a world of hurt.

He pulled a small monitor from his pack and turned it on, waiting for the screen to brighten sufficiently to see in the outdoor environment. The image was being beamed from the drone Marcus Dumond had doing lazy figure eights above.

The security detail was still on high alert inside the courtyard, but nothing in the rhythm of their activities suggested they knew about the storm gathering on their perimeter.

He activated his throat mike, keeping an eye on the image of the men he might soon be up against. "Are you still dead in the water, Stan?"

"Mmmmm hmmmmm."

Coleman set the monitor down and pulled his rifle from its case. Outstanding. He had a cancer-ridden old man cooling his heels in a waiting room, two snipers stuck in the low ground, and Mitch Rapp crawling through a tunnel with the contract killer who murdered his family.

Just another glorious day in the service of the Central Intelligence Agency.

CHAPTER 22

STAN Hurley had chosen a hard, straight-backed chair in the corner over the more comfortable furniture placed throughout the parlor. Its position made a shot at him through the reportedly bulletproof windows impossible while allowing him to keep his back to the wall. Those were only side benefits, though.

In a life that had been lived with no compromises, now compromises were all he had. If he stayed on his feet and walked around the room, his recently replaced hip would start to ache. If he sat in one of the heavily cushioned chairs, he was in danger of falling asleep. And if he sat too long where he was, his knees would start to stiffen up.

Despite the fact that the main purpose of the CIA was gathering intelligence, no one there knew exactly how old he was. His birth on his parents' kitchen table had left no written record, and the last witness to that event—his older brother—had died earlier that year. In fact, Hurley had just turned eighty.

The things he'd experienced over his lifetime astounded even him. Horse-drawn carts in the streets of Bowling Green, Kentucky. Collecting scrap metal with the other kids to support the war effort in Europe.

The rise of the Soviet Union. His old friend Neil Armstrong planting an American flag on the moon.

And Mitch Rapp.

Hurley had done everything in his power—and a few things that were most definitely not—to wash the kid out. In the end, the only thing he succeeded in doing was burning out a bunch of the top special ops guys that made up the rest of Rapp's training class. Things that would have killed the average Army Ranger just made that little pissant stick his middle finger in the air.

On one hand, Rapp still had a way of getting under his skin like no one else. On the other, it was comforting to know that he was leaving Kennedy with someone who would always protect her. Always protect the country that had given them so much.

Hurley stood, subconsciously running through the list of physical ailments that could compromise the op if it got hot. After fifteen or so, he gave up and pulled a Camel from the pack in his jacket. He held a lighter to the innocent-looking white cylinder and inhaled a lungful of smoke. Over the years, he'd been shot, stabbed, garroted, thrown from a ship a hundred miles from shore, and poisoned. The last by a cute little Czech woman he was screwing. Kind of funny that the Grim Reaper had ditched his scythe and snuck up behind him with a tobacco leaf. Just another limp dick in a robe.

He started looking around the room again, getting the blood flowing as he walked. No update from Rapp yet. He was probably still in the tunnel. When he got out and found that the target hadn't been located, he wasn't going to be happy. Not that anyone would blame Hurley, but that didn't matter. This wasn't a business of excuses. You either got the job done or you didn't.

So, what now?

The guard would be standing just outside the closed door, making it impossible for Hurley to simply wander out and play the befuddled old man if he came across anyone. He might be able to bash the man's head in with one of the room's antique knickknacks, but the chance of that compromising the op was nearly one hundred percent.

Hurley felt an all-too-familiar constriction in his lungs and put a handkerchief to his mouth, coughing uncontrollably into it. About halfway through his fit, the door opened and the guard who had led him there appeared. The good news was the desperate hacking would play into his cover as a helpless geriatric. The bad news was that it wasn't an act. Hurley really was struggling to keep from collapsing and the handkerchief really was spattered with bloody specks of what had once been his lungs.

"Mr. Obrecht will see you now," the guard said, apparently unconcerned about the man choking in front of him.

Hurley wiped his mouth with the back of his hand and walked unsteadily toward the door. "Thank you."

"Second floor," the guard said, falling in a pace behind.

Hurley suppressed a smile as he headed for a broad set of steps supported by marble pillars. The timing would be perfect. When Rapp and the frog came out of that tunnel, he'd already have Obrecht wrapped up like a birthday present.

A skylight in the domed ceiling threw a shadow and Hurley kept his eye on the guard's as they began to ascend. The man was three steps back with his assault rifle held against his chest. The image got increasingly dim as they ascended, but not so dim that Hurley didn't see the rifle suddenly begin to rise. He spun, lunging for the man just as the plastic butt caught him in the side of the head. The blow dazed him, but his momentum was still sufficient to send them both toppling down the steps.

When they hit the landing, Hurley's head was swimming, and it felt like someone had jammed a hot knife in his hip joint. The other man had come through the fall in much better condition. Protected from the steps by his body armor and youth, he was on his feet before Hurley could even get to his knees.

This time when the rifle butt came down, there was nothing he could do.

CHAPTER 23

THE emergency lights bathed everything in red as Rapp pulled himself through the tunnel using his elbows. After a reasonably spacious entrance, the shaft had shrunk down to a cramped three feet wide by two feet high.

Rapp had suffered from mild claustrophobia since he was a kid. Years of fighting in the open spaces of America and the Middle East had made it worse for good reason: The speed, endurance, and accuracy that gave him his edge tended to be neutralized in these environments.

The fact that Gould's feet were close enough to his face that he could smell the rubber soles offered some comfort. If anyone discovered them and hosed down the tunnel from the mansion side, the Frenchman would act as a reluctant shield. Even more important, the shaft was too tight for Gould to turn on him.

"I think I see it," the Frenchman said, his whisper echoing through the narrow space. "Twenty meters."

Rapp's grip on his Glock tightened as they continued forward to a steel wall covered in surface rust. They found a keypad similar to the one at the tunnel's entrance and Gould punched in another lengthy code. There was a moment of tense silence followed by the hum of an electric motor.

Rapp lowered the night-vision goggle mounted to his helmet and flipped it on. The next-generation system combined the light amplification of traditional starlight scopes with thermal imaging. Normally, he'd have refused it due to the bulk and weight, but there were enough unknowns about the basement they were about to enter to make it worthwhile. Tests at the Farm suggested the unit would give him a solid view of the ambient environment while highlighting the body heat of human targets.

"You ready, Mitch?"

"Go."

Gould shoved the steel barrier outward and threw himself to the dirt floor on the other side. He rolled smoothly to the right while Rapp went left as planned.

The light amplification capability of the goggle was barely functional due to the depth of the darkness. Thermal picked up a little temperature variation, but other than Gould glowing orange, most everything just read as hazy shades of green. Rapp had to move far slower than he would have liked, avoiding the unidentifiable clutter on his way to an overturned barrel. Gould nearly tripped, but managed to save it and take cover behind something that looked vaguely like an ancient winepress. Rapp spotted a reddish smear at the edge of his peripheral vision but didn't bother tracking it. Most likely a rat.

Other than that, nothing. No sound. No movement. In fact, nothing that would suggest anyone had been down there in years. Rapp swept his gun over a dark hole in the wall that he guessed was a medieval well and then slipped around the left side of the barrel. He motioned Gould forward and the Frenchman moved cautiously to a low pile of rubble. They leapfrogged that way, moving purposefully until they found themselves at the base of the staircase that led up to the main house.

Gould pointed right to a rectangle in the wall that their goggles shaded blue. The cold steel of the entrance to Obrecht's safe room.

Rapp covered the Frenchman as he ran to it and smeared a bead of epoxy into the narrow gap between the edge of the door and the jamb. Not exactly high-tech, but it would be enough to keep the Swiss banker from gaining access should things go south. Obrecht's only option at that point would be the tunnel, where he would flee right into the welcoming arms of Joe Maslick.

Gould returned and led up the stairs with Rapp a few steps behind. They retracted their goggles and removed their helmets when the light bleeding around the basement door became strong enough for them to see. Rapp stowed the helmets beneath a stack of stained towels on the landing while the Frenchman slid a fiber-optic cable beneath the door. The image from the tiny camera read out on his phone, displaying exactly what they'd hoped to see: an empty hallway.

Rapp activated his throat mike and spoke quietly. "We're exiting the basement onto the first floor. Stan, give me a sitrep."

No response.

It was one of the unavoidable drawbacks to their plan. His silence could mean that he was dead and that they were walking into an ambush, or it could mean that he was with Obrecht and not in a position to respond.

"Scott. Update."

"Stan got called in to meet with Obrecht while you were offline. No communication from him since. We're in position and ready to go."

"Roger that. Stan, if you can hear this and you're in Obrecht's office, try to toggle your mike."

He waited for a moment and then the banker's accented voice came over his earpiece.

"I've had my people check on this, and I can assure you that my bank does no—"

The feed went dead and Rapp gave Gould a thumbs-up. Hurley was where he was supposed to be, but couldn't communicate beyond briefly pressing the button on his key fob.

Gould eased the door open and slipped through with Rapp following. The main staircase was to their left, but it was the centerpiece of the mansion's entry hall and in full view of no fewer than six windows. They went right, skirting the kitchen and entering a narrow servant's staircase. Gould aimed his Glock upward as they ascended, with Rapp keeping an eye on their flank.

When they came to the door at the top, Gould did another quick search with the fiber-optic camera and then went through. They were halfway up the wide hallway when they heard a woman's voice singing quietly. The two men ducked into a bedroom and pressed their backs against the wall behind the half-open door.

Of all the rooms in the mansion she could have chosen to clean that day, she picked that one.

Rapp grabbed Gould's wrist when the assassin aimed his silenced pistol at the back of her head. While the proliferation of surveillance cameras throughout the world was a serious drawback for men in their profession, the invention of the iPod almost made up for it. Rapp spotted the ubiquitous white earphones and motioned toward the hallway. She never noticed the two armed men slipping out of the room only a few feet behind her, concentrating instead on the sheets she was unfolding and the latest dance track from Madonna.

They were able to pick up their pace on the thick carpet and it took only seconds to reach the second-to-last door on the right. According to Gould, Leo Obrecht's office was just beyond.

Rapp put an ear to the wall, but it was too thick to hear anything inside. Hopefully, they'd find Obrecht and Hurley having a pleasant conversation over tea. A set of flex cuffs and some duct tape would be all it would take to get their package ready to go back through the tunnel. Next stop, a CIA black site in Bulgaria.

Rapp put a hand on the knob and nodded a silent three count. He didn't throw open the door like he normally would, instead pushing it gently enough that Obrecht wouldn't get spooked if he saw it.

Luck was with them. They slipped inside the study unnoticed, the book-lined walls and tapestries absorbing what little sound they made. At the far side, a heavyset man with his back to them was poking at the embers in a massive stone fireplace. A modern steel sculpture partially obscured both him and a portion of the right side of the room, but not enough that Rapp couldn't immediately determine that Hurley wasn't there.

The man at the fireplace was the size Rapp expected from the surveillance photos and he had the right expensive suit and short-cropped gray hair, but there was something about him that seemed off. The barely perceptible athleticism in the way he stood. The effortless way he handled the heavy iron poker.

Rapp spun toward Gould, but was just a fraction of a second too slow. The Frenchman swept a foot low, taking Rapp's legs out from under him. He hit the carpet rolling just as the man near the fireplace spun around to reveal the MP5 in his free hand. The sculpture obscured his head, but Rapp resisted the urge to go for a body shot. He knew instinctively that the man's bulk was the result of full body armor. It was a perfect way to imitate an overweight banker while making him impervious to small arms fire. There was a weakness in the mercenary's preparations, though: his expensive Italian shoes.

Rapp fired a round into the left one and used his momentum to swing his Glock toward Gould.

"Don't do it, Mitch!"

The assassin had his own pistol lined up in a two-handed grip. And while Rapp could no longer see the merc behind him, the silence suggested he hadn't fallen. If he was tough and disciplined enough to stay upright with the ball of his foot missing, it was likely that the MP5 was also on target.

"Drop the weapon, Mitch. And don't get your hands anywhere near that throat mike."

Rapp let the Glock fall to the carpet.

"And Stan's."

He reached for Hurley's Kimber Gold Match as he slowly stood.

"You've got two guns trained on you, Mitch. And neither one of us are the illiterate goat herders you're used to. Understand?"

"There's no way Obrecht can be paying you enough for this," Rapp said, retrieving the Kimber and then letting it fall from his hand.

"Fifteen million and a new identity so clean even the CIA won't be able to track me. But it's not the money."

"What then?" Rapp said, though he already knew the answer. The truth was, he always had.

"You're my only failure, Mitch. I thought I'd forget about it as time went on, but it just got worse." He eased left to put himself in a position that would allow him to avoid a cross fire if Rapp made a move. "I had you dead to rights in Afghanistan. I can't believe the idiot who hired me blew it like that."

"What about your wife and daughter, Louis? How do they fit in with your new identity?"

It took Gould a few seconds to respond. "Seemed like a fair trade. I lose them but I become the man who killed a legend."

The door opened, but it didn't even cause a flicker of distraction in Gould. He kept his eyes locked on target as Stan Hurley was pushed through. The old man staggered and nearly fell, holding the back of his head with a blood-soaked hand.

"Stan," the Frenchman said cheerfully. "You're just in time to be the icing on my cake."

CHAPTER 24

K ABIR Gadai checked his phone and then laid it back on the table. The screen continued to display Isabella Accorso's daughter in the crosshairs, as it had for the last forty minutes.

He felt the unaccustomed sensation of nervousness spreading from his stomach to his extremities, producing a barely perceptible tremor in his hands. The life he'd led was one of careful plans rewarded with an uninterrupted string of successes. This situation, though, had been beyond his control from the beginning. It was one thing to trust in God, but another to rely on his intervention. Allah might see this as arrogance and punish those involved.

Bianca Accorso was a young woman with highly predictable habits, and Gadai was confident that she would remain sitting with her friends for precisely another seventeen minutes. Taj was certain that this time wouldn't expire without her mother bringing the files, but it would be idiocy not to plan for a worst-case scenario.

A quick return to Pakistan would be the most obvious course of action, but he had been serving Taj for too long to think that was a viable option. If he arrived without the Rickman files, it would be the beginning of his own destruction. Not immediately, of course. Taj was too subtle for that. But within the year, he would find himself accused of treason or assassinated by one of the Taliban loyal to Taj.

If Accorso didn't appear in the next twenty minutes, it seemed almost certain that she had contacted the Italian authorities. Gadai would have no choice but to run. He would never be able to return to his country. He would never see his sons again. His life would become nothing more than an endless procession of days consumed with trying to stay ahead of Taj's assassins.

His Bluetooth earpiece buzzed and he pressed the button to pick up the call.

"Go ahead."

"She's entered the lobby."

"Any sign of the police?"

"None."

Gadai let out a relieved breath and walked across the room to the door. There was no denying that as great as the risks were, the rewards were equally great: a position second only to Taj at the helm of the modern era's first Muslim superpower. He would have a hand in spreading Islam across the globe in a way that had never before been imagined. All while the Americans cowered.

Gadai peered through the peephole, looking across the hallway at room 200. It would be over soon, he reassured himself. Taj had once again been right. While terrifying and unpredictable, he was a great man favored by God.

"She's exiting the stairway," the voice said over his earpiece. "Twenty seconds. No other activity."

Accorso appeared a few moments later with an envelope under her arm. He watched her from behind as she knocked timidly on the door of the empty room.

"Still clear?" he asked.

His men were monitoring the parking lot, the lobby, and all points of entry to the second floor.

"Yes, sir."

Gadai opened the door. "Isabella."

She spun, fear and surprise playing out across her face.

"Come in," he said, keeping his words purposely vague. If she was wearing a wire, the police would assume he was in room 200 instead of being across the hall.

The woman did as she was told and he closed the door behind her.

"Have you brought me what I asked for?"

She gave a short nod and held out the envelope.

Gadai sat at a desk that he'd moved away from the draped window and tore open the flap. He inserted the thumb drive he found into his laptop and began perusing the accompanying single page of paper while it loaded.

The written instructions were somewhat more complex than he'd expected. Files were individually designated and various scenarios were laid out, each with a different release schedule.

"You're following the second scenario?" Gadai asked.

Accorso nodded, perspiration beginning to form on her upper lip. "We were informed that Akhtar Durrani died by an authenticated email. When we didn't hear from the client, we released file D-six on the third of the month."

He nodded noncommittally. It would have contained the information on the Russian mole in Istanbul. The next file to be released, designated R-12, was scheduled for Thursday. What revelations did it contain? The identity of a highly placed informant? A list of bribes to foreign officials? Evidence of wrongdoing by the CIA's administration? It was impossible not to speculate.

"And by 'released' you mean you simply sent it to the email address in the instructions."

"Yes."

"Have you looked at the files?"

"They're encrypted."

"Do you know who the client is?"

"He's anonymous. He contacts me by phone once per week and gives me one of the pass phrases listed on the instruction sheet."

Gadai scrolled through the list of files contained on the thumb drive, feeling a growing sense of elation. They had anticipated twenty or thirty. Instead there were hundreds. How much had Rickman known? What level of access had he enjoyed? Could Taj be right? Could this innocuous data-storage device contain the means to the Central Intelligence Agency's destruction?

"Do you have backups of this information?"

"Yes."

"In the office of the attorney who handles this client?"

"What about my daughter? You said—"

"I said she wouldn't be harmed if you did as I asked. But you're not answering my questions, are you, Isabella?"

He saw the ripple in her cheeks as her jaw clenched in anger, but it was a pathetic display. She was nothing more than a frightened woman who couldn't even hold on to a husband. She would do what she was told.

"Are the backups in the lawyer's office?" Gadai repeated. "Tell me quickly. Your daughter doesn't have much time left."

"No," Accorso said, finally. "He may still have the original of the paper instructions because his secretary made this copy for me. The files are contained on the firm's central computer. It's backed up every night."

Gadai looked up at her. "And do you have a way of deleting those files from both your mainframe and the backups?"

She didn't answer immediately and he just stared at her, letting the seconds tick by.

"Yes. We have a way to do that. Sometimes we have clients who move their business and want their information wiped from our system."

"That's good," Gadai said calmly. "Listen very carefully, Isabella. I want you to eradicate everything about this arrangement from your system. I want it to appear that it never existed."

Surprisingly, she shook her head. "What happens when the client notifies my firm that the files aren't being sent? What will you do to my daughter then?"

Gadai smiled reassuringly. "There will be no such notification. Your client is dead. Forget any of this ever happened, Isabella. When the backups are deleted, your job and your daughter will both be safe."

Of course, it was a lie. He couldn't leave the woman alive. But his words had the intended effect and she relaxed slightly.

"Go back to work," he said. "Tonight, have a glass of wine. Spend some time with Bianca. I promise you'll never hear from me again. Once you've done what I ask, it will be over."

CHAPTER 25

*D*ROP *the weapon, Mitch. And don't get your hands anywhere near that throat mike."*

Charlie Wicker slid forward in the tree stand and sighted through his scope. Rapp had modified his radio to constantly transmit on the frequency Gould had been excluded from. For good reason, it seemed.

Up to that moment, Wicker shared Coleman's take on this op. Gould had crossed Mitch Rapp as bad as anyone ever could and was still breathing. If Wicker had been in the Frenchman's position, he'd have fallen to his knees, thanked Jesus, and slunk away to the far corners of the earth in case Rapp ever changed his mind. This psycho just didn't get it.

"We're copying this, Mitch." Coleman's voice over the comm.

Through his scope, Wicker had a good view of the knoll they'd abandoned. The wind was blowing gently along it, causing the tall grass to wave rhythmically. About halfway up, something caught his eye. A patch that wasn't swaying to the same music as the rest.

"I have movement," he said into his throat mike.

It was the reason they'd surrendered the high ground for this tactical and literal hole. Anyone planning an assault on Obrecht's property would want to take advantage of that knoll, but Gould's anxiousness to put them up there had made Rapp suspicious. He'd expected a betrayal and that was exactly what he was getting.

A camo-covered arm came into view at the bottom of his scope image and then disappeared again.

"Confirmed. One man closing on our former position. I'm guessing there are more just out of sight."

"Can you hit him?" Coleman responded.

If he had his Barrett, it would be no problem. That kind of artillery was impossible to handle in the stand, though. That left him with his M39. An excellent weapon but not exactly built for these kinds of ranges.

"Real low percentage, Scott."

Scott Coleman glanced skyward, but couldn't see the man in the tree above. When Wicker said low percentage, it meant "virtually impossible for the best shooters on the planet." In the years they'd worked together, though, the diminutive SEAL had rarely missed.

"You're my only failure, Mitch. I thought I'd forget about it as time went on but it just got worse."

Coleman ignored Gould's voice over the radio and activated his throat mike again. "What have you got, Bruno?"

"The guards are playing it cool, but they've all pulled back behind the wall. I have no targets."

"Stan. You're just in time to be the icing on my cake."

Coleman confirmed McGraw's report with the video being beamed from Dumond's drone. There was no more time to screw around.

"Wick. Take the shot. If you can't hit him, get close enough to put the fear of God into him."

When those mercs made it to the top of the knoll and found no one, it wouldn't take them long to locate his team's tracks and descend on them. On the other hand, if they lost the element of surprise and found themselves under fire by an unseen sniper, they might retreat. Mercenaries tended to like to push things only so far. It was hard to cash checks with half your head missing.

The familiar puff of Wicker's silenced rifle sounded and Coleman glanced pointlessly up into the tree again. "Report."

"I think I winged him," Wicker said, sounding genuinely surprised. "Yeah. Confirmed. I have blood on the grass. He's still moving, though. Do you want me to try to finish him?"

"Negative. Let him bleed."

A wounded soldier was almost always more damaging than a dead one. If the injury was serious, he might panic or start screaming in pain—two things that could quickly demoralize the most battle-hardened unit. Even if he held it together, his comrades would have to evaluate how bad he was and whether they were going to leave him or attempt a rescue.

"No new targets and the wounded man has taken cover," Wicker said. "They're good. No question of that."

Coleman nodded silently. It's exactly how his team would have reacted. Go still, evaluate the situation, and try to ID the sniper.

"If you get another reasonable target, take the shot. Hurt him bad but try not to kill him. Let's give them something other than us to deal with."

"Roger that."

"Bruno?"

"Still nothing."

Coleman returned to his pack and unstrapped the SMAW rocket launcher secured to its side. This particular unit fired a prototype thermobaric projectile that had been heavy as hell to carry but was guaranteed to make an impression. Its developer at Raytheon had actually laughed out loud when he'd been asked if it could penetrate a reinforced cinder-block wall.

Gould was still talking, but Coleman tuned him out and activated his mike again. "Mitch, Stan. If you can hear this, get ready. Things are about to get a lot less subtle."

CHAPTER 26

SENATOR Carl Ferris and his entourage all rose to their feet when Taj entered the outer office. The American politician strode toward the smaller man, enveloping his hand and smiling broadly.

"Good to see you, Ahmed. It's been a long time."

"Too long, sir. I'm honored that you took time out of your schedule to meet with me personally."

"Deciding which chair Sunny Wicka's ass is in while she drones on about our new aid package isn't much of a priority for me."

The program to be announced at next week's state dinner was yet another example of the bribes that the Americans believed would keep Pakistan docile.

Not that Taj objected to the influx of Western money. He would see to it that only a tiny portion of that billion dollars ever found its way into the hands of Pakistan's poor. The rest would be diverted to the military and the terrorist groups the Americans were so frightened by.

"Please join me in my office, Senator."

Ferris waved at his people to stay where they were and followed the ISI director inside.

"Tea?" Taj offered.

"I'm on a tight schedule, Ahmed."

"Of course. I understand completely."

Ferris had gained a visible amount of weight and was trying unsuccessfully to hide it with a creatively tailored suit. Undoubtedly it was the product of stress. The information given to the politician by Akhtar Durrani would have made for an explosive hearing—endless hours of Ferris hitting Irene Kennedy with specific dates, names, and places, while she stammered and equivocated. A bold first step toward his party's presidential nomination.

Unfortunately, Durrani was dead and Kennedy had discovered Ferris's relationship with the former ISI deputy director. She was keeping the information quiet for now, but the public release of evidence linking the prominent senator to Pakistani intelligence had the potential to devastate his political career.

"Let me say—" Taj started, but Ferris spoke over him.

"Kennedy told me that Durrani kidnapped her man Joe Rickman and was torturing him for information. That they're both dead now."

"Irene Kennedy is a professional liar."

"And you're not?"

"I was appointed to this position specifically *because* I'm not, sir."

Ferris frowned, but there was no skepticism in his expression. Like everyone else, he saw Taj as weak. A pawn to be used and, if necessary, sacrificed.

"So you're saying it's not true?"

"That would be too simple, Senator. Kennedy mixes truth with lies to keep her enemies off balance."

"Is that scotch?" Ferris said, pointing to a crystal service. Taj had his people bring it in specifically for this meeting.

"It is."

Ferris poured himself a glass uninvited. "What's *your* truth, Ahmed?"

"Durrani was little more than a thug. He was not capable of creating a plan this complex. I can assure you that it was entirely Joe Rickman's doing. He had become disillusioned with the CIA in a similar way that you have. He saw it as a corrupt and destructive organization that no longer answered to elected officials like yourself. Unfortunately, he was far more clumsy in his actions than you would have been."

It was untrue to the point of being transparent. Rickman had been a brilliant strategist. He'd spent years devising a plan that had a very real chance of dismantling America's intelligence apparatus. This partisan half-wit would be no more capable of comprehending Rickman's complex machinations than Durrani was.

Of course, the senator didn't see it that way and accepted the blatant flattery without a second thought. "How were they killed? Kennedy didn't say what happened to Rickman and the reports said your man had a heart attack."

"They were shot by one of Durrani's men with the help of an anonymous American."

"An American? Are you sure?"

"Yes. We have recordings of his voice. It's impossible to prove because of the poor quality, but we believe it was Mitch Rapp."

Ferris's face twisted with hate and he stalked around the room for a few moments, processing what he'd heard. Finally he stopped short. "That bitch! She made me believe that Durrani had been playing me and murdered Rickman. She said she'd release the emails between us and make me out to be either a traitor or some naïve patsy. She threatened to have me arrested. Me!"

"She's afraid of you, Senator. She understands your power and your patriotism. That you won't allow her to subvert everything America stands for."

Despite his lifelong devotion to Allah, this was the first time Taj had been absolutely certain he was seeing God's hand at work. What other explanation could there be? His impending takeover of Pakistan, the Rickman files, the billion dollars that the Americans were about to transfer into his pocket. And now Allah had delivered this simpleton who had a very real chance at becoming the president of the United States.

Ferris swilled from his glass, nostrils flaring with anger. "What do you want to bet that even President Alexander doesn't know about this? That she and Rapp assassinated one of your top people and an American citizen with no authority at all?"

"I think it's very likely," Taj responded calmly.

Men like Ferris—ones with delicate egos that had swelled to these proportions—became almost comically easy to manipulate. Undoubtedly, he told himself that he acted out of a love for his country's pathetic Constitution, but that was a lie. The truth was that Irene Kennedy simply hadn't bowed and scraped sufficiently before him. All this was nothing more than the personal vendetta of a feeble little man.

"I doubt she had any admissible evidence against Rickman," Taj said. "Much more likely he knew too much about her and Rapp, and she needed to silence him. It's just the kind of thing that your committee is set up to prevent, no?"

Ferris responded by letting out a long string of expletives.

"To change the subject somewhat, Senator, what are your own lawyers saying?"

Ferris had the potential to become a very useful tool but not if he was under Kennedy's thumb. Recently implemented campaign financing rules were easily subverted and the ISI would be able to quietly funnel as much anonymous money to America's politicians as it pleased.

The cycle of corruption was delicious. Taj used American aid to buy American politicians, who then approved more aid in order to increase the amount of money the ISI had to fill their campaign coffers.

"The lawyers say I'm on solid ground," Ferris said. "As far as they're concerned, a foreign official lodged a confidential complaint about illegal activity by the CIA and I investigated it. The fact that I didn't bring it to the attention of the Intelligence Committee is a procedural issue more than a legal one. I can play it off as being concerned that Senator Lonsdale is in Kennedy's pocket."

"Then your problems are solved."

Ferris looked at him like he was a slow child. "Wake up, Ahmed. It's not that simple. Winning a criminal case keeps me out of jail but fighting it ends my career. I need an army of political consultants to start shaping my message. With the right people, I can come out of this looking like a hero. Those people aren't cheap, though."

"But this shouldn't be difficult," Taj said, feigning naïveté. "You *are* a hero, Senator. You're protecting your country's freedom."

Ferris laughed. "Truth has nothing to do with American politics, Ahmed. Voters are idiots who do what they're told. I just have to make sure it's me—and not that bitch Kennedy—who's doing the telling."

"Of course, I would be happy to contribute to your effort."

"I'm glad to hear you say that, Ahmed. Five million ought to get us off to a good start."

"U.S. dollars?" Taj said, eyes widening.

In fact, the amount was insignificant. Beyond the money flowing in from the U.S. government, the American people provided hundreds of millions annually by purchasing his Afghan-grown heroin.

"Like I said, people like these don't work cheap."

Taj nodded submissively. "You're a good friend to my country and have done nothing but support our efforts to eradicate the terrorist threat. I'll have my people begin preparations immediately."

"That's good, Ahmed. Tell them to work quick, okay? I don't trust Irene Kennedy any farther than I can throw her. We need to slap her down and we need to do it hard and fast."

"Of course. But in the meantime, I think there's more I can do to help you. Information you might find useful."

The man's eyebrows rose. "What kind of information?"

"What if I told you that Rickman is releasing videos damaging to the CIA?"

Ferris waved a hand dismissively. "We all saw the video of him being tortured and talking about Agency assets, Ahmed. It was on YouTube, for God's sake."

"There have been subsequent videos that Kennedy is keeping from your government."

"You said Rickman was dead."

"He is. But he knew that his life was in jeopardy. He feared that

Mitch Rapp would discover that his kidnapping was fake and begin looking for him. Somehow he set up his scheme to survive him."

"What's in these videos?" Ferris said, starting to sound interested.

"We're only aware of one so far. It resulted in Mitch Rapp killing a number of Russian agents in Istanbul. We anticipate further releases in the future."

A broad smile spread across Ferris's face. "Can we prove it?"

"Perhaps soon. It seems like a story your new image consultants would be interested in, no? Kennedy losing control of Rickman as he flooded Afghan warlords and drug dealers with American money. Sloppy security that allowed him to learn far more than he should have. And you trying desperately to stop it while she blackmails you with lies."

Ferris didn't seem to be listening anymore. His eyes stared blankly past Taj, undoubtedly seeing himself crushing Irene Kennedy and then rising meteorically to the Oval Office.

Taj glanced at his watch. "I know you have another commitment in half an hour, Senator, and I fear that traffic will be difficult at this time of day."

That snapped the man out of his trance. He put down his drink and extended a liver-spotted hand. "Good talk, Ahmed. And I look forward to hearing from your people about those contributions."

Taj nodded. "Perhaps we can find time to speak privately when you return with Secretary Wicka's delegation."

"I think that can be arranged."

Taj walked Ferris to his office door, standing by respectfully as the politician barked at his handlers and headed for the exit. Only when he'd disappeared down the hallway did Taj return to his desk.

It was impossible to believe that the culmination of years of planning was only a week away. The assassination of President Chutani at his banquet for the Americans would be a trivial matter. Shaping the aftermath, though, would be more delicate.

The people of Pakistan and the Middle East would have to be made to believe that the United States was responsible. The story was admittedly clumsy. Why would the Americans kill such a steadfast ally? Like in U.S. politics, though, truth was unimportant. People believed what they wanted to believe, and the hatred of America was incredibly powerful in his country.

Following the president's death, Taj would waste no time. Using Shirani's army and his own influence with the Taliban, he would take control.

Pakistan, now a failing patchwork of competing factions, would become a monolith. And the world would tremble.

CHAPTER 27

CAN'T believe it was so easy," Gould said, his gun still trained on Rapp's head. "Either you're slipping or your reputation came right out of the CIA's marketing department."

Rapp remained completely still, eyes locked on the Glock 17. Tom Lewis's psychological profile of Gould portrayed him as a narcissistic sociopath. Once again, the shrink's insights proved correct. The Frenchman had already managed to completely suppress the past, unable to admit that he could ever have been bested. Now he was busy building himself up into the legend he believed he deserved to be.

It was a weakness that could be exploited, but even with that possibility, Rapp recognized that this was about as deadly a situation as he'd ever faced. Nutcase or no, Gould wasn't going to miss at this or any other range. The merc in Rapp's peripheral vision had a crimson puddle growing around his left foot but the blood loss and pain weren't preventing him from holding the MP5 rock steady. Finally, the man who'd shoved Hurley through the door was undoubtedly still standing right on the other side of it.

The old man looked like his head had cleared but that didn't do anything about the fact that he was well past his sell-by date. Unlike

Rapp, though, physical talent and the ability to instantly analyze tactical situations weren't what had made Stan Hurley one of the most effective killers of his generation. He operated entirely on rage, and based on the expression on his face, the decades hadn't dimmed it.

"What are you waiting for?" Gould taunted. "You think Scott's going to rescue you? That knoll's completely surrounded by Obrecht's men. If Coleman's not dead already, he will be soon."

"Mitch, Stan. If you can hear this, get ready. Things are about to get a lot less subtle."

Hurley's fake hearing aid had been taken, making it impossible for him to hear Coleman's warning.

"Scott might just surprise you," Rapp said to get the old man's attention.

He made a subtle motion toward Gould with his thumb. Hurley had the better angle on the Frenchman. That left Rapp tangling with a badly injured, no-name merc while an octogenarian with a freshly replaced hip took on one of the best contractors in the world.

The thermobaric charge worked as advertised, creating an eardrum-splitting explosion and shaking the mansion violently enough to cause Gould's pistol to dip.

Rapp dove toward the mercenary, hoping to draw both men's fire. Surprise and blood loss delayed the merc's reaction, but not Gould's. His shot struck Rapp's flak jacket just above his navel, flipping him onto his side next to the Glock still lying on the carpet. Behind, Rapp could hear the muffled sound of Gould's weapon firing repeatedly. He couldn't worry about that, though. It was Hurley's problem.

The MP5 opened up, stitching holes in the floor as it arced toward him. The statue was still blocking his line of sight to the man's head so Rapp snatched up his Glock and pumped a round into the man's other foot. This time he went down, losing control of his weapon and cutting through the plaster ceiling. Still lying on his side, Rapp lined up on the underside of the fallen merc's chin and blew the top of his head off.

Rapp immediately rolled onto his back and aimed at the door. Predictably, it was thrown open by the man who had captured Hurley.

Rapp squeezed the trigger and put a round through the man's mouth, sending brain tissue, teeth, and shards of skull spraying out into the hallway.

It was only then that he could turn his attention to Hurley and Gould.

They were pressed together face-to-face. Gould's gun was shoved into Hurley's stomach and he was emptying it into the man. The back of Hurley's shirt was torn and wet with blood from numerous exit wounds. His face was buried in the side of Gould's neck but Rapp didn't understand why until his old friend finally collapsed to the floor.

Gould slapped a hand to the side of his throat but it did no good. Bright red arterial blood was flowing through his fingers and from his mouth. He swung his gun toward Rapp and pulled the trigger, unable to process the fact that it was empty. When the Frenchman finally realized that the weapon was useless, he lurched right, stumbling toward the door. He bounced off the jamb and was gone.

The sound of automatic gunfire was starting outside as Rapp crawled to where Hurley was lying on the blood-soaked carpet. His friend stared up at him and for one of the few times in his life, Rapp's emotions made it difficult to speak. "What happened to the belt buckle knife you've been bragging about for the last twenty years?"

Hurley laughed, ejecting a sizable chunk of Gould's neck from his mouth. "Got stuck. Can you believe it? I'm gonna get that old bitch who made it for me."

Rapp stared down at the man, feeling a constriction in his chest that he told himself was the result of Gould's bullet. "I'm sorry, Stan. This was my op. My failure."

Hurley managed to press a bloody hand against Rapp's shoulder. It might have been the first overt display of affection in their long relationship. "No. It was perfect."

And then Stan Hurley—a man who had survived everything from the Soviets to the rise of Muslim extremism—died.

Rapp stood and slipped through the door with his Glock held out in front of him. The scent of chemical explosive was mixing with the gunpowder haze hanging in the air, creating an environment that he'd become all too familiar with. Outside, it sounded like Obrecht's men had regrouped and were hitting Coleman's force hard. The former SEAL would just have to hang on.

The trail wasn't particularly subtle and Rapp followed it down the hallway until it turned into a bedroom on the right. He found Gould sitting on the floor propped up beneath a window. The Frenchman clawed for the empty gun next to him but didn't have the strength to pick it up. His other hand was still clamped weakly to his neck but the entire left side of his body was drenched in blood.

Rapp took aim, thinking of Anna and his unborn child as the assassin struggled to focus. A moment later, he lowered his pistol and went for the door. Even after everything Gould had done to him, this was the old man's kill.

CHAPTER 28

SCOTT Coleman was in a prone position at the bottom of a shallow impression in the dirt. The bushes were dense enough to make him invisible from the mansion but he'd cut away a few to give him a view of the chaos he'd created.

The smoke had dissipated to the point that he could see the massive hole in the wall surrounding Obrecht's property, but not enough for the cameras on Marcus Dumond's drone to provide a reliable overhead feed. Flames were licking the blackened edges of the breach, and burning cinder blocks dotted the ground almost to the tree line.

He swept his scope along the newly created gap, noting two men down. The one lying facedown was still intact but in a grotesque position that suggested there wasn't an unbroken bone in his body. The other was on fire.

"Targets?" he said over his mike.

Wicker and McGraw both returned negatives.

Based on the radio chatter, Rapp was alive and on the move. Hurley and Gould's conditions were more ambiguous.

He activated his throat mike again. Rapp knew he was constantly broadcasting, but it was still unusual for him not to have made a specific report of his status.

"Mitch. Give me a sitrep."

There was a delay long enough to make Coleman start to worry, but then Rapp's voice came on.

"Gould, Stan, and two tangos down in the mansion. This frequency's been compromised. Cut me out."

Coleman let out a quiet breath and did as ordered, mentally assessing their situation. Hurley and Gould were dead. Rapp was running around the building with no way for Coleman to track his position or status. They'd just detonated a projectile that was loud enough to wake people in Madagascar. And, by his count, there were still eight serious shooters digging into what he assumed were hardened positions.

His earpiece produced a series of beeps in the eerie post-explosion silence, notifying him of an incoming encrypted call on his cell phone.

"Done," Maria Glauser said, and then disconnected.

As their logistical support person, she'd carried out their contingency plan for covering up the rocket attack. Rapp had come up with the idea of filling a vacant house in a nearby subdivision with plastique. She'd blown it the moment she heard the blast created by the SMAW and now her people were calling in breathless reports of a gas explosion. It wasn't a permanent solution by a long shot, but it would buy them a little time with the local authorities.

"Movement on the fence line," McGraw said over the radio. "Are you both seeing this?"

Coleman eased his rifle left, finally finding a disturbance in the smoke at the top of an undamaged section of wall. It was too big to be a man and rising with the smooth steadiness of some kind of mechanical platform.

"Take cover!" Coleman shouted, though he knew his men in the trees had a limited ability to do so.

He flattened himself in the shallow ditch just as the familiar buzz of a Gatling gun started up. He could hear the shattering of wood and the crash of falling branches as rounds spewed from the weapon at a rate of three thousand per minute. When the bullet stream passed overhead, Coleman was forced to roll into a ball to protect himself from the debris raining down on him.

Then everything went silent again.

The gunner had no visible targets. He was just sending a message. A very clear one.

"Sound off," he said into his radio.

"No injuries," McGraw said.

The unflappable Charlie Wicker came on right after. "I want to talk about my compensation package."

Coleman ignored him. "Bruno, do you have a line on that guy?"

"Negative. He's completely shielded. At best, he's using cameras for targeting. At worst, the gun's remote controlled."

"Wick?"

"I'm still lined up on the knoll. Can't even see the gun placement."

"Any movement?"

"The explosion seems to have lit a fire under them. Looks like they're retreating and that they're going to just leave their wounded man."

"Joe, did you copy that? Those guys are coming in your direction."

Maslick, who was still covering the tunnel exit, responded immediately. "I copied."

"Do not engage," Coleman said. "I repeat, do not engage. I don't want to do anything to give away your position or change their mind about running. Just stay sharp and watch for Obrecht."

"Roger that."

Coleman crawled forward through the downed leaves and branches. The Gatling gun was fully visible now, moving smoothly back and forth on what he guessed were electric motors. It seemed likely that there was a similar weapon on the southern end of the wall but the damage there was significant enough that he doubted it was something he'd have to deal with. They must have been mounted beneath the wooden promenade behind the fence, keeping them hidden from Dumond's drones.

"Let me know if you acquire a target, but no one shoots without my express order. We can't afford to draw that kind of fire."

He swept his scope over the scene again. The smoke continued to thin, and now he could see a single open window in one of the attic dormers. No doubt there was a sniper just inside and even less doubt that he was top-notch.

"Bruno. You see that window?"

"Yeah, but I got nothing."

It had gone quiet enough that Coleman could hear his own breathing and the light breeze rattling the leaves. It was a sound he was depressingly familiar with—the sound of an operation dead in the water.

Back in the day, this was about the time he'd be calling in air support. Paint the compound with a laser and let the flyboys drop something nasty from the stratosphere. There were times he really missed the navy.

Coleman finally made a decision and enabled Rapp's radio frequency again. "There's a Gatling gun placement on the north side of the wall," he said. "Remember Herat?"

If Obrecht's men were monitoring their communications, they would have no idea what he was talking about. Herat was a city in Afghanistan where he and Rapp had been pinned down for more than an hour by a sniper in the upper floor of a hotel.

As expected, there was no response, but hopefully the message got through. Rapp was in a position to flank Obrecht's men, and if he could just take a little of the heat off, Coleman's team could advance. If not, they would be forced to leave him. Kennedy's orders were clear: At the first hint of Swiss authorities, they were to get the hell out of Dodge.

"Come down and regroup around me," he said, after killing the connection to Rapp again. "One way or another, we're going to have to move fast."

CHAPTER 29

IRENE Kennedy adjusted the lamp for the third time. Finally she was forced to admit that her inability to read the classified documents lying on her desk had nothing to do with a lack of illumination. Her normally unshakable ability to concentrate had simply failed her.

She took off her glasses and looked around the windowless office tucked away at the back of her home. Not that there was much to see. She'd left the overhead lights off, as was her custom.

The semidarkness was usually accompanied by a sense of security. Not that day, though. If anything, it magnified the anxiety and regret building in her. Joe Rickman's files were still out there and it was her failure. She should have seen it coming. Rickman had always been unstable, but he'd also been brilliant. He could do things that no one else could and she had become reliant on—perhaps even blinded by—his talents.

There were no easy problems for the person running the Central Intelligence Agency. Those were dealt with well before they reached her office. Her world was an endless knife-edge balancing act. There were no wins, only scenarios where the rewards slightly outweighed the risks. In the current situation, her careful evaluation of the circumstances had led her to the wrong strategy. Or, as Mitch would undoubtedly simplify it, she'd guessed wrong.

The secure phone next to her began to ring and she reached for it reluctantly. Another drawback to her job was that people rarely called her at home with good news.

"Yes."

"They've blown the fence," Marcus Dumond said. "The smoke's blinding my drone."

"Thank you."

She hung up and felt the knot in her stomach tighten. The Obrecht operation had been authorized entirely on her own authority. Neither the Swiss government nor President Alexander knew anything about it. There hadn't been time for debate, and "no" wasn't an option. It would be easier to offer her resignation than ask permission.

Kennedy reached for the phone again but then withdrew her hand. She had a direct line to Scott Coleman, but it existed only for emergencies. She'd laid out the rules of engagement for this rendition and Coleman would follow her orders to the letter. Rapp and Hurley, on the other hand, would do whatever they wanted. There was no action she could take and no update that would matter at this point. The die had been cast.

Instead of the phone, she used her laptop to check her email account. Automatic notifications had been set up in case she received another communication from Rickman, so she knew she wouldn't find anything. Still, it offered some small comfort to see the empty inbox.

It was just a matter of time, though. Rickman wouldn't let something as trivial as death stop him. He was far too smart and obsessive for that. No, if he'd embarked on a plan this grand, he would have made it foolproof. Unstoppable.

Would she be the director who presided over the disintegration of America's intelligence capability? Was she responsible for recruiting and training the man who would tear down her country's defenses just when the world was at its most dangerous and unpredictable?

Afghanistan was in the process of returning into what Americans considered medieval chaos but the Afghans thought of as normalcy. Various terrorist groups would use the lawlessness and lack of cohesion as cover, but the Afghans themselves posed less of a threat than most people suspected. They didn't much like outsiders and with a little prompting could be used to combat the terrorist groups wanting to use their country as a base.

Iraq was a far more dangerous situation, and one of the keys to the current instability in the Middle East. The truth was that little could be done to remedy the situation militarily and arming moderates in the region was a strategy almost certain to backfire. People who felt moderately about things tended not to fight with the same intensity as fanatics. More often than not, they handed over their American-provided weapons and ran. Or worse, they reacted to the brutality they saw by becoming fanatics in their own right. Sadly, the best answer was for her to insert a brutal pro-American dictator. With a little luck, that would create an environment in which the rest of the region could be stabilized.

Less visceral but perhaps more dangerous were the former and future world powers. Russia was trying to restart the Cold War in order to gain the respect it craved but was incapable of earning with its anemic economy and corrupt institutions. China was trying to take possession of every piece of territory it had ever laid claim to in a cynical effort to distract its people from slowing GDP growth and an environmental disaster that was beginning to bite.

And then there was Pakistan.

As it stood, the ISI was so compartmentalized that one division could be tracking down a particular terrorist cell while another division supported it. Infighting was the norm, with people actively hamstringing operations in order to discredit their rivals and advance their own careers. The director tended to set broad goals, but the real power lay with the deputies who protected their fiefdoms like a pack of wild dogs.

This, among other things, had made the ISI's antiterrorist efforts sporadic and often counterproductive. Problematic? Yes. Destructive to the region? Absolutely. A clear and present danger to the United States? Likely not.

The problem was that the ISI she had set up the CIA to handle was transforming at a pace she would have never thought possible. Nadeem Ashan, the eminently reasonable deputy general for analysis and foreign relations, was under house arrest. Akhtar Durrani, the violent but dull-witted head of the external wing, was dead. And Ahmed Taj had replaced both with men her analysts were unfamiliar with. The S Wing was evolving, too. At first, the CIA had seen the shrinking of the ISI's clandestine division as a good sign. Now, though, it was clear that it was just shedding its weaker agents and stepping farther into the shadows.

She pulled up a photo of Ahmed Taj on her laptop, studying his dull, downturned eyes for a long time. He'd been chosen by Saad Chutani for his competence in logistics, moderate views, and lack of ambition. Beyond that, the CIA had uncovered little about the man. He'd grown up in a poor area of the country where written records were sparse and life expectancy was low enough that human intel about his childhood was little more than thirdhand innuendo. His father had been a pious and talented businessman who had provided Taj a life somewhat more privileged than those around him as well as a university education in America.

What hard data they possessed pointed to mediocrity in all areas of Taj's life: his grades, his extracurricular activities, his military record. Ironically, it was this that had worried the CIA's Pakistan experts most. Many had predicted the ISI fracturing even further with such a weak hand at the helm. And yet the opposite seemed to be true. Under the command of Taj and the ostensibly weak men he had recruited, the ISI seemed to be gaining the discipline it had always lacked.

She glanced at the report she'd been reading and closed the folder. It was yet another analysis of Taj's ISI. More pages of the bizarre intellectual contortions necessary to explain Pakistan's increasingly stable intelligence apparatus. The popular theory now was that it was being held together by the middle managers whom, a few years earlier, the same analysts were blaming for the organization's Wild West culture.

Everything the CIA knew about the modern ISI had been learned by viewing the organization through the lens of Taj's weakness. And every prediction that lens produced had proved wrong. What if their most basic assumptions about the man were inaccurate? What if they were seeing only what he wanted them to see?

She picked up the phone and dialed a number for the third time that day.

"Senator Ferris's office."

"Is he in? This is Irene Kennedy."

"I'm sorry, Director Kennedy, he's not available. I've given him your messages but he just returned from Pakistan and his schedule's full. Do you want me to tell him you called again?"

"No. It's not important," she said, disconnecting the call.

Her sources said that Ferris and Taj had met privately during his fact-finding mission in Islamabad. She was very interested in what the two men discussed.

In the end, though, the influential senator's refusal to return her calls was more instructive than any of the half-truths he'd tell about his meeting. She had always known that her threats against him were only a temporary fix. Like many of his colleagues, Ferris would gladly destroy the CIA, the country, and perhaps even himself before he would allow anyone to get in the way of his ambition.

He had already hired a battery of Ivy League lawyers with PAC money that was impossible for even her to trace. Now he was in talks with some of the country's top political operatives. There could be little doubt that he was looking to turn the tables on her and continue his march toward his party's presidential nomination.

Normally this would be of great concern, but in this case Rapp was right. In the context of the Rickman Affair, this bloated, ridiculous man seemed almost comical. What concerned her more than Ferris's growing army of attorneys and spin doctors was his relationship with

Ahmed Taj. Once again, this outwardly inconsequential Pakistani had appeared at the center of a dire situation.

A quiet knock wrenched her back into the present, and she deleted Taj's picture from her computer screen. "Come in."

The door swung open and she squinted at her seventeen-year-old son, backlit by the sun streaming through her house's windows. She'd completely forgotten it was a beautiful morning.

"Why's it so dark in here, Mom?"

"I have a bit of a headache."

"Maybe that's because you sit around in this closet all the time," he said, playing the exasperated teen to hide his concern. "It's awesome on the back deck."

"You make a good point. Maybe I'll try that."

Tommy didn't respond but also didn't move from the door frame. He obviously had something to say and Kennedy stared silently at him for a few seconds, before admonishing herself. It was a tactic she used to draw information out of her opponents. This was her child.

"What's on your mind, son?"

He looked at his shoes. "Is Mitch going to be at the game tomorrow?"

After their divorce, Tommy's father had moved away and completely lost interest in his boy. Rapp had done a lot to fill that void over the years, taking Tommy to ball games, remembering every birthday, and teaching him the fine art of lacrosse.

"I don't know. He's out of town."

"Where?"

"Surfing, I think."

Tommy laughed and answered her obvious lie with a quote from *Apocalypse Now.* "Charlie don't surf."

He was an extraordinarily intelligent and insightful boy. Straight A's with no effort, nearly a perfect score on his SATs, and every college from Harvard to MIT actively recruiting him. He was also extremely inquisitive, which wasn't always a good thing. He'd made it his business to become an encyclopedia of the CIA, with a particular interest in every bad decision, screwup, and unintended consequence in its long history. As forms of rebellion went, she supposed it was better than alcohol or drugs.

"So you think he might miss it?" Tommy said, sounding a little hopeful. "That he might not be back in time?"

"You seem relieved."

Another brief examination of his shoes. "The guy's, like, a lacrosse genius. Some people still think he's the best player ever. Did you know he can remember where everyone on the field was at any point in a game? It's like you guys installed a computer chip in his brain." He paused. "You didn't, did you?"

"Not that I'm aware of."

"So, he's basically Wayne Gretzky. And I'm just okay."

His assessment was entirely accurate. In fact, the only reason he was even okay was that Rapp had been working with him since he was six. Kennedy admired people who could realistically assess their weaknesses and normally would wonder aloud about the best way for them to minimize the effect of those weaknesses. This wasn't one of her operatives, though.

"You're too hard on yourself, Tommy. Mitch says you're doing really well."

"Give me a break, Mom. He thinks I'm slow, inaccurate, and too passive."

"What makes you think that?"

"Because he told me I'm slow, inaccurate, and too passive."

She made a mental note to talk to Rapp about that. "He just wants you to be the best you can be."

"I know, Mom. But it's a little . . ." His voice trailed off and she smiled sympathetically. What could the kid do? He'd inherited his parents' four left feet.

"Is it fun?"

"Sure. The guys are great. And we have cheerleaders now."

"Then go out there and have a good time, Tommy. Don't worry about impressing Mitch. Worry about impressing those cheerleaders."

CHAPTER 30

RAPP swung his Glock right, tracking motion at the end of the hallway. He lined his sights up on the head of the maid he'd seen earlier and watched her disappear back through the doorway with a strangled scream.

He continued moving along the hazy corridor, clearing rooms as he went. According to Coleman, at least one tango was in the attic with a sniper rifle. Another would be operating the Gatling gun, but there was no way to know if he was doing it directly or remotely. Rapp guessed the latter. When he'd started in this business, setting something like that up would have cost millions of dollars and required an army of engineers. Now it could be done by a couple of teenagers with an iPhone.

As he passed, Rapp closed the door to the room the maid was hiding in. Judging from her expression, she could be trusted to stay put until this was over. Hopefully, Obrecht's other civilian employees were similarly holed up.

Near the end of the hallway, he paused again. The question was whether to take the wide-open stairs that dominated the front of the building or the less prominent servants' access he and Gould had come up. Neither option was good, but he calculated his odds as slightly better on the main staircase. The other offered no room to maneuver and his gut said it was being covered.

On this rare occasion, his gut was wrong. He eased down the steps, staying low behind the railing and searching for targets. Nothing. In the ground-floor entryway, he slipped by an elaborate flower arrangement and passed the entrance to the service stairs unchallenged. With their limited remaining manpower, the mercs appeared to have retreated to prearranged defensive positions—probably concentrated on the front and rear entrances.

Outside, there was still silence. Coleman was stuck and Obrecht's men were satisfied to turn this into a stalemate. Time was on their side. The local authorities were likely already on their way.

Rapp slid with his back against the wall until he came to the closed door leading to the basement. Obrecht would either be down there trying to figure out why he couldn't get his safe room door open, or he'd be in the tunnel heading for Joe Maslick's position. Either way, that little Swiss prick was going to spill everything he knew before Rapp put him in the ground.

He reached out and twisted the knob, throwing the door open. The sharp hiss of a silenced weapon followed immediately and two holes appeared in the wall across from him. Obrecht? Probably not. Based on the speed of the trigger finger and the tight grouping, one of his security team.

The light in the basement was on and Rapp slapped a hand around the jamb, sliding it down the wall and catching the switch. A round hit close enough to send splinters of wood into his unprotected forearm. He ignored the superficial wound and retreated behind a heavy sideboard, using his shoulder to shove it toward the open door. More shots sounded as he squeezed it through the opening, but they couldn't penetrate the thick mahogany. He followed it inside, pushing it along the landing until it tipped partially down the stairs. Movement became audible below as the shooter tried to find an angle.

Rapp grabbed one of the night-vision-enabled helmets he'd hidden by the stairs and slammed the door behind him. The darkness closed in and he heard the man below freeze, suddenly unable to navigate the cluttered space. After toggling the goggles' power switch, Rapp gave the sideboard one last shove.

The heavy piece of furniture careened down the stairs with Rapp following inches behind. The puff of silenced shots joined the crackle of splintering wood as the man below attempted to aim by ear. He was effective enough that halfway down Rapp ducked under the railing and took the short drop, landing next to a stack of decaying pallets.

The sideboard hit the floor a moment later, barely holding together as it came to a stop. Rapp moved right, holding his breath and watching his foot placements to remain completely silent. Everything was bathed in a computer-generated false light and he immediately picked out two separate targets in the bright orange that denoted body heat. The one near the safe room was slumped against the closed door in a seated position. The other was lying in the dirt holding something that Rapp's goggles painted half blue and half red. The cool metal of a gun tipped with a hot silencer.

Every man had his breaking point and the prone merc finally reached his. Trails of color streaked from the hazy image as he switched to full automatic and started spraying bullets randomly around the basement. Rapp ignored the rounds flying past him and ricocheting off the stone walls. He squeezed off a single shot and a moment later the only sound in the basement was emanating from a nicked water pipe.

He approached the mercenary carefully despite the fact that he was picking up specks of body-heat orange spread out around what a moment ago had been the man's head. Satisfied that he was dead, Rapp moved silently toward the tango near the safe room.

It was slow going, but he managed to come within three feet without making any sound at all. Once in position, he reached out and touched his silencer to the side of the man's head.

Nothing.

Rapp retracted the night-vision gear and fished a small penlight from his pocket. He switched it on and found exactly what he'd feared: Leo Obrecht with his throat slit ear to ear. Whatever had been locked up in his head was going to stay there.

Rapp used the penlight to find the tunnel entrance and punched the code Gould had given him into the keypad. The chances of it working were close to zero but it was worth a try. He still needed to retrieve Hurley's body and if he could slip it out this way, there was a good chance his entire team could be on a jet back to the States before sundown. The surviving mercs would tell their story and at the end of a multiyear investigation, the German authorities would chalk this up to Obrecht getting in over his head with a professional assassin.

Of course, Gould's code didn't work. So that left the hard way.

Rapp skirted the sideboard at the bottom of the steps and ascended to the door again. There was no sound on the other side, so he eased it open. A quick check in both directions suggested that Obrecht's guards either were ignorant of what had just happened to their comrade or didn't care enough to come to his aid. Probably the latter.

The servants' stairs still appeared to be unguarded, so Rapp ran for them, ascending the tightly winding steps three at a time. He continued until they dead-ended into a bare wood door leading into the attic. The way it was aligned meant that it should open directly onto the west-facing dormers where the rifleman worrying Coleman would be set up.

Snipers tended to work in teams, so Rapp assumed two men. Based on their vantage point, it would make sense for the spotter to be at the dormer to the right. That would also put him in a reasonable position to cover the door. Based on the architectural plans he'd studied, Rapp put the spotter at two o'clock with the sniper dead at twelve. What would be between him and the two mercs was impossible to know for certain. Even if the attic was as cluttered as the basement, though, he guessed he'd have a shot. They would have moved anything obstructing their line of retreat.

Rapp took a few steps back and charged the door, throwing a foot out into the ancient wood. As expected, it gave easily, and he went sailing through, gun stretched out in front of him.

The spotter was right where he expected him to be. Also as anticipated, he'd been paying close attention to the door. Rapp saw a muzzle flash and felt the sting of a bullet grazing his right shoulder. He lined up his sights and fired, twisting in the air without bothering to confirm if he'd hit his target. When he landed on the wood floor, he was facing the sniper who was spinning in his direction. The rifle was far too unwieldy for him to move quickly, though, and Rapp's shot hit him directly between the eyes.

Rapp got to his feet and moved to the edge of the window, careful not to expose himself to Bruno McGraw, who would be watching for movement. He activated his throat mike, mindful that the frequency had been compromised. "Ended like Herat, too."

Coleman would understand. Rapp had resolved their sniper problem in that Afghan town by scaling the wall and shooting the man through a broken window.

"Roger that."

Rapp was now able to move to a better vantage point without worrying about being taken out by McGraw. He could see the damage to the wall was as impressive as the guy from Raytheon had promised—a burning hole that you could drive a semi through. Other than the two dead men on the ground, none of Obrecht's mercs were in evidence. The Gatling gun was bolted to a platform on the north end of the wall. There was no operator visible, but various cables and flexible hoses were. Definitely remote controlled. But from where?

Rapp started for the exit but then spotted an iPad lying on the floor next to the dead spotter. He was going to stuff it in the waistband of his fatigues for Dumond to examine but stopped when the screen came to life.

It displayed four squares arranged vertically on the left. Three were blank and one was feeding video of the tree line west of the wall. Alongside each square were arrows for up, down, right, and left, as well as a green and red button. He pressed the right arrow next to the live image and it tracked obediently north.

Rapp moved to a position where he could see the Gatling gun placement and tapped the arrow again. If the only man who could help them figure out Joe Rickman's plan weren't lying dead in the basement, he might have actually smiled. The gun obeyed his command.

Now the only question was how cautious the engineers who had set up the weapon were. Rapp would have had its range of motion limited but most people were less suspicious of technology than he was. It turned out Obrecht's men fit into the latter category. By pressing and holding the right arrow, Rapp was able to spin the gun 360 degrees.

He ran a finger down the green buttons on the iPad and watched two of the three other camera feeds come to life. They were gray at first, scanning the interior surface of the wall as the guns rose on hydraulic lifts. In a few seconds, both had cleared the barrier and were showing high-definition images of the surrounding forest.

Using the arrows, he spun the guns to aim at the ground floor of the building, concentrating on the points of entry.

"Get ready to move," he said into his throat mike.

Coleman sounded a bit confused at what he saw as Rapp knowingly giving away their strategy. "This frequency's being monitored. I repeat, this frequency's being monitored."

"In a second, it's not going to matter," Rapp said, swiping the red buttons pulsing on the screen.

• • •

"South corner clear. One tango down," Wicker's voice said over the radio.

"West corner clear," Bruno McGraw followed up. "One man dead. All civilian employees uninjured and accounted for."

Rapp could feel the blood flowing down the back of his flak jacket as he fireman-carried Stan Hurley's body down the stairs. The dust on the ground floor was thick enough to make it hard to breathe. There was a hole about nine feet in diameter next to the door, and a significant portion of the wall to the right of it had collapsed. Scott Coleman was putting flex cuffs on a man lying facedown in a bed of shattered glass. At the other end of the room, the upper half of a torso was on its side in the fireplace. A quick scan of the demolished room didn't turn up the rest of the body.

"One more over there," Coleman said, shaken by the sight of Hurley's body, but trying to hide it.

"That leaves one unaccounted for," Rapp responded.

Charlie Wicker came on the comm a moment later. "There's a man running east toward the wall. I have a shot."

Rapp gave a subtle nod and Coleman brought a bleeding hand to his throat mike. "Take him."

"Affirmative. Tango's down."

The man at Coleman's feet craned his neck around and looked up. Rapp didn't know him but the recognition—and fear—were clear in his eyes.

"You speak English?" Rapp said.

"Yes."

"Louis Gould brought in a team to take out Obrecht," Rapp said to him. "Your men killed Gould but not before he got to Obrecht. The rest of his team got away to the east. You're the only survivor."

"I understand."

"Do you? Because if I find out there was any confusion, I'll come looking for you."

"There's no confusion."

A siren became audible in the distance and Rapp started for the hole next to the door. "Cut him loose and get your men out of here, Scott. Rendezvous at location bravo. And get hold of Maria. Tell her about the change in plan and give her an ETA."

Coleman nodded and Rapp jogged out into the sunlight. He had five miles of hard terrain to cover with a marginal knee and a hundred and fifty pounds of dead weight bleeding all over his shoulder. Somehow he'd always known that Hurley would get the last laugh.

CHAPTER 31

ISABELLA Accorso's nausea reached its peak when her daughter's school came into view through the windshield. She fought the urge to vomit, reminding herself that Bianca had promptly returned her text, as she always did. Still, for the entire drive, she'd been unable to fight back thoughts of police barricades, ambulances, and a single human form lying beneath a bloody white sheet.

The swaying of the car as she turned into the parking area almost pushed her over the edge, but then she saw her daughter leaning safely against the building. She was clutching her backpack to her chest, an expression of concern etched into her normally smooth face. Isabella had given no explanation when she'd requested that Bianca be pulled from class. What explanation could there be?

"Mom?" she said as she opened the car door and slipped inside. "What's going on?"

"Nothing."

Isabella pulled away a little too quickly, once again checking the rearview mirror.

"Seriously, Mom. You're scaring me. Why are you here? Why aren't you at work?"

Isabella felt a tear starting down her cheek and wiped it away, trying to hide the emotions overwhelming her.

The man she'd met that day was deeply evil. She could feel it every time he turned his black eyes on her. There was nothing he wouldn't do to get what he wanted. He would have murdered her daughter and a thousand like her without a second thought. There had been no choice but to follow his instructions exactly.

"Is Dad okay?"

"Of course he is, honey."

She didn't know that for certain, but saw no reason why he wouldn't be. They'd been divorced for four years now. Bianca's father wasn't a bad man, but he'd taken a job in Sweden and their marriage hadn't been strong enough to handle the distance.

"Is it because Dad's getting remarried?"

Isabella smiled. "No. I'm happy for him and Agda. Are you all right with it?"

"Sure. It doesn't matter. I hardly ever see him."

"He's your father, Bianca."

"I know. And I love him. But he's up there, you know? And we're here."

It was one of the reasons Isabella had formed such a strong bond with her daughter. Bianca was everything to her. Probably too much. One day soon she'd be an adult and leave. She'd start her own life. Her own family.

For now, though, they were together. And she was safe.

"Is it something at work?" Bianca probed. "You didn't lose your job, did you? At the Christmas party, Mr. Cipriani said the firm couldn't run without you. I heard him."

She'd been prepared for the subject of work to come up and didn't let the weak trickle of adrenaline show as she accelerated onto a two-lane highway. "My job's fine. Stop worrying. Everything's fine."

"No it's not."

Isabella tried to smile, but it came off as more of a grimace. She'd done everything the man had asked—wiping all trace of the anonymous client from the mainframe. There was nothing she could do about the original copy of the instructions in the attorney's office and the man appeared to understand that. He hadn't seemed angry.

How could she be certain, though? Who was he? Why had these files been so important to him? He was well dressed and looked Arab or Indian but beyond that she knew nothing about him. Was he a drug trafficker? Did this have something to do with the heroin she knew was produced in the Middle East? If so, what business was it of hers? People wanted heroin. There was no stopping it.

"Where are we going, Mom? Home?"

She nodded. "So we can change. I thought we'd go out to dinner tonight. How does La Stiva sound?"

It was Bianca's favorite restaurant, but money had been tight for the past few years and they never went anymore. The budget was hard on her—young girls needed to fit in and that had become an expensive enterprise. She never complained, though.

"It sounds great, I guess. But what's the occasion?"

Isabella almost started crying again but managed to maintain control. The occasion was that her daughter hadn't been murdered.

"You're going to be a woman soon and we might not have time to spend together then," she said, her voice sounding slightly strangled. "I thought it would be nice. We can talk."

Bianca didn't look like she believed any of what she was being told but realized she wasn't going to get any more out of her mother on the drive. No doubt she was scheduling a full interrogation for after a bottle of wine had been opened.

They continued in silence and Isabella felt doubt creeping in. Was the Arab man really gone or would he come back for something else? Was it possible that he wasn't a drug dealer? Could he be a terrorist? Was she putting people in danger by not going to the police?

Ahead, she saw a semitruck approaching in the oncoming lane. It started to swerve, almost rocking up on two wheels as its load of concrete pipes shifted. Isabella slammed on her brakes and threw an arm instinctively in front of her daughter as the truck crossed into the lane in front of them.

CHAPTER 32

W E'RE clear," Wicker said, motioning the team forward and starting to run again.

Mitch Rapp released the tree he was using for balance and lurched forward, falling in behind Scott Coleman. His knee felt like it was full of glass and most of his right side had gone numb. Despite that and a number of offers of help, he'd carried Hurley's body the entire way by himself. He had been in command when his friend was killed. It was his responsibility to get him out.

They finally stopped where the stream took a hard bend, creating a deep pool that shimmered almost black in the late afternoon sun. Joe Maslick dropped to his stomach next to it, reaching down into the water.

"Got them."

He pulled out two large dry bags while the rest of the men peeled off their packs. Rapp nearly fell trying to get Hurley off his shoulder and dropped the man's body unceremoniously into a pile of rocks.

"Scott," Maslick said, throwing a duct tape–wrapped package to Coleman. He reached back into the bag and retrieved another, almost identical package. "This is you, Bruno."

Rapp stripped and dove into the water as Maslick pulled out the bundle meant for Stan. A body bag.

The sudden cold and darkness was strangely comforting, and he stayed under for longer than he should have, reveling in the stillness. When he and Anna lived near the Chesapeake, he swam almost every day. It was one of the many little pleasures from his past that had fallen away.

When he surfaced, his men were cutting open their packages. Business suits, uniforms, and jogging clothes appeared along with wallets full of carefully forged documents. All the things necessary to separate and disappear.

Coleman tore the tape off the package meant for Rapp and tossed him a bar of abrasive soap. He caught it and used it to wash away the dried blood that covered most of his body. Wicker was the first dressed, and he collected everyone's discarded clothing, stuffing it into the dry bags. When he was finished, he headed for the road without a word.

Decked out in running clothes, he would do another ten miles on the shoulder before he got to the car waiting for him. It was a lightly traveled thoroughfare and having all of them drive out at one time could raise suspicion. Staggering the time and method of escape was more critical than getting out fast.

Rapp dunked under again, struggling to get his matted hair clean as Bruno McGraw slipped away in a tailored business suit. When Rapp resurfaced, Coleman was wearing a FedEx uniform beneath an apron and elbow-length rubber gloves. The ease and speed with which he got Hurley into the body bag was a testament to how much practice they all had in such things.

Rapp climbed onto the bank and toweled off, dressing in the jeans, collared shirt, and leather jacket laid out for him on a rock. It felt uncomfortable not to have a weapon, but his Glock was tucked away in the dry bags with the rest of the team's gear. In light of the recent fireworks, running into a roadblock was fairly likely and carrying a gun was too much of a risk.

"We're ready," Coleman said. Everything, including Hurley, had been consolidated into backpacks or bags and was piled up at the west end of the clearing.

Rapp glanced at his watch and picked up two of the packs. "Six minutes."

They needed to ferry all of it to the edge of the road, where a van would pick it up.

"Mitch?" Coleman said, pointing to the side of his nose. "You missed a spot."

Rapp wiped at his face and his fingers came back streaked with blood.

"Okay," Coleman said. "You're good."

They managed to get everything moved in just over five minutes. Another thirty seconds passed before they heard an engine approaching from the south. The FedEx delivery truck slowed and pulled into a narrow indention in the trees just as the second hand on Rapp's watch hit twelve. Next time he was in need of this kind of logistical support, Maria Glauser would be on his short list.

The driver opened the rear doors from inside, revealing boxes stacked floor to ceiling and a hatch open in the false floor. Rapp and Coleman grabbed the body bag first, sliding it inside the space that had been intended for a drugged Leo Obrecht. The driver helped them load the rest of the gear and then closed the well-disguised access door. After another thirty seconds of arranging boxes on top of it, Rapp retreated into the trees and watched the truck accelerate up the road with Coleman in the passenger seat. His blond hair and flawless German would minimize questions if they were stopped.

Rapp started walking south, paralleling the road. The slow pace felt odd, but he was wearing slick dress shoes and drenching himself in sweat wouldn't do much to enhance his cover.

At fifteen minutes, he drifted closer to the road. Once again, Glauser was right on time. He stepped onto the shoulder, and she slowed just long enough for him to jump into the passenger seat.

He immediately leaned back and closed his eyes, trying to let his mind go blank. When he got back to Langley, it was going to be like a bomb going off. What he needed now was a few minutes to clear his head.

"Are you all right?"

Normally, he would have ignored the question, but Glauser's voice was shaking badly enough that even a half-deaf cop would pick up on it.

"Relax, Maria. You did great. It's almost over."

"I was told I'd have to move some people and equipment," she said, the words tumbling breathlessly from her mouth. "You don't transport people in body bags. You transport bodies in them. And were those Gatling guns? They sounded like Gatling guns! I blew up a house. A house! Then I had people call the police and lie about it."

Clearly the subject wasn't going to die on its own. "We told you about the house, Maria."

"You said it was a last resort."

"It was. Now take me to the airport."

"The airport? We're supposed to rendezvous with your people at—"

"Plans have changed."

"But Director Kennedy said—"

"Airport, Maria. And don't talk anymore until we get there, okay?"

CHAPTER 33

KABIR Gadai knocked quietly and then entered the ISI director's office. He found Taj sitting at his desk staring at an empty
wall. The younger man stopped immediately, leaving as much space
between them as the office would allow. Taj's anger had clearly defined
levels, and his deathly stillness was a sign of the last: a rage so intense
that it couldn't be processed. Gadai had seen him like this only once
before and it had ended with seven men from the S Wing being sum-
marily executed along with their families.

Thank Allah he was there to report good news. He had to assume that Taj's anger was the result of the Obrecht operation, which
had been carried out during Gadai's time in Rome. The question was
whether the prudent course was to inquire about it or to ignore the
subject entirely.

"Things went extremely well with Isabella Accorso," Gadai said,
keeping his tone submissive. "Just as you planned."

Taj's eyes remained fixed and his body motionless. It was impossible that he hadn't heard. Gadai began to wonder if he had done something to displease the ISI director. He racked his brain but could come

up with nothing. It mattered little, though. Only what Taj believed was of importance.

The silence stretched out long enough that Gadai could no longer endure it. No one knew for certain what had happened to Taj's previous assistant. The man's broken body was found by people scavenging a trash heap and his death had been quickly deemed an accident. Of what type no one had ever attempted to determine.

If that was to be his fate, it would be better to find out quickly— to have an opportunity to defend himself before Taj's anger grew further. And, if necessary, to beg for mercy for his sons.

"The Obrecht operation, sir? I trust it met with similar success?"

Taj's eyes flickered and Gadai resisted an urge to step back, knowing that the wall behind him would prevent it.

"Obrecht is dead," Taj said finally. "Rapp is not."

Gadai didn't let his relief show. He'd had no hand in planning that operation and in fact had pointed out its numerous potential pitfalls.

The ISI was in the business of knowing everything there was to know about Mitch Rapp. Its files were likely more extensive than those at any other intelligence agency in the world, including the CIA. What those files described was a man who had walked away from certain death on countless occasions, each time leaving in his wake the bodies of men who believed themselves to be assured of victory.

"And Gould?" Gadai prompted gently.

"Also dead."

Gadai nodded. He also had warned against the killing of Abdul Qayem. While it was true that the Afghan general knew far too much to be allowed to fall into the hands of the CIA, it was also true that his death had left the ISI with no obvious path to Mitch Rapp. Qayem could have been used to bait a trap deployed on terrain they controlled: Quetta, North Waziristan, or any of a number of sites in Afghanistan. Rapp could have been isolated and pitted against an overwhelming force.

Of course, pointing this out would be unwise to the extreme. Better to accentuate the positive.

"Gould and Obrecht were loose ends that we would have been

forced to deal with sooner than later, Ahmed. Rapp has done our work for us while allowing us to remain in the shadows. And, in the end, he is only one man."

That caused Taj to spin toward him. "*I* am only one man, Kabir. Sometimes one man is all it takes to change the order of things."

"I hardly think it's a fair comparison," Gadai said. "Mitch Rapp is a simple enforcer constrained by a dysfunctional and cowardly government. You are a brilliant man who will soon lead one of the most powerful countries in the world."

"Don't patronize me, Kabir. I know what you're thinking. Qayem."

"Not at all," Gadai lied smoothly. "In light of Rapp's escape from Switzerland, it's clear that you were right. The risks of leaving the general alive were too great."

Taj's eyes narrowed, but thankfully he chose not to pursue the subject. "I understand you have Rickman's files."

"Yes, sir. And they've been wiped from the law firm's system."

"Including the backups?"

"Absolutely."

"The woman?"

"She and her daughter are both dead. The authorities are treating it as an accident. No criminal investigation has been initiated and none is planned, according to our sources."

He nodded and seemed to relax a bit. Rapp's survival was undoubtedly dangerous, but with the Rickman files in their possession, the assassin could be neutralized. Without the support of the American president and the CIA infrastructure, he would become less than nothing.

"Have you been able to access the information?" Taj asked, though he almost certainly knew the answer to the question.

"They're encrypted."

"You didn't get the key from the law firm?"

"They didn't have it. But the instructions for the files' dissemination weren't encrypted. In fact, the next release is scheduled for tomorrow. Our people think that this is the path to accessing the information."

"Explain."

"We believe the man who is decrypting and sending out the files is some kind of computer criminal. The law firm couldn't be allowed to see the contents of the files because they would have called the authorities. Conversely, a criminal couldn't be given access to all the files at one time, because he might have sought to use them for his own ends. It's the combination of the two organizations—one legal and one not—that made Rickman's system work."

"Then you can find this computer criminal?"

"We believe so. Through his email address."

"You believe so?" Taj said, the volume of his voice rising noticeably. "If we can't access the information in these files, we've learned nothing. Accomplished nothing. We have the tools to crush America's entire intelligence empire in our hands and we can't use them. Find this man, Kabir. Find him now."

"Yes, sir. But I want you to know that doing so will involve some compromises."

Taj's expression turned suspicious. "What kind of compromises?"

"On the surface, his email address is administered through a server in Singapore, so I think we can be confident that he's not a resident of that country. It's simply a gateway. After the email arrives there, it would be forwarded all over the world in the span of only a few seconds, creating a trail that's very difficult to follow."

"But not impossible."

"No, sir, not impossible. We'll get closer with each file release. Eventually, it will lead us to—"

"Each file release? What are you saying, Kabir?"

"That we will have to continue sending the files per Rickman's schedule."

Taj stared silently at him for a few seconds. "It's a dangerous game. We don't know what is in those files and who the ultimate recipient will be."

"I agree, sir, but I think that the risks are acceptable in light of the reward."

"How many releases will have to be carried out before we find the man we're looking for?"

"It's impossible to say for certain, but our hope is no more than five. In the end, though, at least we know that each release will damage the CIA. So if it's more than five—"

"The route to power isn't through clumsy attacks on the CIA, Kabir. It's through subverting the organization. Creating double agents, blackmailing informants and politicians. Turning an intelligence network they spent hundreds of billions to create against them."

"Yes, sir. But chipping away at America's ability to defend itself and the internal chaos that the releases will create is hardly an unattractive secondary strategy."

Taj's frown suggested that he was unwilling to accept anything but complete victory. "Then it's your recommendation that we go forward with the scheduled release tomorrow and continue until we identify the man carrying them out?"

"Yes, sir. The death of President Chutani is less than a week away. Even if there were no hope of getting the encryption key, this would be the most prudent course of action. It will keep the CIA—and Mitch Rapp—focused elsewhere."

Taj just nodded, unwilling to give his authorization aloud. It was clear that he was making Gadai entirely responsible. There would be no reward for success. It was expected. Failure, on the other hand, would be severely punished.

CHAPTER 34

BLACK clouds blanketed the sky, producing heavy drops that roared against Irene Kennedy's armored SUV. Her driver slowed further on the curving gravel road, leaning over the wheel to better see through the overwhelmed wipers. It seemed fitting somehow.

Kennedy stared out the window at the deluge but didn't really register it. The Swiss authorities and Interpol were currently descending on what had been Leo Obrecht's mansion, cataloging damage, identifying bodies, and collecting evidence. An army of European financial regulators had locked down his bank and were starting the process of unraveling what would likely become the largest and most sophisticated criminal financing operation in history.

Her people were quietly leaking fabricated evidence that would lead to the conclusion that Obrecht had gotten in over his head and provoked the wrath of Louis Gould. There were no guarantees, though. It was a mess of epic proportions. Just like Joe Rickman intended.

Her driver rolled to a stop alongside the farmhouse, getting as close as he could to the steps. The features of the man looking down from the covered porch were obscured by the rain, and for a brief moment Kennedy felt the breath catch in her chest. She allowed the fantasy to play at the edges of her mind for a moment, but she knew it wasn't Stan Hurley. It never would be again.

Her door was pulled opened and she ducked beneath the umbrella held by her driver.

"Where's Mitch?" she asked Mike Nash as he moved to open the door for her.

"No one knows."

A flash of anger interrupted her grief, but she knew there was no point to it. Rapp would reappear when he wanted to. Not a moment before.

"What about . . ." Her voice lost its strength for a moment. "What about Stan?"

"We have him," Nash said, leading her inside. "No need to worry."

"I want to see him."

"There's nothing to see, Irene. He's dead."

"I know he's dead," she snapped. "Just take me to him."

Nash let out a long breath and led her into the kitchen. There was a walk-in freezer set into the back wall, installed in case they ever needed to feed a large security team. He pointed to it.

"Seriously, Irene. I don't see the—"

"Open it."

Nash would never be able to understand what she was feeling. He and Hurley had been close, but she had known the man since she was a little girl. Even after she'd become his boss, he'd always seemed bigger than life to her. Incorruptible. Unwavering. And indestructible. Her intellect told her that he was gone but the child who still lived somewhere inside her couldn't believe that the man she'd known as Uncle Stan was dead.

Nash reached for the freezer's handle but then hesitated. "There's something I should probably—"

"Just open it, Mike!" The intensity of her anger surprised her, but he wasn't its target. She was angry with herself. Hurley had died trying to clean up her mess, and now she could feel herself losing her nerve.

She'd approved his involvement in the Obrecht operation knowing he was old and sick. The least she could do was face him.

Nash pulled back the heavy steel door and she stepped inside, her eyes taking a moment to adjust to the lower light. When they did, she found herself unable to move. She'd prepared herself. But not for this.

"That's what I wanted to warn you about, Irene. We laid him out next to the steaks, but for some reason it really bothered Scott. So this is what we figured out."

Hurley was sitting in a chair with a drink in one hand and a cigarette frozen between the fingers of the other. Ice had collected on his eyebrows, hanging down over closed eyes. His suit jacket had been pulled closed to the degree practical but the bloodstained shirt beneath was still visible.

Nash draped a blanket over her shoulders, but she didn't acknowledge it.

"I'll give you a minute," he said, and she heard his footsteps retreat back into the kitchen. For some reason, she could feel neither the cold nor the weight of the blanket. Other than Hurley sitting in front of her, all she could sense was the buzz of the overhead light and the hum of the refrigeration unit.

Her father had been a CIA operative and most of her youth was spent in the Middle East. She'd been no older than six when she'd first met Stan Hurley. He'd come through Baghdad for what she now knew was an extraction in Libya. When her father had been killed in Beirut, his old friend Hurley had done his best to step in. He'd called when he could, made sure she had enough money, and convinced her to pursue her PhD. It had been him who had convinced her to apply to the Agency and he had watched over her career until she became director.

Kennedy approached and put a hand on his arm. "Goodbye, Stan."

When she finally walked out of the freezer, Nash was sitting at the kitchen table. He stood, a sincere expression of concern on his face. Despite being a former Recon marine with more combat commendations than she could be bothered to count, there was a certain gentleness about him. It was most visible when he was around his family but it came out at times like this, too. She and Rapp saw it as weakness despite his impeccable ops record, but now she wondered if she'd rushed to judgment. He was a difficult man to dislike and that could be a very powerful weapon in their business. Sometimes more powerful than the gun.

"Are you all right, Irene?"

She wasn't sure. Handling stress was part of the job, but even she had limits. Rickman's files were still out there, Leo Obrecht was scheduled to be buried later that week, and she was responsible for the death of her oldest friend.

Nash seemed to read her mind. "It would have destroyed him if you hadn't sent him, Irene. If you lost confidence in him. Take it from me, this is better."

She nodded numbly. "What happened, Mike?"

"Gould. Obrecht's people were expecting them."

"How? We had Gould. There was no way for him to communicate."

Nash slid a newspaper across the table and tapped a want ad circled in highlighter. "This newspaper was the only information he got from the outside while we were holding him. Our guys went over it with a fine-tooth comb and found this. It basically outlines the plan. There are similar messages in periodicals and websites worldwide."

"How did Obrecht die? Was it Mitch?"

Nash shook his head. "Looks like one of his guards."

It was what she was afraid of. This went higher than the Swiss banker. Someone had gotten to his security team and given instructions that Obrecht was not to fall into the hands of the CIA.

It had been a mistake to send Gould. She'd underestimated his mental instability. As she had Rickman's. Now was not the time to start questioning her own judgment, but she could feel doubt creeping in. How could it not?

Again, Nash seemed to be able to hear her thoughts. "Sometimes you just have to roll the dice, Irene. Mitch agreed with you that this was our best shot to get to Obrecht and shut down Rickman's machine. We all did."

She leaned back in her chair and tried to work through what was happening. Obrecht would never talk but at least his death provided confirmation that someone was pulling his strings. Someone very well informed and very well funded.

Once again she came back to Pakistan and the ISI. The simple answer was that it was one of Durrani's deputies covering his tracks. But with a new operations director in place, would anyone in the S Wing have sufficient support to pull off something like this? The answer was as clear as it was terrifying: not without Ahmed Taj's blessing.

"Has there been any progress on the lawyer angle?" she asked.

There was no hard evidence that Rickman would use a law firm to release the information he possessed, but the more she considered it, the more the theory made sense. Terrorists and criminals could be useful, but reliability wasn't one of their more prominent qualities. No, if you needed something done confidentially and efficiently, a lawyer was the most straightforward solution.

"Nothing yet," Nash said. "Marcus is working with the NSA on it. Their ability to crunch data is almost unlimited now that they have DaisyChain up and running at their Utah facility. If anything unusual happens at a law firm anywhere in the world and anyone so much as tweets about it, we'll know."

DaisyChain was a quiet—though in this case entirely legal— system that scoured the Internet twenty-four hours a day, seven days a week. It cataloged every news organization website, online magazine, blog, and government site worldwide. Then it translated the pages into English and used artificial intelligence to analyze the information based on whatever search parameters were put into the system.

She'd authorized soliciting the NSA's help but wasn't particularly happy about their involvement. They had an incredible infrastructure in place for this kind of investigation, but the organization had been too much in the spotlight lately. The kind of technology they used was just coming into its own, and they were a bit like a toddler with a new toy. If that toy was a chain saw.

"Then it's a waiting game," she said. "We sit here until another one of Rick's videos is released and another one of our operatives is compromised or killed."

Nash nodded. "For now, I'm afraid so."

CHAPTER 35

THE tiny rental car was struggling with the grade, forcing Rapp to keep one eye on the engine's temperature gauge. When it finally touched red, he parked at the edge of the empty dirt road.

There was no wind at all when he stepped out, only the heat of the Greek sun on his back and the vague scent of chemical explosive still clinging to his hair.

The yellow grass that covered the hill glowed in the light, making the deep green of scattered olive trees seem almost black. Far below, he could see the city and the ocean beyond. Many people considered it paradise and on that particular day, it was hard to argue.

He continued on foot, retrieving a cigarette from the pack in his pocket. He raised a lighter to it but then noticed an unusual sound in the still air around him. His own breathing.

Rapp stopped, squinted up at the winding road and then down at the cigarette. The grade was no steeper than fifteen percent and his elevation above sea level was low enough that he could pick out individual sailboats below.

Two years ago, he'd led a thirty-mile trail-running race through the Colorado mountains, finally turning off a half mile before the finish line in order to avoid the cameras set up to capture the winner. He wouldn't have to worry about anyone snapping his picture or asking for an interview now. Full gas, he'd be lucky to break the top five in a race like that.

Rapp looked out over the ocean, his thoughts turning again to Stan Hurley. In many ways, he'd been a great man. Brave, loyal, patriotic. One of the only people Rapp had ever met who he never even considered worrying about. There was nothing the world could throw at Stan that could knock him off target.

Having said that, it would be a mistake to romanticize him. He'd left three ex-wives, and only two of his five children would take his calls. He'd lived his life at the very edge of control with little concern for himself or those around him. He was probably the best friend Rapp ever had, but also self-destructive, violent, and, as Anna had pointed out on numerous occasions, a bad influence.

Rapp's love-hate relationship with the old man had started out more hate-hate. He could still remember saying that he'd put a gun in his mouth if he ever found himself turning into Stan Hurley.

Yet there he was, living alone in a crap apartment near D.C., smoking and drinking too much in an effort to mask the rage lurking just below the surface. And breathing audibly walking up a hill that he should have been able to do at a full sprint.

The old man was dead. Anna was dead. Gould was dead. His past felt like it had been suddenly stripped away. The question was what he was going to do about it. Would he allow himself to become even more disconnected? To lose even more of who he was? Or would he hit the reset button? At forty-four, there could be a lot of years left.

Rapp wadded up the pack and threw it into the trees before starting up the road again. Strangely, his breathing didn't sound quite as loud. Even with Hurley's death, the inevitable blowback from the Obrecht op, and the impending release of the next Rickman file, he felt a little lighter. Might as well enjoy the illusion while it lasted.

When the farmhouse came into view he slowed, assuming that there was at least one set of crosshairs tracking his head. The building was constructed from stone and white stucco, with blue window frames and a cheerful red roof. It was isolated and easy to protect, but close enough to a tourist town that foreigners went unnoticed. The landscaping was mostly natural and littered with toys—everything from a pink Big Wheel to a dollhouse faded by the sun.

A man appeared on the north side of the house, walking purposefully but keeping a tree between him and his unannounced guest. His plaid shorts, T-shirt, and straw hat looked right at home in the resort area. The expected flip-flops were the only thing missing—replaced by a pair of shoes built for stability and speed. A long-sleeve shirt that hid the veins mapped across his biceps and forearms would have been preferable, but it was a minor oversight.

Hurley had found him in Afghanistan attached to the Green Berets. Rapp recalled that he was an unusually smart kid with a sense of determination that made up for unspectacular natural athletic ability. Bob something. No. Ben. Ben Carter.

"Hello?" the man called out.

His hand was nowhere near the gun he undoubtedly had holstered in the small of his back, but he looked scared. In fact, he looked terrified.

Confused, Rapp started reaching subtly for his own weapon but then stopped when he recognized the problem. Carter had become fond of the woman and child he'd been charged with protecting.

"That's not why I'm here, Ben."

The former soldier let out an audible breath. "I'm sorry, Mr. Rapp. No one called ahead to tell us you were coming."

"Is she inside?"

"Yes, sir. With her daughter."

Rapp went up the gravel walkway, stepping over a sandy boogie board and knocking on the door.

The woman who opened it was as beautiful as he remembered. At thirty-six, her round face was still smooth and dominated by bright, almond-shaped eyes. Her dark hair was a little longer now, and the smile was something he'd never seen. It quickly faded into the deep sadness he recalled from last time. When he'd had a gun pressed to the side of her head.

"Are you here to kill me?" Claudia Gould said in accented English.

His reputation was well deserved, but sometimes he wished it didn't follow him so closely.

"No."

"You're here to tell me something about Louis."

"Yes."

Her eyes closed for a moment and he could see that she was concentrating on not crying. When they opened again, she stepped aside to let him enter.

"Can I get you something?" she said, speaking on autopilot.

"No, thank you."

She was wearing a two-piece swimsuit with a sheer sarong tied around her hips. Rapp didn't allow his eyes to linger.

"Tell me," she said.

The last time he'd visited her home, he'd spared her husband's life. It had been obvious even then that it was a serious tactical error, but he didn't regret it. It happened at a time in his life when he'd needed to regain some of his humanity.

"He's dead, isn't he?"

Rapp nodded.

Claudia switched to her native French. "Did you kill him?"

"No."

Her eyes turned misty, but still there were no tears. Maybe she understood that she was better off. Or maybe she was just tired of crying over the man.

"After what happened to your wife," she said. "After you spared us, I thought it was enough to make him see clearly. I was stupid to believe that he'd quit. I let myself be blinded."

"It's not your fault, Claudia. He had everything. It just wasn't enough."

"Was it . . ." Her voice faltered. "Was it quick?"

"He never knew what hit him," Rapp lied. There was no reason to make her suffer any more than she already had.

"Bonjour!"

Rapp turned and managed a smile at the sight of a girl skidding to a stop on bare feet. She was seven now, with disheveled sun-bleached hair and a swimsuit similar to her mother's. The sunscreen on her face hadn't been completely rubbed in, leaving a white streak across her nose that smelled like coconuts.

"Bonjour," Rapp said. Claudia had named the girl after his wife and he found it hard to say aloud. "You must be Anna."

"That's right. Who are you?"

"My name's Mitch. I'm an old friend of your mother's. You and I met once, too, but you were just a baby."

"I don't remember stuff from when I was a baby."

"Me neither."

"Are you coming with us to the beach? You're not dressed."

"I don't think so. I just need to talk to your mom for a couple of minutes."

"I'm going to see if Ben wants to make castles. He's really good at it. He can even make the things that look like teeth on top of the walls."

"Merlons."

"What?"

"The teeth are called merlons and the gaps between them are called crenels."

"Are you making that up? How do you know that?"

The sad truth was that it was because he was an encyclopedia with only one chapter: things that could be used for war.

"I saw a TV show on it once."

"I'm going to ask if Ben knows that."

Rapp watched her run out before turning back to Claudia.

"Beautiful girl."

"I don't deserve her." She motioned around the house that Irene Kennedy was paying for. "Or this."

"Everyone makes mistakes. What matters is that we try to make up for them."

He dug an iPhone out of his pocket and handed it to her. The display had a screenshot of a mutual fund statement. "We consolidated all of Louis's accounts into this one. It's all clean and the taxes have been paid. You don't have anything to worry about."

Her eyes widened. "There's almost thirty million dollars here."

Rapp nodded. "The account is under the name Claudia Dufort. We're working with the French government to get you a new passport, a legend, and everything else you'll need to stay off Louis's enemies' radar. Irene got you permanent residence in South Africa, and she used some of your money to buy you a house in the wine country. I think Anna will like it. There's a good school close by and plenty of space for a horse or two."

The tears finally came. She threw her arms around him and began to sob. "I'm so sorry, Mitch. I'm so sorry for everything I've done to you."

CHAPTER 36

IRENE Kennedy pushed her reading glasses onto her forehead, tying to chase the image of Stan Hurley from her mind. There would be time to mourn him later. Right now her only responsibility was to ensure that no more of her people ended up like him.

The handwritten list on the desk in front of her had been pulled almost entirely from her impeccable memory. It looked as innocuous as a guest list to one of her son's birthday parties, but in fact it was the most sensitive catalog of names ever put to paper.

It included every significant spy or informant currently controlled by the CIA from the Middle East to China to Europe. Even South America and Australia were represented.

Three numbers accompanied each name. The first ranked the likelihood that Rickman would be aware of that individual's existence on a scale of one to ten. The second used an inverse scale to rank each operative's importance to America's security. Finally, the third number was the sum of the first two.

The twenties—people who were low level and unquestionably known by Rickman—were already being prepared for extraction. Too much risk for not enough reward. The twos—critical personnel that

Rickman would likely be unaware of—would be staying where they were. The question was, how far down did she go with extractions? Fifteens? Tens? How many lives would she jeopardize in the interest of America's intelligence efforts?

Once again, Hurley intruded on her thoughts, this time whispering in her ear. *You took this job, Princess. Suck it up and do it.*

There was a knock on the door and Mike Nash poked his head in. "Bad time?"

She flipped the list facedown on her desk. "A welcome interruption. Are you bringing me good news?"

He entered but didn't respond to her question.

"I'll take anything at this point, Mike."

"Coffee machine's fixed."

Kennedy smiled. She still wasn't sure about Nash, but her view of the man was evolving. She'd been doing some detailed research into his background and discovered that he'd always been the charismatic charmer. Voted most popular in high school, class president in college, and the beneficiary of almost fanatical loyalty from the marines he'd led in combat.

It was a gift that few people had and one that couldn't be taught. Kennedy had many competent people working for her, but their personalities often left a bit to be desired—mostly insufferable wonks, slick politicians, and swaggering cowboys. Then there was Mitch, who wasn't exactly a favorite on Capitol Hill. At best, he elicited nervousness from Congress. At worst, fear and hatred.

Kennedy didn't exempt herself from her clear-eyed evaluation. She was largely seen as an icy intellectual alone in a sea of people who made decisions based on their gut instead of their head. It was a trait that made people question whether there was anything she really believed in. The answer was that there was. She believed in getting the job done.

Nash could be a bit of a handwringer, but admittedly an extremely intelligent one. He'd performed well since Rapp had forced him out of the field and behind a desk. He was good at handling the overblown egos on the Hill and a near prodigy at motivating people. While she and Nash were very different, who was to say that her approach was right and his was wrong? As her mentor, Thomas Stansfield, had been fond of saying, there was more than one way to skin a cat.

"Unfortunately, I'm a tea drinker. Where are we on finding the people disseminating the Rickman files?"

"Let's just say we're moving generally forward," he said, sitting in one of the chairs lined up in front of her desk. "Everyone agrees with your idea that he'd go to an attorney, but the category Every Ambulance Chaser on the Planet is a pretty big one."

"Is the NSA producing?"

"That's the problem. Their AI's ability to filter out the junk is less impressive than they let on. We're getting everything from a bunch of lawyers in D.C. who won an intermural softball game to a London firm that signed on to represent J. K. Rowling in a plagiarism suit."

"Nothing useful, then."

"We thought we had something with a break-in at a firm in Buenos Aires, but it turned out to be a drug addict who got caught two days later pawning their laptops. We have people working around the clock sifting through all the hits. Anything that looks even vaguely interesting gets sent to me."

"What about Marcus?"

"He's working on the next step under the assumption that the NSA will eventually turn up something we can use. He figures that the files are being released by some kind of hacker—someone crooked enough to be willing to decrypt and send out classified material but smart enough to keep it from being traced back to him. Finding a guy like that should be right in Marcus's wheelhouse."

Kennedy took a sip of her tea, not sure how much to say. It was in her nature to keep secrets, but if things went as badly as she expected, Nash would need to be aware of her suspicions.

"We have even less time than you might imagine, Mike. I believe that we're not just in a race against Rick, but that we're competing with another organization."

Nash nodded. "The Pakistanis."

She was pleased that he'd come to the conclusion on his own. "Please go on."

"It's hard to believe that Akhtar Durrani was the only person in the S Wing who knew about Rick's files. And if they're aware they exist, they want them something awful. Depending on how much Rick knew, the ISI could co-opt our entire network in the Middle East. Maybe worldwide."

"But who?" Kennedy prompted.

"One of Durrani's men? If you work for the ISI, getting hold of the CIA's throat wouldn't exactly be bad for your career."

It was a reasonable hypothesis—maybe even the right one—but she was concerned Nash was thinking too small.

"What about President Chutani?"

Nash's expression turned thoughtful. "There's no question that Chutani would like to take a peek at Rick's files and hold some of them over us, but I'm not sure he has that kind of penetration into the S Wing yet."

"I tend to agree. Have you considered Ahmed Taj?"

"Yeah. He's a lot more interesting."

"How so?" Kennedy said, wondering if Nash recognized he was being tested and just wasn't letting on. She hoped that was the case.

"I've met the guy a couple times and I've read all the files we've got on him. Everything points to him being weak. I'm starting to wonder, though. Durrani's death would have created quite a power vacuum at the ISI. We should have seen a lot of fireworks but we didn't. I've seen successions in my kid's Boy Scout troop go harder than that."

Kennedy remained silent, taking another sip of her tea.

"So do you think I'm totally off base here, Irene? Maybe Chutani's got a better handle on the ISI than I'm giving him credit for."

"No. Unfortunately, I find myself nursing the same suspicions. Our analysts have been telling me for years that Taj is too feeble to control the ISI, and in the same breath they tell me that the ISI is becoming increasingly effective. Somewhere there's a disconnect between theory and reality. If you discard the conventional wisdom that Taj is just a figurehead, it's amazing how quickly the picture comes into focus."

"I hope you're wrong," Nash said. "Because I'd rather see those files in the hands of al Qaeda than the ISI."

Before she could respond, an alarm sounded on her laptop. She felt her heart rate accelerate. That particular chime was set to sound only when an email arrived from Joe Rickman.

"Rick?" Nash said, noticing her sudden pallor.

She nodded and opened her inbox as he moved to a position where he could look over her shoulder.

The attachment was another video. Kennedy felt her mouth go dry when she started the playback.

"Hello, Irene. I'd say it's good to see you but I can't see you because you had me killed."

He was sitting with his boots on the desk again, wearing the same clothes he had in the last communiqué. Knowing Rickman, he'd recorded these all in one caffeine- and amphetamine-fueled push.

"I hope it drives you nuts trying to figure out how I got all this intel. Take my advice and don't bother. I'm just smarter than you." He paused dramatically, letting the seconds tick by. "Freaking out yet, Irene? Want to know what I've got? 'Cause this one's way bigger than Sitting Bull. I mean, who really gives a crap about the Russians? Nothing but a bunch of vodka-swilling losers."

"I can't tell you how much I wish I'd been there when Mitch splattered this prick's brains all over the wall," Nash said.

Kennedy motioned for silence.

"Okay, I guess you've waited long enough," Rickman said. "I sent the Iranians a detailed file about how their ambassador to the U.K. is on your payroll. Names, dates, bank account numbers. Even a few nice glossy eight-by-tens." He smiled and reached for a remote on his desk. "Have fun."

"Is that true?" Nash said when the image went black.

Kennedy was too stunned to answer. It was absolutely true. Kamal Safavi was their highest-placed Iranian asset, a man well versed in both his country's fledgling nuclear weapons program and its increasingly severe political power struggles.

"What time is it in London, Mike?"

He glanced at his watch. "Around midnight."

Kennedy shut down her email and pulled up Safavi's information. She clicked on the text button and sent him an innocuous message that he would recognize as a warning. The contingency plan they'd created was for him and his family to immediately proceed to a safe house, where they'd be met by her London station chief. The question was whether Rickman had left time. Would he have seen it as more destructive to let the United States take the man and weather the inevitable Iranian demands for his return? Or would he want the ayatollah to take him and extract everything he knew about the CIA's Iranian operations?

"Where's Mitch?" Kennedy asked.

"We still don't know. He said he had some personal business to deal with and took one of the Gulfstreams we have hangared in Europe."

"During this?" Kennedy said, letting a rare flash of anger show. "You're supposed to keep track of him, Mike. And the Agency's planes aren't his private limousines."

"Then that's a conversation you should have with him, Irene. Because sometimes he gets a look on his face like he's trying to decide whether it would be more efficient to argue with me or just kill me. As far as I'm concerned, he can do whatever he wants with those planes."

Kennedy's line buzzed and she picked up. Ken Barrett, her London station chief, was on the other end. He'd been copied on the text she'd sent.

"I have people on the way to the safe house, Dr. Kennedy. Do you want me to send anyone to the ambassador's residence?"

She didn't answer immediately. Maybe Rickman had timed this to provoke a confrontation between the CIA and the Iranians on London's streets. What she didn't need to do was to create a violent incident in the backyard of America's strongest ally.

"Quietly," she said finally. "No one does anything but watch unless I give the order. And call Charlie. We need to bring MI6 in on this."

Kennedy hung up and dialed Mitch Rapp's cell number. Until now, she'd left him alone. He rarely disappeared like this, so it stood to reason that what he was doing was important to him. She couldn't wait any longer, though. Wherever he was, his vacation was over.

Her stomach tightened with each ring but finally the line clicked and Rapp's voice came on.

"Yeah?"

"Where are you?"

"Greece."

"Get to London. Now."

CHAPTER 37

KAMAL Safavi remained as still as possible, trying not to wake his wife in bed next to him. It was just after midnight and he'd been lying awake for almost two hours. The meeting at the Foreign Office that day had gone predictably badly. MI6 had reports—correct as far as he knew—that Iran had just accepted a delivery of advanced centrifuges from North Korea.

Based on his country's history with America, he could understand and sympathize with his masters' paranoia regarding the West. The affronts that so consumed them, though, now existed only in history books. They needed to be concerned the future. They needed to acknowledge that the nuclear program they believed would keep Iran safe was strangling the country's economy. Paralyzed by their misguided fears of an American attack, Iran's government was dooming its population to a death by a thousand cuts.

So much foolishness and hate served no purpose. Iran was a rational and stable island in a region that was in the process of tearing itself apart. Only the shortsightedness of their respective politicians prevented the two countries from laying the foundations for an era of cooperation.

It was a sentiment that Irene Kennedy shared. She was an eminently reasonable woman who saw the potential of normalizing relations between Tehran and Washington. She understood that Iran's youth had little memory of the shah or the revolution. They wanted freedom and prosperity. They wanted to occupy a place of respect in the world.

There was a static-ridden cry from his nightstand, and he glanced over at the baby monitor as it went silent again. His young daughter was dreaming. But about what? A future of unbounded opportunity? A life in a society that treated her as an equal? Peace and security?

Probably not. That was his dream. For her. For all of his people.

A moment later, a more urgent sound emanated from the direction of his nightstand. For a few seconds he was disoriented by the shrillness, unable to remember what it meant. His confusion didn't last long, though, and he snatched up his phone to scan the text on the screen.

"Get up!" he said, throwing the covers to the floor and leaping from bed.

In the dim glow of the alarm clock, he saw his wife's eyes flutter open.

"What is it?" she said, reaching for the lamp by her side of the bed. "Is it Ava? Is she awake?"

He grabbed his wife's wrist before she could get to the switch. "Don't turn it on. Just get up and put your robe on. Quietly. We're leaving."

"Leaving?" she said, alarmed. "What are you talking about?"

He had never told her or anyone else about his relationship with Kennedy. He'd thought it was safe. That it was important. Now all he could feel was guilt for what he'd done. His family was in danger. And for what? The idealism that his father had warned him about so many times as a youth.

"There's no time to explain," he said in a harsh whisper. "We have to leave. Now!"

Safavi ran in bare feet to his daughter's room, finding her fast asleep. He lifted her carefully. They had to be silent. Their staff consisted only of a woman who did the cooking and cleaning, and an aging security man who spent most of his time shuttling them around the city. He could afford to wake neither.

"Kamal, you're scaring me," his wife said, appearing in the doorway. "What's happening?"

"I'll tell you later," he whispered. "Now we have to get to the car. It's parked right out front."

"But I need to get dressed. I don't even have shoes. We—"

Fortunately, his daughter was still small enough to hold in one arm, and he clamped his free hand around his wife's bicep. The apprehension on her face turned to fear when she felt the force of his grip.

"Kamal, you—"

"Silence!" he whispered as he dragged her toward the stairs.

Light from the courtyard filtered through the windows, providing enough illumination to navigate through the furniture arranged in the entryway. Kennedy had warned them in time. They were going to make it.

The door was suddenly thrown open with enough force to nearly rip it from its hinges. Safavi's wife screamed as three men ran into their home, shouting in Persian.

A forearm hit him in the face and he held his daughter tight, trying to protect her as he was slammed to the floor.

"No!" he shouted as she was torn away from him.

His wife continued to scream and he turned his face toward her as his hands were secured behind his back. "Don't hurt her! She doesn't know anything!"

The man didn't listen, grinding a knee into her back as she was bound with flex cuffs. Their driver appeared at the end of the hallway but stopped short when he recognized the intruders as being from the embassy's security team.

Ava was wailing now, her shrieks echoing eerily through the house. Safavi couldn't breathe with the weight of the man on top of him, but he barely noticed. His wife was sobbing, still having no idea what was happening. He had done this. He was responsible for the terror his wife and child felt.

An arm snaked around Safavi's neck and he felt himself being dragged backward. Their maid appeared and ran instinctively toward the man holding Ava, but was hit in the side of the head with a pistol butt. She collapsed to the floor and went completely still.

The arm cutting off his air tightened as they exited into a light London rain. Only then did the man holding him speak. "The ayatollah is looking forward to seeing you and your family, Kamal."

CHAPTER 38

PULL over."

The traffic was almost nonexistent on the dark London high street. To his right, Rapp could see a narrow alleyway swirling with the blue flash of a police cruiser's lights.

"Here?" the cabbie said. "But the address you gave me is another six blocks."

Rapp had decided to take a taxi instead of getting someone from the CIA to pick him up at the airstrip. His goal was to slip in and out of Britain with as little fanfare as possible. The Istanbul operation was still bringing down a fair amount of heat, and the EU's intelligence community was starting to suspect him in the death of an Islamic propagandist in Spain two months earlier. Entirely true, but proper protocols hadn't been followed, so Kennedy was doing everything she could to shift the blame to the Mossad. Its director owed her and he seemed amenable to taking responsibility.

Rapp retrieved a hundred-pound note and held it out for the driver. "I'll walk the rest of the way."

The vehicle rolled to a stop near the sidewalk and Rapp got out without looking back. The dark overcoat he'd found on the plane was enough to keep the rain off, but not enough to hold back the damp cold. He flipped up the collar, partially for warmth, but mostly because London was the most videotaped city in the world. Constant adjustments to the angle of his head kept his face in shadow as he moved across the cobblestones.

The uneven surface ended at a street that ran through a posh neighborhood lined with turn-of-the-century buildings. Normally, it would have been quiet at such a late hour, but that night almost every light was on and he could see people standing at their windows looking down into a crowded street.

Rapp turned toward a set of yellow barriers blocking off the area in front of an especially impressive stone building. There were twenty or so civilians talking among themselves near the police line, and he kept his distance, skirting the far edge of the rain-soaked barricade.

"Sir!" a cop shouted, starting toward him with a nightstick in his hand. "This is a restricted area."

"Shut up."

The man paused for a moment, confused by Rapp's reaction, but then started running at him. He got within five yards before one of the two men Rapp was striding toward waved him off.

"Charlie," Rapp said, keeping his hands in his jacket pockets as he stopped in front of a man wearing an impeccable Burberry trench coat and bowler. Charles Plimpton was one of MI6's top men, and he reveled in his role as a British spy. When he'd started out, he'd been vaguely competent, but now political aspirations had set in. Apparently, his wife was the second cousin to King Arthur's maid or something. She felt entitled to a higher station in life.

"I wish I could say that it's good to see you, Mitch. But whenever you arrive in my country, disaster follows."

The other man was Ken Barrett, the CIA's London station chief. He had the more appropriately disheveled look of a man woken in the middle of the night: wrinkled jeans, a hooded parka, and waterproof boots.

"What happened?" Rapp said.

Barrett was the first to speak. "Irene called me a couple of hours ago and told me Safavi had been compromised. I got in the car and called Charlie. Unfortunately, we were too late."

"Meaning what?" Rapp said.

"Safavi and his family were already gone when we got here."

"For how long?"

"About fifteen minutes, according to the cameras."

"Did you track the car? There's no traffic and they're either going to their embassy or an airport."

"Their embassy," Plimpton said.

"So you intercepted? Do we have them?"

Barrett cast his eyes down and Plimpton answered in his place.

"We didn't, Mitch. He's an Iranian diplomat being protected by a car full of Iranian security."

"They're not protecting him, Charlie. They're fucking kidnapping him. They're going to take him back to Tehran, throw him in a hole, and force him to watch while they cut his family apart."

"I'm sympathetic to your viewpoint," Plimpton said in an accent that seemed to get more posh every year. "But this is the CIA's cock-up. We aren't going to create a diplomatic incident trying to set your problem to right."

"Our problem?" Mitch said, struggling to keep his voice low enough not to be heard by the people rubbernecking near the police perimeter. "You think it's going to help the U.K. if Iran builds a bomb?"

"I've spoken with the prime minister personally and we've agreed that getting dragged into this isn't in the best interest of Her Majesty's government."

"I don't give a shit what you've agreed," Rapp said, grabbing the man by the front of his coat. "Quit thinking about using your ass to polish a chair in Parliament and do your fucking job. Safavi's put everything on the line for us. Now you're going to just turn your back on him because your wife doesn't feel like she's getting invited to the right parties?"

"Mitch," he heard Barrett caution from behind.

"Shut up, Ken."

"Cops, man . . ."

Three uniformed men were edging toward them, obviously not certain what to do. Rapp shoved Plimpton back hard enough that he nearly stumbled over his four-hundred-dollar shoes and grabbed Barrett by the arm.

"Where is Safavi now?" he said, dragging the London station chief into the shadows at the far end of the square. "The embassy?"

"Yeah. I have people out front. No activity."

"They can't keep him there forever. He and his family will have to be transported."

"I know what you're thinking, Mitch, but it can't happen. Not here."

Rapp locked eyes with Barrett, who took a hesitant step back. "Easy, man. You know I'd follow you through the gates of hell, but we've lost this round. Even if I wake up the FBI guys, we have no manpower. And the minute we make a move, Charlie's going to have us thrown in jail."

Rapp balled a fist, but managed not to slam it into Barrett's face. He had always been a solid man. Given the chance, he would have pulled out every stop to rescue Safavi. But he wasn't being given that chance. Rickman had nailed down every detail. Every contingency. Like he always did.

Rapp brushed past the man, dialing his phone as he walked across the street.

"I understand the situation has deteriorated," Irene Kennedy said when she picked up.

"Safavi's barricaded in the Iranian embassy."

"It's what we feared. Rickman is randomizing his methods to keep us off balance. This time he made sure we wouldn't have time to intervene."

"That piece of shit Charlie Plimpton's not going to let us make a move as long as Safavi's on British soil. The Iranians are going to have to get him back to Tehran, though. It's possible that we could intercept the plane."

"I've talked to the president and he says no. He's been working to thaw the relationship between the U.S. and Iran since he took office, and this is a big enough setback as it is. Interfering with their flight would put us on a war footing."

"So I'm just supposed to do nothing so we can make sure no one's political career gets bruised?"

"I'm sorry, Mitch. There's nothing I can do."

"I don't want to hear that, Irene. Rick's just getting warmed up. He's going to bleed us until there's nothing left."

"I might have some good news on that front. Can you get to Rome?"

"Why?"

"Mike's already on the way. He can brief you."

"I don't like it, Irene. Istanbul. London. Now Rome. Rick's leading us around on a leash. We can't afford to keep reacting. We need to get ahead of this."

"You ask me to trust you. Now I'm asking you to trust me."

He glanced upward as the rain started coming down harder. "Italy."

"I'll let Mike know you're on your way. Oh, and Mitch?"

"What?"

"Let him do the talking, okay?"

CHAPTER 39

BUT, sir, I—"

"Shut up and listen!" Saad Chutani shouted.

Taj cradled the phone handset between his ear and shoulder as Pakistan's president continued his rant. Of course it was necessary to provide the occasional frightened grunt or affirmation to indicate his rapt attention, but in reality he was scrolling through his email.

"I want this journalistic hack silenced, do you understand? I will not have distortions and lies spread by our newspapers."

Four days ago, the Pakistani Taliban had attacked a girls' school that Chutani heavily supported. In fact, he had personally attended its opening, hailing it as the foundation of a new Pakistan. There had even been champagne and an absurd Western-style ribbon cutting. Now it was a burned-out husk surrounded by the bullet-riddled bodies of young girls who should have been at home under the supervision of their fathers and brothers.

"Answer me, Ahmed!"

Taj frowned. He'd assumed the question was rhetorical and the fool would continue to shout endlessly while saying nothing of consequence. A gift all politicians had but that this one excelled at in particular.

"Sir, there was simply no question that the press was going to cover this incident. I have the article you're concerned about in front of me and while it lays out the facts, I don't find it disrespectful to you or your administration. It—"

"Not disrespectful? Can you read, Ahmed? It makes me look powerless. How could this have even happened? It's your job and the job of the S Wing to control these events."

It was an interesting choice of words. Not "prevent" but "control." And indeed Taj did. He had personally planned and authorized the attack. It was all part of the delicate balance he was attempting to strike. While Chutani's assassination—ostensibly by the Americans—needed to be an event that stoked Pakistan's nationalism, the dead president couldn't be *too* popular. He needed to be portrayed as a good man who wasn't equal to the task. The people had to understand that Pakistan needed a stronger leader. Someone who could achieve the order that the democrats had so miserably failed to deliver.

"The death of Akhtar Durrani created a period of blindness, Mr. President. I assure you that his successor has now fully transitioned into his position. Making that transition completely seamless, though, was impossible and the Taliban knew it. They took advantage of the brief period of weakness."

"Excuses!"

"I'm sorry," Taj said, conjuring a hint of fearfulness. "I'm doing the best—"

"We have to deal with the reporter, Ahmed. Now. There's nothing we can do about your incompetence in letting the attack succeed, but we can certainly shape the aftermath."

"The article has already been published, sir. There's no way to—"

"It's emboldening the other media outlets!" Chutani shouted. "In the last two days, there have been two articles critical of my involvement with the American drone attacks, and a newscaster has come out publicly against secular education. Without consequences, there is no way to know what they'll say next."

Chutani wanted to impress the West with a free press just so long as it was entirely supportive of his administration. And when it wasn't, he called the man he'd hired for his weakness, expecting him to suddenly transform into an assassin.

"What kind of consequences are you talking about, sir?"

"We don't need a press like the Americans have, Ahmed. One that spews lies and distortions twenty-four hours a day in search of profits. Pakistan needs fair and patriotic media outlets dedicated to moving the country forward. This recent activity sets a dangerous precedent."

Taj smiled. Of course, the politician wouldn't give a specific order. He had to have deniability. Should the coercion of Pakistan's news-people become public, he would need Taj and the ISI as a scapegoat.

"Private media is dependent on advertising dollars, Mr. President. I'll have my people speak to the companies that support these outlets and ask them whether it's in their best interest to encourage this kind of journalism."

There was a long, disappointed silence. Chutani undoubtedly wanted the man dead and Taj completely understood. After he had closed his fist around Pakistan, a man like this would watch his entire family die before being exterminated like the animal he was. However, now wasn't the time to be pulled into something this controversial. He would need the Americans' unwitting support during his rise to power, and the assassination of a journalist could jeopardize that support.

"I assure you, this will be quite effective," Taj continued. "No media company can afford to be painted as unpatriotic, and a large number of their advertisers have significant ownership by the army and ISI. They'll publish no more articles critical of you, and if we proceed carefully, I think we can coerce a retraction. Or at least a clarification that highlights the difficulties of stamping out terrorism and provides examples of how effective your administration has been thus far."

"If this is your recommendation, I will accept it," Chutani said, still unwilling to make demands that could be traced back to him. "But I expect results, Ahmed."

There was a knock on his office door and a moment later Kabir Gadai entered.

"I think you'll be quite satisfied," Taj said, watching his assistant approach. "We should be able to resolve the situation without undue risk to you or your government."

"Tomorrow morning, Ahmed. I want a briefing on your plan's specifics tomorrow morning."

"I'll have my people schedule a meeting."

The line went dead and Taj hung up the phone. "Our president can be quite the hysterical woman."

Gadai smiled and took a seat.

"What news do you have for me, Kabir? Have you determined what was in the Rickman file that we released?"

"I believe I have, sir." He held out a manila envelope containing a number of eight-by-ten photographs, and Taj began flipping through them. He recognized the city as London and two of the men behind the police barricade as being from MI6 and the CIA, but other than that, the images meant little to him.

"Those are stills from security cameras installed near the Iranian ambassador's residence. Our resources say that he and his family were taken by Iranian security in the middle of the night. They're being recalled to Tehran."

"Was a threat made against him? This might have been done for his own protection."

"That's what we thought at first, too."

"What changed your mind?"

"Do you see the man in the black coat? The one whose face is always turned away from the camera? We believe that's Mitch Rapp."

Taj spread out the photos in front of him and studied the man in question. It was difficult to determine detail but, in a strange way, that's what made the images stand out. In the middle of London, during a well-lit police operation, there wasn't a single definitive photo.

Taj leaned back in his chair and met his assistant's gaze. "So, you're saying that Kamal Safavi was on the CIA's payroll?"

"It seems likely. Since this occurred, there's been a huge increase in diplomatic traffic between Iran and the United States, including a reported personal conversation between the ayatollah and President Alexander. It's the first direct communication between the two men that we're aware of."

Taj felt the perspiration break across his forehead. If he'd had an asset this highly placed, only one or two of his most trusted people would have known. Kennedy operated no differently. If Rickman had access to this level of intelligence, what else could be hidden in his files? What did he know about the Israelis? About America's politicians and allies? Indeed, what did he know about Pakistan?

"It's a massive blow to the U.S.," Gadai said, sounding typically prideful. "The thawing of relations between Iran and America was one of the cornerstones of Alexander's Middle East strategy. He hoped to build a Shiite bulwark against the expansion of Sunni militias."

"Don't be too pleased with yourself, Kabir. The loss of Safavi has harmed America but if we'd had access to this information instead of being forced to release it, we would have had the tools to turn one of the CIA's highest-placed assets. He was a well-liked moderate with political aspirations. Who knows how useful he could have been in keeping the Iranians in their place. This wasn't a victory, it was an opportunity missed. Don't ever forget that."

"Yes, sir," Gadai said, averting his eyes appropriately.

Taj needed to keep the young man's arrogance in check, and highlighting the negative side of the situation was a good way of doing it. Having said that, it was admittedly difficult not to revel in this particular failure. A partnership between Iran and America would significantly extend the West's influence in the Middle East. It was a natural alliance that had been made impossible by a powerful—but largely empty—animosity between the two countries. Now the flames of that fire would once again burn bright.

"The question I'm interested in, Kabir, is whether the file release got us any closer to finding the man who can decrypt the files."

"Yes, absolutely," Gadai said, recovering quickly from his reprimand. "My people were able to trace it even farther than they originally thought. Perhaps as few as two more releases will lead us to his location."

"And the next one is scheduled for when?"

"Tomorrow."

Taj nodded thoughtfully. It was difficult not to speculate what that dispatch contained. What damage it would do to the country that believed it had the right to rule the world.

"Unfortunately, we have no choice. You have my authorization."

CHAPTER 40

T HE sun was up by the time Mitch Rapp's Gulfstream landed at the private airport in Rome. It had barely rolled to a stop when a black BMW with heavily tinted windows pulled alongside. Rapp jumped out of the plane without lowering the stairs and walked briskly across the runway. Inside the car, Mike Nash leaned over the seats and threw one of the back doors open. Rapp slid inside and a moment later they were accelerating toward the highway.

"Your suit and tie are in the garment bag," Nash said. "There's a passport in the breast pocket with the name Mitch Kruse. The entry stamps have you arriving last night. You were on a Turkish Airlines flight out of Dulles."

Typically thorough but, ironically, Rapp wasn't the problem on that particular day. His operations on Italian soil had all gone relatively smoothly. Nash, on the other hand, had been betrayed during a rendition in Sicily a few years back and was now a wanted man in Italy. This little excursion must have been important if Kennedy was willing to risk sending him to Rome.

"Who are you?" Rapp asked, unzipping the garment bag.

"Michael Blake, aka a guy who's very anxious to finish this little errand and get out of here."

Rapp started stripping off his clothes as they merged into traffic. The suit was his, one of a few he kept in a locker at Langley. So was the Glock 19 and the custom shoulder holster that contained it. A silencer hung from the side opposite the weapon, as did a spare magazine. Hopefully, neither would be necessary. The heat coming down on the CIA from enemies and allies alike was starting to take its toll on ops all over the globe.

"Where are we going?"

"To see an attorney. Our luck might finally be changing. We had DaisyChain searching for mentions of law firms—"

"You got the NSA involved?"

Rapp didn't trust those tech freaks. He spent more time worrying about them monitoring his communications than he did about foreign intelligence agencies.

"No choice, Mitch. We just don't have that kind of computer fire-power."

London had already put him in a dark mood, and the involvement of Fort Meade wasn't making it any better.

"We'll talk about that later," Rapp said, pulling the partially but-toned dress shirt over his head. "What did they come up with?"

"More stuff than I want to remember. All complete crap until they turned up an obituary from an Italian newspaper. A woman named Isabella Accorso was killed in a car accident along with her daughter."

"How is this interesting to me?"

"Well, first, she worked at a large law firm managing trusts and payments to clients. She's the person who'd administer the kind of sce-nario we think Rick set up. We figure he'd check in with someone like her on a given schedule, and if he didn't, she'd start sending the files he gave her."

"That's it?" Rapp said.

"No. The crash was a head-on with a truck that crossed into her lane. The driver was an undocumented Pakistani immigrant."

"Thin."

"It gets better. Irene strong-armed the Italians into giving us the records from the law firm's Internet service provider. We found heavily encrypted files going out the day before the Rickman stuff hit the streets."

"Is he alive?"

"Who?"

"The Pakistani driver."

"Yeah."

"Can we get to him?"

"Well, he's in an unguarded hospital room if that's what you mean."

"I take it that's not as good as it sounds."

"He apparently wasn't wearing a seat belt and the part of his brain you'd want to communicate with is still on the inside of the windshield. So we're on our way to talk to the managing partner of Accorso's firm."

Rapp finished dressing and did the best he could to smooth his unruly hair. The reflection in the side window suggested that despite the month's salary he'd spent on the suit, it didn't have the power to make him look respectable. His grooming was aimed more at being able to walk around Kabul unnoticed than blending into American boardrooms.

He sat back and watched the ancient buildings pass by. Italy had always felt like a second home to him. He'd spent many happy—if infuriating—months living there with a fashion designer who had a way with ice picks. Probably not the right woman for him, but also not entirely the wrong one. She understood and accepted the life he'd chosen, neither judging him nor worrying every time he didn't make it home for dinner. On the other hand, he'd never been able to sleep well lying next to her. There was no question that there was a price at which she'd turn that ice pick on him. A high price, to be sure, but he'd still found himself habitually searching the bed for hidden weapons while they were having sex.

He'd resigned himself to the fact that another Anna Reilly would never come along. Trying to find a replica of her would only make him and the poor woman he ended up with miserable.

Anna had been everything to him, but as time went on he could start to see the flaws in their relationship. She'd come to terms with what he did but had never become comfortable with it. He could see now that the dissonance had been slowly driving her insane. Anna believed strongly that people were fundamentally good and that violence inevitably led to disaster. He'd developed a somewhat different philosophy.

It was time to change his life before it was too late. Shaking off the habits he'd picked up from Hurley was a good start, but there was going to be a lot more to it than that. Selling the burned husk of his and Anna's home would have to finally happen. And getting out of the dank apartment he'd landed in wouldn't hurt, either. Most of all, though, he needed to figure out how he could be in a relationship that didn't end with an ice pick in the ear or his partner having a nervous breakdown.

For now, though, he had to shove all that into a dark corner of his mind. If he didn't stop Rickman, his elaborate plans for self-improvement wouldn't be necessary. More than likely, he'd end up the subject of a very public witch hunt led by the politicians who had spent the last two decades demanding his protection.

Rapp didn't realize he'd dozed off until the BMW glided to a stop in front of a building with a series of flags hanging over the entrance. He stepped out, looking up at the six-story glass structure.

"Irene says I'm supposed to take the lead. We're not dangling anyone out of windows today," Nash said.

"They don't open."

Nash wasn't sure whether that was meant as a joke and flashed a nervous smile before starting toward the lobby. Rapp dragged his feet behind. He hated lawyers and was dreading the meeting. If Kennedy really didn't want him to do anything, why was he here? Clearly she expected results and wasn't certain that Nash's honey tongue was enough to get them.

There was no security beyond a friendly woman who used her broken English to give them directions. Nash looked a little apprehensive as they rode the elevator to the top floor—an emotion the former marine never displayed when getting shot at or blown up. He was still transitioning into his new job and wasn't yet comfortable with his role as management. Also, the knowledge that Rapp and Kennedy were watching his every move wasn't doing much to calm his nerves.

Two men were already waiting for them in a conference room nestled in a quiet corner of the executive floor. Nash strode in with an easy smile.

"Mike Blake," he said, shaking hands with the older of the two men. "It's good to finally meet you, Mr. Cipriani."

"Please, call me Marcelo," the man said with a light accent. "May I present my attorney, Dante Necchi?"

Nash's smile broadened while Rapp's own expression darkened. The lawyer they'd come to see had a lawyer. Outstanding.

"Good to meet you, Dante." He motioned behind him. "This is my colleague Mitch Kruse."

Rapp sat in an empty chair and stared straight ahead, unwilling to shake hands with either man. He just wanted to get what they were here to get and head back to the plane. Maybe after a quick stop for a plate of carbonara. He hadn't eaten anything for almost twelve hours.

"What is Mr. Kruse's role in this meeting?" Necchi said, looking a bit bemused. "To intimidate us?"

"Don't be ridiculous," Nash said. "He's part of our legal team."

Neither man seemed convinced, but they let it go. Necchi laid a cell phone on the table.

"I assume you won't object to this meeting being recorded?"

Nash continued his valiant effort to be disarming. "Not at all. Now we have—"

"And by 'we' you're referring to America's Central Intelligence Agency."

"I'm referring to the U.S. government in general. Now, may I continue?"

"By all means."

"We have reason to believe that classified information stolen from us has been given to your firm."

Both men looked a bit startled, and Nash raised his hand before that surprise could turn to indignation. "Unknown to you, of course. We are not suggesting any impropriety on your part. It would be in the form of a series of encrypted files that you would be asked to release if you aren't contacted by your client on a given schedule."

Rapp kept his gaze locked on the managing partner, who in turn kept his on Nash so as to avoid eye contact.

"We have many clients who have many schedules for many things," Necchi said. "All completely legal."

"Again, I'm aware of your firm's sterling reputation and that you would have no way of knowing what's in these files."

"I assume that you're not just here to tell us this? That you want something from my client?"

"In the past weeks your firm has been responsible for releasing information that's compromised our national security and gotten a number of people killed. For obvious reasons, we'd like to see that stopped."

"And how would you know what files this firm has released?"

"I don't think that's important right now."

"Does this have anything to do with the Internet video of your Joe Rickman being tortured?"

"I don't think that's relevant to our discussion, either."

"I, however, believe it is. And I find it odd that a group of jihadists would use a law firm to administer a series of schedules and triggers. Why wouldn't they just release the information into the public domain?"

"Hard to say."

"Do you understand what you're asking, Mr. Blake? I presume your legal counsel Mr. Kruse does. You're asking us to completely ignore our legal obligations in regard to this matter. In light of that, your equivocations are rather insulting."

Rapp took a deep breath and let it out slowly. He was willing—

actually anxious—to let Nash handle this. But there was a limit to how long he was going to sit there and listen to this bullshit.

"If that's the case, Dante, I apologize. I certainly didn't intend to give offense."

"I have to wonder . . ." Necchi said, warming up to the subject. "Since I think we all agree that jihadists hiring this firm is absurd, who might have? Is it possible that Rickman himself is responsible? Perhaps he was afraid he was being targeted by your organization and was using the threat of releasing these secrets to protect himself?"

"That's an interesting piece of speculation, but we seem to be ranging pretty far from the subject, don't you think?"

"Is Mr. Rickman dead?"

"I don't know Rickman's status."

Necchi clearly wasn't buying that. "The CIA may be all-powerful in the United States, Mr. Blake. But not in Italy. We have laws."

Rapp couldn't help laughing out loud, and everyone turned toward him.

"I'm sorry," he said. "I was just thinking about the scientists you put in jail for not predicting an earthquake and the fact that your former prime minister spent most of his time screwing underage hookers. But by all means tell us more about the integrity of your legal system. This meeting's finally starting to get entertaining."

Necchi lost his train of thought for a moment but recovered quickly. "For all we know, your organization murdered Mr. Rickman because he was trying to expose your illegal activities."

Rapp leaned back in his chair and when he did, Cipriani fixated on the bulge in the side of his jacket.

"Is this man armed?" he said, alarmed.

"Don't be ridiculous," Nash said, still trying to remain civil. "It's just bad tailoring."

"This meeting is over," Necchi said, standing. "If you want to speak to us further, you can make a request through the appropriate political channels."

"Isabella Accorso was handling the files, wasn't she?" Nash said.

Cipriani had started to stand but at the mention of her name sank back into his seat. "Why do you say that?"

"Because she's dead."

"It was a traffic accident."

Nash shook his head. "Since you've taken your shot at speculation, let me have a turn. Someone contacted Accorso and demanded that she give him copies of those files. She was scared, so she did it. Then, when this person got what he wanted, he had her killed. One of the reasons you're fighting us is because you don't want to admit that you've lost those files. Right now, you've got your tech people searching for them in your backups but they're coming up empty."

"That's absurd!" Necchi said. "Isabella and her daughter died in a car accident. We are not as gullible as the American people, Mr. Blake. You can't come in here and wave an American flag, expecting us to roll over. Using the deaths of these two women to further the CIA's agenda is outrageous! More than that, it's disgusting!"

Rapp had given Nash every opportunity to resolve this and he was getting nowhere. These idiots had let the Rickman files fall into the hands of one of America's enemies, and if he had to listen to another ten seconds of their fake indignation, someone was going to get pistol-whipped.

"Enough!" Rapp said, slamming his palm down on the table. "People are already dead because of your firm, including one of your employees and her daughter. Now you're going to be good citizens and give us every scrap of information you have on this."

"Are you . . ." Necchi stammered. "Are you threatening us?"

"What threat?" Nash said, trying to regain control of the meeting. "I didn't hear a threat."

"In that case, I apologize for not being clear," Rapp said, picking up Necchi's phone and enunciating clearly into it. "If one more of our people is harmed because of this firm's lack of cooperation, I'm going to pay Mr. Cipriani here a visit. After that you can file as many diplomatic protests and lawsuits as you want. It's not going to do him a whole lot of good."

The room got very quiet as Necchi searched for some piece of legalese that would have any meaning at all, and Nash tried to figure out a way to spin Rapp's words into something benign.

Surprisingly, it was Cipriani who broke the silence. "Our firm certainly wouldn't want to see harm come to the courageous men and women who protect our countries from terrorism."

"Marcelo," Necchi cautioned. "You have a responsibility—"

"And I take those responsibilities very seriously, Dante, but we're being told that Isabella was murdered because of our involvement with those files. This situation has clearly escalated beyond something our firm can handle and has become a matter for the intelligence community."

"You've made the right decision, Marcelo," Nash said. "Your cooperation is going to save lives. Now, can I assume that I was right when I said that you're looking into this?"

"Yes," Cipriani responded, his eyes flicking briefly toward Rapp. "After Isabella's death we immediately did an audit of her responsibilities in order to make certain our clients received the uninterrupted service they've come to expect from us. The files from one of those clients had been wiped from our system."

"The backups as well?"

"Yes. I'm told they're completely unrecoverable."

"Bull," Rapp said.

Cipriani's voice rose a bit in pitch. "I swear that I'm telling you the truth."

"Of course you are," Nash said, delivering a subtle kick to Rapp's leg beneath the table. "But we may have capabilities that you don't. In fact, we've got a very nice young man named Marcus who specializes in resolving these kinds of problems. Can I assume you'd be willing to give him access to your system?"

Cipriani chewed his lip for a moment before answering. "Of course."

"Thank you, Marcelo. That's very helpful. Now, is there any other information you can give us?"

Cipriani nodded. "The client is completely anonymous, but we have a hard copy of his instructions. They include various scenarios and schedules for file release."

"I'd love to have the original of that as well as your assurance that no copies exist."

"I'll arrange it."

That was apparently more than Necchi could bear. "Marcelo. This is malpractice. You can't—"

"Shut up, Dante," Cipriani said before Rapp had to. "I don't think I need you anymore. Why don't you go back to your office."

"But—"

"Now, Dante!"

He reached for his phone, but Rapp beat him to it and smashed it against the table.

"I don't think it benefits either party to have a recording of this conversation," Nash said as Rapp stood and headed for the door.

He pulled out his wallet and tossed a few hundred-euro notes on the table to cover the damage. "Now, if you could get us that original, it looks like we're leaving."

CHAPTER 41

"IS Mitch all right?" Marcus Dumond said. "He looks dead."

"Not yet," Rapp said from his position lying on the couch in Irene Kennedy's office. He didn't bother to open his eyes when the young hacker walked in. More than forty-eight hours without sleep had made them feel like they were full of sand.

"You sure?" Dumond said. "You kind of smell like it."

Also, more than forty-eight hours without a shower, he was reminded.

"What did you find?" Kennedy said as Rapp pushed himself into a sitting position. She was at her desk with Mike Nash in one of the facing chairs. He was fresh as a daisy in neatly pressed khakis and a golf shirt. No matter what the circumstances, Nash always looked like the former Eagle Scout he was.

"Not much," Dumond admitted. "The computers were wiped clean."

"Not what we wanted to hear," Rapp said. "Are you sure?"

"Mitch, please. Do I tell you how to shoot people?"

Rapp didn't react other than to frown imperceptibly. In his current mood, anyone else ribbing him would have found themselves with their face shoved through a wall. He had a soft spot for this kid, though. Dumond had always reminded Rapp of his younger brother Steven. But with an Afro.

"Could they be holding out on us?" Nash said. "Dante Necchi didn't look happy about handing us the keys to their kingdom."

Dumond shook his head. "The files were overwritten the day Isabella Accorso died. They have a system in place for eradicating data and making sure it's unrecoverable. All very thorough and professional."

"We've looked into Accorso's background, and there's nothing to suggest that she had some hidden involvement in this," Kennedy said. "I don't think there's any question that she was threatened and told to wipe the system after she delivered the files. The only reason we have the hard copy of the instructions is because they were stored in a filing cabinet that she didn't have access to."

"Speaking of which," Nash said. "Isn't the next release scheduled for today?"

Kennedy nodded. "Ten minutes from now."

"Do you think it's still going to happen?" Rapp said. "If I had those files, I'd want to know what was in them before I splashed them across the 'Net. Controlling information is more useful than releasing it."

"It'll go out," Dumond said, sounding typically confident. "I know the level of encryption Rick used, and I can tell you it's not trivial. Even with unlimited resources, we're talking years to crack it. Maybe decades."

"So you're telling me that whoever has the files will just keep on going. They'll carry out Rick's plan to destroy the Agency just the way he set it up," Rapp said.

"I didn't say that," Dumond responded. "I think they're going to use the releases to track down the person sending them out. The person who has the encryption key."

"That's possible?" Rapp said.

"Definitely. Every time our mystery man sends a file, it bounces all around the world on its way to the recipient. With every release, they can zero in a little tighter."

"How long until they find the person they're looking for?" Kennedy said.

"Depends on their technological capability."

"But it's safe to say that at some point the person with the files is going to find the person with the encryption key," Nash said. "And then they'll have instant access to everything Rick knew."

"Yes."

"How long would it take you?" Rapp asked.

"With access to some of the NSA's bandwidth, probably three releases."

The room fell silent for a moment. Kennedy finally broke it. "Marcus, I don't want you to ever repeat the question I'm about to ask you. Is that understood?"

"Sure."

"What if the ISI has the files?"

He thought about it for a moment. "I'm not an expert on their capabilities, so I'll have to confirm this, but I'd guess four releases. I doubt more than five, and they'd have to be brain-dead not to get it in six."

"We need to make sure no one ever puts those files together with the password to access them," Nash said. "You understand what's at stake, right, Marcus? Our people's lives and the lives of a whole lot of innocent civilians."

Dumond started looking uncomfortable, and Rapp felt a spark of grudging respect when Nash immediately reacted by taking his rhetoric down a notch. There was a fine line between motivating Dumond and paralyzing him.

"You're the best at this, Marcus. You know that and we know that. Whatever resources you need, you get. You want Utah? We'll hand you the keys to the NSA's building. You need a hundred million dollars in cash? Just tell us where to send the forklift. Right, Irene?"

"There are no secondary considerations," she agreed. "This isn't our first priority, Marcus. It's our only priority."

Dumond nodded. "I have an idea, but I need to work through it in my head."

Nash glanced at the clock, confirming that it was a little over two minutes before Rickman's next file was scheduled to be released. He stood and threw an arm around the younger man's shoulders, leading him toward the door. "Let's go down to your office and you can tell me all about it."

When they were gone, Rapp moved to the chair Nash had abandoned. Neither he nor Kennedy spoke while they waited for the quiet chime that would announce the arrival of Rickman's email. When it came, she turned her laptop partially toward him and opened the attached file.

No video this time. Instead it contained a detailed dossier on Fahran Hotaki, an Afghan who had helped the CIA fight al Qaeda and obstruct the Taliban's efforts to drag his country back into the eleventh century. This had been an easy one for Rick—he'd been Hotaki's handler. The dossier included names, dates, photographs, and account numbers—any one of which would have been enough to get the man decapitated.

"Can we contact him?" Rapp said.

Kennedy pulled up his information on her computer. "We gave him a sat phone that he's supposed to always keep with him. There's a predesignated text to warn him that he's been compromised and to direct him to a safe location."

Rapp grabbed Kennedy's phone and began dialing.

"What are you doing?"

"I know Hotaki. I've fought with him. He'll consider a text telling him to put his tail between his legs and run an insult."

With every static-ridden ring, Rapp felt his anger and frustration grow. Finally a familiar voice came on.

"Yes."

"You've been compromised."

"Mitch? Is that you?"

"Listen to me, Fahran. You need to get to extraction point Delta. Do you understand? Delta. We'll have people there waiting for you."

"No. I don't think so."

"Can you not move? How long will you be able to hole up? I can be on a plane in half an hour."

"It's good to hear your voice, Mitch," Hotaki said, sounding infuriatingly unconcerned. "How long has it been? Two years? You've been well?"

"We'll talk about it when you get stateside."

"Oh, no. You have a beautiful country, I'm sure. But my home is here."

"You like desert hellholes? How about Arizona? We'll get you a crappy house right on the border near the drug violence. You'll never even know you left."

"That's very generous, but is it what you'd do, Mitch? If it was America and not Afghanistan being taken over by radicals? Would you have the Europeans pick you up and give you a new home and a comfortable pension? No. Like you, I'm alone. My family is dead. Taken from me by the people I've sworn to stop."

"Okay, forget the house. How about a job? A really dangerous one with lousy pay. I can almost guarantee you'll be dead in a year."

Hotaki laughed. "I would like very much to fight with you again, Mitch. But I must decline. It's been a privilege to have known you."

The line went dead, and Rapp threw the handset hard enough to drag the phone off Kennedy's desk.

"Rickman's mixing it up like we thought," she said as Rapp stalked back and forth across her office floor. "With Safavi, he picked a critical asset and didn't give us time to get to him. Hotaki is the opposite. A relatively unimportant asset with—"

"Unimportant asset?" Rapp shouted. "He's an important *man*, Irene! I've bled with that guy. I watched his brother die in his arms."

"I understand, Mitch, but you have to ask yourself why Rickman chose this *particular* Afghan fighter. There's no question that he's courageous, but there's also no question that he's largely inconsequential. I'd say it's because of your feelings toward him. Rick wants to hurt you. And he needs to keep you off balance."

Rapp stopped pacing and forced Hotaki out of his mind for the moment. "If the ISI's behind these releases now, who are we talking about specifically? This feels like something Durrani would pull, but I saw him die."

"What would you say about Ahmed Taj?"

"I'd say I've never been impressed."

"Were you impressed when you first met me?"

It was an interesting question. The intelligence behind her eyes had been immediately clear but would he have thought she was capable of the things she'd done since? No way. She hid behind that cool, polite exterior better than anyone else he'd ever met.

"So you're saying there's more to him than he lets on?"

"I have no proof. But we both know that the ISI is operating too smoothly to be run by a man everyone agrees isn't up to the task."

Rapp considered the theory and found the ramifications hard to fully wrap his mind around. If a bunch of jihadists got those files, it would be a disaster but not Armageddon. The likelihood that they'd ever succeed in decrypting them was remote, and even if they did, they'd just dump them all onto the Internet in one chunk. Unimaginably destructive, but mercifully quick. The ISI was a completely different animal. Their chance of actually accessing the files was sky-high. And worse, they had the resources to wield them to maximum effect. They'd keep the information close to their vest, using it to undermine America's intelligence efforts and sow the seeds of distrust between the United States and its allies. The Agency would spend the next quarter century with no idea who to trust.

She slid a single sheet of paper across her desk. "I want you to take a look at this."

He sat and scanned the names it contained. Only about two-thirds of them were recognizable, but it was enough to understand the importance of the list's order.

"So the people at the top are noncritical assets that Rick would definitely know about. At the bottom, you've got critical assets who he probably wouldn't have had access to."

She nodded. "I'm not sure it's worth much, though."

"Fahran Hotaki's name is near the top. That proved right."

"But Sitting Bull and the Iranian ambassador are near the bottom. We still haven't been able to determine how Rick got hold of their identities. On the surface, it seems impossible."

"Certainty is hard to come by in this business. Particularly when Rickman was involved."

"Do you see anything on that list you disagree with?"

"You're thinking about pulling people out?"

"I'm not sure I have any choice at this point. We'll start at the top and quietly work our way down."

"You can't pull them all. You'd do Rick's job for him. You'd collapse our entire network. Where are you drawing the line?"

"I haven't figured that out yet."

Rapp grabbed a pen off her desk and began going down the list. At the seventh name, he stopped and crossed it out. "Ghannam is a scumbag who's gone through over a million dollars of our money and not given us shit in return. Let him burn."

He stopped again halfway down. "Prifti's given us some good intel, and I think he's got a lot more in him. He controls a pretty serious organized crime outfit in Albania—petty stuff like tobacco smuggling and racketeering, but big money. Tell him to get back there until we straighten this out. His guys can protect him."

He handed the list back to her. "The rest I agree with, but are you sure this is a good idea? The video of Rickman being tortured already spooked a lot of people and we've had a hard time keeping them from running for the nearest U.S. embassy. If it gets around that you're extracting people, we could end up getting stampeded by every sewer rat we ever gave ten bucks to."

"To answer your question, no," she said. "I'm not sure it's a good idea. Rick would have anticipated it. In fact, he might have been able to write out the list I just showed you verbatim. Every move I make, I have to wonder if I'm playing into his hands."

She walked to a level-six shredder and fed the page into it. "We need to end this, Mitch. Now. Because tomorrow might be too late."

CHAPTER 42

THE ancient stone window frame had only a few shards of glass still clinging to it. Probably the result of an American bomb, but that was by no means a certainty. It could have been shattered in the 1980s by a Russian rocket, or even decades before that in one of the tribal conflicts that predated either of Afghanistan's most recent invaders.

Fahran Hotaki stood with his back pressed against the wall, looking down on the unpaved street below. The sunbaked car on the other side was well known to him—it hadn't run in years. The pedestrians were equally familiar, moving back and forth at the strangely unhurried pace of people aware that their lives offered few options. In the facing building, families he knew well were taking advantage of the quiet afternoon to go about the business of survival.

The outward peacefulness of the scene was an illusion that would be short-lived. Joe Rickman had seen to that.

It had been five years since Hotaki's family was murdered but his hatred for the men responsible wasn't diminished. None of the killers were Afghan—they were mostly Saudi, with a few Egyptians and

Lebanese. These outsiders came to his country to tell his people how to live. How to worship. And they butchered anyone who resisted their twisted view of Islam.

Before al Qaeda had spilled over his country's borders, Hotaki had been a simple farmer. He'd lived in a remote region of Afghanistan untouched by politics or technology or foreigners. He and his people had inhabited that place for more generations than anyone could remember.

What had been built over the course of a thousand years had taken less than an hour to destroy. He'd seen his sons beheaded, his wife and daughters raped and left to die from their wounds, and his village consumed by flames.

Hotaki had been bound and on his knees when they'd finally come to kill him. The gun had been pressed to the side of his head, but the trigger was never pulled. Instead they left him there among the blackened bodies of all those he had loved, the sound of their laughter ringing in his ears.

It was shortly thereafter that he had joined with Mitch Rapp and the Americans. Not because he believed in their futile and unwelcome efforts to turn Afghanistan into a modern democracy. No, he'd simply seen them as a powerful ally in his quest to kill the men responsible for taking away his life.

The Americans were a confused and naïve people, but generally the champions of peace and stability. Occupations were not in their nature. Unlike the fanatics who had converged on his country, the Americans could be counted on to leave.

A pickup truck appeared in the distance, slowing but continuing inevitably forward. The people on the street immediately recognized the armed men in the bed, as did he. Not foreigners, but almost as bad. They were members of a Taliban enclave who wanted to extend their influence over the tribal areas and subject Afghanistan to their fundamentalist stranglehold.

The steps of his neighbors quickened as they scurried back to their homes. Hotaki opened a wooden crate at his feet as the rumble of the approaching vehicle mingled with the sound of people barricading their windows.

He put on the flak jacket he found lying on top and retrieved a silver Desert Eagle .44 Magnum that had been a gift from Stan Hurley. A bit garish but highly effective. Much like the man himself. He took the spare magazines but left the silencer and helmet. These men should hear the bullet that killed them. And they should see the face of the man who fired it.

A nearly identical pickup filled with similar young men appeared on the other end of the street but this one stopped. Clearly it was there to cut off the escape of the man they mistakenly thought was their prey.

Hotaki knew that there would be no help from the Americans. As angry as he had sounded, Mitch Rapp could be trusted to respect his wishes. He knew what it was to lose loved ones in this endless war. And more than any other American Hotaki had met, he understood what it was to be Afghan.

The first pickup continued forward, finally coming to a halt directly beneath his window. Was it arrogance or just complacency? The Taliban had elicited so much fear for so long, they had come to expect their targets to do nothing but cower and beg. On this occasion, they would be disappointed.

He could hear them arguing and used the time to ponder his strategy. The handgun was hardly an appropriate weapon when faced with a truckload of armed men. He had an AK-47, but even that would leave a great deal to chance. Certainly, he would kill or wound a number of them, but the rest would take up positions across the street and in the stairwell leading to his apartment. He would be trapped.

Finally, he selected a grenade. It was reported to have a seven-second delay and he wondered how accurate that was. The Americans were normally quite precise about such things but it didn't really matter. He didn't own a watch.

Hotaki pulled the pin and began counting. What was the word the Americans used when they did this? It was one of their states. *Mississippi*. Yes, that was it.

When he got to seven, he held the grenade out the window and let go.

Allah, in his infinite mercy, decided to smile on him. The explosive detonated just after Hotaki withdrew his hand behind the safety of the wall. It sent shrapnel raining down on the vehicle and the men in it, as well as disintegrating part of the window's upper frame in a cloud of eye-stinging dust and smoke. Beyond being entirely deaf—a relatively trivial problem since it was unlikely he would survive another five minutes—Hotaki was completely unharmed.

He heard the spinning of tires on the south side of the street and threw himself out of the window. It was a three-meter drop, but the bodies in the truck's bed provided a comfortable landing. He immediately leapt to the ground, pulling open the driver's door and dragging the man from behind the wheel. He was bleeding badly from his head and neck as a result of shrapnel that had penetrated the roof. Hotaki slid into the seat and shoved the accelerator to the floor. The vehicle fishtailed into the road as the other pickup closed from behind.

The man in the passenger seat next to him suddenly regained consciousness and began asking what had happened in a panicked voice. He'd been blinded by the grenade and had no idea that his comrade was choking to death in the road behind them.

Hotaki leaned across and threw open the passenger-side door. He swung close to a cart full of hand-hewn cooking utensils and pushed the Taliban fighter out as they passed. The door caught the edge of the cart and nearly severed the man's legs as he fell to the street. The door was ruined, so Hotaki used the side of a building to shear it the rest of the way off.

Automatic gunfire started behind him, and Hotaki swerved around a tight corner before skidding to a stop. He adjusted the mirror and pressed himself back into the seat, bracing himself as he waited.

A few seconds later, the pickup chasing him came drifting around the corner. The driver, focused on aiming a submachine gun through his open window, realized too late that Hotaki was stopped in the road.

The impact felt less powerful than expected, probably due to the

considerable weight of the bodies in the back. His vehicle was propelled forward a few meters, and he gripped the wheel as two men flew
over the top of him and landed in the road.

Hotaki depressed the accelerator again, swerving in a lazy S pattern to run over the men as they tried to shake off the impact and rise
to their feet. He hoped Allah would forgive him the intense pleasure he
felt as they were pulled beneath his wheels.

CHAPTER 43

IRENE Kennedy followed as Nash weaved confidently through the maze of cubicles. She'd never been in this part of the building and its inhabitants' faces reflected that. At first, expressions ranged from mild shock to outright fear. By the time she neared the back wall, though, word had spread. Every head was down, focused on computer screens, phones, or whatever documents were at hand.

Apparently Marcus Dumond was starting to be affected by the pressure of the job he'd been tasked with and Nash felt that dragging him up to the seventh floor would make matters worse. The hope was that Dumond would be more relaxed on his home turf.

The office was what she'd expected—indeed what he'd asked for when he'd signed on. Nearly as big as hers but windowless, it looked a bit like a garage sale right before the doors opened. There was nothing that even vaguely resembled office furniture. Paper files and books were stacked on a sagging Ping-Pong table, vintage La-Z-Boys provided seating, and there was an unmade twin bed beneath a Washington Redskins poster in the corner. Mitch Rapp was sitting on a threadbare sofa next to what appeared to be a week's worth of dirty clothes.

He didn't look up from the *Sports Illustrated* he was reading when they entered. Dumond, on the other hand, jumped to attention and began tossing stuff off a recliner centered in the room.

"That's all right," Kennedy said. "I can stand."

"Are you sure?"

She nodded. "I'm told you've come up with a plan, Marcus."

"I guess. I mean, yes . . . I have."

She was glad she hadn't insisted on him coming upstairs. Nash was right. She'd seen the young computer genius nervous before, but the deer-in-the-headlights look in his eyes was new.

"I'm anxious to hear it. You know we have nothing but confidence in you, right, Marcus?"

"Yeah. . . . Thanks," he said before falling silent.

"Come on, big guy," Nash prompted. "It's a great idea. Tell Irene just like you told me."

"Okay. I still have friends who are . . . well, hackers. I mean, *I* don't do any of that stuff anymore. No way. But I've stayed in touch with a few people from back in the day." His gaze fell to the floor. "You know. Here and there."

Kennedy just smiled blandly. It was an outrageous lie. Just last week, Dumond and a few of these friends had broken into the Walt Disney Studios site and replaced the new Star Wars trailer with a vulgar—but beautifully produced—interpretation of their own.

As long as it was harmless fun and he covered his tracks, Kennedy wasn't inclined to intervene. In a way, the competition and coopera- tion with other hackers helped keep his skills sharp. While people on her end of the spy business tended to benefit from their years of experi- ence, time worked against the tech gurus.

Dumond's comment got more of a reaction from Rapp, who finally looked over the top of his magazine. "Loved the Star Wars video, ass- hole."

The young man froze. "You know about that?"

Rapp scowled and went back to his article. "Are we going to do this anytime this year?"

Nash leaned into Dumond and spoke reassuringly in his ear. The hacker gave a few jerky nods and continued.

"Rickman needed someone to send his files to the Russians or the Iranians, or whoever, right? He'd have to find someone good enough to cover their tracks, and since they'd have to decrypt the data first, they'd also have to be kind of lunatic fringe. Crooked enough not to care that the stuff they're handling could get people killed and nuts enough to not care about pissing off the CIA."

"Your point?" Rapp said.

"It's a pretty short list—people smart enough to have a chance of keeping me off them and big enough jerks to get involved."

"Do we have that list?" Kennedy asked.

He slipped a piece of paper from his back pocket and carefully unfolded it. Kennedy took the damp page and scanned down it. "There must be fifty names here. And probably thirty nationalities."

"Yeah. But it's better than seven billion names, which is what we've got now."

"So let's say our guy is on that list," Rapp said, putting down his magazine. "How do we narrow it down?"

"I send out a phishing email."

Rapp's suspicion of technology had made him somewhat ignorant of it. In his mind, it was better to just stay away from things that evolved on an hourly schedule and could be grasped only by teenagers.

"Like the ones you get pretending to be your bank and asking for your password?"

"Exactly. We'd send a file from that Italian law firm's server to everyone on the list. The guy we're looking for would try to decrypt it, but I'd make it so it comes up corrupted. Whoever responds and asks for us to resend it is the person we're looking for."

"And you'd be able to trace that email?"

"If I'm ready for it and you were serious about giving me access to a whole lot of the NSA's bandwidth, yeah. I can trace it."

Kennedy was the first to raise an objection. "Fifty seems like a lot, Marcus. You hackers communicate, don't you? In private chat rooms and forums? Isn't it likely that someone will mention getting this email? And that other people will say they did, too? Won't that raise suspicions?"

"It's definitely a risk. But it's the best thing I can come up with."

"Why can't we narrow it down?" Rapp said.

Everyone looked over at him. "How?" Nash asked.

"Rick would pick the best one."

"I agree," Kennedy said. "But that's a subjective concept. What's 'best'?"

Rapp stood and took the list from her, spreading it out on the Ping-Pong table before motioning Dumond over. "Rick never made a move without knowing all the angles. He researched everything to death and had more contacts in more places than anyone in the Agency."

"I don't understand what you're getting at," Dumond said.

"How many of these people are you friends with or have you collaborated with in the past? Rick would know we'd give you the lead on this, so it seems pretty unlikely that he'd hand the job to someone you're close to. Mark off all your friends."

"Hey, Mitch . . . like I told you, the people on this list are pretty bent. I wouldn't hang out with guys who'd do something like this."

Rapp turned toward Dumond and the hacker again let his eyes drift to the floor.

"Look at me, Marcus."

"Mitch, I—"

"You know what kind of people I deal with every day?"

"Yeah, I guess," he mumbled.

"Then you'll believe me when I say that I couldn't give a fuck about a bunch of people running around stealing credit card numbers. What I care about—all I care about—is you putting me in front of this guy."

Dumond reluctantly pulled out a pen and began marking through names. It turned out to be more than Rapp would have guessed. When he was finished, there were only about twenty names left.

"Mitch is right," Kennedy said. "But let's take it one step further. How many of the remaining people have you hurt, Marcus? Blocked, stolen from, or made look foolish? How many hate you enough that they'd fight you every step if you ever tried to get to them?"

He scanned through the list. "Maybe four."

Rapp tapped the page with his index finger. "Then that's where we start."

• • •

Rapp followed Irene Kennedy into her office and closed the door behind him.

"What do you want to talk to me about?"

Normally Rapp avoided headquarters like the plague, and that day he'd been forced to take the full tour—public elevators, the basement, and more crowded hallways than he could count. As a man who valued anonymity beyond all other things, being gawked at and backslapped by half the Agency wasn't going down well.

"Please have a seat."

He would have preferred to stay close to the door, but there was a weight to Kennedy's tone that suggested the meeting was going to be neither quick nor easy.

"What is it?" he said, doing as she asked.

"I have a meeting with the president scheduled for later this afternoon."

"Let me guess. Kamal Safavi?"

Tensions between the United States and the Iranians continued to escalate, with accusations being flung from both sides. Tehran had completely shut down diplomatic relations, and President Alexander was talking about a new round of sanctions. In the meantime, the fledgling cooperation between the two countries with regard to controlling the Sunnis was dead in the water.

"Iran's one item on the agenda."

"What are the others?"

"The Russians. Fahran Hotaki. The fact that someone has the Rickman files and there's no way for us to be certain they haven't accessed them. What Rick knew and how he got that information . . ." Her voice trailed off.

Rapp didn't envy her. There was nothing politicians liked to do more than Monday morning quarterback decisions that they themselves wouldn't have the guts to make. As long as things were going well and they were getting reelected, they were content to stay in the background. But when things got tough, they didn't just abandon the sinking ship, they drilled holes in the hull on their way out.

"Is that all?"

"No. I assume the subject of my resignation will come up."

"You've got to be kidding."

"I'm afraid not. We had a lot of history with President Hayes, but the situation with Alexander is completely different. He wants to do the right thing but at some point politics wins."

"So we have the walls coming down around us and they're going to install some political hack to make it look like they're reining us in? If he gets in my way, Irene, I swear I'll put a bullet in the back of his head."

"I wish you wouldn't say things like that."

"I'm not joking. If anyone tries to stop me from turning this situation around, they're going to have serious problems. The choice between some wound-up bureaucrat and one of our guys in the field is pretty easy for me."

"I think we can avoid it coming to that. With all the gridlock and posturing that goes along with getting a new director confirmed, a temporary head of the Agency will have to be named. I think the president will strongly consider any recommendation I make."

"I feel like you're giving up too easily, Irene. You almost sound okay with this."

"I'm not giving up, but there's blood in the water and I've made more than my share of enemies in Washington. It would be stupid for me to go to this meeting unprepared for the president to ask me to step down."

"Who then?"

"You're too controversial and I assume you wouldn't take the job anyway."

"I'd rather put a gun in my mouth."

"Then Mike Nash."

Rapp didn't respond, instead leaning back in his chair and staring past Kennedy through the window behind her.

"He's the American hero you insisted on making him, Mitch. Any politician who takes a stand against him will run a serious public relations risk."

While Rapp wasn't exactly enthusiastic about the idea, Kennedy was likely right. Nash had the resume, and despite a tendency toward moral paralysis, he was no coward. When it came time for things to get bloody, he could be counted on to be there.

"Mike wouldn't be permanent and I don't think he or anyone in Washington would want him to be," Kennedy continued. "The goal here is to put someone in my chair who can keep the politicians off your back long enough for you to resolve the Rickman problem."

Rapp still didn't respond.

"Mitch? I need you to say something. If you can't work with him—technically *for* him—you have to tell me who you'd prefer."

"Fine."

"What does that mean?"

"It means that I might have to knock him on his ass a couple of times, but I can work with him."

"*For* him," she repeated.

"I said fine."

She was visibly relieved. "Like I said, I hope it won't come to that, but we have to be ready."

"Yeah," Rapp said, trying to swallow his anger. Putting Irene Kennedy out on the street with everything that was going on would be unimaginably stupid. The problem was that unimaginably stupid had become a job requirement in Washington.

CHAPTER 44

IT was good to be out of the city.

The air blowing through the missing door was still hot despite the sunset fifteen minutes before. Dust rising from the road swirled inside the cab, attacking Fahran Hotaki's eyes and working its way into his mouth, but it didn't bother him. In fact, he found it strangely nostalgic. A reminder of his life before the war. Of days spent tending livestock and raising children.

He had no photos of his village or his family. Cameras, as well as phones and computers, had been of little use to him then. They'd become part of his life only after he'd joined the fighting.

Living a life cut off from the outside world was appealing in so many ways. The unchanging rhythm of it, the intimate familiarity with everything that made up his universe. He'd known nothing of economic swings, the Internet, or nuclear weapons. Nothing of tensions between nations, pandemics, or environmental disasters. There had been only him, his people, and the vast, empty land around them.

It was a level of simplicity that should have been easy to preserve— one that would make his country of little interest to outside forces.

For some reason, though, Afghanistan could never just retreat into its primitive, insular culture.

Would-be conquerors had come in seemingly endless waves since the dawn of history. In his lifetime, Afghanistan had endured the Russians, the Taliban, countless foreign terrorist groups, and now the Americans.

Why would Allah not let this rocky corner of the planet exist in peace? Why must there be constant tests of His people's faith? How many horrors would God force them to suffer before He was convinced of their devotion?

"Allahu akbar," Hotaki said over the whistle of the wind. His growing habit of questioning the god he would be meeting later that night was the height of arrogance. Still, he hoped there would be some kind of explanation. He wanted so badly to understand.

The stars were beginning to ignite and he glanced down at the truck's gas gauge while there was still sufficient light. Less than a quarter of a tank. He could extend the pickup's range by emptying the bodies from the bed, but it was unnecessary. There would be no return trip.

Hotaki came over a small rise and saw the encampment he was looking for. There were a few modern lights but most of the illumination was emanating from a bonfire in the central square. Behind were the mountains, black silhouettes that seemed to swallow the universe he'd only recently learned about.

Hotaki rolled to a stop and examined the scene below. The village was simple—a rough circle crisscrossed with dirt roads and low stone houses. It was inhabited by a particularly brutal group of Taliban looking to reassert control. In his mind, it made them worse than the others. Outsiders owed Afghanistan nothing. If they had the power to conquer it, they had the right. These men, though, were murderers. Killers of their own people.

He pressed the accelerator and started down the back of the rise, suddenly free of the deep sadness that had plagued him since the death of his family. By the time he reached the curving wall surrounding the village, all that was left in him was hate.

"Stop!"

A man with an AK-47 appeared from the shadows and approached the truck. Hotaki had the headlights off in order to obscure the corpses he was hauling, but it was unlikely that the precaution was necessary. The guard wouldn't acknowledge even the possibility of danger. Like the men Hotaki had already killed that day, this one was confident in his righteousness and invincibility.

The young man didn't even have his finger on the trigger of the weapon when he leaned toward the open window. "Who are you?"

Hotaki answered by shoving a broken bottle he'd found on the floorboard into the man's neck. Surprise more than fear or pain froze him long enough for Hotaki to pull him partially through the window and hold his head as he bled. The dying man began to struggle, but he couldn't free the gun pinned between his chest and the door. Instead, he swung his fists uselessly, slamming them repeatedly into the cab's rusting metal as the life drained from him.

When he finally went still, Hotaki released his body and pushed the truck's accelerator to the floor. The back wheels struggled for traction before catching and propelling him through the narrow opening in the wall.

The village's men were right where he expected them to be, huddled around the central fire. They turned when they heard the approaching vehicle, but their eyes were adjusted to the glow of the flames and couldn't penetrate the darkness beyond. None realized what was happening until it was too late. He plowed into them, pulling some beneath his wheels and knocking others into the fire. The ones who managed to avoid being hit scattered.

Smoke filled the cab as the oil-soaked chassis ignited. Hotaki leapt out, using an American-built AAC Honey Badger to spray the men trying to scurry away. It took only a moment for the pickup to be engulfed and his advantage was lessened by the blinding glare.

A round hit his flak jacket from behind, nearly knocking him off his feet. He spun, holding the trigger of his weapon down and sweeping from left to right. The scent of charred human flesh filled his nostrils as he charged forward, dodging the burning logs his arrival had strewn about. More rounds struck his vest, their force trying to drive him back. His thigh was hit but the bullet missed the bone, weakening but not destabilizing his leg. A sudden burning in his neck and the subsequent taste of blood in his mouth heralded the death blow he'd known was coming, but it wasn't enough to stop him. Not yet.

He suddenly found himself amid the men. The flash from their gun barrels and the roar of automatic fire were all around him. He realized that his weapon was empty and dropped it, pulling the .44 Magnum from his waistband. He knew he was being repeatedly hit but could no longer feel anything.

Hotaki was vaguely aware that he had dropped to his knees and that his gun was again empty, but still he didn't stop. His finger continued to pull the trigger, tracking on the shifting shadows created by the firelight. Finally, the darkness descended.

God is great.

CHAPTER 45

H E'S there. Next to the kitchen entrance."

Ahmed Taj looked past his assistant toward a heavyset American man in a dark suit. Having arrived in the country only that morning, he'd already taken command of the Secret Service team tasked with providing security for the American secretary of state. Even the Pakistani detail seemed to be deferring to him—a shameful display of weakness that Taj would deal with later.

"Who is he?"

"Jack Warch," Kabir Gadai said quietly. "He's retired now but he was the head of President Hayes's security when the White House was attacked years ago. Officially, he's here only as an advisor, but there's no question that he's in charge."

They moved from their position beneath the ballroom's windows in order to let a banquet table be deposited there. Chairs were being brought in on wheeled pallets, and decorations were going up on the walls. Freshly polished silverware was arranged in velvet-lined boxes and crystal glasses were being held to the light by kitchen staff in search of spots.

President Chutani had spared no expense. This state dinner was to commemorate a new beginning in Pakistan's long relationship with the United States. And to demonstrate to Chutani's enemies the strength of his friendship with the most powerful country in the world.

The real outcome would be quite different. Dramatic pictures of Chutani choking on his own blood while American security men drew their weapons would whip the country into a frenzy that Taj would ride to power.

"Will Warch be a problem?"

"I don't anticipate it. He's inundated us with questions and requests, but I've been handling his demands personally. Obviously, his primary focus is on the safety of the American delegation."

"What have we given him on Chef Marri?"

"Everything," Gadai responded, lowering his voice further. "There's no information connecting the two of you, so there was no reason to make any alterations that could raise suspicion. The entire staff, including Obaid Marri, has already been cleared by the Americans."

Taj tried to quell the nervousness growing in the pit of his stomach. His preparations had been painstaking and Allah had smiled on them, he told himself. There was nothing to fear.

On the other hand, perhaps it wasn't fear of failure that was eating at him. Maybe it was the inevitability of success. Much of his life had been consumed with the creation and implementation of this plan and it was strangely disorienting to know that those machinations would soon be over. In three days, he would begin the violent, but in all likelihood short, battle for control of Pakistan. After that, he would have the power he had craved for so long.

It was the much more difficult task of wielding his newfound power that was beginning to worry him. The Americans were not to be underestimated. They would fight the new order of things with every fiber of their being, doing everything possible to prevent him from asserting dominance over the Middle East. In the end, though, they would fail.

President Saad Chutani entered through the east archway and stopped, taking in the activity around him with a satisfied smile. When his eyes fell on his intelligence director, he motioned. Taj scurried obediently to the politician's side.

"How are things going?" Chutani asked.

"No problems at all, Mr. President. I think you'll be happy in the coming weeks with the resolution to your press issues, and security preparations for the banquet are entirely satisfactory."

"You're certain? There's been a rise in terrorist activity in the north recently. Apparently, the loss of Akhtar Durrani is still being felt by your organization."

In fact, Taj had far greater influence over Pakistan's radical elements than Durrani ever did. "I'm confident, sir. The men you approved for this detail are some of the finest in Pakistan, and the people the Americans sent are quite impressive as well."

"We don't want to test those assertions, Ahmed. Even a thwarted attack would be a disaster. We need to demonstrate that we're in control and project Pakistan as a stable, modern country. A worthy ally for our American friends."

"I completely understand, sir."

The president waved to someone and Taj glanced back to see the infamously volatile Obaid Marri jabbing one of the waitstaff in the chest. Spittle actually few from his mouth as he berated the man. Most people thought it was the arrogance wrought from his restaurant receiving its third Michelin star, but Taj knew that wasn't true. Obaid had been this way since he was a child.

"Have you met the chef, Ahmed?"

"I haven't had the pleasure."

"Come, I'll introduce you."

Marri spotted them approaching and gave the man a shove toward the kitchen. When Pakistan's most renowned restaurateur turned toward them, his red face had turned respectful.

"Obaid!" Chutani said, embracing the man. "I'm honored that you've come to personally oversee the setup."

"Everything must be perfect, Mr. President. And I fear your staff is . . ." His voice trailed off.

"Incompetent," Chutani said with a tolerant grin.

"I was going to say 'in need of polish.'"

"I'm certain you were." The president indicated to Taj. "I don't think you've met Ahmed."

Marri extended his hand. To his credit, there wasn't so much as a hint of recognition in his eyes—only a slight nervousness that was hardly uncommon when faced with the head of the vaunted ISI. "It's a pleasure, Director."

"The pleasure is mine."

Marri was from a village not far from where Taj had grown up. Their fathers had regular business dealings and the two boys had known each other since they were toddlers. More important, Marri shared Taj's thirst for power and vision for Pakistan.

"Have you eaten at Obaid's restaurant?" Chutani asked.

"I'm afraid I haven't had the opportunity."

"You must make the time. It's truly magnificent."

"Mr. President, please . . ." Marri protested halfheartedly.

Kabir Gadai appeared on the opposite side of the room and immediately began trying to get Taj's attention. Excellent timing, as usual. Marri was doing well with their meeting, but it was dangerous to put the man under too much stress. While he had enthusiastically agreed to be part of this plan, in the end he was just a cook.

"Would you excuse me?" Taj said. "My assistant seems desperate to speak to me and I want to make sure it's nothing urgent."

"Of course," Chutani said. "Thank you, Ahmed."

He started toward Gadai, who was disconnecting a call and slipping his phone into his pocket.

"We released another Rickman file this morning," he said, leaning into Taj's ear. "It was all we needed. Our people have tracked it to an Internet service provider in Russia."

Taj nodded solemnly. It was another in a long line of miracles bestowed on him by God. There was no other explanation. He would soon control not only a nuclear arsenal but America's entire intelligence network.

"I want you to go personally."

"But—"

"No arguments, Kabir. I trust no one else in this matter."

"Of course," Gadai said, clearly reluctant but wise enough not to press the issue. "My team is assembling as we speak."

CHAPTER 46

WHEN Irene Kennedy entered the Oval Office, President Josh Alexander immediately strode across the room to shake her hand. The former Alabama quarterback had the gait of an athlete despite having turned fifty-one a few months before. His sandy brown hair was still thick and the elongated dimples that had so captivated the press were still noticeable when he smiled.

Not everything was the same as when they'd first met, though. The suits that had been a bit too shiny now exuded understated elegance. Teeth that had been a few shades too white now were more in keeping with the constituents he served. And a little gray had cropped up at his temples as it always seemed to with men in his position.

Despite the fact that he kept as much political distance as he could from her—and even more so from Mitch Rapp—she admired the man. He understood and accepted that he couldn't stay entirely clean in the fight they were in.

"It's been too long," Alexander lied. "Always good to see you, Irene."

"I appreciate your time, Mr. President."

"You know Barbara and Carl."

Barbara Lonsdale didn't get up from the sofa, but raised a hand in greeting. She was the chair of the Senate Intelligence Committee and at one time had been the CIA's most rabid detractor. After her closest friend was killed in a terrorist attack, though, she'd had a change of heart.

Carl Ferris, in contrast, did rise. He came toward her with his hand outstretched.

"I appreciate you including me on this," he said, though he knew full well that she had nothing to do with approving the attendees at a White House meeting.

Kennedy wondered how his new legal and marketing teams were coming along with spinning his relationship with the late Akhtar Durrani. The senator's arrogant smile and attempt to crush her hand suggested that their work was going well.

"I hope you don't mind," Alexander said. "Carl asked to be here, and I thought it wouldn't hurt to have the Judiciary Committee's input. More importantly, though, he's going to Pakistan with Sunny's delegation and he's understandably concerned about his safety."

"Actually, I'm glad we're finally connecting. I've been trying to get in touch with him about his meeting with Ahmed Taj."

"Really?" Alexander said, obviously surprised that Ferris had met the ISI director without his knowledge.

"My schedule since I got back has been extremely hectic, Director Kennedy. And the meeting was purely social. Ahmed invited me to his office for a drink."

A rather sloppy lie since the man was a devout Muslim. It was far more likely that they discussed how expensive Ferris's new people would be and how they would be paid.

Everyone sat and Alexander refrained from offering her tea, as was his custom. Undoubtedly the oversight was intended as a subtle display of displeasure—one she'd pick up on but that would be missed by the others.

"I know Irene won't mind if we dispense with the pleasantries and get right to business. The Rickman situation. First let me say that trying to assign blame is a waste of time at this point and very much not on the agenda. What we need to talk about is a resolution. Ignoring for the moment minor players like Fahran Hotaki in Afghanistan, this thing has caused us serious problems with Russia and the Iranians."

"A complete disaster," Ferris added.

Alexander frowned at the interruption. There was no love lost between him and the chairman of the Judiciary Committee, but Ferris was a powerful man and he couldn't be ignored.

"Now I'm told we've had another leak this morning," Alexander continued. "In Saudi Arabia this time. Irene, could you brief us on that?"

She nodded respectfully. "Mohammed Kattan, a high-level employee at Saudi Aramco, was exposed as a CIA informant. We were able to notify him and he made it to the U.S. embassy in Riyadh."

"Not necessarily helpful," Ferris interjected, struggling to sound solemn.

While his thinly veiled glee was despicable under the circumstances, he wasn't wrong. Rickman had given them just enough time to warn the man but not enough for an extraction. He'd wanted to create an international incident where the Saudis would demand their citizen's return and the United States would refuse. It had worked beautifully. The demonstrations around the embassy were growing in intensity and had the potential to turn violent at any moment.

"Irene," Alexander admonished. "We have an agreement with the Saudis that we don't spy on each other."

"Completely ignored by both sides," Barbara Lonsdale said, speaking for the first time in the meeting.

"True. But that mutual understanding only works when no one gets caught."

"With all due respect," Lonsdale said. "Screw the Saudis. They're the biggest supporters of terror on the planet and their treatment of women is beyond disgusting."

"They're also the major force in OPEC and this country runs on oil," Ferris said. "You can make all the moral arguments you want, but the American people aren't ready for ten-dollar-a-gallon gas."

"Look," the president said, leaning forward and propping his elbows on his knees. "We've dealt with the Russians, and the Saudis are going to kick up some dust that we can handle. The situation with the Iranians is different. It's going to set back our negotiations at least a year. But, honestly, I've never been sure if those talks are going anywhere or if I'm just falling on my political sword over nothing."

Alexander was being so understanding about Iran less out of benevolence and more due to the fact that the angry protests from Tehran had actually strengthened him politically. The American people were skeptical about his outreach policy and this demonstrated that he wasn't as naïve about the country as his opponents charged. A rare miscalculation by Rickman.

"This can't continue, though. We can't spend the next five years chasing leaks and groveling to foreign governments."

When she didn't immediately answer, Ferris saw the chance he was waiting for. "Dr. Kennedy told me that Akhtar Durrani had kidnapped Rickman and was torturing him for information. Based on the fact that classified documents keep getting released after both men's deaths, this appears to not be true."

She'd told him that in order to stop his grandstanding attempt to discredit the CIA. It had been a necessary measure to put out an immediate fire, but she'd known it would provide only brief cover. Perhaps she should have taken Rapp up on his offer to get rid of the problematic senator.

"It appears that Joe Rickman became unbalanced," Kennedy admitted.

"You mean he's a traitor," Ferris said.

"It's more complicated than that but, in the end, yes."

"I don't understand how something like this can happen," Ferris said, warming up to his subject. "First of all, why would he know anything about a Russian informant or an Iranian ambassador? Are you tacking top-secret files to the lunchroom bulletin board?"

"Spare us the soapbox speech," Barbara Lonsdale said. Alexander, on the other hand, remained silent. While he didn't want to assign blame, he wasn't above letting someone else do it.

"What does the CIA do?" Ferris continued. "Spy on people, right? Isn't that its whole multibillion-dollar purpose? Why wasn't Rickman being watched? Why was he exempted?"

"This is a difficult business full of difficult people," Lonsdale said. "It happened. Now let's figure out how to fix it."

"You can downplay this all you want, Barbara, but it's a disaster. An *ongoing* disaster. Apparently, Dr. Kennedy has no clue what Rickman knew or how he got the information. How many files are there? Ten? A hundred? A thousand? And why would we think Rickman would lead with his best stuff? I wouldn't. What did he know that I don't? Hell, what did he know that President Alexander doesn't? What we've seen so far might just be the tip of the iceberg. But we don't know if that's the case and neither does Dr. Kennedy. Are we certain that her other people and operations are secure? Because, with all due respect, she doesn't seem to know."

"What are you proposing, Carl?" Lonsdale said. "Disbanding the CIA?"

"What do they really do for us?" Ferris said. "Occasionally solve a problem that they themselves created? At the very least, I think it's time to consider a complete restructuring of the organization."

"Maybe we should get rid of the military while we're at it?" Lonsdale said sarcastically.

Ferris shrugged. "Almost a trillion dollars a year and they haven't been able to deliver a clear win since the Japanese surrendered in '44. Obviously, the United States needs a strong defensive force, but I wonder if that couldn't be achieved for half the current budget."

"I think we're getting well off the subject at hand," Alexander said.

Ferris grinned. "My apologies, Mr. President. As you know, I have a passion for theoretical tangents."

Ferris could be dangerously charming when he chose to be. The very real prospect that he could become president and turn some of his bizarre philosophical musings into legislation was terrifying to Kennedy.

"Irene," Alexander said. "Where are we with plugging these leaks?"

"We have a strong lead, and it's my hope that we'll be able to stop them shortly."

The president was no happier with her response than she herself was. "I'm getting hammered on this, Irene. From our enemies, from our allies, from voters. And all you can give me is that you're working on it?"

"Rickman was a brilliant man," she said honestly. "That's why he was in the position he was. I'm confident that we're going to resolve the issue but I'm reluctant to make promises I may not be able to keep."

"I suppose that's the end of that conversation, then," Alexander said, not bothering to hide his frustration. "What about Sunny's delegation going to Pakistan? Things are looking pretty volatile over there and I'm sure Carl would prefer not to find himself in the middle of a Taliban attack."

"I'm really not that concerned," Ferris said.

Kennedy noted his response with interest. Ferris cared only about himself and had proven over and over to be a coward on virtually every level. His sudden lack of interest in his own safety flew in the face of everything she knew about the man.

"The Secret Service is taking this very seriously," Kennedy said. "And, as you can imagine, the Pakistanis are putting their top people on President Chutani's detail. Again, though, if you're asking for guarantees, I can't provide them."

President Alexander glanced at his watch, hinting that the meeting was coming to a close. "I'm disappointed that we weren't able to accomplish more here today. Does anyone have any other questions?"

"About a thousand," Ferris said. "But it seems that Dr. Kennedy can't answer any of them."

"I'm confident that she'll be able to soon," Barbara Lonsdale said.

Alexander stood. "Thank you all for coming. Irene, could I have another moment of your time?"

Lonsdale leaned into her as she passed. "Chin up, Irene."

Alexander went to his desk and sat but didn't offer Kennedy a chair. "That didn't go well."

"No, sir, it didn't."

He spun a piece of paper on the blotter in front of him and slid it in her direction. It was immediately recognizable as the letter of resignation she'd signed on her first day as DCI.

The president could accept it anytime he chose but instead he pulled it back and put it in a drawer. Point made.

"I'm behind you, Irene. Your job is like mine. Pretty much impossible. You have thousands of people working for you and some of them aren't the most stable or cooperative in the world. It's a miracle things like this don't happen more often."

"Thank you for the vote of confidence, sir."

"Don't thank me too quickly. I'm not going to lie to you, Irene. This is bad. If I could think of a single person who could run the CIA better than you, you'd be looking for a job right now."

"I understand, sir."

"Then fix it, Irene. Not tomorrow. Not next week. Do it now."

CHAPTER 47

MITCH Rapp eased his Dodge Charger into the trees at the side of the dead-end road. He grabbed a pizza box and a six-pack of Coke from the passenger seat but then couldn't bring himself to open the door. There was a reason he never came here. A lot of them.

He wasn't sure how long he sat there but finally he reached for the handle. Not so much because he was ready but because it was about time for Mrs. Randall to start her afternoon walk. She was a nice old lady, but the last thing he needed was a woman in a tracksuit cooing sympathetically at him.

Seven years of wind and rain had cleared out the loose ash, leaving only the blackened skeleton of what had once been his and Anna's home. The second floor was gone, as was most of one side, but there were still enough upright two-by-fours to conjure memories of what it had once been.

Rapp headed for the only intact structure—a sooty brick fireplace standing against the cloudless sky. He chose a place behind it that would obscure him from the street, then unscrewed the top of a Coke and sat. Beer—maybe a whole case—would have been more appropriate but it was time for him to give that up until he pulled his life together.

The afternoon sun reflected off the water of Chesapeake Bay, and he squinted at the dock extending into the water. It looked like one of his neighpapers had cleaned it up and taken over maintenance duties.

He used to run off the end of it in the early mornings and pound out a three-mile training swim. When he returned, he'd inevitably find Anna drinking coffee and reading through a teetering stack of newspapers. She'd feign surprise at how fast he was and then offer a less than heartfelt apology for not having started breakfast. That was usually followed by compliments about his cooking that were actually a thinly veiled effort to get him to whip up a couple of omelets.

Rapp grabbed a piece of pizza and took a bite. Before Anna died, they'd started building a new house on a secluded lot outside the Beltway. The foundations were poured and a few walls were framed, but that was all that had been done before he shut the project down.

The general contractor had been calling, offering to finish it for cost. He was a decent guy who was hit hard by Anna's death and had been having a great time figuring out how to integrate all of Rapp's security measures. Maybe it was time to return his calls.

The years had begun to run together in Rapp's mind. One crisis after another. Lost friends. Dead enemies. A lengthening list of wounds and injuries. Every day had become similar to the last. Every scenario a familiar twist on one of the horrors that preceded it.

But that might be about to change.

President Alexander was a pragmatist, which made him easier to work with than the ideologues on either side of the aisle. But he was also a politician. If he saw the CIA becoming a threat to him, he'd move to deal with that threat. It was entirely possible that Kennedy would be out by the end of the day.

If that happened, Rapp had decided that he would deal with the Rickman mess and then get out. Without her to insulate him from politics, he would have killed half of Washington by now. That left a long and uncomfortably empty road ahead of him. What reason would he have to get out of bed in the morning? Thanks to his brother's investment skills, Rapp had more money than he could ever spend, and his resume wasn't one you took to an employment agency.

There was no way he was going to hire himself out to one of the foreign governments that would undoubtedly come calling, and he couldn't picture himself protecting some celebrity or billionaire whom he'd just as soon shoot in the back of the head. While he didn't necessarily like what he did every day, at least it was quasi-legal and made a difference.

Going back to triathlons would be an interesting challenge, but he had to be realistic. The years and bullet holes would make it impossible for him to return to the top level. And that was less a life than it was a time killer.

The phone in his jacket began to vibrate and he pulled it out. Mike Nash. Rapp let out a long breath and picked up.

"Yeah."

"She's out of her meeting with the president."

"And?"

"Rumor has it that we're still gainfully employed."

A sailboat came into view and Rapp followed it with his eyes. "I guess that's good news."

"Might not last long."

He and Kennedy had decided not to tell Nash about his role in their succession plans. He had enough pressure bearing down on him and they weren't sure how he'd handle more. There weren't many people better in combat, but running the Agency was different. Having someone shooting at you was, in many ways, the simplest of problems. You knew who the enemy was and you knew the issue was going to be quickly resolved in either your favor or the other guy's. Once you sat down in the DCI's chair, the shit came at you from every direction and it never stopped.

"Anything new with Rickman?"

"Maybe. A high-level asset disappeared in Venezuela."

"No gloating?"

"No email, no video. Rick would keep changing things up to keep us guessing. We think that's what we're seeing here."

It seemed like a good bet. Rickman had been well connected in Venezuela through its membership in OPEC. Not that it mattered. He seemed to have had the ability to shine a light into any dark corner he wanted.

"What about Marcus's phishing emails?"

"They've been sent, but we haven't gotten any responses yet."

"Do you think they're on to us?"

"Not likely. Marcus is monitoring the chatter and there hasn't been any mention of the emails. Hackers are a pretty secretive bunch, and for now that's working in our favor."

"Yeah, but we're running out of time. Maybe Irene didn't get her walking papers today but she will next week. Or the week after that."

"I understand, but there's nothing we can do but wait. This is our shot, Mitch. If it doesn't work . . ." His voice faded and Rapp understood why. They'd have to shut down virtually their entire network and walk away. In all likelihood, Congress would gut the CIA and piece out its duties to everyone from the FBI to the Park Service. All while America's enemies danced on the Agency's grave.

CHAPTER 48

CARL Ferris looked at the White House through the windows of his idling limousine. Activity was limited, consisting primarily of Secret Service agents and dogs patrolling the grounds.

Dialing the satellite phone in the heightened security environment made him sweat a bit, but Ahmed Taj had assured him the encryption was unbreakable. Why doubt the man? The ISI had been playing America's intelligence agencies for fools for more than a decade.

Predictably, Taj picked up on the first ring. "I trust the meeting went well?"

Ferris confirmed that the barrier between him and his driver was sealed before responding. "Better than either of us expected. That icy bitch embarrassed herself more times than I can count. Rickman has her by the short hairs. I won't have to lift a finger. The great Irene Kennedy is going to get taken down by a corpse."

"The president didn't ask for her resignation?"

"No. But he will soon. For some reason he still has confidence in her but he's not going to commit political suicide. No one has any idea what's in these files and he knows he could be one release away from a scandal that will break his administration. Plausible deniability will only get you so far. When the American people see the CIA for what it really is—a bunch of psychotics who think they're above the law—he'll want to be as far from her as he can get."

"I'm disappointed that she's still at Langley, but I trust your judgment," Taj said. "With that woman and Mitch Rapp in place, we'll never be able to forge a relationship of trust and friendship between our two countries. I sincerely believe that it will be you and President Chutani who are remembered by history for laying the groundwork for peace in the region. I look forward to seeing you when you arrive with Secretary Wicka's delegation."

The line went dead and Ferris put the phone back in his briefcase. The American people were tired of endless war and Homeland Security overreach. It was the right issue at the right time. Along with the Pakistani money quietly flowing into his campaign coffers, this was the platform he needed to take the leadership of his party and gain the presidential nomination. Once in the Oval Office, he'd pull the CIA's teeth one by one. America and Pakistan would stop their clandestine war against each other and join forces. Their fledgling partnership would allow him to do what his predecessors never could—stabilize the Middle East.

There was a tap on the glass in front of him and Ferris glanced up to see his driver motioning through the windshield at a woman walking down the White House steps.

Ferris threw open his door but didn't get out of the vehicle. "A word, Dr. Kennedy?"

She slowed, turning her dead eyes on him before managing an unconvincing smile. Of all the people Ferris had ever met, she was the one he hated the most. His uncanny ability to read people was the main reason he'd risen so meteorically through the political ranks. This woman gave away nothing. Even beneath the withering stare of the president of the United States—likely the only ally she had left—Kennedy portrayed only supernatural calm.

She indicated for her driver to wait. "Of course, Senator."

"Perhaps we could talk inside?" he said, slipping deeper into his limousine. She followed, closing the door behind her. Normally, he'd move in a little too close, using his superior bulk to intimidate her, but in this case it would work against him. The woman made him nervous, and her close relationship with Mitch Rapp amplified that nervousness to fear. It infuriated him that they could make him feel that way. He was likely the next leader of the free world and Rapp was nothing but an eighty-five-thousand-dollar-a-year thug.

"It seems that our fortunes have reversed," he said.

Irene Kennedy didn't respond to the senator's statement. She'd known many men like him but very few whose pathological narcissism had reached this level. The lack of term limits allowed politicians to stay in their jobs long enough to be twisted by them, and Ferris was the current generation's best example of this. His ego had grown to the point that its tendrils had invaded every part of his mind. He'd come to believe that *he* was America. That what was good for him was good for the country. That the expansion of his own influence was critical to its survival.

Ferris could rationalize anything based on his all-encompassing belief that he—and no one else—must be in charge of every aspect of American life. The idea that he might be wrong or that opposing views might have some validity was so alien to him that he was sincerely baffled when anyone brought up the possibility. In his mind, there was no sacrifice that shouldn't be made in order to protect his privileged status. As long as those sacrifices were made by others.

"I've given copies of the emails between myself and Akhtar Durrani to my lawyers and new campaign consultants. The emails you threatened me with. None of them see any problem. A foreign official lodged a complaint against the CIA and I began an investigation. Now that I know you lied to me—that your man Rickman was in fact a traitor—it appears that my decision to look into the matter was well founded."

"I assume this is going somewhere, Senator?"

He smiled. "I can call a press conference this afternoon, admit my relationship with Durrani, and then come after you with guns blazing.

But since your ship's already sinking, I don't think you'll be able to take much of that. And it sounded to me like the president's skirt is no longer available for you to hide behind."

"Would you also admit to your relationship with Ahmed Taj?"

He was clearly prepared for the question. "Why wouldn't I have one? He's a witness to CIA wrongdoing, including what I suspect was your assassination of his external wing commander. In fact, if this comes to a committee hearing, I might call him to testify."

Ferris wasn't particularly intelligent, but he was smart enough to hire good people. She was convinced that much of his financing was coming from Pakistan and believed that she would soon be able to prove it. The revelation that his campaign was being fueled by an unstable Muslim nuclear power—even if his attorneys managed to make it technically legal—would do irreparable damage to his ambitions. For now, though, she would remain silent on the subject.

"Mitch Rapp threatened not only my life but the life of one of my people. You're drowning in this Rickman thing. The CIA's being exposed for what it is. I don't think it's time for you to start throwing stones."

Her phone vibrated in her pocket and she reached for it. Only communications from Mitch, Mike Nash, and Marcus Dumond were enabled while she was at the White House. "Excuse me a moment."

The text on her screen was written in Marcus Dumond's brief but emphatic style.

GOT IT!!!!! SERVER IN RUSSIA!

ON MY WAY TO MEET MITCH AND SCOTT @ AIRPORT.

The message was followed by an emoji of his caricature wearing sunglasses and flanked by two thumbs-up.

"It's been nice talking to you, Senator, but I'm afraid there's something I need to attend to."

When she reached for the door handle, Ferris grabbed her wrist. "You don't want me as an enemy, Irene. When I become president, the

CIA *will* come under political control and Mitch Rapp will spend the rest of his life trying to stay out of prison. The question is what happens to you. You can fight me and end up like him or you can be a good little girl and walk away with a pension and a high-paying private sector job. If you're smart—and I know you are—I'd suggest you give some thought to which future you see for yourself."

CHAPTER 49

THE snow was light but the wind was strong enough to rattle the windows of the scattered buildings. It was 2 a.m. and the small industrial park was all but abandoned. What little illumination existed was provided by a few icy security lights glowing over doors locked down for the night.

Kabir Gadai approached on foot, taking a circuitous route that kept him in complete darkness. His team leader was crouched at the edge of the only parking lot in the area still containing cars. The windows of the building on the far side were about half lit, with hazy human figures visible moving inside.

"How many people?" Gadai asked as he slipped in behind his man.

"We don't know, sir."

Normally he would have carefully researched the company and sent an advance team to determine its rhythms before embarking on an operation like this. Once again, though, Taj had made those kinds of precautions impossible. His desperation to acquire Rickman's files continued to grow, turning incaution into outright volatility. Any call for premeditation would have done nothing but throw the man into a rage.

"Maxim and Raisa Durov?"

"All evidence points to them both being inside. Their house is empty and their car is in the lot. There's no way to be entirely certain, though."

The Durovs owned the small Internet service provider that hosted the email address connected to the Rickman files. Based on what little Gadai had been able to find out, the former hackers had a very exclusive clientele of oligarchs and organized criminals who valued the privacy the couple could provide. It was a shame there would be no opportunity to look deeper into their organization. Undoubtedly they had access to a great deal of information that could benefit Pakistan, Islam, and him personally.

"Do we have schematics of the building?"

"No, sir."

Gadai let out a frustrated breath. Their entry into Russia had been less than careful, and now they were embarking on a completely improvised operation. He was beginning to wonder if these files were a gift from Allah or a punishment from the devil.

"Your people all know what the Durovs look like?"

"We were provided photographs."

"Then you have my authorization to begin."

The former soldier spoke into a microphone on his wrist, and a moment later, Gadai saw movement west of the building. A man in a long gray coat walked across the parking lot and knocked on the glass door leading to the reception area. A young woman sitting behind a curved desk stood and walked toward the front of the building. She appeared to be unarmed and her relaxed gait suggested that she was unconcerned by the late-night visitor. Either this was a common occurrence in an industry without set hours or she was confident that the company was well protected by its client list.

She unlocked the door and leaned out, saying something in Russian. Gadai's man spoke the language fluently, but didn't respond. Having confirmed that this wasn't Raisa Durov, he grabbed the woman's long hair in one hand and chin in the other. A violent twist created a soft crunch that carried across the lot. Gadai began to move as soon as it reached him. More men—his team numbered six in all—appeared from hidden positions and headed for the building.

Gadai entered and went immediately to the desk while the woman's body was dragged behind it. As he'd hoped, there was a bank of monitors streaming security camera video from throughout the building. With no floor plan, it was impossible to connect the images with specific locations, but at least he would be able to get an idea of what they were dealing with.

"Ten people in all," he said to the men gathering around him. "Six are asleep—either in cots or on the floor. The remaining four are working behind terminals. Maxim and Raisa are separated from the others in what appears to be their office. I think we can assume it's on the top floor. We'll use the stairs and clear the four floors two at a time."

Gadai led, splitting his force. One went through a metal door at the back of the lobby while he ushered the men staying with him into the stairwell. They ascended quickly, coming out on the second floor and clearing the bathrooms before continuing silently down the hallway. The first few rooms were empty, but the last contained a woman and two men who looked to be in their late teens or early twenties. All were asleep on cots, and he motioned to his men, assigning targets. They each fired a single shot from their silenced pistols.

"Second floor clear," he said into the microphone attached to his wrist. "Three contacts down. Continuing to the fourth floor."

The response over his earpiece was immediate. "First floor clear. One contact down. Continuing to the third floor."

They entered the top floor with no resistance. All doors in the corridor were open but only one had a light on. Gadai moved toward it as his men checked for people asleep in the other rooms.

He stopped next to the entrance to the lit office. Two of his three men accompanied him, while another stood in a doorway down the hall and signaled with one finger. The flash and the muffled pop of his Beretta 92F were loud enough to cause the clack of keyboards in the office to go silent.

Gadai moved through the door with his weapon in front of him. Raisa Durov let out a strangled chirp of a scream and her husband's eyes widened as he raised his hands.

"Stay where you are," Gadai said as his men fanned out behind him.

"What . . ." Maxim stammered. "What do you want?"

"Information."

"Do you know who really owns this company?" Raisa said incredulously. "You can't do this."

"Shut up, woman!" Gadai said, approaching and pressing his silencer to the side of her head. She cringed in fear and he locked eyes with her husband. "Do you want her to die?"

"No! Please. Don't hurt her."

Gadai handed him a piece of paper. "This email address. Who does it belong to?"

"How would I know? People don't have to give me their real names or locations when they set up an address. It could be anyone."

It was an absurd lie. His ISP wasn't Google. It was private, expensive, and highly selective. Maxim would have access to everything that went through his server.

"Third floor clear," came the voice over his earpiece. "Three contacts down."

Gadai turned his gaze to the young woman for a moment. She was in her late twenties, with a thin body and vaguely Asian features. Her dark hair had a streak of blue that was nearly identical to the color of the sweater stretched tightly over her breasts. Another whore like the one who had been sleeping with the men below.

"Do what you want with her," Gadai said, taking a step back and adjusting his aim to Maxim's head.

His men grabbed the woman and threw her to the floor. One used a switchblade to cut off her sweater, leaving a thin red line where the blade had contacted her skin.

"No!" Maxim shouted. "Stop!" He tried to get out of his chair, but Gadai slammed a boot into his chest.

One of his men had a hand clamped over the woman's mouth and her arms pinned behind her. She fought wildly as the other cut through her pants.

"Stop!" Maxim said, the panic rising in his voice. "I'll tell you what you want to know."

"Too late." The woman's bra and jeans were in tatters on the floor now, leaving her wearing nothing but a pair of bright red panties. Gadai was enjoying watching the terror in her eyes.

"Please! Whatever you want to know, I'll tell you," Maxim begged. "If you hurt her, though, I'll lock the whole system down. I swear you won't get anything."

It was an empty but expected threat. A hierarchy had been established, and Maxim was well aware of where he and his wife existed on it.

"Since we seem to understand one another," Gadai said, "my men will stop."

The disappointment was clear on their faces, but it made sense to pull back before the woman was completely naked before them. It provided a line that her husband would not want crossed.

"Who does that email address belong to?" Gadai repeated.

"I have to use my computer to find out."

Gadai nodded and the man turned slowly in his chair, reluctant to take his eyes off the men holding his wife.

"I have people monitoring every access point into this industrial park," Gadai said, pressing his gun to the back of Maxim's neck. "If you send out a warning and we see someone approach, I'll make you watch my men cut your wife apart."

"I'm not going to warn anyone. We handle thousands of email addresses. You can't expect me to remember them all."

In fact, Gadai didn't. He had always known that this information would need to be pulled off the server and that there was danger in giving a man like Maxim access to a keyboard. Unfortunately, it was a danger he could do nothing to mitigate.

Gadai watched the Russian type, not understanding what he was seeing but doing everything possible to give the impression that he did.

"Where are the others?" Maxim said as he worked. "Are my people all right?"

"Of course. And they'll remain that way as long as you give me what I want."

He scrolled down a list of email addresses, finally clicking on one near the bottom of the screen. A name, and nothing else, came up. Pavel Katdsyn.

"Where can I find him?"

"I don't know. I—"

Gadai spun the chair so that Maxim was once again facing his wife and nodded. She was still being held from behind, now with one of his men fondling her breasts. The knife came out again and a moment later her panties were being thrown across the room.

"Wait!"

Gadai held up a hand. "Why? Why should I stop my men when you're telling me nothing but lies?"

"I know where Pavel lives. I can't guarantee he's there right now, though. I—"

"Where?"

"I have to use my computer again. If I turn around your men won't hurt her? I have your word?"

"I want only the information I came for, Maxim. The fact that I don't have it is the only thing keeping me here."

The young computer expert went back to his keyboard, pulling up a Russian mapping site and zeroing in on a remote region to the north. "He's here."

There was no city or town marked, only what looked like an empty expanse of wilderness.

"You're trying to tell me this man lives in the forest?"

Maxim switched from map view to satellite view and a small outpost revealed itself. One street with what looked like four buildings on either side.

"What is this?"

"It's a . . ." He searched for the English word. "Commune. About thirty people live there."

"Criminals," Gadai said. "Staying out of the reach of authorities."

"Yes."

"Part of Russia's organized crime network?"

"No. Mostly spammers and con artists. They traffic in a few stolen goods, but it's mostly Internet scams."

"What's the closest access point?"

"You could fly into Ukhta."

"That's still more than a hundred kilometers away. How would I get to their location?"

Maxim ran a finger along a barely visible line leading from the commune. "It's hard to see, but this is a road. It's packed with snow this time of year, but they maintain it well enough to get a snowcat through. It's how they bring in supplies."

Gadai nodded. "You've done well."

"Then you're going to leave? You're going to let us go?"

The Pakistani smiled as Maxim turned back toward his wife. The knife that had been used to disrobe her was now drawn across her neck. Maxim screamed as the blood sprayed across the room, splattering his legs and bare feet. Gadai grabbed him by the hair, forcing his head down and firing a single round into the back of it.

Gadai started for the door as his men cast off the still-thrashing woman. "Burn everything. And tell our pilots to lay in a flight plan to Ukhta."

CHAPTER 50

THE plane's left side dipped violently, stretching the seat belt across Mitch Rapp's lap and slamming his head into the window. He awoke and squinted through the glass, but there wasn't much to see. A wing with a disconcerting number of rivets missing, heavy snow streaking past the lights, and the darkness beyond.

Another violent gust struck but this time the plane rose, shoving him down in his seat with impressive force. He closed his eyes again. The weather was the pilot's problem. And while the Russians couldn't do much right, they did blizzards better than anyone.

A long, terrified scream became audible but he ignored it and let himself drift again. It was the first time in days that he'd been able to get fully asleep. There would be no more posthumous chess games with Joe Rickman. No more talk. Finally, he and his team had an opportunity to take action.

Marcus Dumond—the source of the scream—believed that if their competition really was Pakistan, enough files had been released for the ISI to have traced the location of the hacker they were on their way to find. In fact, S Wing operatives might have already been there, obtained Rickman's encryption key, and gone. If that was the case, the trip to Russia would be a complete waste of time but still better than standing around Langley waiting for another gloating video to hit Kennedy's inbox.

Rapp felt a hand close on his shoulder followed by the voice of Scott Coleman shouting over the roar of the wind and straining engines. "We're going in!"

"Crashing or landing?"

"I'm not sure. The good news is that the pilot says we'll be fine. The bad news is that it looks like he's been crying."

Rapp just nodded and went back to sleep.

• • •

"Mitch! Rise and shine. We made it!"

Rapp opened his eyes and stretched, looking around at the carnage on the small plane. Most of the overhead bins had given way during landing, leaving some of their gear strewn across empty seats and the rest on the floor. Charlie Wicker and Bruno McGraw were gathering everything up while Marcus Dumond clutched his laptop, looking queasy. He was standing near the cockpit as their sweat-soaked pilot threw a shoulder repeatedly against the door. It finally came free with a blast of wind nearly strong enough to knock him over. That didn't deter Dumond, though. He leapt through the opening and into the snow.

The cold was both immediate and lung searing. Rapp pulled on a white parka designed to camouflage him against the winter landscape and headed for the front. The stairs were down now and he descended, pulling Dumond out of a snowbank and dusting him off.

"I shouldn't be here, Mitch. I'm a tech guy. This is ops. It's fucking freezing and we're a hundred miles from the middle of nowhere. We could get trapped out here. How would anybody help us? No one even knows we're here, do they? I told my girlfriend I was—"

"Marcus. Shut up and try to relax."

Rapp moved away, studying what little he could see. Beyond the circle of illumination generated by the plane, there was nothing but blackness. Inside the circle, there was nothing but snow. If anyone was out there, they'd have an advantage, but not much of one. Even a shooter with state-of-the-art optics would have to be within ten yards to even pick out a target, let alone hit it.

His men started throwing duffels out the door just as the muffled hum of a motor separated itself from the storm. A set of lights appeared a few moments later, mounted to a bright red tracked vehicle. Rapp unzipped his jacket for better access to his weapon as it came to a stop. The logo was Cyrillic but below was an English translation: Shulyov Hunting and Snowmobile Tours.

They'd gotten lucky when Nash found the outfitter. Their camp was only about thirty miles from where the Rickman files were being released by a Russian crook named Pavel Katdsyn. Their cover was as a last-minute booking by a corporate team-building group. There wasn't time to create an elaborate legend, so Rapp just had to hope that Nash hadn't missed anything. After Istanbul, it wasn't a great time for him to get recognized in Russia.

A figure in a North Face Himalayan suit jumped out of the vehicle and started running toward them. It wasn't until the person got within a few feet that Rapp could make out the face inside the hood. The woman's skin was a bit more windburned than the pictures he'd seen but still unlined, with dark eyes and a long, straight nose. She was only twenty-nine and as far as the CIA could tell had spent nearly all of those years in this wilderness. Her father had started the company after leaving the Soviet army and had run it until his death two years ago.

"Mr. Kramer!" she said, extending a gloved hand. "I'm Irena Shulyov. I'm so sorry I wasn't here to meet you. We only just got word from the pilot that you were coming in. We never expected him to fly in this weather. Are you and your people all right?"

"Fine," Rapp said, regretting not putting Scott Coleman front and center to deal with her. He did easygoing charm a lot more convincingly. "There was a little turbulence there at the end, but not too bad."

Her expression was incredulous, and he realized that he'd over-played his attempt to be disarming. Shulyov's clientele were probably accustomed to safer and more luxurious travel methods. In contrast, he and his men had spent half their lives stuffed into the back of C-130s. At least the aircraft they'd come in on that day had windows and wasn't a prime target for every radical old enough to lift a rocket launcher.

"We heard there's a wolf pack in the area," he said, changing the subject. "Do you think we'll have a chance to get a few photos?"

She looked past him at Coleman, who was still tossing duffels to McGraw and Wicker on the ground. Dumond had carved out a rough seat in the snow and was planted in it, trying to calm down.

"That's a lot of gear."

"We weren't sure what to bring, so I guess you could say we brought everything."

"This is no problem," she said, still looking a bit confused. "Let me help you carry your bags to the truck."

She started around Rapp, but he blocked her path and thumbed toward Dumond. "We can handle it. My friend over there got a little airsick on the way in, though. Maybe you could take him to your rig. A little sympathy wouldn't hurt, either."

"Oh, I'm so sorry! Of course."

Shulyov rushed to his side and helped him up. Keeping an arm locked in his, she chatted encouragingly as they made their way across the snowpack.

"Cute," Charlie Wicker said, coming up next to Rapp.

"Your kind of woman."

Wicker was debatably one of the top five operatives in the world and undisputedly one of the top three snipers. He'd grown up in a small town in Wyoming hunting with his brothers. When he was twelve, he'd gotten separated from them in a storm not unlike this one. After three days, everyone assumed he was dead and that they wouldn't find him until the snow melted in the spring. On day four he'd emerged from the wilderness without a scratch, dragging an antelope he'd shot.

Rapp originally thought it was just a legend, but when Wicker left the SEALs to join Coleman's company, he'd pulled the man's file. In it was a copy of the news story, complete with a photo of a skinny kid with a big grin and a rifle towering over his back. Since then, not much had changed.

"Grab the gear and let's get out of here," Rapp said. "I want to be on the trail in an hour."

CHAPTER 51

RENA Shulyov seemed to be piloting the vehicle entirely by memory. The powerful headlights illuminated nothing but a disorienting tunnel of snowflakes that looked like they were being shot from a cannon. Powerful windshield wipers swept manically across the glass, but appeared to have no purpose other than to create an electric whine that competed with the howl of the wind.

According to the Agency's weather forecasters, the storm would continue through the night with temperatures dipping into the single digits. Windchill would be in the negative-twenty range. Not exactly Rapp's favorite operating conditions.

A few years back he'd acknowledged this gap in his skill set and joined a couple of SAS friends on a two-month-long training session in Antarctica. To this day, he remembered it as sixty of the most miserable days of his life—a blur of frozen appendages, unruly sled dogs, and hypothermia.

Rapp had managed to be the first to drag himself across the finish line of a hundred-mile self-supported race across the tundra. He could still hear the instructor's comment: "Well, you can't ski for shit, but you've sure got a big motor." Even fresher in his mind was the frost-bitten chunk of his right thumb that turned black and fell off. It eventually grew back, but he still didn't have full sensation.

"I don't want you and your friends to worry!" Irena Shulyov shouted over the ambient noise. "We have a high-pressure system coming in tomorrow. Blue skies and no wind. It will be a perfect day for touring and taking photos."

That jibed with what he'd been told but unless things went very wrong, he and his team would be long gone before visibility got much over a mile.

"Sounds great."

"How is your friend doing?"

Rapp glanced back at Dumond, sandwiched between Coleman and Wicker. It was a bit hard to tell in the dim light but he seemed a little less green than he had back at the plane.

"Fine. He's really looking forward to taking in the sights."

Rapp couldn't see her face, but the giant hood she was still wearing moved forward and back in what he assumed was a nod.

"Is there anything in particular you and your friends would like to do? I see you brought skis. Avalanche danger will likely be considerable but there are some lower-angle slopes that will remain stable. We're expecting at least two meters out of this storm."

She spoke a little too fast, jumbling her passable English. It was possible that the nervousness was just a holdover from having her clients coming in on such a dangerous flight, but he suspected it was more than that. It would be pretty clear to anyone with even a room-temperature IQ that they weren't middle managers from Procter & Gamble. So now Irena Shulyov found herself alone in the wilderness with a group of men who would probably be familiar to her from her father's time in the Russian military.

"What kind of work do you do?" she asked, the silence obviously magnifying her discomfort.

"Product development."

"What kind of products?"

"How long have you lived here?" Rapp said, changing the subject.

"All my life. I went to college in St. Petersburg but hated the city. The people, the cars. The buildings blocking the sky. I can't imagine being anywhere else."

Rapp was about to ask another question to keep the conversation focused on her, but she pointed through the windshield.

"We're here. That's the main building. My guides have prepared food and we have drinks available there if you like. If you're tired, though, I can take you directly to your cabins."

"Are all of your guides in the main building?"

"Yes."

"How many do you have working for you?"

Rapp knew he was being less than subtle, but there wasn't time to screw around.

"Only two," she said. "My permanent men. In the high season I have as many as six."

"Why don't we swing in for a drink, then," Rapp said. "I'd like to meet them."

"Of course."

Irena relaxed a bit and it was no mystery why. According to Nash's intel, her two guides were brothers, both in their mid-thirties and both born and bred in the area. One was former army and the other had spent eight years roughnecking on oil rigs. They weren't to be underestimated.

She pulled up in front of a log building and Rapp twisted around to face the rear seats before getting out. "Irena's going to introduce us to our guides."

Coleman gave a barely perceptible nod. The hope was that this would go smoothly, but the only thing that really mattered was that it went fast. The clock was ticking.

Snow blasted the exposed skin on Rapp's face, turning to ice on his beard as they passed through a rough-hewn door. Inside, it was probably only about forty degrees, but that temperature felt like the tropics by comparison.

"The main building is a bit rustic," Irena apologized. "But don't worry. The cabins were completely updated only a year ago."

The modest heat was generated by a single greasy woodstove in the corner. The room was approximately thirty feet square with a restroom at the back. The door to it was open and Rapp confirmed that it was unoccupied. Both guides were standing next to a low table arranged with liquor and food. They looked as formidable as expected.

Dumond went straight toward them, giving each a polite smile before going for the vodka. His actions were more the product of his near-death experience on the plane than a preconceived plan, but they worked nicely to divert the men's attention. Coleman used the opportunity to check out a shortwave radio near the building's only window. Wicker and McGraw took up positions on either side of the door.

"Alexi, Stepan," Irena said. "I'd like to introduce you to Mitch Kramer."

Rapp shook their hands and exchanged a few pleasantries before pointing to a map on the wall. The CIA had some broad-stroked stuff and a few high-resolution photos, but this looked quite a bit more detailed.

"So where are we?"

Irena tapped her finger near the center while her men took drink orders from the rest of his team. "Right here. Tomorrow we'll go out through this shallow canyon to the north. The plateau it leads to is where the wolf pack has been seen. With the weather clearing, I think we have a good chance of getting close enough for photos."

Rapp ignored the tourist route and followed the elevation markings toward a dotted line that dead-ended about thirty miles to the east. "What's that? A road?"

"Of sorts," Irena said. "It leads to a small commune. It's kept relatively clear in order to get supplies in and out."

"What kind of commune? Are they artists? My wife loves pottery."

"No. They keep to themselves. We won't be going anywhere near there."

A cold blast of air hit them and she turned to wave a cautionary hand at Wicker and McGraw as they pulled the door open. "It's dangerous outside in this kind of weather. If you'd like to go to your cabin, I can send one of my people with you."

"No worries," Wicker said. "We're just going to stand under the light and have a smoke."

"This isn't America. You can smoke in here."

Wicker smiled and they disappeared outside.

Irena motioned for one of her men to follow but Rapp moved to intercept. "They'll be fine. How about you make me a drink? Vodka."

He looked at Irena and she shook her head, motioning again toward the door. Based on her expression, she wasn't sure what was happening and this was her way of finding out. Probably inevitable, but not the way Rapp had wanted it to go down.

He blocked Stepan's path again, this time shoving him backward. Surprise flashed across the Russian's face and then he reached out to grab the front of Rapp's jacket. He was a bear of a man typical in this part of the world—six one, 240, with thick forearms covered in dark hair and tattoos. Someone best dealt with quickly.

Rapp grabbed Stepan's thumb and bent it back before sweeping the man's right leg just below the knee. He executed the maneuver about half speed—enough to put the Russian on the ground, but not enough to do any permanent damage.

The air rushed out of Stepan's lungs, but he looked more surprised than injured. More problematic was the fact that his equally burly brother had come around the makeshift bar and was in full charge. He made it only a few steps before noticing Coleman tracking him with a silenced Glock. That was enough to bring him to a halt, but it was an open question whether he was smart enough to stay that way.

"Irena," Rapp said. "You own this company, right?"

She was completely frozen, eyes locked on the gun. Finally, she managed to answer. "Yes."

"Then you're in command and these men are your responsibility. You understand you can't win, right? All that can happen is that you and your people get hurt."

She said something in Russian and Alexi helped his brother to his feet. Then both retreated to the bar.

"We . . . We don't have anything worth stealing," she said, trying to decipher what was happening. "What do you want from us?"

"I want you to go to bed," Rapp said. "Tomorrow morning I want you to sleep in. Your fees have been paid and we'll be wiring another fifty thousand U.S. dollars to cover damages."

"Damages?"

Right on cue, McGraw came back through the door. "They use walkie-talkies for local communication and the shortwave is connected to an antenna out back. We've cut the wires and Wick's on the roof dismantling their satellite dish."

"What about the snowmobiles?"

"All well maintained and gassed up. We've loaded the gear on the five newest ones and disabled the others. Keys are in 'em." He glanced at his watch. "Wick said he'd be ready to go in four and a half minutes."

Rapp loved working with Coleman's team. No complaints, no hesitation, no detail too small or timeline too tight. He turned back to Irena. "Do we have a deal?"

CHAPTER 52

THE Russian-built snowcat was shut down, leaving an icy world illuminated only by a distant glow. Travel up the makeshift road had taken almost nine hours and had involved digging a path through three drifts too dense for the vehicle's front shovel.

Kabir Gadai stared through the windshield, letting his eyes adjust to the gloom. Spindrift swirled from the towering banks on either side, but with less violence than it had only an hour ago. The snowflakes were still thick and heavy, but now floating straight down at a predictable rate. With the engine off and the storm subsiding, the breathing of the five ISI operatives packed in behind him now dominated.

Based on what he knew from the odometer and intermittent GPS signal, the source of the dim light was Pavel Katdsyn's village, perhaps a half kilometer to the east. As had become customary, there was no time to collect detailed intelligence or recon the area. They were in a race against America's Central Intelligence Agency and once again Gadai would have to endure risks that would normally be unacceptable.

According to his FSB informants, the village was inhabited by approximately ten families, some of which included children. Focused on hacking and Internet scams, they weren't involved in any activity that could create territorial disputes, and they paid significant protection money to both organized crime and the police. Combined with the remote setting, this suggested—but by no means guaranteed—that they would have light security.

"I'll go in using the road," he said as his men began piling out of the vehicle. It was the most straightforward of the three attack plans they'd devised. Unfortunately, it was also the most dangerous. With visibility so limited, though, the risks were outweighed by the benefits. Every moment of delay increased the potential for a confrontation with the Americans.

Gadai started the snowcat and propelled it forward. His men would follow at a distance that allowed them to remain in darkness.

At first, he thought the entrance to the village was completely unguarded, but then he spotted a man running toward him. He was wearing mismatched down pants and jacket, both in garish colors that made him stand out against the white background. The rifle over his shoulder hung up as he clawed at it, finally coming free and allowing him to aim the weapon in Gadai's general direction. It was a pathetic display that confirmed his suspicions about security. No doubt the men of the village took turns on watch with no regard to ability or training.

Gadai slid the driver's-side window down and shouted a greeting in Russian as the man cautiously approached. Satisfied that he posed little threat, Gadai turned his attention to the small enclave beyond his windshield. The photos he'd seen appeared to be accurate. The village formed a rough U shape, with four buildings on each side of a snow-packed street and one at the end. All were two stories, constructed primarily of local timber and metal sheeting. A single snowcat and various snowmobiles were visible but showed little sign of use. None could be dug out quickly enough to be used as escape vehicles and fleeing into the wilderness on foot would be suicide.

When the man got to within a few meters, he called out to Gadai. The Pakistani smiled in an attempt to put the man at ease, but also in reaction to his own good luck. He possessed only a single blurry photo of Pavel Katdsyn and had assumed that he would have to question the guard out of fear that it could be him. The man's pure-blood Asian features made that unnecessary.

Gadai lifted the silenced pistol from his lap, aiming it through the open window and squeezing the trigger. The round hit the man directly between the eyes and he crumpled to the snow without so much as a whimper.

Gadai's team appeared a moment later, running past the snowcat and fanning out in a well-coordinated pattern. He jumped down to the snow and sprinted toward the first building on the left as his men began accessing the others.

The door was unlocked and he went inside, entering an open room with threadbare sofas and a kitchen stacked with dirty dishes. There was a set of stairs to the left and he began to ascend, dragging a hand against the wall as a guide in the darkness. He heard a muffled scream from outside and picked up his pace, concerned that it might wake the house's occupants.

His instincts were right. When he slipped into a room on the upper floor, he found a man desperately searching an old chest of drawers for a weapon. He spun when Gadai stepped on a loose floorboard and instinctively threw an arm in front of his face. He was wearing only a pair of briefs, but his long hair provided a convenient grip point that Gadai used to drag him down the stairs and out into the snow.

He began to babble in Russian, but Gadai ignored him, scanning the upper windows of the buildings for any threat. There was nothing, though. His men had control of the situation and were marching people out of their homes at gunpoint. Men, women, children, and even infants appeared, some fully dressed and others naked or in bedclothes. His team lined them up on their knees, standing behind them with weapons at the ready. Some were shouting angrily, others pleading. The children wailed, already shivering as their skin reddened in the frigid temperatures.

"Who here speaks English?" Gadai said.

They all looked at each other but no one answered. Normally, he would have just stood there and let them freeze but he had neither the time nor patience for that. Despite his heavy clothing, he himself was beginning to suffer from the bitter climate.

"I'll ask only one more time. Who here speaks English?"

"What do you want?"

Gadai turned toward the man who had spoken. He was fully dressed but his daughter, probably no older than six, was wearing only a long T-shirt. He had wrapped his arms around her for warmth and was trying to quiet her sobbing.

"I want Pavel Katdsyn. Are you him?"

"No. Pavel isn't here. He left weeks ago."

For a career criminal, he was an almost laughably bad liar.

Gadai raised his pistol and aimed at the girl. The man tried to put himself between her and the weapon, but the cold made him a fraction too slow.

CHAPTER 53

RAPP'S team had abandoned their snowmobiles about a mile back and were now making slow progress through the wilderness on skis. Gaps had formed in the clouds, creating intermittent splashes of stars. Not much light, but with the snow reflecting it, there was enough to proceed without night-vision equipment.

Since this frozen landscape was fundamentally indistinguishable from Charlie Wicker's backyard, Rapp had put him on point. McGraw was breaking his own trail thirty-five feet left and Coleman was keeping roughly the same interval to Rapp's right. Just ahead, following unsteadily in Wick's tracks, was a very unhappy Marcus Dumond.

Despite the young hacker being dressed head-to-toe in white, his outline was clearly visible. When it started to waver, Rapp swore under his breath and accelerated to a near run. Once again, he was too late. Dumond tipped right, overcompensated, and ended up buried in the deep snow. When Rapp pulled alongside, Dumond was thrashing like a drowning man, digging himself in deeper in an attempt to keep his nose and mouth clear.

"Marcus, stop moving!" Rapp said in a harsh whisper. "This stuff's like quicksand."

"What am I doing here?" he whined, sounding like he was on the verge of breaking into tears. "I'm freezing and I'm exhausted. Just leave me. Just leave me here to die."

There had been no choice but to bring Dumond along. Coleman was probably the best computer guy they had on the ops side, and he still hadn't fully figured out texting.

"Spare me the melodrama, Marcus. Now grab my pole."

Dumond threw out a mitten-clad hand and after a few tries, Rapp managed to get him back on his skis. "Slow and steady, kid. Okay? If you feel like you're starting to lose your balance again, stop before it's too late to get it back. Understand?"

"Mitch, I—"

"Do you understand?"

"Yes."

He gave Dumond a full minute's lead before starting out again. To his right, he could see Coleman pacing him. Wick and McGraw were out of visual range, but they would have stopped, too, in order to keep the intervals he'd stipulated.

Miraculously, the next ten minutes passed without any more problems. The wind had died down and the snow absorbed sound with startling efficiency. Beyond the hiss of his skis, the only thing audible was the occasional dull *whup* of snow dropping from overloaded tree branches.

Rapp came to an abrupt halt when the silence was broken by the faint echo of a gunshot. "Marcus, stop!" he said into his throat mike. "Crouch down on your skis and don't move."

There was no follow-up shot and all his men checked in safe. After staying motionless for almost a minute, it seemed clear that whoever had fired wasn't aiming at them.

"Wick. Can you get a bearing?"

"Hard to say with the acoustics but I'm pretty sure it came from the village. It's dead ahead less than five hundred yards."

Rapp accelerated, stopping next to Dumond to pull him back into a standing position. "Stay. Just stand here and don't do anything."

"What? Alone? Are you crazy?"

"You'll be fine."

"What if . . . What if something happens to you? What if you don't come back?"

"That's not going to happen, Marcus."

"But what if it does?"

Patience wasn't Rapp's finest trait and what little he had was starting to fail him. "Then you're probably going to die."

He took off, staying in Wicker's tracks and leaving a speechless Dumond to himself. Coleman was out of sight now, having headed southeast while McGraw went north. After a hard four-minute effort, Rapp saw Wicker's track disappear into a dense stand of snow-encapsulated trees. He released his bindings and covered his skis before half-crawling, half-swimming into a depression beneath trees.

He found Wicker lying partially buried with an eye to his rifle scope. The long silencer on the end of his barrel was covered in a silicone sleeve to prevent heat shimmer from interfering with the optics.

They were at the western edge of the village as planned. Its inhabitants—twenty-five or thirty in all—were in the middle of the street in various stages of undress. Most were on their knees being guarded by three armed men in white jumpsuits identical to the ones his team wore. The one exception was a child lying in the snow with half her head missing.

Of more immediate concern was the armed man running north, dragging along with him a man wearing a T-shirt and boxer shorts. Pavel Katdsyn.

"What have we got?" Rapp whispered.

"Pakistanis," Wicker said. "You can always tell by the mustaches."

"Four tangos visible from our position," Rapp said into his throat mike. "Three in the square and one running west with our potential target. Bruno, give me a sitrep."

"I have eyes on your runners. They're headed for the building at the end of the road and they're going to make it before I can get an angle.

No other movement. Windows look clear but it seems unlikely that they don't have anyone up there."

"Scott?"

"I'm at the entrance to the village. One dead local and one armed tango. Judging by the tracks coming out of a snowcat, I make it six men total."

That left one tango unaccounted for and it wasn't hard to guess where he was. To his left, Rapp saw the two men disappear through a door in the building at the far edge of the village. It wouldn't take Katdsyn long to access those files. Most likely a matter of minutes.

"Scott. Do you have a shot at the man guarding the entrance?"

"One hundred percent."

"Take it and move into a position to cover the east-facing windows."

"Give me a minute and a half. Two at the most."

"Bruno. How long to get into position to cover the west-facing windows?"

"The same."

"Do it."

Rapp pointed to the men guarding the civilians in the street. "Can you take the two on the right, Wick?"

"No problem."

Rapp slid the rifle off his back and lined up on the head of the man to the left. He was scanning the area for anything unusual, no longer having to pay much attention to his prisoners. The intense cold was doing his job for him. A number of the children had slipped into un-consciousness and their parents looked like they were on the verge of doing the same. Another fifteen minutes and they'd all be dead.

Coleman's voice crackled over his earpiece. "Tango's down and I'm in position."

A few seconds passed before McGraw came on. "I'm ready."

"Okay, then. On three."

Rapp counted them off and then squeezed the rifle's trigger. His target's head exploded along with the head of the man next to him.

Rapp immediately dropped the rifle and vaulted the low snowbank. He made it to the street just as the third Pakistani was swinging his rifle into position. Rapp ignored the threat and sprinted up the road. A moment later the puff of Wicker's silenced rifle sounded and he knew without looking back that there were no tangos left alive behind him.

Rapp retrieved his Glock from beneath his jacket and made it about a hundred yards before a cloud of snow and ice kicked up to his left. As anticipated, the Pakistani assault team had put a man in the upper floor of one of the buildings. Fortunately, the sniper had underestimated Rapp's speed and failed to lead him enough. Wicker had turned Rapp on to a pair of Dynafit ski boots that didn't weigh much more than his running shoes. They allowed him to hold a faster pace on the hard-packed snow than many college sprinters could on a track.

The shooter wouldn't make the same mistake twice, though.

The sound of shattering glass reached him as he continued to run along the fronts of the buildings. Coleman's voice came over his earpiece a moment later. "Sniper's down."

Rapp slid on his hip, ending up behind a pillar bowing visibly under the weight of an overhang piled with snow. He crawled to the door the two men had disappeared through and found it unlocked. Before entering, he glanced back into the street. It was as if nothing had happened. The locals were still slowly freezing to death, watched over by three armed men in white jumpsuits. The only difference was that now those men were his.

Rapp would have liked to give the order to take at least the children to safety, but it was impossible. The man holding Pavel Katdsyn would be unlikely to miss something that obvious. If he looked out the window—and he would—Rapp couldn't afford for him to see anything but exactly what he expected to see.

CHAPTER 54

GADAI shoved his prisoner through the door and watched him fall to the floor. Pavel Katdsyn curled into a fetal position on the warm surface, pulling his hands to his bare chest in an attempt to warm them. His feet appeared to be completely numb, making it unlikely that he would try to escape.

"Your computers," Gadai said, scanning the room and finding only telephone headsets set up on desks piled with paper files. "Where are they?"

"Up . . ." was all Katdsyn could get out. His teeth were chattering audibly and his shivering had become so violent that he appeared to be in the throes of convulsions.

Gadai forced the man to stand. He couldn't walk on his own, making it necessary for the Pakistani to support much of his weight as they ascended a set of stairs. Normally, he would have made his prisoner go first as a shield. In this case, though, Gadai would have to rely on his skill and the bulletproof vest beneath his parka. Until the Russian decrypted Rickman's files, he had to be protected at all costs.

Despite the darkness, entering the second floor with any stealth was made impossible by the whimpering man. Gadai dropped him on the landing and slapped the light switch before stepping out with his Beretta held in front of him. The upper story was a single open space similar to the one below, but lined with computer equipment. He dragged Katdsyn to the nearest terminal and propped him in a chair.

"You've been decrypting and releasing a set of files sent to you by a law firm in Rome. Do you know the files I'm speaking of?"

Katdsyn managed only a weak nod and Gadai pressed his gun to the side of the man's head. "Speak!"

"Yes!" Katdsyn said, his voice shaking with panic and cold. "I know them."

"I want the encryption key."

Katdsyn hesitated. "My people. You have to release them. Let them leave here and I'll give you whatever you want."

Gadai had been through this scenario already with Maxim Durov and his patience had run out. He reached for a letter opener next to the computer but then hesitated. While it would be a pleasure to ram it into the man's leg and start making threats, Katdsyn was already compromised by hypothermia. If he lost consciousness, it would accomplish nothing but cause further delays.

He pulled Katdsyn from his chair and forced him to the window at the far end of the room.

"Look!"

The Russian tried to turn away but Gadai shoved his face into the icy glass. The people of the village were just barely visible through the falling snow. A few were still on their knees but most had collapsed at the feet of the men keeping watch over them.

"They're dying, Pavel. Not an hour from now. Not in ten minutes. They're dying now. And you can stop it. Only you."

"I—"

Gadai twisted the man's head around and stared directly into his eyes. "I don't care about you. I don't care about your people. Give me what I want and you can go to them. You can get them to shelter and care for them. But do it now, Pavel. Because it may already be too late for the children."

Katdsyn pulled away and this time Gadai allowed it. He watched the Russian stagger back to the computer and peck awkwardly at the keyboard with dead hands. It took an excruciating two minutes before the screen suddenly filled with a solid block of nonsensical characters.

"That's it," Katdsyn said. "That's the encryption key."

Gadai shoved him to the floor and sat, peeling off his jacket as the sweat broke across his forehead. He pulled a thumb drive from a pocket in his vest and inserted it into the computer's USB slot. When he tried to open one of the Rickman files it contained, the screen prompted him for a password. He pasted Katdsyn's key into the window and held his breath. A moment later, the individual documents appeared on the screen.

Gadai opened one, skimming a dossier relating to a CIA mole inside the Chinese defense ministry. A second file opened with similar ease and contained a detailed account of the illegal rendition of a French citizen living in Yemen.

His mouth went dry and he leaned back for a moment, staring at the screen. It was done. With the proper cunning and the unwitting help of Carl Ferris, there was no limit to the damage Taj could do to the Americans.

"I've given it to you!" Katdsyn said. "Have your men take my people inside."

Gadai ignored him and opened a browser, navigating to Gmail on the village's satellite link. He typed in the address Taj had given him and pasted the key into it. After pressing the SEND button, he leaned back in his chair again. Katdsyn was struggling to get to his feet, pleading in broken English, but Gadai was consumed by the words on the screen.

YOUR MESSAGE HAS BEEN SENT.

Praise be to God.

CHAPTER 55

MITCH, I'm getting really cold and freaked out."

Marcus Dumond's voice over his earpiece.

Rapp stayed in the shadows beneath the overhang, unbuckling his boots and sliding along the building's wall until he reached the door. A gentle twist of the icy knob suggested it was open, but he didn't immediately enter. The storm had kicked up again and the gusts were coming with a predictable rhythm. He waited a couple of cycles to solidify the timing in his mind and then used the roar to cover his entry.

"Mitch?" Dumond prompted again, the fear in his voice notching higher. "Are you still out there? Are you okay?"

Coleman responded. "Stay off the comm, Marcus. Everything's fine. Just a few more minutes."

Rapp crouched and swept his Glock across the room. No movement. Light was flooding down a staircase to his left and he could hear muffled voices at the top. There was no other way up, so he padded toward it in damp socks. The ancient wood looked like it was barely holding together, forcing him to test each step for sound before fully committing his weight.

He paused on the landing, listening for evidence that his approach had been noticed. Nothing.

Rapp swung around the wall and into the room with a single fluid motion. Pavel Katdsyn was trying unsuccessfully to stand, fear and pain etched deeply into his face. The Pakistani was carelessly sitting with his back to the entrance, staring intently at a computer screen in front of him.

Katdsyn spotted him and Rapp put a finger to his lips. Unfortunately, the Russian had been pushed well beyond the point where he could comprehend an instruction that subtle. He reached out with a shaking hand. "Help me!"

The seated man had made an amateur mistake by putting himself in that position, but the speed of his reaction suggested it was an aberration. He leapt to his feet, simultaneously spinning and kicking the wheeled chair backward. Rapp was forced to dodge right, but didn't lose his line on the head of the Pakistani drawing a pistol from a holster strapped over his bulletproof vest.

Rapp's finger tightened on the trigger but at the last moment he lowered his aim and fired three rapid shots into the man's sternum. When he jerked backward, Rapp charged, knocking him to the floor and pinning the Beretta beneath his foot.

The man's eyes and mouth were wide open but he wasn't making a sound. The rounds Rapp was using hit like a Mack truck. His sternum would be broken, most likely along with a few ribs. Painful as hell, but probably not fatal. On the off chance he was unable to get in a breath and suffocated, at least his face was intact for an ID.

Rapp reached down and relieved him of his weapon, noting the burning hatred in his expression before rolling him over and looping a set of flex cuffs over his wrists.

"I'm clear in here," Rapp said into his throat mike. "Get those people inside."

"Roger that," Coleman responded. "Can I send Wick for Marcus?"

"Yeah. Bring him here."

A hand closed around Rapp's ankle and he turned to see Pavel Katdsyn looking up at him. "Thank you."

In acknowledgment of his gratitude, Rapp brought his silencer to within an inch of the Russian's forehead. "Good people are dead because of you, you son of a bitch."

Katdsyn tried to pull back, but Rapp followed with his weapon.

"Please!" he whimpered.

"What did he want?"

"The . . . The encryption key to some files."

"From a law firm in Rome?"

"Yes."

"Did you give it to him?"

"He was letting my friends freeze to—"

Rapp hit him across the cheek with his silencer. *"Did you give it to him?"*

"Yes! Yes, I gave it to him. I had no choice."

The door opened on the ground floor and Rapp heard footsteps on the stairs. A moment later Marcus Dumond appeared. His hair was dusted with snow and he was shaking a bit, but otherwise he didn't look much worse for the wear. Spotting the computer, he went directly for it, kneeling in front of the keyboard and ripping off his mittens.

"Katdsyn says he gave up the encryption key," Rapp said.

"Yeah, I see it here. And there's a thumb drive. Looks like Rickman's files are on it."

"How many?" Rapp said, leaning over the younger man's shoulder.

"Two hundred and three."

Rapp let out a long breath. The number was higher even than the worst-case scenario he and Kennedy had come up with.

"Let's see if it works," Dumond said.

He chose a file at random and was prompted for a password. A moment later, Rapp was reading a detailed account of a series of assassinations that had taken place in the UAE without the local government's knowledge. He himself had pulled the trigger on two of them and as near as he could tell all the information was accurate.

"Did he send it anywhere?"

"Sorry, Mitch. The key went out a couple of minutes ago via email."

"Can you intercept it?"

"No way. It's gone."

Rapp swore under his breath. "Where?"

"A Gmail account. There's no way to know who it belongs to. I doubt even Google does."

There was a quiet chime from the computer and Dumond leaned into the screen. "Hold on, we've got a response."

"What's it say?"

"Key received and fully functional. Well done. Destroy everything."

Rapp stepped back and stared out the window at the storm. Two hundred and three files. Ops, agents, informants, and God knew what else. Endless scenarios were churning through his mind, each one more catastrophic than the last.

"Do you want me to reply?" Dumond said.

"Just say 'understood.'"

Dumond typed the word while Rapp went to the man on the floor and rolled him onto his back. He was breathing, but in shallow gulps that barely provided enough oxygen to keep him conscious.

"Who did you send it to?"

The Pakistani actually managed a strangled laugh. "The CIA is done," he gasped. "We have your entire network."

It wasn't bravado, Rapp knew. The Rickman files would contain enough fodder for years of grandstanding hearings by the self-serving political hacks back home. They would portray the Agency as being completely out of control and, now with its network compromised, completely useless.

"Marcus. Can you get me a secure video link to Irene?"

"Yeah."

"Do it."

Rapp knelt next to the man on the floor. "I'm going to ask you one more time. Who did you send that email to?"

He tried to spit on Rapp but didn't have the strength and ended up just drooling down his cheek.

"Link's up, Mitch."

"Irene, can you hear me?"

"Barely," came the crackling response over the computer's speakers. "What's your situation?"

Rapp grabbed the man by the bulletproof vest and dragged him toward the webcam above the monitor. The pain from his damaged chest stopped his breathing again, leaving him silently opening and closing his mouth as he struggled not to asphyxiate.

"Can you see?" Rapp said. "Get a screenshot and run his face through our computers."

Kennedy's image was badly pixelated by the weather's effect on the sat link but he could see her shake her head.

"I don't have to, Mitch. That's Kabir Gadai. Ahmed Taj's personal assistant."

Rapp let the man go and he collapsed to the floor next to Pavel Katdsyn.

"Do you have the encryption key?" Kennedy asked.

"Yeah, but I'm not the only one. Gadai emailed it out before I could get to him."

There was a long pause before she responded. "Then you're saying Taj has access to the files?"

"All two hundred and three of them."

"That many?"

She raised her hands to her temples, rubbing them in slow circles as the image broke up.

"Marcus. Send her the files and the encryption key."

At least now they wouldn't have to guess. She could start damage control and try to get ahead of the ISI. Not that it was likely to do much good. A little like putting a Band-Aid on a severed limb.

"We've . . . We've won," Gadai said weakly. "The ISI will dominate the world intelligence community for the next half century. And it was all made possible by your work and your dollars."

Rapp wanted nothing more than to leap into the air and land with both feet on the man's broken sternum, but he held back.

"God rewards His servants," Gadai continued. "And He punishes His enemies."

Rapp stepped back and looked down at the man, finding him willing—maybe even anxious—to lock eyes.

Everyone had a weakness. For some it was intolerance to pain. Others had a faith that was less unshakable than they imagined. Gadai's was suddenly clear: arrogance. Despite the agony speaking must have caused, he continued to gloat. To demonstrate his superiority. Deep down, he wanted to talk. He wanted the Americans around him to know how thoroughly and easily they'd been beaten.

"Don't get too far ahead of yourself," Rapp said. "We have access to the files now and Taj doesn't know it. We'll pull in the people we need to and the others we'll watch. We'll tie the ISI up in so many knots you won't trust your own mothers."

"You're a fool," Gadai gasped. "When I don't come back, Taj will assume you have the information. We've outsmarted you at every turn and he will continue to do so."

Rapp glanced up at Kennedy and she gave a slight nod, indicating that she'd heard. Gadai had just unwittingly confirmed that Taj was behind this.

"The CIA's network will be destroyed and after tomorrow night, there will be nothing you can do about it," Gadai continued. "Run. Both of you. Before your own politicians set out to destroy you."

Rapp smiled and pressed his foot down on Gadai's damaged chest. Not hard, but enough to silence the man. "Tomorrow night. What happens tomorrow night?"

The surprise on the Pakistani's face was easy to read. He realized he'd said too much.

The door downstairs opened again, followed by the sound of footsteps running up the stairs. Dumond retreated against the wall as

Rapp aimed his pistol toward the landing. He lowered it when Scott Coleman appeared.

"Where do we stand?" Rapp asked.

"All the people are inside. Wick and Bruno are working on them. The easiest way out is going to be the snowcat these guys came in on. We can bring in a plane that can better handle the weather and rendez-vous with it in Ukhta."

Rapp nodded and pointed to Gadai. "Take him."

The Pakistani couldn't walk and he let out a gurgling cry when Coleman lifted him into a fireman's carry. Rapp pointed to Katdsyn and Dumond took the hint, helping the man to his feet and following Coleman out.

Rapp waited until he was alone before he turned back to the image of Irene Kennedy. "Tomorrow night is President Chutani's reception for the secretary of state, isn't it?"

She nodded. "Sunny's already arrived in Islamabad with a congressional delegation led by Carl Ferris."

"But why kill her? Or a bunch of congressmen? What good would that do? As far as I'm concerned, he'd be doing America a favor if he gets rid of Ferris."

"I don't think he's after our people, Mitch."

"Then what?"

She stared intently out from the screen. "If President Chutani were killed at that function, it wouldn't be hard for Taj to convince Pakistan that we're responsible. It's already one of the most anti-American places on earth."

Rapp had to admit that there was a certain twisted logic to it. Coups were the national pastime in Pakistan and the timing was perfect. Taj could run the CIA ragged with Rickman's files while he took control of the country and its nuclear arsenal.

"So you think we should warn Chutani?" Rapp said.

Kennedy remained silent. Her expressions were always hard to read, but the poor image quality made it impossible.

"What?" Rapp said.

"In the context of that region, Chutani is a reasonable man. But I don't think either of us has any illusions about him. He's a violent, power-hungry dictator who allies himself with us because it's in his best interest. If he gets Taj, then it's likely he also gets the files. I'm not sure I want to spend the next twenty years being blackmailed by him."

"Agreed."

"How fast can you get to Islamabad?"

"Figure eight or so hours to get to Ukhta and then flight time."

"Do it. And extract as much as you can from Gadai en route. I'll try to determine our next step from here."

CHAPTER 56

IT was after midnight and Ahmed Taj was still hunched over his desk. Behind him, large windows looked out on the well-lit campus of ISI headquarters. The traffic beyond the gate was light as it always was this time of the morning and armed guards patrolled in the same pattern they always did. The familiarity of it was little more than an illusion, though. Everything had changed. Everything.

The goal he'd constructed his life around was less than twenty-four hours from being achieved and Taj knew he should be attending to the myriad last-minute details. It was impossible, though. He couldn't tear himself away.

The ISI director clicked on another of Rickman's files and scanned through its contents. This one had no taunting video attached, only reproductions of handwritten CIA reports from Ukraine. It seemed that a man high up in the Russian separatist movement had been lining his Swiss bank account with American dollars.

Only when his eyes could no longer focus did Taj finally slide his chair back and turn away from the screen. There were still well over a hundred files he hadn't yet examined. What secrets did they contain? How devastating would their impact be?

Allah had provided so much more than his faithful servant could have imagined. Tomorrow, Saad Chutani would die. His last breath would mark Taj's inevitable rise to rule Pakistan and eventually the Middle East. These files would not only accelerate his plans, but expand them in ways he never could have imagined.

Taj stood and began pacing across his dimly lit office. The scale of what he would accomplish was just beginning to settle its weight on him.

The brilliant Joe Rickman had been planning this attack for years. He'd put together files not only on the Middle East, but on China, Russia, and countless U.S. allies. There was damning intelligence on American politicians, descriptions of unsanctioned assassinations, and detailed accounts of unlawful domestic operations carried out by CIA operatives.

Taj would use this information to create a worldwide outcry for the dismantling of America's spy network, and Carl Ferris would be the perfect tool to lead that effort. Taj now had much more than just money to offer the man. He had classified information on many of Ferris's political opponents. The combination of the two would almost certainly be enough to put him in the White House.

With Ferris leading America and Taj pulling his strings, the country would quickly go from the most powerful in the world to completely dysfunctional. A nation distrusted by its allies, blind to the activities of its enemies, and reviled by its people.

He returned to his desk and started a video from one of the file folders still open on-screen. He'd seen it before but the excitement in the pit of his stomach was even more intense upon the second playing.

Joe Rickman was wearing a cowboy hat and holding a beer bottle in one hand. He stared directly into the camera, eyes glistening and wild.

"Howdy, Irene. Thought we'd go for a change of pace on this one. I figured I'd help you out and tell you that I'm about to release proof that your buddy Ben Friedman at the Mossad is the one behind the destruction of Iran's nuclear research facility a few years back. And that it was Mitch who came up with the BS cover story you fed the world. Add that to the fact that Kamal Safavi's probably spilled everything to the ayatollah by now, and I'm thinking that Alexander's little Iranian lovefest isn't going so well. May I suggest a fruit basket? In my experience, those always seem to smooth things over."

The video faded to black and Taj wiped at the perspiration building on his flushed cheeks. The temptation to give the files to a team of ISI analysts was overwhelming but impossible. It was far too sensitive to allow anyone else access to. He would have to personally sift through all of the information, cross-referencing it with the ISI's data banks and determining how it could be used to generate the maximum impact.

There was little question that Irene Kennedy and Mitch Rapp would end up in an American prison. It was a sweet irony that two patriots who had so brilliantly defended their country would die in cages fashioned by the very people they had dedicated their lives to protecting.

These were largely trivial matters, though. The Rickman files generated far grander questions that Taj was just now daring to ask. Was there enough information to provoke a military confrontation between America and Russia? Or, even more devastating, China? Could the former Soviet bloc countries be turned away from the West? Could he gain enough sway over Middle Eastern oil producers to create an oil shock that would collapse the American economy?

Taj closed the computer files and moved them to a heavily encrypted drive that only he had access to. He stared at the progress bar as they were transferred but didn't feel the sense of security he had hoped for. The reason was obvious. Kabir Gadai.

The younger man had been a loyal and highly competent assistant for years but he was also ambitious. Had he kept copies of the files and encryption key? Did he have designs on using them for his own benefit?

It was unlikely, but the possibility was too great to risk. After he helped Taj close his fist around Pakistan, Gadai would have to be quietly dealt with.

Accusations of treason or bribery had the potential to reflect poorly on Taj's fledgling administration and therefore could not be tolerated. No, an accident or perhaps even martyrdom. Gadai would become yet another inspiring symbol of the rebirth of Pakistan. A shining example to others as the country rose to its rightful place as the world's first Muslim superpower.

CHAPTER 57

SCOTT Coleman was standing in the plane's aisle, shouting into a satellite phone as he struggled to maintain his balance in the turbulence. The CIA pilot was more conservative than the Russian who had flown them to Irena Shulyov's camp and had wanted to fly around the storm. Rapp quickly made it clear that they were taking the shortest route—the only question was who was at the controls.

Coleman finally turned off the phone and tossed it onto an empty seat. "Four dead including the girl who was shot. Everyone else is stabilized and the team's getting ready to take the sleds to Ukhta. They'll be back stateside tomorrow morning."

Rapp nodded. Pavel Katdsyn's people—particularly the children—had been in bad shape. He'd left McGraw and Wick to save as many as they could. Whatever was going to go down in Islamabad, it wouldn't be a frontal assault on the heavily guarded presidential palace. The difference between him having three men and one wasn't going to matter.

"Get some sleep, Scott."

The former SEAL thumbed back at their prisoner. "You don't want help?"

"I've got it."

Coleman retreated to a sofa mid-plane and fell onto it, nodding off almost immediately. The ability to rest whenever possible was stressed in special forces training, and it was a lesson Coleman had learned well. Unfortunately, sleep wasn't an option for Rapp. He was on a laptop paging through everything the CIA knew about Kabir Gadai. None of it came as much of a surprise: Well educated, military background, impeccable record. Wife, three sons, and two daughters. A golden boy since the day he'd been born.

More interesting were the few paragraphs of new intel on Ahmed Taj. Kennedy had started digging into his background when she'd first begun having suspicions about the man. None of it was particularly shocking considering his success in the murky world of Pakistani intelligence, but there were unquestionably a few useful revelations. Whether they would be enough to get the job done remained to be seen.

The plane dipped and Rapp glanced over the top of his screen. Gadai was strapped into a seat at the back with his hands still secured behind him. The pain generated by his broken sternum had been working on him for hours now, and a thin trail of blood ran down his chin where he'd chewed through his lip. When their eyes locked, Rapp could see that the hatred burning there had intensified—a trend that needed to be reversed before it reached the point of no return.

Gadai wasn't some run-of-the-mill jihadist. Based on his stoic performance in the snowcat and his unbroken silence on the flight, he'd been well trained in the art of dealing with physical suffering. Of course, he would break eventually—everyone did—but that would take time they didn't have.

Rapp grabbed a bottle of OxyContin from the seat next to him and started down the aisle. The Pakistani watched his approach with an admirably blank expression. He was aware of Rapp's reputation and had prepared for what he believed was coming. Any sign of weakness or fear would be hidden for as long as possible.

Gadai's jaw clenched, anticipating the first of many blows. There was nothing Rapp would have liked more than to oblige him. Unfortunately, circumstances demanded a different strategy.

He shook two pills from the bottle and held them out. "For the pain. I've taken shots like that to the vest and I know how bad it hurts."

Gadai was predictably suspicious. His jaw tightened further and he turned his head away.

"Come on," Rapp said, sitting in the chair facing him. "If I wanted to drug you, I'd use a needle."

"I'll take nothing from you."

"I know you think we're enemies, but we're not."

Gadai let out a short laugh, wincing perceptibly at the pain it caused.

"We protect our countries, our homes, and our families," Rapp said. "We do what we believe is necessary. If you'd been born in America, you'd probably be working for me."

"I serve only the one true god."

"I have no problem with that. And if you and Taj take control of Pakistan, I figure I'm better off. Nations aren't a problem for the United States—we've been dealing with those kinds of enemies since we signed the Declaration of Independence. Chaos is a real thorn in our side, though. You and I both know that all this democracy talk from American politicians is bullshit. Muslim countries need a strong hand at the helm."

"I don't know what you're talking about."

As planned, Gadai was confused by how the conversation was playing out. "What do you want from me?"

"We know that Taj is going to kill President Chutani at the state dinner tonight."

"What? Where did you get this information? It's absurd."

He was a good liar, but the pain, fatigue, and unexpected line of questioning were straining that skill past its breaking point.

"You told me as much a few hours ago," Rapp said in a calculatedly bored tone. "Honestly, it doesn't matter. We've been onto Taj for a long time. He's great at staying under the radar and playing the bland servant, but come on. Irene Kennedy wrote the book on that trick."

Rapp tapped the bottle of pain medication again. "Are you sure? You look like you're really suffering."

Gadai just stared defiantly at him.

"The way I see it, Kabir, we both have serious problems."

"You more than me," Gadai responded. "All you can do is kill me. Send me to paradise."

"Actually, I can do a lot more than that, but let's forget about that for the moment. I think you know what I'm worried about."

"The files," Gadai said proudly. "The first step in the inevitable destruction of your corrupt and godless country."

Rapp rolled his eyes. "America's not going to be destroyed, Kabir. You're a smart guy. Let go of your ideology for a minute and think. For all the money we've poured into it, your military has never managed to win a war. And that's against the Indians. We're not the Indians."

"We'll destroy your intelligence network. Leave you defenseless and your government in turmoil. We'll cut off your oil. And unlike you, we're prepared to use our nuclear arsenal. You profess to have faith in your god but it's a lie. Christians fear death. They fear everything."

"I'm sure that was the plan, but what do you think I'm going to do? Just sit back and let Taj make his move?"

"He's too clever for you. Too dedicated. And too powerful within Pakistan."

Rapp slammed a hand down on the table between them, causing Gadai to jerk back in surprise.

"You want to sit here with stars in your eyes about Pakistan taking over the world?" Rapp shouted. "Fine. I'll call President Chutani and tell him what's going on at the ISI. He'll spend the next two years cutting little pieces off Taj while I do the same to you."

Rapp pulled out a switchblade and Gadai tried futilely to twist away, but in the end the knife just cut through his flex cuffs. Once they were severed, he moved his swollen hands to his lap, careful not to bring about another flash of rage in his captor.

"It gets worse for both of us," Rapp said, folding the blade and moderating his tone again. "I don't trust Chutani. I don't want him to have those files any more than I want Taj to."

He let that statement hang, deciding to force the Pakistani to ask him to say more. Unsatisfying as hell but it was how these standoffs were won. One small victory at a time.

"And how does it get worse for me?" Gadai said after almost a full minute of silence.

"If I keep you, then Chutani's going to move against your family. He'll figure there's a chance they know something that can help him. And he won't stop trying to get that information until they're dead."

Gadai's eyes began to shift back and forth, focusing on everything in the small plane except the man in front of him. It wasn't hard to convince him of his wife and children's bleak future for one simple reason: It was the truth.

"I heard a rumor that Chutani took a page out of Saddam Hussein's book," Rapp said, looking out the window into the darkness. "He likes to lower people's kids into vats of acid while their parents watch. Makes quite a mess, and I understand the smell is horrible."

It wasn't an observation that demanded a response but Rapp waited anyway.

"The rumor is true," Gadai said finally.

"Then let me ask you a question, Kabir. Do you think anything I've said to you tonight is a lie?"

"No."

Rapp was in a virtually impossible situation even if Gadai started talking. They were scheduled to land only an hour before the start of Chutani's state dinner and he had no idea how he was even going to access the heavily guarded palace, let alone deal with Taj.

"I've spent most of my adult life in the Middle East, Kabir, so I know how people like you think. You sit in your fundamentalist echo chamber and talk about creating a thousand-year dynasty. About how God loves you best and how He's going to help you turn the world into some half-assed caliphate. But you graduated near the top of your class with a degree in history, right? So you know that Pakistan has a hard time going a week without a coup. If Taj takes over, how long is it going to be before the military figures out a way to get rid of him? Hell, how long is it going to be before he pisses off our president so bad that he sends *me* over to deal with the situation? It's a pipe dream, Kabir. The whole world will line up against you like they did against Hitler. And Pakistan's not Nazi Germany. It's a mess of kooks and semiliterate fanatics who'd just as soon shoot each other as shoot us."

"You want me to betray Taj."

Rapp shrugged. "It's what he plans to do to you."

"What are you talking about? I've been with him since I was a child. We're from the same family."

"Maybe you're right. Maybe blood is thicker than water. But from what I heard, his last assistant ended up rotting on a trash heap."

Kennedy had warned that the intel about Taj's involvement in that death was little more than hearsay, but the flicker in Gadai's mask suggested he'd heard the same story.

"Rickman's files are the key to Taj's power and you've seen them. You have the encryption key."

"He knows I'm loyal to him. That I would die for him."

"Correction: He's *pretty sure* you're loyal to him and probably no better than fifty-fifty on whether you'd die for him. Put yourself in his place, Kabir. Would you take that chance?"

Gadai didn't respond.

"If you just let go of this world domination crap and take a clear-eyed look at your situation, you'll see that Taj is going to kill you. You don't owe him anything. He sent you to Russia with my team closing in. What do you want to bet that he would have taken a more cautious approach if it had been his neck on the line instead of yours? You're sitting here because of him."

"If I agree to cooperate, what becomes of me?"

Normally, it was the question Rapp would be waiting for—an indication that Gadai was willing to deal. In this case, though, it was a dangerous crossroad. Did he lie and risk that Gadai would pick up on it or tell the truth and risk Gadai not being able to handle it? In the end, he decided the latter path posed the least risk.

"There is no you, Kabir. Chutani's going to want to get his hands on you something awful and we have no legal authority to keep you."

"Tell him I'm dead."

"He's not stupid. He's going to want a body."

"So you're offering me a bullet to the back of the head?"

"I'll leave the method to you, but that's the long and short of it. All I'm selling is the safety of your family."

"And I'm to believe that you can guarantee this?"

"If I save Chutani's life, he's going to owe me. I'll call in that marker for your family. He won't have a problem with that. Your wife isn't the type to be involved in something like this and your kids are too young. He's not going to cross me over some vague suspicions and a piece of pointless revenge."

"Why would I trust you?"

Rapp slid the OxyContin across the table and this time the man accepted. "You've read everything the ISI has on me, right?"

"Yes."

"Then you know what I'm capable of. But you also know that I'm a man of my word."

CHAPTER 58

"WHERE are we going?"

Rapp didn't look at the man driving and didn't immediately answer. Bill Drake had been the station chief in Islamabad for years now and he enjoyed Kennedy's confidence more than Rapp's own. There was no question that he had a decent head for the constant push-pull between Pakistani factions, but he was an observer by nature. When it came time to act, Drake always had a reason that more data was necessary and more experts needed to be consulted. Paralysis by analysis.

Rapp reached for the rearview mirror and adjusted it so he could see behind them. "Keep going east."

Coleman was still trying to get into the dark gray suit Drake had brought. Rapp's fit better but not much. The fact that the pants were an inch too short was less a problem than the obvious bulge his Glock made beneath his right shoulder. Not that it was Drake's fault. Rapp had waited until the last minute to contact him and the clothes were the result of the man sprinting through the only department store on the way to the airport.

"The traffic's not too bad right now, but the farther we go, the worse it's going to get. President Chutani's dinner for Sunny Wicka is tonight and they've got everything around the presidential palace blocked off."

"You heard me."

"Is there anything I need to know?"

"No."

Rapp inserted an earpiece and dialed Kennedy on a secure sat phone. Not surprisingly, she picked up on the first ring.

"Are you on the ground?"

"Yeah."

"Time's tight, Mitch. We're less than an hour from the start of the dinner."

True to Drake's word, traffic was getting worse. A flatbed teetering with bales of cotton cut them off, forcing the station chief to slam on the BMW's brakes. The gap that opened between them and the back of the truck was immediately filled with motor scooters. The cause of the jam was just ahead and hard to miss—a tank parked sideways in the road.

Beyond, Rapp could see the massive, bunkerlike presidential palace illuminated with colored spotlights. A single limousine was gliding toward a set of barricades guarded by a group of soldiers. Other vehicles trailed at intervals designed to limit damage from a potential attack.

"We're approaching the palace now," Rapp said. "It doesn't look like we're going to be able to get the car close, though."

Drake gave him an inquisitive look and Rapp pointed left. They diverted onto a narrower street but soon found themselves stopped in a sea of blaring horns.

"Do you have a plan to get in?" Kennedy asked.

The truth was that he still didn't. He had no intel on Pakistani security, no layout for the building, and no guest list. Even the event schedule he had was just something pulled off a Pakistani news site. Not exactly something he wanted to bet his life on.

"I'm still working on that," he said, feeling around on the floorboard for the electric razor Drake brought.

"They have tanks," Coleman said loud enough for her to hear. "Tanks are usually not a good sign."

Rapp started into his beard with the clippers, debating whether to leave the mustache favored by ISI men. His skin wasn't quite dark enough to pass, but he might be able to create a second of hesitation on the part of anyone lining up on him. In the end, he decided against it and went with the clean-shaven look of the Secret Service.

"Then I think I have some good news for you," Kennedy said. "Guess who's consulting on the security for Sunny's delegation."

"I'm not in the mood for games, Irene."

"Jack Warch."

Rapp stopped the razor midway through his chin. Warch was a former Secret Service executive who had started a private security firm a few years back. He was a solid man and a good friend. More important, he owed Rapp his life.

"With all the instability in Pakistan, the government decided to bring Jack in to stress-test the Secret Service's protocols," Kennedy said.

"No, our luck's even better than that," Rapp responded. "If Jack's here, he's not doing stress tests. He's in charge. No one at Secret Service is going to question him and no one will have the guts to do anything but exactly what he tells them."

"I suspect you're right. I spoke to him earlier and he seems to have a solid handle on things."

"Our chances of pulling this off just went from zero to ten percent. Did you tell him what's happening?"

"I thought you'd prefer to do that yourself. He's going to meet you outside the pedestrian gate on the palace's north side. But he's not happy about it."

"He's never happy."

"Like you."

Rapp ignored the jab. "Does Sunny know?"

"No. She's not the target and we can't afford to have her looking nervous."

"Understood."

"You haven't told me if you were able to get Gadai to talk."

"He talked."

"So you know Taj's plan?"

"Unless he was lying."

"Do you think he was?"

"Sixty–forty not."

"Where is he now?"

"Dead."

"Dead?" The pitch of her voice rose perceptibly. "What do you mean, dead? What happened?"

"It was part of our agreement."

There was a brief silence over the line. "We'll discuss that later."

"Have you talked to President Alexander?"

"I got off the phone with him ten minutes ago."

"And?"

"He wants to have the banquet canceled and tell Chutani what we know. Let him deal with Taj."

"That's going to leave Chutani with the files."

"In his mind, that's an acceptable compromise."

"If Alexander believes the president of Pakistan won't sell us down the river the second it's in his best interest, he's nuts. And even if Chutani were the Boy Scout we know he's not, are we sure he can keep that data under wraps? What happens when some ISI mole gets his hands on it? Or one of the eight hundred terrorist groups operating here? What happens when there's another coup?"

"My argument to him exactly."

"And?"

"He's given us authorization to assess the situation. But under no circumstances are you to act without his express authorization."

"What's that? You're breaking up."

"I thought I might be."

"So I deal with Taj. Tonight."

"Neither of us is naïve about these kinds of situations, Mitch. If it all goes right, our sins will be forgiven. If it goes wrong . . ."

She didn't have to finish the thought. Her expectation was that she would take the political bullet and he would disappear to the far corners of the earth. The world's governments would try to find him, of course, but he knew most of the people they'd send. Some would put on a show and cash their expense checks, but none would be stupid enough to succeed.

Rapp dropped the razor on the floorboard and brushed the hair off his suit. He'd already made his decision. If he could get this done without exposing his involvement, he would. But if the only option was to beat Taj to death while his security detail emptied their guns into him, that's the way it would have to be.

One way or another, Ahmed Taj wasn't going to see the sun rise.

CHAPTER 59

AHMED Taj extricated himself from a conversation with two of Pakistan's members of parliament and walked toward the center of the room. A uniformed waiter offered a tray of Obaid Marri's tiny creations and Taj took one. He assumed that the other guests would find it exquisite but he had never seen food as anything more than sustenance.

President Saad Chutani was holding court on the south side of the hall, laughing easily with the American secretary of state. His wife stood next to him wearing an immodest Western dress and holding a glass of wine produced locally by another of Pakistan's anti-Islamic economic initiatives.

It was a display that made Taj wonder even more about the politician. Until that night, he had seen Chutani as the West's puppet—an ultimately weak man desperate to prove himself to his masters. Now, though, Taj's eyes were open. Chutani wasn't playing a role to ingratiate himself with the Americans. He was one of them. It was his identity as a Pakistani and a Muslim that was a lie.

Predictably, Carl Ferris was at the bar. Despite having only recently arrived, his gait was already a bit unsteady. Not surprising. Taj's people reported that the American senator had consumed a quarter of a bottle of scotch in his hotel suite.

Ferris started in his direction, but Taj scanned past him at the room itself. Soon it would be his. The presidential palace would become the center of modern Islam and a base for spreading sharia law throughout the world. All while the Americans watched helplessly.

Chef Marri appeared in the kitchen doorway and surveyed the growing crowd, looking understandably nervous. He was carrying the poison Taj had given him hidden on his person. It was not the exotic toxin Taj had originally planned to use in order to further implicate the Americans. Instead he'd chosen a mix of common compounds that would generate a much more sensational and horrifying death for the traitor Chutani. A death that would stir the rage and nationalism of even Pakistan's growing secular elite.

"Ahmed!" Ferris said as he came within earshot. "Nice party."

Taj smiled warmly as they shook hands. "I'm glad you approve."

"And I have to say that the security is impressive. They can't even keep people from climbing over the White House fence in my country."

He was speaking loudly enough to be overheard by people around them and Taj made sure his response was sufficiently diplomatic. "Your Secret Service is to be given a great deal of credit for what you see, Senator. My men have felt privileged to work with them."

Ferris frowned and looked around him at the dark-suited men blending in near the walls. Most were American, with much of the Pakistani detail doubling as waitstaff. Jack Warch, the consultant who had been so much trouble, was nowhere to be seen. Perhaps Gadai had overestimated the man's diligence.

"At least you don't have to deal with the CIA. I'm telling you, it's one screwup after another. We could use a man like you to straighten it out."

Implausibly, the idiot's voice had grown even louder. A man and woman Taj didn't recognize glanced inquisitively in their direction. Ferris was unquestionably a destructive force, but there was no telling from one moment to another what kind. Taj had hoped to use him as a scalpel to slowly slice at America's heart. Based on his recent behavior, though, his destiny might be more as an indiscriminate bludgeon. Less effective, but still blessedly ruinous if enough force was applied.

"The world has become a complex and chaotic place, Senator. I'm glad to be heading a much more modest organization. I wouldn't want to be in Director Kennedy's position."

"Too bad," Ferris said, swilling his drink. "Because if I have anything to do with it, there'll be a job opening soon."

Taj put a hand of Ferris's back and nudged him toward the knot of people surrounding Sunny Wicka and the president. "I haven't yet had the pleasure of meeting your secretary of state. Perhaps you would introduce us."

"Sure. Why not?"

"You go ahead, Senator. I'll be there in a moment."

Ferris forced himself into the group and immediately hijacked the conversation while Taj found the head of Pakistan's security detail. "Rearrange the place cards so Ferris is next to me."

The man nodded and Taj returned to the senator's side. He would have to keep a close watch on the man while he was in Pakistan. It would be impossible to deliver this half-wit to the White House if he couldn't get through a simple state dinner without compromising himself.

CHAPTER 60

THE Secret Service man was waiting in the shadows of a well-manicured stand of trees. Five hundred yards beyond, the presidential palace was lit up in yellow, green, and white. Pakistani special forces were everywhere, clad in dress uniforms but armed with automatic weapons that were in no way ceremonial. In addition to the tank Rapp had seen earlier, there were no fewer than five armored vehicles within view—three of which had mounted guns.

"I've been told to take you to the side gate," the man said. Rapp didn't recognize him but the young agent's nervousness suggested he knew exactly who he was dealing with. Coleman and Rapp followed along, keeping their heads down and managing not to attract any attention. Just two more Americans in dark suits patrolling the area.

Rapp studied the security in the palace courtyard as they skirted the fence. It was understated in an effort to seem welcoming to Sunny Wicka's delegation, but still solid. The fence itself was only about six feet tall, with bars eight inches apart. Easily climbable, but with the firepower in the area, it was unlikely that anyone trying would still be recognizable as human when they hit the ground on the other side.

They found Jack Warch standing with his back against the bars, scanning the area in a calculated pattern. The retired Secret Service assistant director would have to be close to sixty now, Rapp knew. Backlit the way he was, fine details were impossible to pick out, but it was obvious he had a lot less hair and a lot more midsection than he'd had during his days protecting the president.

"The private sector's made you fat," Rapp said as they approached. Their escort peeled off and headed for the main gate without a word.

"And the Agency's made you crazy if you think you're just waltzing into my operation like this. Bad things happen when you're around, Mitch."

No one shook hands. It might seem suspicious to anyone watching. Warch did give a nod to Coleman, though. They'd known each other for years.

"Chutani's going to be poisoned," Rapp said simply.

Warch remained silent for a moment, processing what he'd just heard. "How do you know?"

"I know."

"Who's making the move?"

"Taj."

Warch's expression turned skeptical. "My ass. He can barely get out of his own way. That's why Chutani put him in as head of the ISI."

Rapp just stared at him.

"All right. Fine. I only have authority over U.S. security but I'll talk to my counterpart on the Pakistani side. I'm not sure he trusts me but he'll listen to a potential threat. Do you know how it's going to go down?"

"I might."

"Give me the details then. That should help."

"We're not getting him involved, Jack. You and I are going to handle this."

"Yeah, Irene told me you'd say something like that. Listen, Mitch. Security is wall-to-wall and there's a lot of tension on both sides. Basically, you've got a powder keg ready to go off, and what I don't need is going in there throwing matches."

"I've always liked and respected you, Jack, but right now I don't care what you think. Get me inside. And do it now."

Warch hesitated for a moment and then reached into his pocket. Rapp assumed the man wouldn't do anything stupid but crossed his arms in a way that brought his hand closer to his weapon inside his jacket. There was too much at stake to take chances.

When the former Secret Service man's hand reappeared, it held a laminated badge. "This guy looks as much like you as anyone I have. I've pulled him and you're going to take his place." He glanced at Coleman. "I'm sorry, Scott. You'd stand out like a sore thumb in there. I don't have any blond guys."

"Mitch—" Coleman protested.

"Go back to the car and keep your eye on Drake. Make sure he doesn't lose his nerve and take off."

"The car? Shouldn't I be closer? I can cover—"

"Not up for discussion, Scott. If this goes right, I'm going to walk out the main gate. If it goes wrong there's nothing you or anyone else is going to be able to do for me."

Rapp glanced down at the badge, noting the name, and then hung it around his neck. "Let's go, Jack."

They walked to a heavily guarded service entrance where Warch cut left and went around the metal detector. He lectured Rapp about some imaginary screwup loud enough that everyone understood they were together and angrily enough that no one dared interrupt. When they were out of earshot of the checkpoint, Warch lowered his voice and looked down at the ground to obscure his lips from anyone watching through a scope.

"We're in a shoot first, ask questions later environment, Mitch. With the terrorist shit storm going on in this country, Chutani's made it clear that this dinner is to go off without a hitch. If it doesn't, his security people and their families are going to end up in a hole somewhere. Every finger on every trigger is shaking as near as I can tell."

"Where does that leave your guys?"

"We have a fairly free hand. The head of Chutani's security knows that having us here can't do anything but help him. Best case he's got a bunch of extra guns. Worst case he's got a scapegoat."

They entered the presidential palace through an unassuming door isolated from the pomp and circumstance of the main entrance. This time Warch greeted the Pakistani soldier manning the security station by name and asked after one of his children. Rapp was completely ignored.

They continued down a broad hallway, passing no fewer than five Pakistani security personnel and a man carrying a silver tray who looked suspiciously fit and alert. At the end of the corridor, they ducked into a room lined with monitors. The two men watching the various video feeds immediately stood. Warch thumbed toward the door. "Why don't you guys take a break."

As they passed, Rapp began to suspect that Warch's initial protests had been just for show. The Americans seemed prepared for his arrival, and it was hard not to notice that all the security checkpoints had been manned by Pakistanis whom Warch was on friendly terms with.

When the men were gone and the door was closed, Rapp approached the largest of the monitors. It depicted a richly decorated room full of well-dressed people grazing on food arranged on a central table. Sunny Wicka was one of a small group that included Saad Chutani and his wife. More interesting, though, was Ahmed Taj, who appeared to be making an effort to stay close to Carl Ferris. The senator had a good-sized scotch in his hand and already looked drunk.

It was a match made in hell, Rapp knew. A foreign intelligence czar who wanted to take down the CIA and a megalomaniacal American senator with exactly the same goal. How deep was Ferris in this thing? Would it be worth putting the screws to him? Probably not. He was a moron and Taj would be smart enough to keep him in the dark. The Pakistani would just play on Ferris's ego and greed for power. He wore both on his sleeve.

Rapp recognized a few other members of Congress, but none were ⟨im⟩portant or dangerous enough that he had bothered to remember ⟨their⟩ names. Warch's men were also in evidence, trying to blend into the walls. No Pakistani security presence was obvious, but Rapp suspected he knew why.

"Are all the waitstaff ISI?"

"Yeah. It's driving that prick of a chef nuts. They've been training for a month but some of them still don't know a dessert fork from a hole in the ground."

"When this thing hits the fan, get Sunny and her people out first."

"When what hits the fan, Mitch?"

Rapp ignored the question. "Where's the dinner being served?"

Warch used a computer mouse to switch to a view of the dining room. The only people in it were a few kitchen staff and a man in a chef's uniform screaming at someone trying to straighten a listing ice sculpture.

"Is that Obaid Marri?"

Warch nodded. "The only person my guys are more afraid of than me. He hit a Black Stork with a frying pan for knocking over a flower display. Nearly cold-cocked the guy."

"I'm surprised he got away with that."

"Totally protected. I guess he's some kind of hot shit cook. Chutani loves him."

Marri shoved the man working on the sculpture and then stalked toward a set of double doors. A moment later, he appeared on the monitor displaying video from the kitchen.

"I'd like an introduction."

"To Marri? Trust me, you don't." Warch glanced at his watch. "Look, Mitch, they're going to start seating people for dinner in less than two minutes. After that, you've got maybe another fifteen before the soup starts rolling out. Are you going to tell me what we're doing here?"

"Take me to Marri," Rapp said. "I'll fill you in on the way."

They entered the kitchen and Rapp stopped for a moment, flipping his ID badge to face his chest and surveying the tightly controlled order. Obaid Marri ran his kitchen like an African dictator and one

of his standing orders was that no waitstaff was allowed inside unless they were serving. That meant no ISI. With the exception of him
and Warch, everyone in the room was a professional cook. And by the
looks of them, they were all terrified of the man in charge. Only a few
dared even a brief glance in their direction before returning to whatever they were chopping, stirring, or arranging.

No one but Marri spoke and he was too absorbed in doing just that
to notice Rapp and Warch approaching from behind. Finally, he heard
their footsteps and spun. He fell into a stunned silence for a moment
before jabbing a chef's knife in their direction. "What are you doing in
here? Get out! Do you hear me? Get out!"

That turned out to be enough for everyone to stop what they were
doing and watch—a problem Rapp had anticipated. "Chef Marri? I'm
Mitch Keller."

"What? Why are you speaking to me? Why do I care who you are?"

"I'm Thomas Keller's brother," Rapp said, using a name he'd pulled
off the Internet on the way there. Apparently, Keller was one of America's top chefs.

Marri lowered the knife. "From The French Laundry?"

Rapp smiled and nodded. "He wanted me to send his compliments
if I got a chance. He's planning a trip to Pakistan next year and was
hoping to get a chance to meet you."

Rapp extended his hand and Marri, still looking a bit confused,
reached for it. With the fireworks over, the kitchen staff went back
to concentrating on their tasks. So no one noticed when, instead of
shaking hands, Rapp grabbed the chef's testicles and gave them a hard
squeeze.

Marri doubled over, his breath coming out in a loud rush. Once
again, all eyes were on them.

"Chef? Are you all right?" Rapp said, feigning concern. He slid an
arm beneath Marri's and pulled him upright. The man was trying to
speak but, as planned, the pain and surprise prevented it.

"It's the heat," Warch said to the staff as Rapp led the man to a walk-in refrigerator. "He'll be fine. Just keep doing what you're doing. We have to stay on schedule."

It was one of the drawbacks to treating your staff like slaves, Rapp reflected. None had the courage to question or take charge. In the absence of Marri screaming orders, they'd listen to anyone with a plan and an authoritative manner.

Warch rushed ahead and opened the thick metal door, following Rapp and Marri inside before pulling it closed.

"Are you . . ." the chef managed to get out. "Are you insane? Do you know who I am? President Chutani—"

Rapp gave the man an open-handed slap to the face that was hard enough to knock him to the floor.

"Mitch . . ." Warch cautioned.

"If you can't handle this, Jack, get out."

"I'd just like to avoid getting shot or thrown in jail."

Marri raised his arms defensively and Rapp knocked them out of the way before grabbing the front of his coat. "We know all about your plans with Taj."

"What? You're crazy!" Marri looked up at Warch. "Get him off me. I don't know what he's talking about. I don't even know Ahmed Taj! I work for the president."

"Really? Because I hear that you grew up in the same town. That you both attended a madrassa financed by Taj's father. Not too many people know that, though, do they? Because the place burned to the ground and the administrators are all dead."

"It isn't true! Who told you this?"

"Kabir Gadai."

The fear in his eyes grew but he repeated his protest, this time even more emphatically.

Men like him were all the same. They became accustomed to their position of unshakable authority and it made them prone to panic when it slipped away.

"Where's the poison?"

"Poison? I—"

Rapp clamped a hand around the man's throat, silencing him while he searched through the pockets of his chef's jacket. It was possible the vial could be hidden in the kitchen but it seemed unlikely. Too easy for someone to stumble upon it.

There was a hesitant knock on the refrigerator door and Warch opened it a crack.

Rapp heard a quiet voice and he tightened his grip on Marri's throat.

"Is the chef all right?"

"He's fine," Warch said in a reassuring tone. "The heat of the kitchen got to him but he's feeling better. He'll be back out in a moment."

By the time he pushed the refrigerator door closed again, Rapp was finished with his search. He'd come up empty.

"Please tell me your informant didn't lie to you," Warch said.

"Shut up, Jack."

"Come on, Mitch. This guy's famous all over the world and Chutani thinks the sun shines out of his ass. You'll walk away but I'm screwed. I'm paying for grandkids in private school and I've got a daughter getting married next month."

Rapp was convinced that Gadai had been telling the truth and that the hyperventilating man on the floor was the one lying. But with no way to prove it and time running out, he was left with only one option. To walk into the dining room and put a bullet in Taj's head with half the world watching.

"Get off me!" Marri said, swinging a fist in what passed for a weak right cross. Rapp blocked it easily, and when he did, something caught his eye. The edge of the chef's thumbnail had been filed to a sharp point. Rapp examined it for a moment and then dropped a knee into the man's chest.

"Mitch!" Warch said from behind him. "This has to stop. It's time for you and me to get out of here before anyone finds out this happened."

Rapp pushed up the left sleeve on Marri's chef's coat. He knew he was onto something when the man suddenly found the strength to start thrashing. Rapp rammed the back of his head into the concrete hard enough to daze him but not hard enough to knock him out. The groan that followed came from Warch, not Marri.

Rapp finally found what he was looking for on the underside of the man's forearm. The tiny blister pack was completely invisible, colored to perfectly match Marri's skin and glued down seamlessly. The only way he could tell it was there was the soft, fluid feel.

"Got it," Rapp said. "On his arm."

Warch let out a long breath. "Thank God."

When the effects of his head hitting the floor faded, Marri started to whimper.

"Everything stays the same," Rapp said, dragging him to his feet. "Except you put that in Taj's food instead of Chutani's."

"I won't. Ahmed Taj is a great man. He will create a new Pakistan that will—"

Rapp had heard enough of this Muslim superpower bullshit from Gadai and his patience was finished. The dossier on Marri had been thrown together at the last minute from public domain information but it didn't paint a picture of a man with any real convictions. He was neither a religious fundamentalist nor a political radical. No, Marri was just a pathetic little man looking to better his social status. He had no desire to martyr himself.

Rapp glanced back at the slabs of meat hanging near the rear of the refrigerator. Finding an empty hook, he grabbed Marri with both hands and began driving him back. When they were less than three feet from the steel spike, he lifted the chef off his feet.

"Stop!"

Marri's scream was loud enough that it would have been heard throughout the palace if they hadn't been closed up in the refrigerator. Rapp didn't stop, though. He accelerated. Marri's back was only inches from the hook when Rapp pulled right and slammed him into a wall stained with dried blood.

The man was blubbering now and his legs wouldn't support him. When he crumpled to the ground, Rapp went with him, grabbing the back of his hair and forcing him to meet his gaze. "Decision time, Obaid. I leave you here on a hook or you do exactly what I tell you."

"I'll . . ." he stammered.

"You'll what?"

"I'll do it."

Rapp pulled the man to his feet and shoved him toward the door. Marri stumbled but Warch caught him. He straightened the man's coat and wiped away the tears that had started to flow down his soft cheeks. "Stay calm, Chef. It'll all be over in a few minutes."

CHAPTER 61

RAPP kept his eyes locked on Obaid Marri.
The red marks on this throat and right cheek were still visible and he was sweating profusely, but those things were plausibly explained by the heatstroke story. If the kitchen crew had any curiosity about what happened in that refrigerator or why there was a security man standing watch over the kitchen, they didn't show it.

Marri was working on a bowl of soup, carefully arranging sprigs of cilantro before tapping chili powder artistically over the top.

"Secretary of State Wicka," he said to the server waiting obediently at the end of his worktable. The man took it and hurried toward the door. Despite actually being an ISI operative, he passed by without giving Rapp so much as a glance. Such was the power of Chef Obaid Marri to beat down anyone in his presence.

He continued to personally adorn the dishes of the most important guests, prioritizing them based on the complex protocols that politicians were so obsessed with. While Rapp spent his time being shot at in places without electricity or running water, the world's elected officials filled their days worrying about who got the shiniest fork.

Jack Warch entered the kitchen and took up a position next to Rapp. "I've got nothing. I'm sorry, Mitch."

The former Secret Service agent had been poring over building plans and manpower distribution charts to find an escape route for Rapp in case he had to take Taj out himself. The result wasn't much of a surprise. Warch and the Pakistanis had specifically designed their security to be foolproof.

If Marri failed, Rapp's best option would be to just stride into the room and put an unsilenced round into the back of Taj's head. The panic would be immediate and he could use that. With luck—a lot of it—he might be able to disappear into the chaos and make it to the main gate.

Marri glanced at a list clipped to the shelf in front of him and froze. When he began moving again, it was to push up his left sleeve.

"This is it," Rapp said quietly.

Warch brought his wrist to his mouth. "We have a report of a potential threat. Don't make any overt moves, but stay alert."

Warch went for the door to the dining room as Marri casually scratched his arm. It was an admirably practiced motion that brought the poison packet right over the bowl. Even anticipating the move, Rapp was barely able to track what was happening. A moment later, the garnish was in place and Marri was handing the bowl to a server.

"Ahmed Taj."

The man took it with a curt nod and headed for the dining room. This time Rapp followed, taking up a position along the south wall where he would be behind Taj. President Chutani was standing next to Sunny Wicka, making a speech about friendship and cooperation. Warch had moved as close as was practical to the secretary of state and his eyes were silently taking in the positions of the guests, his men, and Pakistani security.

Chutani began acknowledging individual guests as the last of the soup bowls were delivered. Ahmed Taj looked on respectfully, reacting with appropriately enthusiastic nods and smiles as the president outlined his vision for Pakistan. The ISI director was good—of that there was no question. He exuded the same calm neutrality that Kennedy had mastered, but added to it a vague dullness that she could never pull off.

Finally, President Chutani sat down and, after a few cheerful words to Wicka, began eating. Rapp focused on Taj as the room was filled with the metallic clink of guests picking up their spoons. He had absolutely no idea what to expect. His best guess was that the ISI director would abandon his normal subtlety in favor of something spectacular. He'd picked a public venue full of Americans for a reason. This was about making a statement.

It started surprisingly innocuously. Taj coughed, wiping at his mouth and reaching for a glass of water. He brought it to his lips, but wasn't able to swallow, struggling for a moment before spewing it across the table. The man next to him seemed to think that Taj was choking and slapped him on the back.

The scene seemed to slow down as Rapp moved a hand toward his weapon. Warch's men were edging in Wicka's direction while one of the ISI men doubling as a waiter started toward Taj. All conversations had gone quiet and everyone's full attention was on the intelligence director. Faces at this point reflected concern but not fear. It was clear that he was breathing and everyone assumed he'd swallowed something wrong. That he would be fine in a moment.

The next time Taj spit something up, it wasn't water. It was blood. He grabbed at his throat and tried to stand, knocking his chair to the floor and then tumbling backward over it. The guards went into motion, drawing their guns and sprinting toward President Chutani and Sunny Wicka. The panic started when Taj vomited a flood of dark fluid and security began shoving people and furniture out of the way in an effort to evacuate the guests of honor.

The attendees were going for whatever exit was closest—some rushing toward the kitchen, others following Chutani and Wicka as they were ushered toward the arch leading to the entry hall. Rapp fought against the momentum of the crowd, forcing his way toward Ahmed Taj.

A Pakistani guard reached the stricken man first, aiming his weapon at Rapp when he saw the CIA man closing in.

"I'm a medic!" Rapp shouted over the chaos around them.

Ironically, it was true. He had an advanced EMT certification and was very interested in Taj's condition, though not for the reason most would suspect. The Pakistani lowered his gun and allowed Rapp to roll Taj onto his back.

Blood and tissue continued to flow from the ISI director's mouth with each convulsion, but the force was subsiding as his muscles lost their ability to contract. The whites of his eyes had gone red with burst blood vessels and his gaze wandered blankly until it fell on the American hovering over him. Recognition was immediate and he suddenly gained the strength to shoot a hand out and grab Rapp's shoulder.

"Relax, Director, you're going to be fine," Rapp said, pulling free of the man's grip and pointing to the guard. "If you don't get him to the hospital in the next half hour, there's not going to be any point. Do you understand? There are emergency vehicles out front. Go!"

The guard gave him a short nod and began to lift Taj, mistaking the man's thrashing for panic. In fact, he was trying to communicate who Rapp was, but with his throat eaten away all he could do was gag and struggle uselessly as he was dragged toward the door.

Rapp smiled and the expression made Taj fight even harder. The guard managed to maintain his grip but it didn't matter. The ISI director would suffocate on his own blood before they made it to the front door.

The crowd shifted when the main exit became jammed with people and Rapp once again found himself being buffeted by the panicked guests. To his right, he spotted a freshman congresswoman who had stumbled and was unable to get back to her feet in the melee. He started toward her and made it to within a couple of yards when someone grabbed him from behind. He spun, prepared to deal with one of the Pakistani guards, but instead found himself face-to-face with a terrified Carl Ferris.

"Where do you think you're going? Get me out of here, you idiot!"

Too much booze and the mayhem around them combined to lengthen the time it took Ferris to realize whom he was talking to. When he finally did, Rapp expected him to scurry away. Surprisingly, he did no such thing.

"What the hell are you doing here? No, don't answer. Just keep your mouth shut and get me to my limousine!"

Clearly the young congresswoman on her knees didn't concern him. And neither did the fact that he'd dedicated much of his life to destroying the CIA in general and Rapp in particular. Now that he was in danger, Ferris assumed that Rapp would do whatever was necessary to save him.

"Don't just stand there like a—" Ferris was clipped from behind by a woman running in shoes that should have made running impossible. The senator grabbed the front of Rapp's jacket, partially for balance but also to try to force him toward an exit.

They were next to an abandoned table and Rapp reached for it, retrieving a salad fork and jamming it into Ferris's thigh. The politician let out an earsplitting scream and collapsed as Rapp went for the congresswoman. He put a hand beneath her arm and pulled her to her feet, supporting her weight as they joined the irresistible current of the fleeing crowd.

EPILOGUE

RAPP'S opponent was faster than anticipated and had a gift for using the terrain to his advantage. The sun was out for the first time in a week, filling the air with water vapor rising from the manicured grass. Rows of dew-covered tombstones created a glare that overpowered Rapp's sunglasses and rendered shadows dangerously opaque. He angled left, but then thought better of it and instead slipped into the narrow space between two mausoleums.

There was a flicker of movement ahead and he picked up his pace, staying silent as he broke out into the open again. His target was just ahead, crouched behind a low hedge. Rapp abandoned all stealth and accelerated to a full sprint, coming around the south edge of the bush and grabbing his quarry by the back of the collar.

Mike Nash's four-year-old son squirmed wildly as he was lifted off his feet, but the hand-me-down jacket was too tight for him to slip out of.

"The jig's up, kid."

Chuck had escaped ten minutes ago, disappearing in a rare moment when both his parents lost focus at the same time.

"I'm bored, Mitch!"

"Tough," Rapp said, putting him back down. "Now march."

Rapp followed, noting that Chuck glanced back every few moments to calculate the odds of another successful escape. To his credit, he recognized that he was beat and decided to play it cool until another opportunity presented itself.

Ahead, the small knot of people surrounding Stan Hurley's coffin came into view. Chuck ran toward his annoyed mother while Rapp aimed for Irene Kennedy, who was hanging back in a long black coat and a hat that shadowed her face.

A man with Stan Hurley's past should have had a much bigger turnout but the guest list was complicated. Despite his profession, he'd outlived his siblings, and the ex-wives who were still alive wanted nothing to do with him. Two of his five children had showed, but the other three didn't speak to him. Most of the surviving people he'd worked with over the years were either out of the country or understandably reluctant to publicly acknowledge their relationship. Flowers were everywhere, though. Many sent by people who owed Hurley their lives.

Scott Coleman and his team were there, as were a scattering of retired CIA operatives. Two attractive foreign women Rapp didn't recognize were most teary. The odd mix was rounded out by an elderly priest who had served with Hurley in Europe before attending seminary. He was keeping the Bible reading to a minimum, focusing on old war stories instead. While Hurley had been a fundamentally religious man, he'd made it clear that he had no interest in a heaven that would accept him.

It was hard for Rapp not to wonder if this was a preview of his own end. A week propped up in a freezer before being quietly planted. A handful of guests, a few mumbled toasts in dives scattered across the globe, and a collective sigh of relief from the enemies who had managed to stay one step ahead.

What would Anna have said? Probably that life and death were about choice, not destiny. That he had the ability to evolve.

But into what? There would never be another Anna, and he'd come to believe that was a good thing. She was the love of his life but that had put him in a terrifying position. He had worried constantly not only about her safety but about what she saw when she looked at him.

The coffin began to glide down on its hydraulic lift just as he came alongside Kennedy.

"I'm going to miss him," she said.

It had been a long and complicated relationship for both of them. She'd known Hurley since she was a child and, in a way, he had, too. From their early days of trying to beat each other to death to the man frozen in a chair next to the steaks, it had never been normal. Or boring.

"I'm sorry, Irene. It was my op. My failure."

The smile that spread across her face was uncharacteristically broad. "He'd have said that it was his op and you were just tagging along."

"Yeah. I guess he would."

"I was staying in touch with his doctors, Mitch. He wasn't going to last much longer, and the death they described . . ." Her voice faded for a moment. "I've come to believe that it was better this way."

Rapp just nodded. It was a scenario that had scared the hell out of him. Hurley would have never killed himself—survival was woven into every fiber of his being. And that would have left it to Rapp to slip into the hospital late one night as the shifts were changing. What would it have felt like to press a silencer to Hurley's temple while the old cuss goaded him on?

"Are Rickman's files safe?" Rapp asked as the coffin hit bottom and the funeral started to break up. Chuck was the first to take off, and this time Nash gave chase while the rest of his family dabbed at their eyes with a shared handkerchief. Coleman's people drifted away, leaving only their boss to stare stoically down at the hole.

"President Chutani has started an internal investigation. We have a man in his administration who tells us the files were stored on a computer that Ahmed Taj kept in his office safe. Marcus is familiar with the encryption protocol he used and says that it'll take the Pakistanis a minimum of thirty years to crack it. By then the information will only be interesting to historians."

They didn't speak again until they were the only mourners left, watched discreetly from the trees by the men charged with covering Hurley up.

"Senator Ferris was trampled during the panic caused by Taj's poisoning," Kennedy said. "Six cracked ribs, a broken wrist, and a puncture wound in his thigh. Last night he was transferred to Bethesda and he insists that you're responsible. That you stabbed him with a steak knife. Is that true?"

"No."

"You're certain?"

"Positive. It was a fork."

"He told the White House that you tried to kill him."

"I don't try to kill people, Irene. I either do it or I don't."

"That's essentially what I said to President Alexander. And Chutani is extremely grateful for your intervention. According to him, the security footage was somehow corrupted. He also says that he has two men who will sign affidavits stating that Ferris was drunk and that you were nowhere near him when he fell."

"Problem solved, then."

"That was pushing the limits, Mitch. Even for you."

"We needed to send a message to that piece of garbage. Consider it sent."

"Fortunately for both of us, President Alexander privately agrees. Having said that, he did mention that if you ever do anything like this again, he's going to personally come to Langley and kick your ass."

Rapp laughed and started toward his car. "Tell him any time."